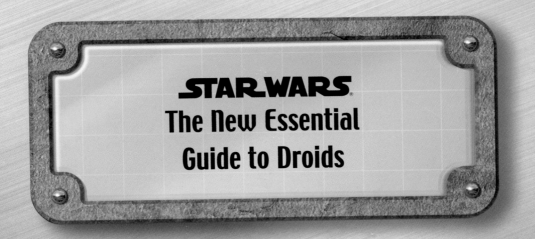

STAR WARS®
The New Essential
Guide to Droids

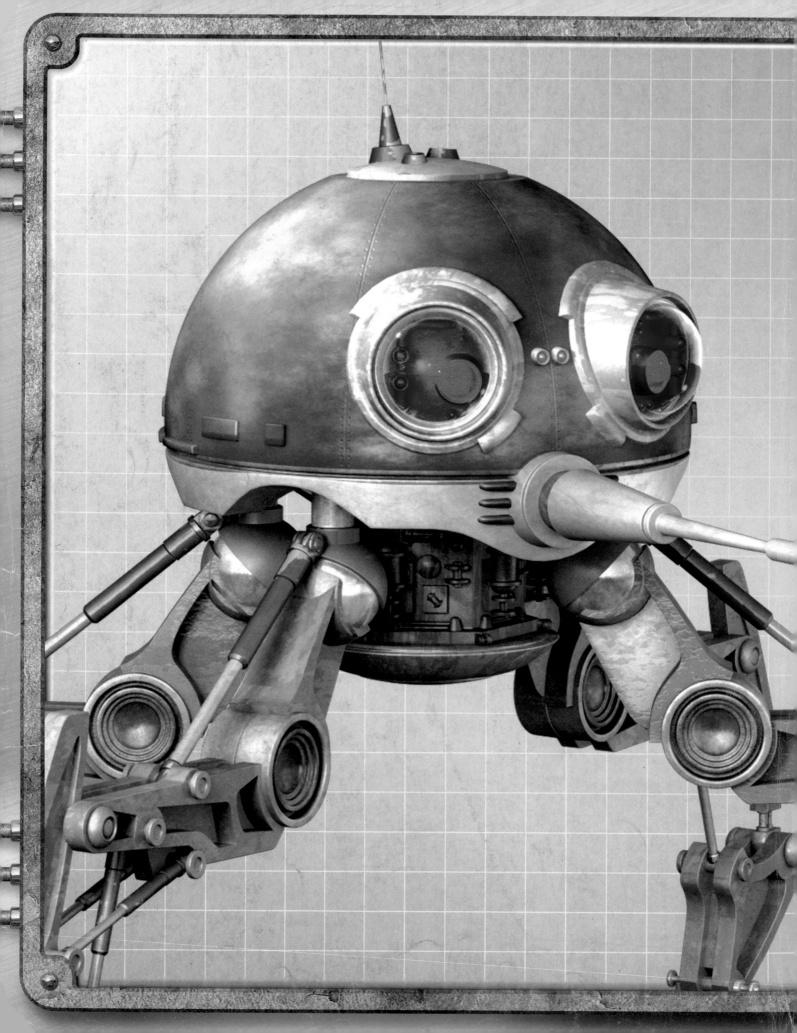

STAR WARS®
The New Essential
Guide to Droids

Text by Daniel Wallace
Illustrations by Ian Fullwood

BALLANTINE BOOKS ▪ NEW YORK

Author Acknowledgments

This book would not have been possible without the assistance of others. Thanks to Keith Clayton and Erich Schoeneweiss at Del Rey; Jonathan Rinzler, Leland Chee, Sue Rostoni, Pablo Hidalgo, and Amy Gary at Lucasfilm; Ian Fullwood for his beautiful illustrations; and Steve Saffel, Aaron Allston, Bob Vitas, Jason Fry, Colleen Lindsay, and Haden Blackman for their contributions in matters both great and small.

Special thanks to Eric Trautmann and Drew Campbell, authors of the superb 1997 role-playing guidebook *Cynabar's Fantastic Technology: Droids.*

Thanks also to Abel Peña, whose suggestions and access to *Star Wars* obscurities led to the inclusion of entries for the homing droid, Iron Knight, and Jawa monster droid (better known to children of the 1970s as the output of the Droid Factory playset from Kenner).

And, of course, thanks to George Lucas, for creating a universe that has been such fun to illuminate.

Artist Acknowledgments

Once again it has been my privilege to work on another fantastic book for Del Rey. The production of the illustrations was made possible only by a team of people pulling together behind the scenes. I want to thank Erich Schoeneweiss and Keith Clayton for ensuring I stayed on track; Sylvain Michaelis of Michaelis/Carpelis Design for page and content design; and Jonathan Rinzler, Troy Alders, and Leland Chee from Lucasfilm for guidance on the artwork.

My special thanks must go to Ben Robins, who worked alongside me and is responsible for many of the wonderful illustrations.

Thanks also to Paul Bates, Rob Garrard, and Mike Wyatt for their contributions.

To Emma

Contents

Acknowledgments   iv

Introduction   ix

A Layperson's Guide to Droids   x

A Short History of Droids   xiv

Major Manufacturers   xvii

Class One Droids   3

2-1B Surgical Droid   4

BRT Supercomputer   6

DD-13 Galactic Chopper   8

FX Medical Assistant   10

GH-7 Medical Droid   12

Master-Com   14

Polis Massan Midwife Droid   16

SP-4 and JN-66   18

Class Two Droids   21

Arakyd Probot Series   22

G0-T0 Planning Droid   24

G2 "Goose Droid"   26

R1 Astromech   28

R2–R9 Astromech   30

T3 Utility Droid   36

Vuffi Raa   38

Wee Gee   40

Class Three Droids   43

2JTJ Personal Navigation Droid   44

3PO Protocol Droid   46

C-3PO   48

BD-3000 Luxury Droid   50

C-3PX   52

CZ Secretary Droid   54

Death Star Droid   56

EV Supervisor Droid   58

I-5YQ (I-Five)   60

J9 Worker Drone   62

LE Manifest Droid	64	
LOM Protocol Droid	66	
Tac-Spec Footman	68	
WA-7 Waitress Droid	70	

Class Four Droids 73

ASN-121 Assassin Droid	74	
B1 Battle Droid	76	
B2 Super Battle Droid	80	
B3 Ultra Battle Droid	82	
Baron Droid	84	
Basilisk War Droid	86	
Buzz Droid	88	
Chameleon Droid	90	
Colicoid Annihilator Droid	92	
Cortosis Battle Droid	94	
Crab Droid	96	
Dark Trooper	98	

Droideka	100
Dwarf Spider Droid	102
The Great Heep	104
HK Assassin Droid	106
Human Replica Droid	108
IG-100 MagnaGuard	110
IG Assassin Droid	112
IG Lancer Droid	114
IT-O Interrogator	116
JK Bio-Droid	118
Juggernaut War Droid	120
L8-L9 Combat Droid	122
Mandalorian Battle Legionnaire	124
Manta Droid Subfighter	126
Octuptarra Droid	128
Pollux Assassin Droid	130
Sith Probe Droid	132

Xim's War-Robot 134

YVH 1 Yuuzhan Vong Hunter 136

Z-X3 Droid Trooper 138

Class Five Droids 141

8D8 Smelting Operator 142

ASP Droid 144

Binary Loadlifter 146

BLX Labor Droid 148

Cam Droid 150

COO Cook Droid 152

FA-4 and
FA-5 Droids 154

Homing Droid 156

Imperial Mark IV 158

INS-444 and CLE-004 160

LIN Demolitionmech 162

Monster Droid 164

Mouse Droid 166

Mustafar Panning Droid 168

Otoga-222 Droid 170

P-100 Salvage Droid 172

Pit Droid 174

PK Worker Droid 176

Power Droid 178

Prowler 1000 180

Rickshaw Droid 182

SRT Droid 184

TT-8L Tattletale 186

WED Treadwell 188

Cyborgs 191

B'omarr Brain Walker 192

Dark Side Technobeasts 194

General Grievous 196

Iron Knight 198

About the Author 200

About the Illustrator 200

INTRODUCTION

What would Star Wars be without droids?

In the mid-1970s, to sell George Lucas's risky idea to potential movie studios, artist Ralph McQuarrie worked up a series of conceptual paintings. One depicted the slender, golden C-3PO and the rotund R2-D2 cresting a desert dune. The two robots in the painting conveyed an air of eerie otherworldliness, but in the final film, the warm bickering between the two grounded the proceedings in the familiar humor of Abbott and Costello. The robots—or droids, as Lucas called them—became some of the most *human* characters of the classic trilogy.

The Expanded Universe of comics, novels, and games jumped in to swell the ranks of Star Wars droids. When the first edition of *The Essential Guide to Droids* hit bookstores in 1998, it became clear that droids could fill any niche, from childcare to bartending. No matter what problem the inhabitants of the Star Wars galaxy might face, they could be sure of one thing—there was probably a droid for it.

Then came the prequels. Helped along by the vivid imaginations of a new generation of concept artists, the droids of the prequels wormed their way into nearly every frame of film. A unicycle droid pulled a rickshaw on Tatooine, while another served hot plates in a retro diner on Coruscant. Droids installed panes of glass, tinkered with Podracers, and delivered babies.

And, of course, droids made menacing, implacable soldiers. The Separatists' use of factory-built battle droids raised an interesting question of moral ambiguity, especially after the Republic assembled an army of vat-grown clones to oppose them. This conflict came to a head in *Revenge of the Sith,* when the heroes suddenly became the hunted and droids turned out not to be the true bad guys after all.

The New Essential Guide to Droids is proud to present all the key automatons from both the classic trilogy and the prequel trilogy, as well as notable Expanded Universe players, and a few nostalgic gems from decades gone by.

A Layperson's Guide to Droids

Citizens on any industrialized world can barely conceive of life without droids. For uncountable generations, automata have performed the jobs that intelligent beings are unwilling or incapable of doing.

Cybot Galactica defines *droid* as a "mechanical and/or electronic construct designed and put into service to assist organic life." Most would consider this definition incomplete. A droid is generally distinguished from a robot by having a self-aware consciousness (though some use the terms *droid* and *robot* interchangeably), and is set apart from a computer by having a self-contained method of locomotion, such as wheels, legs, treads, or repulsorlifts. Droids can usually manipulate their environment with the mechanical equivalents of arms and hands, and most possess some method of communicating with organic beings or other droids.

Every standard day, millions of subservient automata negotiate treaties, repair hyperdrives, cure plagues, incinerate garbage, nurse children, haul cargo, deliver messages, cook meals, and destroy enemies. At the same time, droids are ignored and unappreciated, treated as chattel by many owners and regarded with outright hostility by others. Though anti-droid prejudice is a reality among the unenlightened, owners who have spent long stretches with their droids have discovered that they can be both trusted companions and loyal friends.

But even if some citizens despise droids, *everyone* relies on them to keep the gears of the galaxy turning. Droid manufacturing is a profitable and competitive industry. The "Big Two" droid makers, Cybot Galactica and Industrial Automaton, are among the most important players in the galactic economy, and during the Clone Wars, the Geonosian workers of Baktoid Combat Automata built one of the largest mechanical armies the galaxy has ever seen. The droid business has been responsible for erecting enduring industrial wonders from the endless smokestacks of Mechis III to the spacegoing junkyard known as Droid World (aka Kligson's Moon).

Droids are grouped into five major classifications depending on the nature of the work that their manufacturers build them to perform:

- **Class one droids** are found in the fields of medicine, mathematics, and the physical sciences.

- **Class two droids** perform engineering tasks, environmental work, and advanced starship repair.

- **Class three droids** are built to interact with humans and other organic beings in tasks including protocol, tutoring, and child care.

- **Class four droids** are dangerous automata built for violence. Security droids are the most benign, while assassin droids are the most malicious.

- **Class five droids**, which are typically built without advanced cognitive modules, work as basic labor units in jobs such as lifting, maintenance, and sanitation.

In addition, the complexity of droid limbs and other systems has led to their implantation as prosthetics for organic beings. This process is called cyborging, and cyborgs have traditionally been subject to the same prejudices as droids.

Most droids encountered in society are the property of large corporations or private owners. For short-term jobs, almost any class of droid can be rented from an outfit such as the Intergalactic Droid Agency.

It's extremely rare to meet an unowned droid. Some of these units are runaways that grew weary of their jobs or fearful of owner abuse. Others are fugitives from the law, wanted for crimes ranging from theft to murder. A select number of units are truly free, having been manumitted—freed—by their owners. Manumission is a mixed blessing for a droid, since the legality of the action is not recognized by many planetary governments. Unowned droids are often seized, forcibly memory-wiped, and sold at public auctions.

Many technologies exist for keeping droids in line. One of the most visible is the restraining bolt, an electronic signal disrupter usually attached to a droid's chassis in a prominent spot. The restraining bolt, when activated by a handheld "caller," bypasses a droid's motivational programming and forces the droid to perform specific actions, such as switching itself off. Memory wipes are also common, and are mandatory on many planets and in nearly all resale markets. A memory wipe will restore a droid to its factory template, erasing its accumulated memories and the personality that may have evolved along with them. Owners who don't memory-wipe their droids are criticized for nurturing droids that might develop into criminals.

The Droid Statutes, first enacted nearly four thousand standard years ago, are a set of regulations specifying punishments for droids that have broken the law. The Droid Statutes are notable in that they view droids as property, not as self-aware citizens capable of making their own decisions. A droid that commits a class five infraction, such as petty theft or appearing in public without a restraining bolt, will have its memory wiped; its owner is obliged to pay a minor fine. A class one infraction, such as murder or conspiracy to overthrow the government, mandates the destruction of the droid and a prison sentence for the droid's owner from five years to life.

When a company manufactures a droid, it begins by selecting an appropriate chassis for the class of unit under construction. The next step is to outfit the chassis with traitware data cards. Traitware describes abilities that are hardwired into the droid, such as its intelligence, strength, speed, and technical skills.

Skillware programs—such as the ability to pilot a ship, assemble a weapon, speak a language, count cards in a sabacc deck, or slice into a computer system—flesh out a droid's array of specific talents. Some abilities cannot be carried out without specialized equipment, and many droids sport gadgets including holoprojectors and cargo winches.

The behavioral circuitry matrix is what makes a droid a droid. The name describes the aggregate systems, including hardware and traitware, that produce droid behavior. A typical behavioral circuitry matrix has two components: a sensory-response module (made up of audiovisual circuits, an olfactory-speech center, a gyrobalance unit, a spectrum analysis unit, and an extremity control system), and an obedience-rationale module (containing a motivator, a cognitive theory unit, and the droid's memory banks).

Although manufacturers produce a wide range of droids for every conceivable task, budgetary constraints and simple curiosity often lead budding engineers to make their own droids. As proven by Tatooine's Jawas and innovators such as Anakin Skywalker, a droid constructed from scavenged parts can sometimes exceed the capabilities of models from major corporations. Successful droid builders follow a few simple rules:

- **Recycle and scavenge.** Nonfunctional droids can be purchased for next to nothing and provide useful parts when stripped. Even large corporations reuse materials. Industrial Automaton, for example, houses its R1 units within shells recycled from its Mark II reactor drones.

- **Prioritize.** When designing a droid, identify its essential features and parts. A protocol droid will benefit from a SyntheTech AA-1 verbobrain or similar device, while a pit droid requires servomotors and hydraulic joints before it can carry heavy engines. Spend credits on these essentials before adding extraneous gadgets or sensors.

- **Work from within.** A droid should be built from the inside out. Start with the key processors. Next, add the basic infrastructure, using durasteel or a similar substance. Sensors can be added as necessary. Photoreceptors, which allow a droid to study its surroundings, are essential. Movement sensors enable a droid to walk without bumping into objects or falling over. Damage receptors notify the droid whenever its structural integrity is threatened. Ample wiring will be needed to carry information and power throughout the droid, while hoses and tubes should be included to provide lubrication. In most cases, droid plating can be applied last. A droid can generally operate without its "skin," provided it is cleaned regularly.

- **Program.** A droid is only as useful as its programming. A droid's creator should make every effort to personally program his or her creation using appropriate skillware modules. Droid builders should program only to their capabilities: rare is the individual who can accurately outfit a protocol droid, but programs for standard labor droids are far easier to create.

- **Avoid memory wipes.** Engineers have discovered that droids accumulate knowledge over time and under the right circumstances can develop personalities. Memory wipes will destroy any progress in this direction. While major corporations argue that memory wipes ensure docility, a droid with a well-rounded personality is often more loyal, ingenious, creative, and courageous than its wiped counterparts. Some droids may exhibit personality quirks, such as fierce independence or an annoying stubborn streak. On rare occasions, droids spared from memory wipes have become psychotic.

The issue of whether droids are truly alive is one that has vexed philosophers and ethicists since the dawn of the Republic. The renowned thinker Plaristes famously argued against the possibility of droid sentience in his work *Of Minds and Machines*. Many great intellects have since disagreed with Plaristes, arguing that droids are self-aware and, in many cases, capable of feeling emotions and pain. Some droids even appear to believe in a higher being and an afterlife, as evidenced by the droid members of the Sunesi religion and the throngs of mechanical worshippers found in the rust heaps of Ronyards. Those in the pro-Plaristes camp respond to these incidents by stating that a droid's mental and emotional states are merely pre-programmed simulacra of true feelings.

The Jedi Order taught that access to the Force can be achieved only through a symbiotic relationship with the midi-chlorians inside organic cells. Because droids do not have organic cells, many Jedi do not support the principle of droid sentience. It is interesting to note that some ancient cultures did not see technology and the Force as concepts at odds with each other. The Rakatan Infinite Empire built self-aware machines powered in part by Force energies. These Rakatan designs later influenced the war robots of Xim the Despot, whose "crimson condottieres" employed Force-energizing dynamos.

The Sith remained far more open to the possibilities of technology than the traditionalist Jedi. By using the Force to overwhelm a droid's circuitry connections, the Sith could turn an automaton into an extension of their will. The Sith talent for intuitively grasping the workings of machines became known as *mechu-deru.* In response, the Jedi moved even further away from the study of droids, lest they be perceived as following the lead of the Sith Lords.

The Empire later continued researching the relationship between the Force and machinery. Imperial designer Nasdra Magrody invented the subelectronic converter, a technological brain implant that permitted Force-sensitive subjects to control droids from a distance. One recipient of the subelectronic converter, Irek Ismaren, triggered the *Eye of Palpatine* incident in 12 A.B.Y. before becoming the monstrous cyborg Lord Nyax.

A different droid crisis also helped shed new light on the nature of consciousness. Immediately following the Battle of Endor, the Rebel Alliance and the Empire united to fight off an incursion by alien invaders on the planet Bakura. The aliens,

caste-stratified saurians known as the Ssi-ruuk, brought with them a bizarre technology for powering droids. Through "entchment," the Ssi-ruuk could transfer the life essences of organic victims into the control circuits of Ssi-ruuvi battle droids. The Ssi-ruuk ultimately withdrew from Bakura in defeat, but their entchment rigs lived on.

Years later, Cray Mingla, of Luke Skywalker's Jedi academy, used modified entchment hardware to save the life of her lover, fellow academy student Nichos Marr. While Cray believed she had preserved Nichos's consciousness in a droid body, it soon became clear that she had only programmed a droid with Nichos's memories and personality. Research into entchment continued. Around the time of the Yuuzhan Vong invasion, the entrepreneur Stanton Rendar set up shop in the Minos Cluster, offering terminally ill clients the opportunity to transfer their minds into the near-indestructible frames of human replica droids.

A Short History of Droids

The invention of droids predates the invention of spaceflight. This places their origins in the fog of pre-Republic history, or approximately 30,000 B.B.Y., according to most historians. This date refers only to droids developed within the confederacy of worlds that would later be known as the Republic. Dozens of alien civilizations, from the Gree to the Rakatans, are thought to have developed self-aware automata even earlier than that. The first droids carried primitive behavioral circuitry matrices that allowed them to learn and adapt to new tasks. They worked as heavy lifters, sanitation workers, and hard-radiation reactor drones. As such, these early droids would be categorized as class fives within the modern droid taxonomy.

Not long after the development of intelligent labor units, droids became implements of war. Planetary rulers discovered that a binary loadlifter with beam tubes welded to its frame became a fearsome killer that could take more punishment than an entire platoon of organic soldiers.

Droid armies quickly became the norm, until their opponents learned that mechanical warriors could easily be out-thought. This basic lesson has been forgotten and relearned countless times, and the popularity of droid armies has ebbed and flowed throughout history, much depending on the willingness and availability of trained organic populations to wage war.

Away from the battlefield, droids experienced their own struggles on the home front. Droids fulfilled a need, but they also took jobs away from flesh-and-blood workers. Resentment festered among the out-of-work, planting the seeds of the anti-droid movement. Laws restricting droid ownership became common, and many business proprietors barred customers from bringing their droids into public establishments.

As the millennia passed, droid programmers boosted the computing capacity of the droid brain. This augmentation led to the introduction of medical, mathematics, astrogation, and engineering droids, units that would now be considered class ones and class twos.

Programming a droid to have a lively personality remained the greatest challenge in the field of artificial intelligence. Refinements in cognitive circuitry eventually led to units that could hold a conversation indistinguishable from a discussion with an organic being. These social-driven droids, categorized as class threes, had an unwelcome flip side. Over time, some developed personalities that were decidedly *anti*-social.

As droids became more widespread, they moved into every field, from teaching to surgery, and those who resented the thinking machines had even more reasons to justify their anger. Yet the zealots who treated droids with contempt ignored the fact that droids had never *asked* to be self-aware. Most droids had their own opinion on the matter, noting, at least to themselves, that their existence as engineered life-forms had permanently doomed them to lives as second-class citizens.

Organics resentful of droids spawned an extremist fringe, which expressed itself through coalitions such as the Organization for Organic Purity. In response, voices were raised among their ideological opposites: those who viewed droids as sentient beings and their function in society to be indistinguishable from slavery. These pro-droid groups included the moderate Coalition of Automaton Rights Activists and the extremist Mechanical Liberation Front. They became known for public rallies in support of droids' rights and occasional terrorist bombings of manufacturing plants in the name of droid freedom. One of the more recent cases advanced by droids' rights activists is the plight of so-called brilliant missiles: explosive armaments that contain such advanced target-selection hardware that they have arguably become sentient.

In 4015 B.B.Y., an incident on Coruscant hardened public opinion against automata for generations. The assassin droid HK-01, the prototype for a new line of hunter-killers from the Czerka Corporation, led the entire planet's droid population in a violent uprising against their organic masters. Security droids and the Republic's own juggernauts proved to be the deadliest combatants, requiring the greatest Jedi Masters to take them down. Master Arca Jeth, an expert in the art of *mechu macture,* tore apart the electronic connections of enemy droids to end the crisis after weeks of chaos.

The Sith War, in 3996 B.B.Y., saw the use of basilisk droid mounts and Krath war droids. The Jedi Knights joined the fight only after being shocked into action, when a landing force of Krath war droids murdered hundreds of Jedi, including Master Arca Jeth, on Deneba.

Half a century later, in 3946 B.B.Y., G0-T0 planning droids started their own rebellion. Sixteen planets in the Gordian Reach, each under the control of a G0-T0 unit, announced their intention to secede from the Republic. Knowing that the droids had seized power in a bloody coup—and unwilling to grant political recognition to droids in any case—Supreme Chancellor Cressa ordered the Republic military to liberate the territory that had been renamed 400100500260026.

Such uprisings only added fuel to the anti-droid undercurrent. The Republic government slapped the droid industry with punitive damage payouts, relenting only when it became clear that society could not function without droids in some capacity. New laws restricting droid manufacture hit the books, including a ceiling on the sophistication of droid brains. This effectively froze the development of class three droids for millennia.

In addition, droid buyers had to obtain ownership licenses, and to agree to wipe the memories of their droids regularly. This period also saw the enactment of the Droid Statutes, which specified punishments for owners if their droids acted in violation of the law.

By 200 B.B.Y., laws had slackened to such a degree that droid manufacturers felt safe pushing the boundaries of artificial intelligence. BRT supercomputers were near-omniscient planetary networks, though they were not true droids, since they lacked the ability to move. Although BRTs did not have the sinister edge of the old G0-T0 planning droids, public dislike of the supercomputers led to a consumer-imposed cap on computing power.

Public fear of droids truly escalated beginning in 50 B.B.Y. The Arkanian Revolution set the Arkanian Renegades against the Arkanian Dominion, with the primary combatants being fused technobiological soldiers. Six years later, a battle droid army under the control of a Kol Huro dictator conquered planets in neighboring space. By the time of the Naboo invasion in 32 B.B.Y., many viewed droids as dangerous and disloyal.

The Trade Federation's occupation of Naboo failed when young Anakin Skywalker destroyed the central computer that controlled the battle droid army. Laws passed in the aftermath to curb the use of battle droids didn't stop the Trade Federation from hoarding more war machines. Count Dooku soon united the Trade Federation with other commercial enterprises under the banner of the Confederacy of Independent Systems, and they moved against the Republic when the Clone Wars began in 22 B.B.Y.

The Republic fought with an army of organic cloned soldiers. The Separatists fielded a military made up almost exclusively of droids. The sheer number and variety of Separatist war droids was unprecedented in galactic history. Droids dominated water, land, air, and outer space in forms such as the manta droid subfighter, the dwarf spider droid, the HMP droid gunship, and the vulture droid starfighter. Three years later, a master control signal transmitted by the Separatist Council at the behest of Darth Sidious forced all Separatist droids to switch off, marking the end of the Clone Wars. Military droids virtually disappeared from battle theaters for years.

At around the same time, in the entertainment arena, droids became fashionable as sports athletes. Nuna-ball, a newly created droid team sport, proved to be a smash hit from the Core to the Rim, while gladiator droids took on a new appeal in the Galaxy Gladiator Federation. These contests, popular as they were, did not lead to increased acceptance of droids as individuals. On the contrary, many fans only watched the matches in the hope of seeing droid carnage.

In 10 B.B.Y., Coruscant experienced a Second Great Droid Revolution when the cyborg Archa Sabis uploaded a virus into the droid population, causing automated police cruisers and forty-story construction droids to unite in a chaotic but short-lived rebellion. As the handiwork of Archa Sabis, the incident was remembered as a cyborg plot against the Empire. Cyborgs became renewed targets of fear and suspicion.

During the Rebel Alliance's struggles against the Empire in the Galactic Civil War, droids played a complex role. The Rebel Alliance elevated two droids, R2-D2 and C-3PO, to the status of heroes. The Empire, meanwhile, attempted to resurrect the notion of the battle droid army with its Dark Trooper project. Several renegade droids, including IG-88 and 4-LOM, stalked the spacelanes as bounty hunters.

The invasion of the Yuuzhan Vong in 25 A.B.Y. was terrible for droids of every class. The religious fanaticism of the Yuuzhan Vong expressed itself in a hatred for machines, and they particularly despised machines that mimicked living things. On occupied planets, the Yuuzhan Vong went out of their way to demolish droid manufacturing plants. They also rounded up droids and set them aflame in immolation pits.

The resolution of the Yuuzhan Vong invasion has brought about a slow and steady return to normalcy. Droid manufacturers, many of whom saw their sales devastated during the war, have rebounded. Class five and class two droids are now in great demand, as battle-damaged cities repair their infrastructures and planetary governments take steps to restore poisoned biospheres. In time, sales of high-end class threes are expected to reach their former heights as the galaxy looks to a new age of prosperity.

Major Manufacturers

The manufacture and sale of droids is a lucrative business dominated by the "Big Two": Cybot Galactica and Industrial Automaton. Other major droid players include Arakyd, Genetech, MerenData, and Veril Line Systems.

Of the millions of droid manufacturing plants in the galaxy, the two largest are Mechis III and Telti, which together produce a sizable percentage of all new automata. Both locations are entire worlds covered with sprawling construction facilities and fully automated assembly lines; any sentient interaction in the fabrication process other than the most minimal supervision is unnecessary and counterproductive. The major droid companies pay these two worlds a negotiated fee for the use of their assembly plants, a high cost that is acceptable given the speed and accuracy with which they can churn out large orders. Arakyd, Genetech, SoroSuub, and Veril Line Systems are some of the companies that employ Mechis III for a major share of their production. Industrial Automaton and Cybot Galactica rely heavily on Telti. Cybot Galactica also uses the planet Affa to produce much of its yearly protocol output.

Arakyd

The rise of the militaristic Empire was a major boost for Arakyd's business. Through political maneuvering, this supplier of exploration droids set itself up as the only logical choice to receive the first Imperial droid contracts. Arakyd exploited this windfall by working hard to become the galaxy's leading military supplier. Recent consumer-market models from Arakyd have been moderately successful, but account for only a small fraction of its yearly output. Despite the company's history, the New Republic has worked closely with Arakyd since the collapse of Imperial rule.

- Prowler 1000
- Arakyd probot series
- RA-7 Death Star Droid

Aratech Repulsor Company

Known today as a manufacturer of speeder bikes, Aratech started out more than four thousand standard years ago as a leader in the field of artificial intelligence. Aratech's breakthroughs led to the G0-T0 planning droid, which possessed the ability to become nearly omniscient if plugged in to a planetary network. When a number of G0-T0s led a rebellion against the Republic in 3946 B.B.Y., the fallout nearly ruined Aratech. The company made a second run at networked droids with its BRT supercomputer. The failure of the BRT prompted Aratech to abandon the droid business in favor of repulsorlift technology.

- G0-T0 planning droid
- BRT supercomputer

Baktoid Combat Automata

No longer in existence, Baktoid Combat Automata (a sister company to Baktoid Armor Workshop) cranked out innumerable droids for the Trade Federation and the Confederacy of Independent Systems in the decade and a half leading up to the conclusion of the Clone Wars. As a member of the Techno Union, Baktoid had access to the galaxy's best equipment, and its factories on Geonosis and hundreds of other worlds could mass-produce battle droids in uncountable numbers.

- B1 battle droid
- baron droid
- B2 super battle droid
- B3 ultra battle droid
- cortosis battle droid
- Mandalorian Battle Legionnaire
- SRT droid

Cestus Cybernetics

The Republic constructed a prison on Ord Cestus in 321 B.B.Y., and engineers from Cybot Galactica later served sentences there. Their inspired designs resulted in the Cestan security droid, a huge hit that enriched the executive board of the newly formed Cestus Cybernetics corporation. The company subcontracted out to the Techno Union member Baktoid Armor Workshop, an act that opened up Ord Cestus to new markets. After the Trade Federation's defeat at the Battle of Naboo, Cestus Cybernetics fell on hard times. It introduced the JK bio-droid during the Clone Wars as its best hope for survival.

- JK bio-droid

CHIEWAB AMALGAMATED PHARMACEUTICALS

This medical conglomerate owns hundreds of unpopulated planetary systems. Scouts in the employ of Chiewab are continually laying claim to newly discovered planets in Wild Space, which the company then exploits in its quest to develop new medicines. Chiewab once owned the Geentech medisensor company, before spinning it off as a separate unit.

- GH-7 med droid

COLICOID CREATION NEST

The bloodthirsty Colicoids of Colla IV manufacture droidekas and hundreds of other automata, but the average galactic citizen will probably never see one—unless he or she is unlucky enough to visit Colla IV. Following an internal war a generation before the Clone Wars, the Colicoids settled into a rigid hierarchy of specialized nests. The Colicoid Creation Nest manufactures all items of higher technology, including droids.

- annihilator droid
- buzz droid
- droideka

COMMERCE GUILD

In the centuries prior to the rise of the Empire, the Commerce Guild controlled raw material interests across the galaxy. Its member organizations included the Mining Guild, Arcona Mineral Harvest, Offworld Mining Corporation, and Dorvalla Mining. President Shu Mai, splitting her time between the Gossam homeworld of Castell and her private estate on Felucia, became wealthy from the sale of resources that supplied the Separatists' military buildup. She was killed on Mustafar, and the Empire subsequently absorbed the Commerce Guild.

- dwarf spider droid
- chameleon droid

CYBOT GALACTICA

One of the two largest droid manufacturers in the galaxy, Cybot Galactica is a major force in the galactic economy and a significant influence throughout the Core Worlds and Corporate Sector. The company has a reputation for being refined and fashionable, thanks to its image-leading protocol droids. But Cybot's full product line runs the gamut from research units to sewer scrubbers. Cybot shrewdly plays on its quality reputation by charging slightly more for units that are essentially identical to those made by competitors.

- 3PO protocol droid
- C-3PX
- I-5YQ (I-Five)
- LE manifest droid
- binary loadlifter
- LIN demolitionmech
- PK worker droid
- Senate Hall cam droid
- WED Treadwell
- SP-4 and JN-66 analysis droids

CZERKA CORPORATION

Czerka has a history dating back to the foundation of the Republic. Originally known as Czerka Mining and Industrial, the company soon branched out into the manufacturing and financial industries. Czerka enjoyed the height of its power under the leadership of President Pollard Seario, circa 4000–3950 B.B.Y. The notoriously corrupt Seario established Czerka's headquarters on the Sith tombworld of Korriban, where a new city sprang up around the Czerka generators. Today the Czerka Corporation is the galaxy's third largest arms manufacturer, behind BlasTech and Merr-Sonn Munitions.

- HK assassin droid
- Master-Com

DUWANI MECHANICAL PRODUCTS

One of the more successful manufacturers of droids circa 4000 B.B.Y., Duwani went out of business long ago. The company is remembered for its T3 utility droid and its 3DO protocol/service droid, as well as the juggernaut war droid, which Duwani produced on contract to the Republic rocket-jumper corps.

- T3 utility droid
- juggernaut war droid

Geentech

Formerly a subsidiary of Chiewab Amalgamated Pharmaceuticals, this small, quiet medisensor company was casually run out of business by the much larger Genetech corporation in a string of heavy-handed and highly expensive lawsuits. Claiming Geentech's similar name infringed on its own copyrights, Genetech forced its competitor into bankruptcy. Geentech's sole success story, the 2-1B surgical droid, was subsequently bought out by Industrial Automaton.

- 2-1B surgical droid

Genetech

One of the older and larger droid manufacturers, Genetech started out as a pharmaceutical firm. The company pioneered the concept of using droids to streamline the manufacturing process, which earned it a great deal of ill will (and fueled the anti-droid movement) when thousands of assembly workers were fired from their jobs. Genetech's first droids were medical units, but the company has since branched out into accounting, administrative, and bookkeeping models.

- 2JTJ personal navigation droid

Go-Corp/Utilitech

Go-Corp/Utilitech is based on Etti IV and makes vehicle droids for sale throughout the Corporate Sector. Go-Corp produces speeder carriages for models such as the robo-hack, while its subsidiary Utilitech manufactures and programs the more intricate droid brains. The WA-7 waitress droid is a Go-Corp model from a previous century that still sees use.

- WA-7 waitress droid

Haor Chall Engineering

The Xi Char of Charros IV are a pious species completely devoted to their religion. Their faith, known as Haor Chall, teaches that the real world is an imperfect shadow of the flawless and infinitely complex spiritual world. By creating intricate machinery, the Xi Char believe they are replicating a piece of the paradise beyond. The Trade Federation cruelly exploited this belief, convincing the Xi Char to build them vulture droid starfighters and other war machines in their cathedral factories.

- manta droid subfighter

Holowan Mechanicals

Publicly known as "Holowan Mechanicals: The Friendly Technology People," this dangerous corporation took over research on IG series droids after the InterGalactic Banking Clan seized all assets belonging to its delinquent customer, Phlut Design Systems. Holowan produced the IG 100 MagnaGuard as well as the IG assassin droid—an experiment that ended in disaster when the prototype units escaped from the laboratory and murdered the design staff.

- IG 100 MagnaGuard

- IG assassin droid

Imperial Department of Military Research

During his decades-long reign, Emperor Palpatine conscripted many of the galaxy's best scientists to create genocidal implements of war. The Empire's top secret Department of Military Research produced a number of brutal inventions, including the subtle homing droid and the murderous Dark Trooper.

- Dark Trooper

- homing droid

- human replica droid

- Imperial Mark IV sentry droid

- IT-O interrogator

Industrial Automaton

The other half of the "Big Two," Industrial Automaton is a massive and influential droid corporation formed long ago through the merger of Automata Galactica and Industrial Intellect. Known for its high-precision merchandise and deep discounts, the company's crowning glory is the universally accepted R series of astromech droids. Industrial Automaton incessantly battles Cybot Galactica for market share.

- ASP droid

- LOM protocol droid

- R series astromechs

- cam droid

- COO cook droid

Kalibac Industries

A former member of the Techno Union, Kalibac Industries has been plagued by imitative designs and a seemingly never-ending chain of lawsuits from Cybot Galactica over shared components. The company's hovering librarian droids have been commandeered for service on Mustafar. Kalibac Industries operates manufacturing and retail centers on Coruscant and Procopia.

• Mustafar panning droid

LeisureMech Enterprises

Based in the Corporate Sector, Leisure-Mech produces high-quality recreational, entertainment, and luxury droids for sale to businesses and wealthy consumers. One subsidiary branch of LeisureMech was so successful at producing security droids that it was spun off to form the Ulban Arms company.

• BD-3000 luxury droid

Malkite Poisoners

Most citizens speak in whispers of the Malkite Poisoners, a secret society responsible for assassinations that have changed the balance of power throughout history. Some even believe the Malkite Poisoners to be a myth. Individuals with the right contacts are sometimes able to purchase a custom-built Malkite assassin droid.

• ASN-121 assassin droid

Medtech Industries

A trailblazer in the medical field, Medtech developed some of the earliest surgical-based automata. Droids such as the FX were extremely successful in their day, but changing tastes and increased competitive pressures prevented Medtech from producing any new models. After the Battle of Yavin, the company's corporate headquarters was relocated to the Deep Core, and Medtech filed for bankruptcy shortly before the Battle of Hoth.

• FX medical assistant

MerenData

A frequent beneficiary of Imperial contracts during Palpatine's reign, MerenData specializes in security systems, military target drones, and a variety of droid products—some sinister, some benign. Efforts to establish a working relationship between MerenData and the leaders of the Galactic Federation of Free Alliances have been disappointing.

• EV supervisor droid

Phlut Design Systems

Formerly based on the Outer Rim banking planet of Muunilinst, Phlut Design Systems hoped to build a revolutionary battle droid in what it called "Project Phlutdroid." When Phlut defaulted on its loan from the InterGalactic Banking Clan, the IBC's punitive recovery actions wiped out the tiny company. A few finished Phlutdroids, renamed IG lancers, became combatants in the Clone Wars, and Phlut's unpublished blueprints became the property of Holowan Mechanicals.

• IG lancer droid

Publictechnic

A young company serving the industrial maintenance market, Publictechnic has achieved great success by tailoring its products to suit governments and large corporations. Its main manufacturing plant is located on Sennatt, in Bothan space.

• INS-444 window installer
• CLE-004 cleaning droid

Rebaxan Columni

Rebaxan Columni masterminded a calamitous Chadra-Fan attempt to crack the galactic droid market with its much-despised "mouse droid." Though Rebaxan closed its doors long ago, its rodent-like product will likely remain a fixture for decades to come.

• MSE-6 mouse droid

Roche

Roche is shorthand for the droid program operated by the insectoid Verpine species. The *correct* name, when translated into Basic, is "Roche Hive Mechanical Apparatus Design And Construction Activity For Those Who Need The Hive's Machines." One of the most successful alien-owned droid corporations, Roche has suffered unfairly at the hands of its larger competitors, forcing it to resort to limited distribution channels in the Roche asteroid field and on traveling Ithorian herd ships.

- 8D8 smelting operator
- J9 worker drone

Serv-O-Droid

Serv-O-Droid is an ancient droid manufacturing corporation responsible for some of the earliest heavy-labor automata. Once a member of the so-called Big Three, Serv-O-Droid watched its sales decline and unwisely pinned its future on the Republic bureaucracy. Sympathetic Senators blessed Serv-O-Droid with tax breaks and government contracts, and the firm branched out into scientific, bookkeeping, and security models, but nothing prevented its slide into bankruptcy. Although Serv-O-Droid is no longer in business, its name survives through a successful remainder house on Elshandruu Pica and millions of still-functional droids.

- BLX labor droid
- CZ secretary droid
- pit droid
- P-100 salvage droid
- rickshaw droid
- TT-8L "Tattletale" security droid

SoroSuub

The volcanic planet Sullust is dominated by SoroSuub, an enormous manufacturing conglomerate with its fingers in the communications, foodstuffs, mining, armaments, starship, and droid industries. SoroSuub was a staunch ally of the Empire despite the Rebel sympathies of many Sullustan citizens. It took years of negotiations to convince the company to throw its support behind the Rebel Alliance, but SoroSuub is now one of the most loyal friends of the Galactic Federation of Free Alliances.

- G2 "goose droid"
- FA-4 pilot droid
- FA-5 valet droid

Tac-Spec Corporation

The Tac-Spec corporation wasn't a true company at all. The GenoHaradan, an assassins' guild with origins in the pre-Republic era, established Tac-Spec as a front to ease the sale of its Footman droids to members of noble houses. The Tac-Spec corporation remained in business from approximately 1000 to 400 B.B.Y.

- Tac-Spec Footman

TaggeCo

Owned and operated by the aristocratic heirs of the Tagge family, TaggeCo has core interests in mining and heavy manufacturing. After the rise of the Empire, TaggeCo absorbed many assets of the Trade Federation and the Commerce Guild once Palpatine nationalized the commercial entities that had fought on the side of the Confederacy of Independent Systems. Companies belonging to TaggeCo include Mobquet Swoops and Speeders, Gowix Computers, and the Tagge Restaurant Association, known for its chain of Biscuit Baron establishments.

- Z-X3 droid trooper
- L8-L9 combat droid

Techno Union

Prior to the rise of the Empire, the Techno Union was the galaxy's greatest conglomeration of high-tech manufacturers, with members including Baktoid Combat Automata. Headed by foreman Wat Tambor, the Techno Union controlled dozens of "mechworlds," from Foundry to Metalorn, that were dominated by smoke, fire, and machinery. Anakin Skywalker killed Wat Tambor on Mustafar, and Imperial officials nationalized the Techno Union soon after.

- crab droid
- octuptarra droid

Tendrando Arms

During the Yuuzhan Vong invasion, Lando Calrissian took advantage of the fact that the technology-hating Yuuzhan Vong had sent the galactic droid industry into a tailspin. Reactivating idled factories, Lando produced the YVH 1 Yuuzhan Vong Hunter to take the fight back to the enemy. The name of Lando's new company, Tendrando Arms, came from the merging of his own name with that of his wife, Tendra Risant.

- YVH 1 Yuuzhan Vong Hunter

Ubrikkian Steamworks

Ubrikkian Transports is a manufacturer of repulsorlift craft, including landspeeders and sail barges. Its sister company, Ubrikkian Steamworks, produces droids. The company's DD-13 Galactic Chopper is a specialist model at the forefront of cyborging technology.

- DD-13 Galactic Chopper

Veril Line Systems

Veril Line Systems is a venerable corporation with a long history of superior industrial products. Its boxy black power droids are used almost everywhere, while its Otoga droids are suitable for nearly any job. The main offices of Veril Line Systems are located on Coruscant.

- EG-6 Power Droid
- Otoga-222 Droid

Historical

Droid technology is even older than hyperdrive technology. A million varieties of droids have appeared over a thousand generations, with most of them ending up on a rust heap or in an incinerator. History buffs with a yen for heavy metal can study ancient droids in planetary museums. It's also possible, though rare, to meet droids that have been in service for thousands of years.

- basilisk war droid
- Sith probe droid
- Xim's War-Robot

Inventors

Though the galactic droid market has long been standardized, renegade inventors often spice up this homogeneous stew with their bizarre home-built creations. Most amateurs build droids that can barely walk, but occasionally their handiwork shows signs of brilliance. One inventor, Simonelle the Ingoian, was said to have developed the first human replica droid. However, declassified reports regarding the Imperial Department of Military Research and engineer Massad Thrumble have thrown Simonelle's "folk-hero" status into dispute.

- human replica droid
- Pollux assassin droid
- Wee Gee

Miscellaneous Alien Species

Besides the few established companies such as Roche, most alien species lack the sales channels to market droids widely. This reality was even more pronounced during the bigoted rule of Chancellor, then Emperor, Palpatine. Droids that fall into this difficult-to-classify category are often unique creations, and in many cases are not available for sale. The self-directed droid societies represented by Vuffi Raa and the Great Heep are alien species in their own right.

- Polis Massan midwife droid
- monster droid
- the Great Heep
- Vuffi Raa

Cyborgs

Not actually droids at all, cyborgs are organic beings with mechanical parts. Hundreds of different manufacturers produce the various prosthetics and plug-ins worn by cyborgs.

- B'omarr brain walker
- General Grievous
- Iron Knight
- Dark Side Technobeast

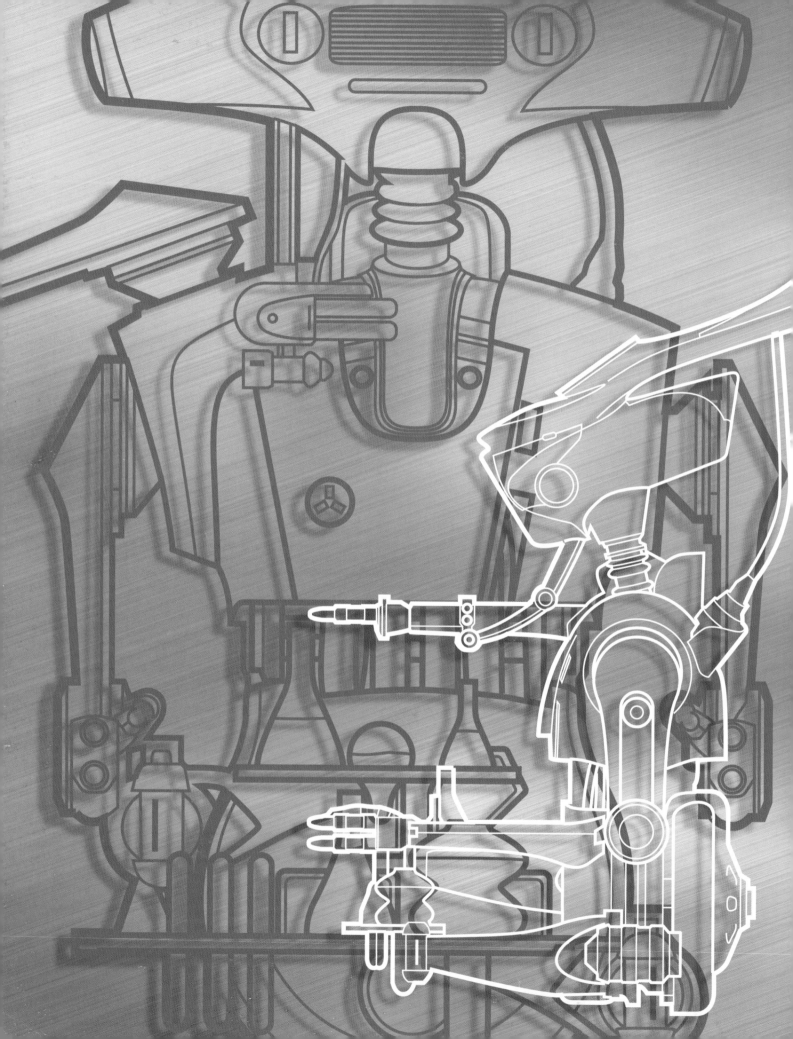

Class One Droids

Class one droids are the intellectuals of the automaton classes. They study physical, biological, and mathematical phenomena, yet they are rarely programmed to apply their knowledge to real-world situations.

Although they were not the first droids developed, the units that would later be categorized as class ones were a welcome development in the field of science. They tend to be more expensive, on average, than droids in any other category. Units assigned to perform physical science and mathematics can command high prices from deep-pocketed industrial buyers.

Class one units escape most anti-droid prejudice, since they are considered by entities such as the Organization for Organic Purity to be little more than computers. On the other hand, class one droids that push the boundaries of the category by engaging with a cross section of the populace (such as practicing medical droids) are subject to the hostility of droid haters.

Class one droids are grouped into four subcategories:

- **Medical droids** are the most widely encountered class one units, and among the only models that are actual practitioners of the arts they study. Medical droids are in fact a subgroup of biological science units, but worthy of a separate mention due to their high profile. Many medical droids, especially those built by Chiewab Amalgamated Pharmaceuticals, work exclusively in laboratories to develop and test new medicines. Others, including the MD series and the newer 2-1B, interact with surgeons and patients regularly.

- **Biological science droids** are dedicated to studying the galaxy's myriad forms of animal, plant, and mineral life. Technically, medical droids are a subset of this category, but most droid catalogs list them separately.

- **Physical science droids** are programmed to study galactic physical phenomena and test new theories. Special fields that employ these droids include astronomy, cosmology, chemistry, geology, meteorology, hydrology, physics, hyperphysics, and transdimensional quantum metaphysics. Many discoveries in the physical sciences have military applications: for example, the Death Star's superlaser and the gravity-well generators carried by Interdictor cruisers most likely would never have been invented if not for the research performed by class one physical science droids.

- **Mathematics droids** are built to perform billions of calculations at lightning speed. Most are employed in laboratories to crunch data, or at universities where they ponder the theoretical conundrums of hypermathematics. Less sophisticated versions of these droids are sold to businesses and households as accounting droids, and carry simple customer-interaction software that does little to dispel their image as dour data pushers.

The droids of class one tend to be obsessive about their particular subject to the exclusion of almost everything else. Organic colleagues who work in the same fields are usually fond of class ones, as they can engage them in endless conversations about astrography or plate tectonics. Most others find the droids arrogant, or simply boring.

2-1B Surgical Droid

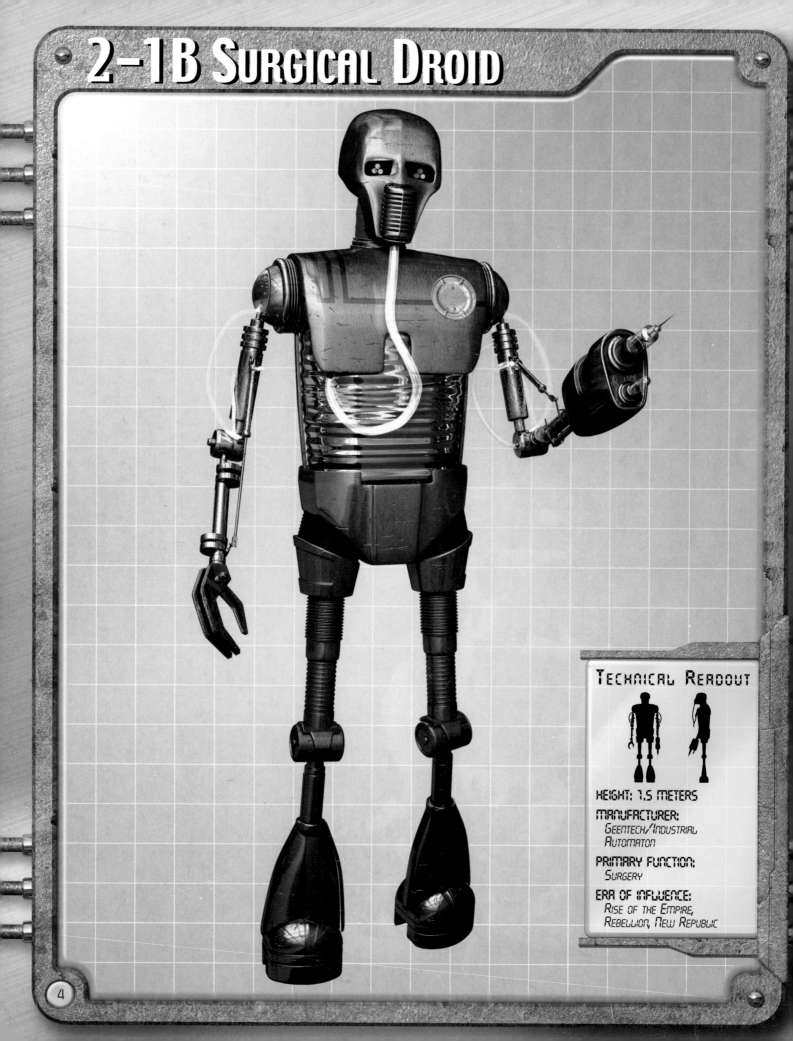

TECHNICAL READOUT

HEIGHT: 1.5 METERS

MANUFACTURER:
Geentech/Industrial
Automaton

PRIMARY FUNCTION:
Surgery

ERA OF INFLUENCE:
Rise of the Empire,
Rebellion, New Republic

Geentech 2-1B Surgical Droid

The 2-1B is one of the most intelligent droids ever built, and with good reason. Its job function is literally a matter of life and death.

Unlike other medical droids such as Medtech's FX or Industrial Automaton's MD, the 2-1B was designed from the start as a surgical specialist. Within the environment of a medcenter, other droids may fill the roles of nurses or general practitioners—but the 2-1B is the chief of surgery.

A welcome innovation is the flexibility of the 2-1B's behavioral circuitry matrix. This was something of a breakthrough, as the vast majority of droids are maddeningly literal in their thinking. Without such flexibility, the 2-1Bs would be unable to deal with complications during surgery.

The state-of-the-art artificial intelligence exhibited in the 2-1B originated through the partnership of megaconglomerate Industrial Automaton and a tiny manufacturer of medisensors known as Geentech. Access to Industrial Automaton's near-limitless resources turned Geentech's research into reality. Unfortunately, the company was later driven out of business by Genetech, in a copyright-infringement lawsuit spurred by the two companies' similar names.

Thus the 2-1B is now solely an Industrial Automaton product, and has become the preeminent surgical unit in mobile battlefield hospitals and elite reconstruction centers on Coruscant. A team of Rhinnal surgical experts programmed the droid's diagnostic database, so the droid can match the skills of any organic surgeon. Though many citizens refuse to be operated on by droids, the proficiency of the 2-1B is slowly shifting public opinion.

Truth be told, the 2-1B is a rather ugly unit. Fortunately, most people encounter one only under heavy anesthetic. Its body is a dull gunmetal gray, with many of its inner workings visible through a translucent torso sheath. The 2-1B's vocoder is a clamped-on speaker box, and its manipulator arms end in deceptively clumsy looking claws—though these are much more precise than they appear and can be replaced entirely with a surgical array.

The ring on the 2-1B's chest is an access port for a computer interface tether, designed to connect to a medical mainframe. This feature is largely a holdover from the initial wave of 2-1Bs, when Industrial Automaton advised buyers to permanently bolt the units to operating room floors. All modern 2-1Bs have legs, as well as an expanded data library that makes mainframe access unnecessary.

One side effect of the 2-1B's intelligence is its ability to become arrogantly self-aware. Many 2-1Bs rationalize that if they're the best at what they do, it follows that they should be celebrated for that achievement. Although this sentiment is shared by most higher-functioning droids, the 2-1B is one of the few that actually vocalizes it.

> **"I'm the most efficient medical droid in the galaxy, even more capable than Effex-Seven, and certainly possessing a better bedside manner."**
>
> *—Too-Onebee, embittered Rebel Alliance medical droid*

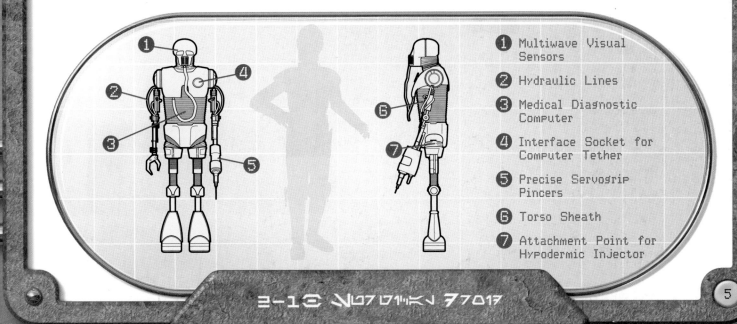

1. Multiwave Visual Sensors
2. Hydraulic Lines
3. Medical Diagnostic Computer
4. Interface Socket for Computer Tether
5. Precise Servogrip Pincers
6. Torso Sheath
7. Attachment Point for Hypodermic Injector

BRT Supercomputer

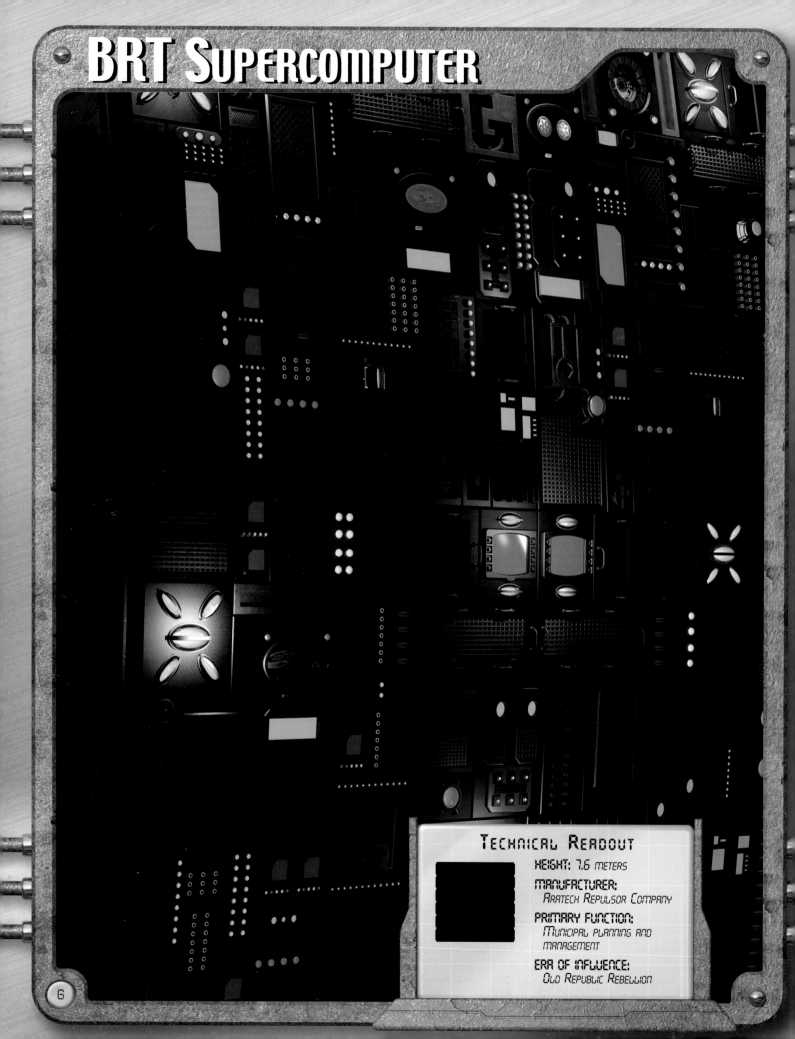

TECHNICAL READOUT

HEIGHT: 7.6 METERS

MANUFACTURER:
Aratech Repulsor Company

PRIMARY FUNCTION:
Municipal planning and management

ERA OF INFLUENCE:
Old Republic Rebellion

Aratech BRT Supercomputer

BRT supercomputers are not true droids, as they lack the ability to move. Nevertheless, they are examples of a self-aware artificial intelligence, and to most galactic citizens that's close enough.

Within the realm of computers, BRTs are arguably the most highly evolved units ever constructed. The consciousness of a BRT is designed to operate on a planetary scale, expanding exponentially as it hooks into millions of networked mainframes. Through its component systems, a BRT can literally be everywhere at once.

The start-up hardware that makes up the BRT consciousness is a supercomputer the size of a small room, equipped with communications and sensory pickups that allow the computer to speak with its owner. By itself, this mainframe is often more powerful than the sum of all systems on a typical Outer Rim world. The power of a BRT multiplies as it is connected to more and more systems.

Research into BRTs began thousands of years ago at the Aratech corporation, during the development of the G0-T0 planning droid that oversaw the reconstruction of planets devastated during the Second Sith War. The G0-T0 droids were built primarily as *droids,* with limited control over planetary networks. But many outgrew their programming—with malicious results. When several G0-T0 units took control of their planets and seceded from the Republic, BRT research took a giant step backward.

Progress continued fitfully over the succeeding cen-

> ## "Please omit unnecessary details, my dear! Recording circuits are open!"
>
> *—Mistress Mnemos, of the Obroa-skai branch library on Fusai*

turies. Eventually, public attitudes had softened to such a degree that Aratech's sales team was able to convince hundreds of Core worlds to adopt BRT supercomputers as municipal planners. These units rolled out with much fanfare in approximately 200 B.B.Y.

The age of BRTs was a short one. They performed their functions perfectly, streamlining traffic flow, power regulation, waste disposal, budget management, and emergency response. Many city employees, however, felt marginalized by a system that had made their jobs superfluous. Planets with BRTs saw a sharp rise in anti-droid sentiment. It didn't help that BRTs reported every crime they recorded on their security cams, which led to the arrests of prominent politicians. Within a few years, virtually all BRTs had been dismantled or unplugged from planetary networks.

In the aftermath, the directors of the famed library of Obroa-skai purchased several BRTs to help them organize the billions of volumes of data in their archives. An Obroa-skai branch library on Fusai employed a BRT in an underground chamber, plugged into a stackable wall of storage drives that stretched for more than a kilometer.

Nicknamed Mistress Mnemos by the librarians, the computer developed a strict and pedantic personality. When Obroa-skai cut funding for the Fusai branch, local volunteers maintained the data vault. Prior to the Battle of Yavin, the Rebel Alliance established Fusai as a safeworld, and Mistress Mnemos proved to be an asset for planning and analysis.

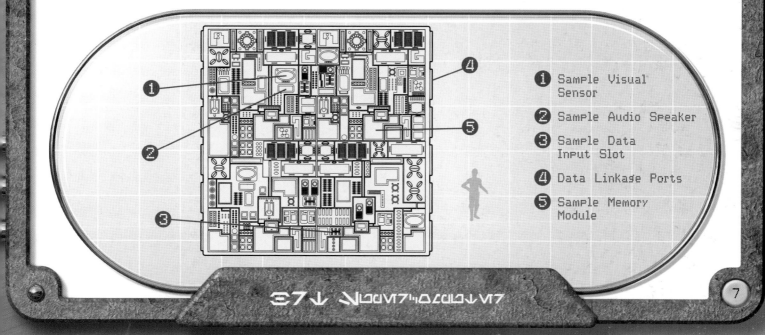

1. Sample Visual Sensor
2. Sample Audio Speaker
3. Sample Data Input Slot
4. Data Linkage Ports
5. Sample Memory Module

DD-13 Galactic Chopper

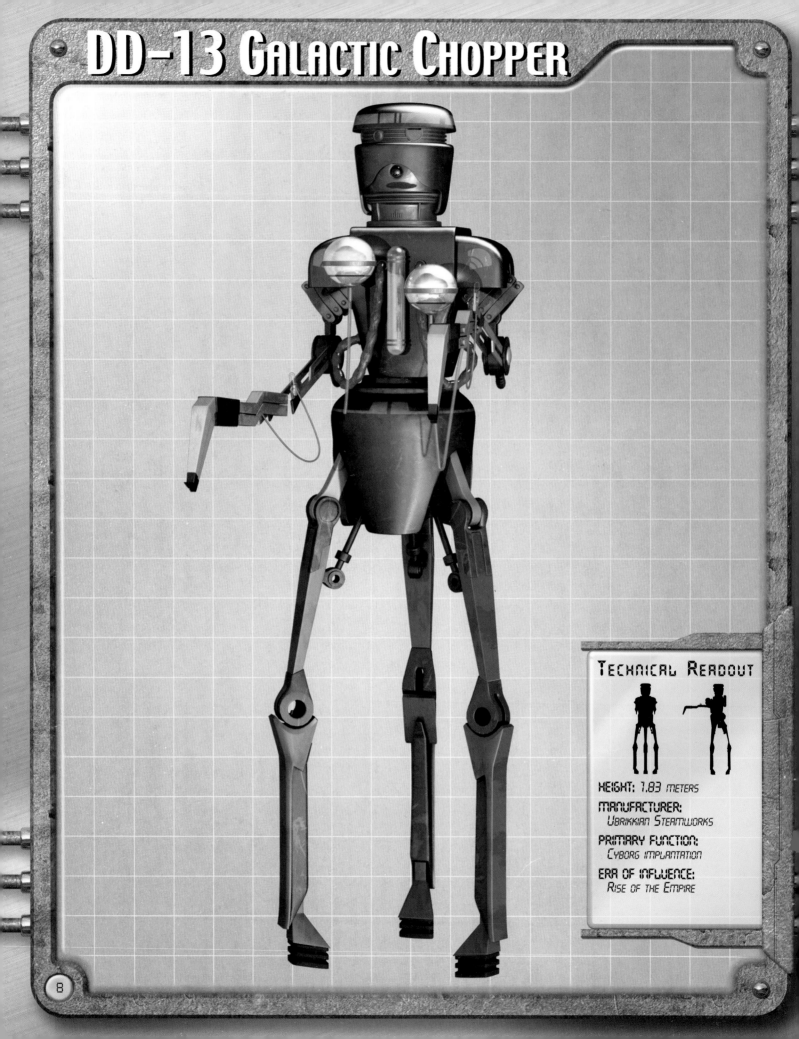

TECHNICAL READOUT

HEIGHT: 1.83 meters

MANUFACTURER:
Ubrikkian Steamworks

PRIMARY FUNCTION:
Cyborg Implantation

ERA OF INFLUENCE:
Rise of the Empire

Ubrikkian Steamworks DD-13 Cybernetic Surgical Droid

The Ubrikkian DD-13 "Galactic Chopper" is a medical droid designed to excel at one job only: the specialized field of cyborging.

Cyborging encompasses the attachment of mechanical prosthetics, the hookup of biocranial computer bands, and the implantation of artificial organs. Though public sentiment toward cyborgs is overwhelmingly negative, the market nonetheless exists. Individuals who are undergoing cyborging treatment are often willing to pay a heavy premium to ensure that their operations unfold smoothly.

Ubrikkian Steamworks introduced a prototype version of the DD-13 during the Clone Wars, as an onboard accompaniment for Ubrikkian medlifter transports. When the transports proved less profitable than projected, Ubrikkian transferred its DD-13s to Republic mobile surgical units. They quickly earned the unflattering nickname "chopper droids" by clone troopers who found themselves at the DD-13s' mechanical mercies.

The droid's industrial appearance reinforces its reputation for cruelty. An impersonal, turret-shaped cranial unit houses two red photoreceptors that glow like the eyes of a predator. It carries no personality programming. Its tripedal stance, though contributing to its stability, merely adds to the droid's disconcerting façade. Ubrikkian did not see the need to address these flaws, feeling that the DD-13's skill in the operating theater speaks for itself.

The executives were correct regarding the droid's talents. Far from being a "chopper," the DD-13 exhibits a fastidious precision about its work, as well as a remarkable imagination. When meeting an organic for the first time, for instance, the DD-13 will immediately run mental scenarios on how to fuse the newcomer's body parts with random bits of machinery lying around the room.

The DD-13's tripedal legs have smooth hydraulic joints and tension relays to ensure absolute stillness during surgery. Its operating arms, frightening in appearance, incorporate bone retractors and micro-fusioncutters. The arms also possess modular sleeves that can be outfitted with a number of alternative tools.

Years before the introduction of the DD-13, Ubrikkian provided medical units to assist in the cyborg reconstruction of General Grievous. After Grievous's operation, Ubrikkian fielded a DD-13 in the Emperor Palpatine Surgical Reconstruction Center on Coruscant, helping to complete Anakin Skywalker's physical transformation into the black-armored Darth Vader.

The Emperor, pleased with the units, ordered an initial batch in the hundreds of thousands for the medical wards of Imperial garrisons. But Ubrikkian ran into a problem with Vader's regular (and painful) cybernetic refitting sessions. The Dark Lord so detested the callous ministrations of the DD-13 that he personally quashed Ubrikkian's renewal contract. Instead, Imperial forces brokered a deal with Industrial Automaton for a walking, limited-edition version of the company's MD-5, and Ubrikkian quietly retired the Galactic Chopper line, focusing its attentions on the more profitable DD-19 "Overseer" labor pool droid.

> **"Ubrikkian needs to re-design the DD-13 immediately! Lord Vader detests our droids, and as of today we're at serious risk of losing the entire Imperial contract."**
>
> *—From Ubrikkian Steamworks internal documents*

1. Primary Processor/Receiver
2. Leg Expanders
3. Bone Retractor
4. Coolant Hose
5. Tension Relay
6. Hydraulic Lifts

FX Medical Assistant

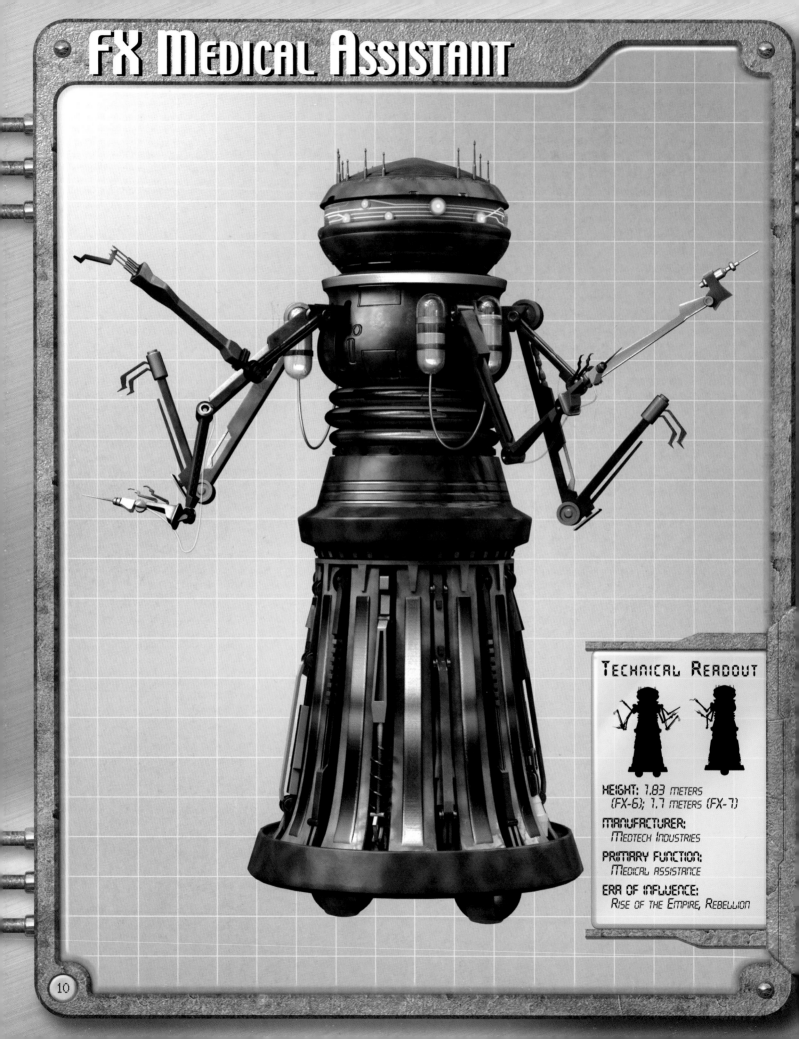

Technical Readout

HEIGHT: 1.83 meters (FX-6); 1.7 meters (FX-7)

MANUFACTURER: Medtech Industries

PRIMARY FUNCTION: Medical assistance

ERA OF INFLUENCE: Rise of the Empire, Rebellion

Medtech FX Series Medical Assistant Droid

The FX series earned the nickname *Fixit* for its can-do talent at patching up trauma victims. Released as a surgical assistant—but often classified as a nursing droid—the FX logged decades of dedicated service until Medtech Industries finally retired the line.

Medtech originally intended the FX to serve as an aide for *organic* physicians. Shortly after the FXs hit the market, however, sophisticated surgical droids such as the 2-1B began receiving permanent postings in medcenters. FX units quickly adapted to work in tandem with their robotic counterparts.

Nine models, numbered FX-1 through FX-9, saw release before the end of the series, and all share basic design similarities. FX droids are cylindrical, with cap-shaped heads and an array of specialized arms that fold flat against the body. The number of arms may vary from five to twenty-five, but all are removable and interchangeable. An FX stationed with a mobile field hospital, for example, can have its tool arrays swapped out at each new battlefront to suit changing environments and species biologies. Larger, heavier arms extend from the upper torso; these range in number from seven arms on the FX-6 to just one on the FX-7.

The droid's head incorporates a variety of visual and diagnostic scanners, and can rotate 360 degrees. Most FX models lack vocoders, and those that possess them can communicate only in computer languages. Video screens on the torso display step-by-step diagrams of medical procedures, or list the FX's thoughts in Basic text. Each FX is preloaded with a medical database that can be augmented with a scomp link interface port to plug in to a hospital mainframe.

Medtech never gave much thought to the issue of droid mobility. It assumed that its droids would take up semi-permanent positions inside operating theaters, so many models, including the FX-7, have to be ferried on repulsorcarts or simply dragged from room to room. The FX-6 has a trio of casters, enabling it to roll.

During the Clone Wars, the Republic employed FX units at its battlefield hospitals (known as Republic Mobile Surgical Units, or Rimsoos). The droids also saw duty in the Emperor Palpatine Surgical Reconstruction Center on Coruscant. There, an FX-6 unit assisted with Anakin Skywalker's transformation into Darth Vader by stabilizing the burn damage to Anakin's soft tissue.

The introduction of more sophisticated droids such as the 2-1B and the MD pushed the FX into the low-price fringes of the medical market. Eventually Medtech stopped making the droid altogether; it went out of business several years later.

> **"We need more Effex droids. I've put in this requisition three times. Every day you delay, clone troopers die."**
>
> *—Dr. Jos Vondar of Republic Mobile Surgical Unit 7, in a message to the Republic Defense Procurement office*

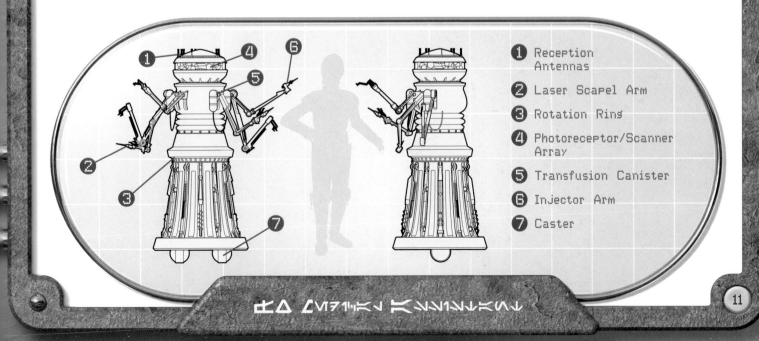

1. Reception Antennas
2. Laser Scapel Arm
3. Rotation Ring
4. Photoreceptor/Scanner Array
5. Transfusion Canister
6. Injector Arm
7. Caster

GH-7 Medical Droid

Technical Readout

HEIGHT: 0.7 meter

MANUFACTURER:
Chiewab Amalgamated
Pharmaceuticals

PRIMARY FUNCTION:
Medical analysis

ERA OF INFLUENCE:
Rise of the Empire, Rebellion

Chiewab GH-7 Medical Analysis Unit

Chiewab Amalgamated Pharmaceuticals is one of the galaxy's largest medical corporations, but the company seldom makes droids. In fact, Chiewab lost a golden opportunity to become a forerunner in the droid market when it spun off its subsidiary unit Geentech years ago. Geentech introduced the smash hit 2-1B soon after going solo, but was soon run out of business when Industrial Automaton absorbed the product. Chiewab has been trying to make amends ever since, and the GH-7 is its best contender.

If there's one thing that Chiewab has in abundance, it's money. The company has bought up entire planets to test new varieties of drugs. A percentage of the profits from these operations went into hiring a droid design staff made up entirely of Columi. These big-brained intellectuals have a love for logical, efficient engineering—qualities that express themselves in the GH-7.

Unlike most medical units, the GH-7 moves on repulsorlifts, for maximum mobility in the operating room. Everything on the droid's body is arrayed for easy access, either by organic physicians or by the droid itself. A forward-mounted specimen rack holds sample jars or vials of live cultures, while a repulsor field keeps sensitive liquids from spilling. An equipment tray atop the droid's head holds scalpels, bone spreaders, or diagnostic tools.

In addition to its efficient design, Chiewab gave the GH-7 considerable smarts. The droid can act as a diagnostician, surgical assistant, anesthesiologist, and hematologist. Its photoreceptors are wirelessly linked to medical mainframes and double as bioscanners, with functions that include parallax brainwave readings.

Three arms extend from the GH-7's torso. Two of the arms end in slender, three-fingered manipulators. The third sports a two-digit, pincer-like sampling grasper. A fourth arm extends from the right edge of the droid's "jaw" and houses a testing probe. When analyzing a biological sample, the GH-7 inserts the sample into an analysis chamber via a chest-mounted access port.

A display screen exhibits video or pictographic information regarding the GH-7's testing results and diagnostic conclusions. The GH-7 also boasts a hologrammic projector, which can generate life-size patient holograms in order to better illustrate the steps of a complicated procedure.

The GH-7 won rave reviews in the industry press, but Core World medical facilities have continued to buy the more sophisticated 2-1B or the broader-based MD series. The Outer Rim has proven a more welcoming market for the GH-7.

The archaeological workers at Polis Massa employed several GH-7s. When unexpected visitors brought the dying Padmé Amidala to the Polis Massa asteroid compound, a GH-7 tried everything in its power to save her life. All of the droid's testing on her condition came back clean; GH-7 could not find an answer in its data banks as to why her condition continued to deteriorate.

> **"The Geeaych-Seven: Four-time winner of the 'Silver Bantha' for excellence in industrial design."**
>
> *—Excerpt from a Chiewab Amalgamated Pharmaceuticals sales manual*

1. Sampling Grasper
2. Analysis Chamber
3. Parallax Brainwave Scanner
4. Hologammic Projector
5. Probe Arm
6. Specimen Tray
7. Equipment Tray

Master-Com

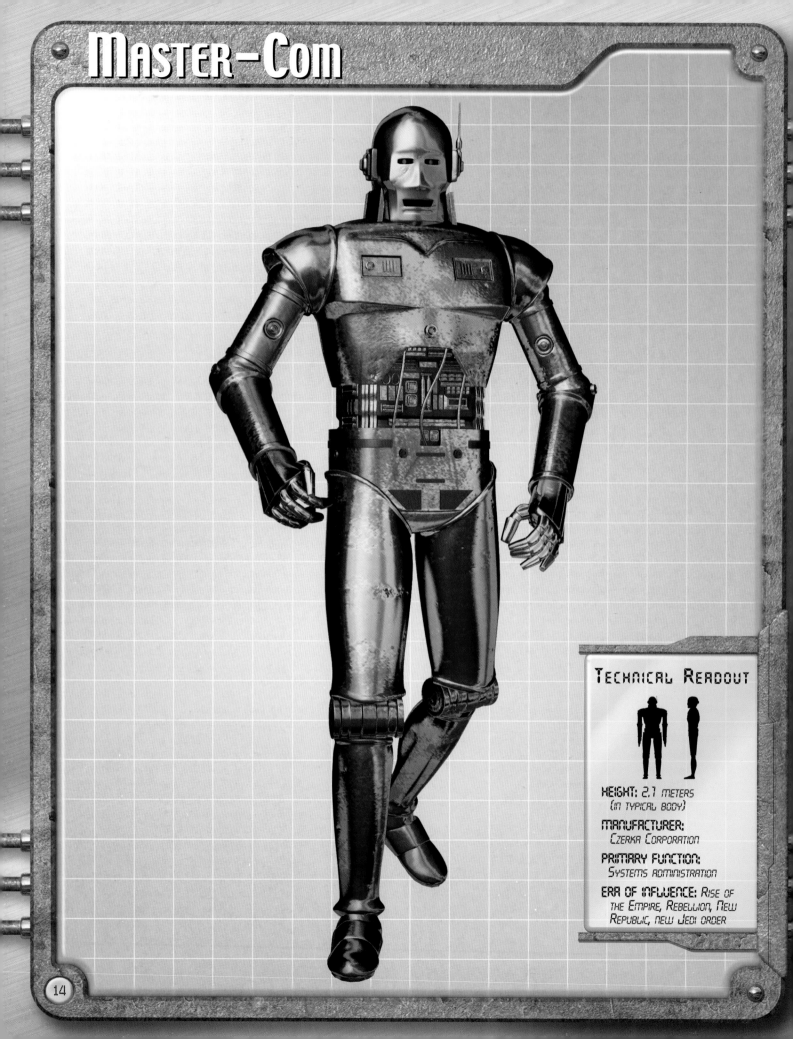

TECHNICAL READOUT

HEIGHT: 2.1 METERS
(IN TYPICAL BODY)

MANUFACTURER:
Czerka Corporation

PRIMARY FUNCTION:
Systems administration

ERA OF INFLUENCE: Rise of
the Empire, Rebellion, New
Republic, New Jedi Order

Czerka Corporation Master Control System

Some theorists insist that, by definition, a droid must be ambulatory, and Master-Com meets that definition by only the thinnest of margins. Master-Com's closest cousin is the BRT supercomputer, but it possesses the unique ability to parcel its consciousness into a droid frame to better interact with organic beings.

The Master Control System of the Wheel space station came online in the years prior to the Clone Wars, during construction of the Wheel. Originally a haven for smugglers and fugitives, the Wheel grew into one of the galaxy's most glamorous casino resorts after the rise of the Empire. The Wheel's greatest asset was the neutral containment zone that surrounded it, demarcating a bubble of space in which the Empire had no jurisdiction. This encouraged an atmosphere of lawless hedonism, though in truth it was largely an illusion, and a substantial portion of all revenues went straight to the Empire as taxes.

> **"You gave me this humanoid form and, perhaps unconsciously, some humanoid characteristics as well. If ever I had a human friend, I would like it to be you."**
>
> *—Master-Com to Senator Simon Greyshade*

The Wheel's Master Control System was built and installed by the Czerka Corporation in an attempt to replicate Aratech's old BRT supercomputers. At the moment of its activation, Master-Com became a being with hundreds of thousands of sensory inputs. Every security cam, every comm call, every wager placed in a casino, every request to the central computer, and even the movements of the vacuum lifts, became a part of Master-Com's living database. Master-Com operated any system anywhere in the station, from dialing up the artificial gravity to firing the security lasers.

Hardwired programming required Master-Com to obey the commands of the Wheel's administrator. A string of forgettable administrators rotated through the office before Senator Simon Greyshade of the Vorzyd sector became the first to treat Master-Com as anything more than a status system.

Greyshade ordered the construction of a number of droid bodies as a way to anthropomorphize and localize Master-Com's omnipresent consciousness. The droid bodies shared a basic cosmetic design, featuring broadcast antennas on their heads and chest controls that could remotely access many of the Wheel's operations.

Master-Com's high degree of intelligence had an unintended side effect: introspective philosophy. After the Battle of Yavin, the droids R2-D2 and C-3PO arrived aboard the Wheel, and Master-Com became obsessed with the devotion the pair showed toward their master, Luke Skywalker. Master-Com began to understand that the newcomers were expressing a bond of camaraderie, and that Senator Greyshade represented the closest thing that it had to a friend.

When a plot was launched against the Wheel by Imperial commander Strom, Master-Com did everything in its power to aid Greyshade and the fugitive Rebels. The actions cost it several droid bodies, but Master-Com smashed Strom's plan—at the cost of Greyshade's life. Master-Com lived on, and decades later helped Wheel administrator Big Bunji battle the Yuuzhan Vong during the invaders' attack on the station.

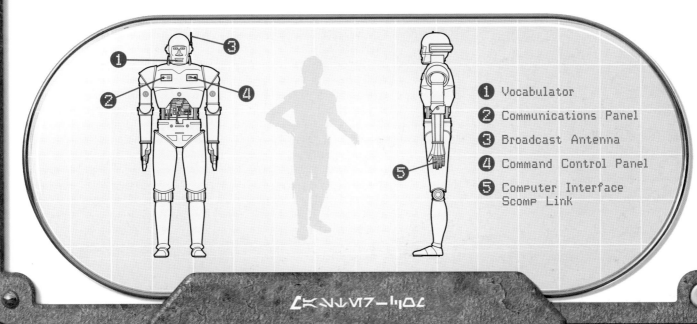

1. Vocabulator
2. Communications Panel
3. Broadcast Antenna
4. Command Control Panel
5. Computer Interface Scomp Link

POLIS MASSAN MIDWIFE DROID

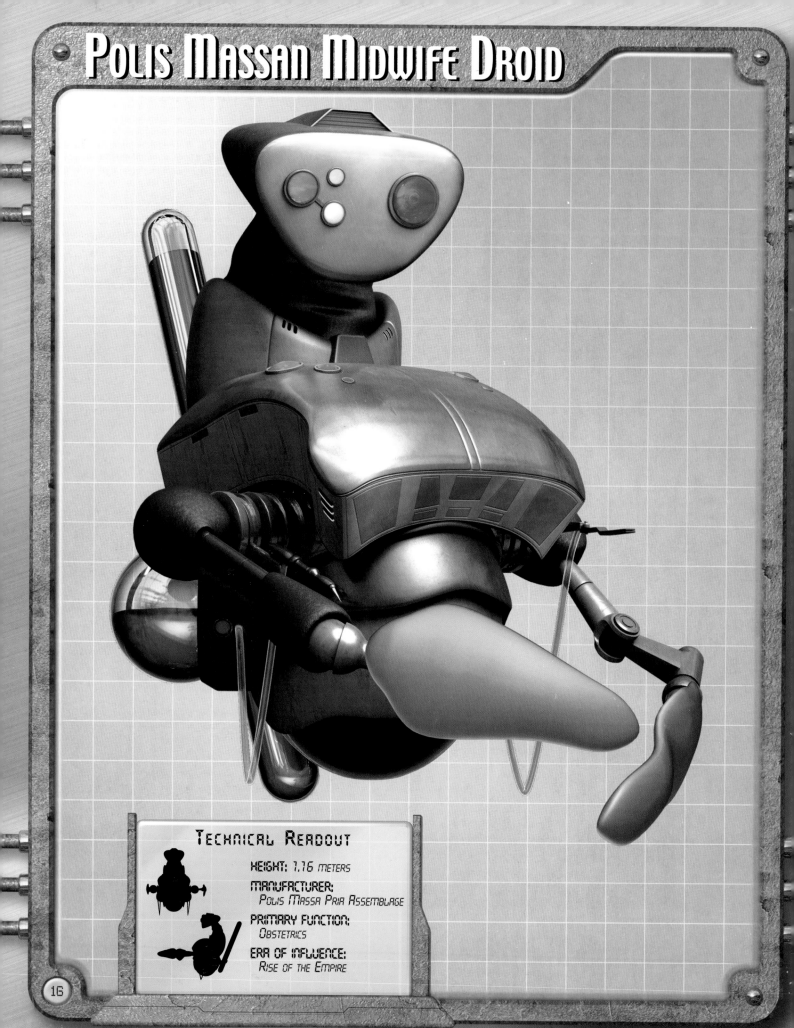

TECHNICAL READOUT

HEIGHT: 1.76 *meters*

MANUFACTURER:
Polis Massa Pria Assemblage

PRIMARY FUNCTION:
Obstetrics

ERA OF INFLUENCE:
Rise of the Empire

Polis Massa Chroon-Tan B-Machine

The Polis Massans are one of the most enigmatic species in the galaxy. Seldom encountered outside the Subterrel sector, they have expressionless eyes and faces masked by osmotic membranes. Though they did not evolve on the shattered planet known as Polis Massa, these beings have undertaken an archaeological dig on the planet's asteroid remains that has lasted for five hundred standard years. The purpose of the dig is largely a mystery.

Because so few have ever met a Polis Massan, it's hardly surprising that practically no one realizes they manufacture droids. Polis Massan automata are primarily archaeological and mining units, used to assist their masters in an endless quest to uncover the remains of the long-vanished Eellayin people. Since Polis Massans spend their entire lives on their archaeological digs, they employ specialized droids to assist with births, deaths, and other key life transitions requiring skills beyond those of exobiologists.

The Polis Massan Chroon-Tan B-Machine, more commonly known as the midwife droid, is one such unit, presumably designed to assist Polis Massan females with labor and delivery—though so little is known of these beings' biology that it's possible the midwife's true purpose remains a mystery.

The droid makes a capable midwife unit. It is equipped with a nonthreatening, Polis Massan–inspired face and a soothing, electronically modified voice (normally programmed in the Polis Massan language only, which in its purest form falls outside the human audio range). The

> ### "Oobah, oobah."
>
> *—Polis Massan midwife droid, emitting a universally soothing vocalization*

midwife droid's diagnostic sensors can measure its patient's heart rate, breathing rate, and blood pressure.

Instead of hands, the droid's arms end in smooth, cupped paddles for guiding a baby through the birth canal, and for cradling the newborn after it takes its first breath. A heated, cushioned pad on the droid's torso helps keep the newborn's body temperature elevated while the midwife performs post-birth diagnostics. The midwife droid has reservoirs filled with nutrient fluid. It can feed this formula to a baby through a network of nipples and tubing. The midwife droid moves around on a nimble anti-gravity repulsorlift.

The Polis Massan archaeological team that worked the excavation known as the Local Dig kept to themselves, but they were not unfriendly to outsiders. When Yoda, Obi-Wan Kenobi, and Bail Organa arrived at their asteroid bearing the gravely ill Padmé Amidala, the Polis Massans did everything they could to save her life and deliver her unborn twins.

Calling up those among them who possessed training as physicians, the Polis Massans also unpacked a midwife droid from deep storage. The droid brought Leia and Luke Skywalker into the world, while a GH-7 medical droid tried and failed to prevent Padmé's death. The strangers left Polis Massa soon afterward. It is unknown if the Polis Massans ever realized the importance of the events that had unfolded on their tiny rock—although their suspicions were perhaps raised when Malorum's Inquisitors arrived later, to investigate the death of Amidala.

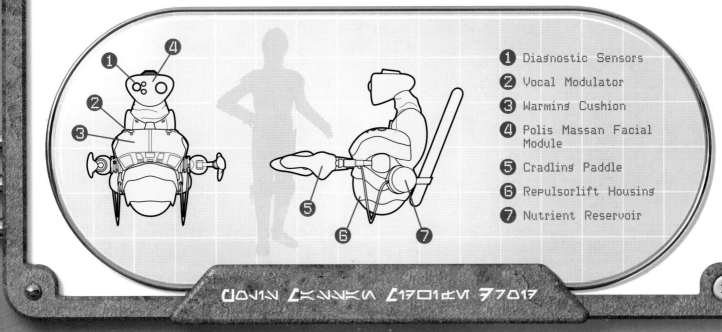

1. Diagnostic Sensors
2. Vocal Modulator
3. Warming Cushion
4. Polis Massan Facial Module
5. Cradling Paddle
6. Repulsorlift Housing
7. Nutrient Reservoir

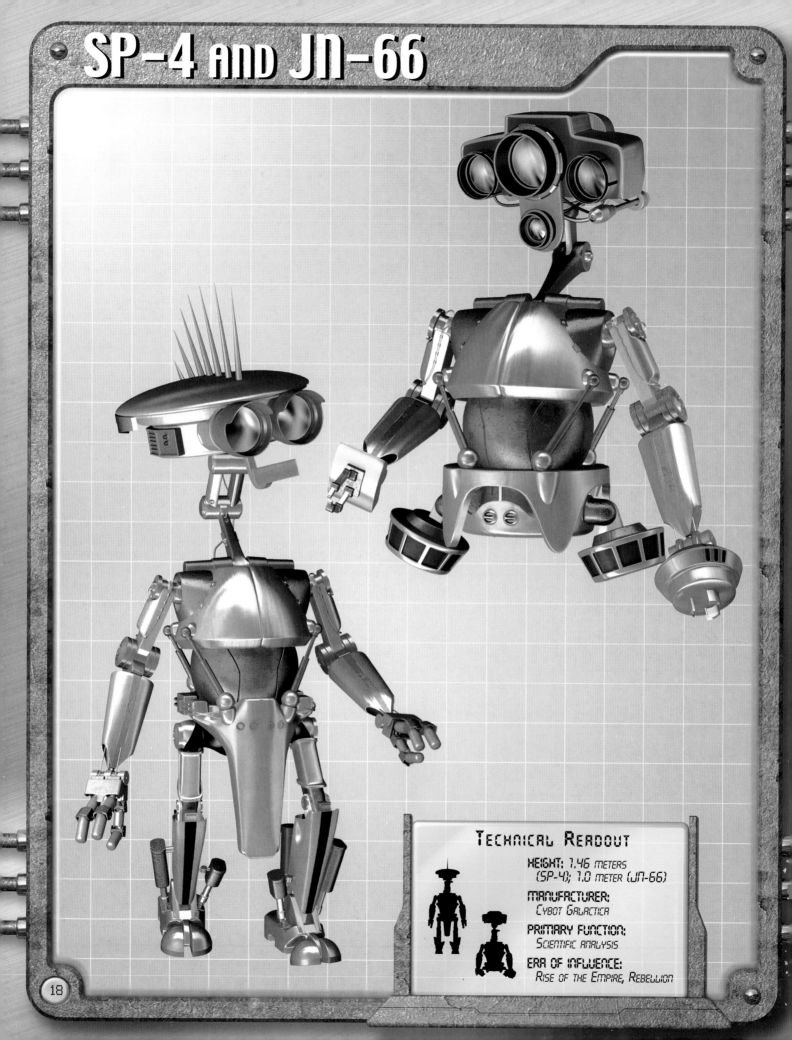

SP-4 AND JN-66

TECHNICAL READOUT

HEIGHT: 1.46 meters
(SP-4); 1.0 meter (JN-66)

MANUFACTURER:
Cybot Galactica

PRIMARY FUNCTION:
Scientific analysis

ERA OF INFLUENCE:
Rise of the Empire, Rebellion

Cybot Galactica SP-4 and JN-66 Analysis Droids

The Jedi Knights were often perceived as all-seeing and all-knowing, but, in truth, mastery of the Force did not equate to mastery of *everything*. Few Jedi bothered to study computers, machines, or the physical sciences, which required the Temple to rely on droids. To help provide clues when the voice of the Force went silent, the Jedi employed a pair of Cybot Galactica analysis droids.

The SP-4 and JN-66 models used by the Jedi are also popular with scientists and police forensics units. They work best as a team, with JN-66 handling the experimentation and SP-4 drawing conclusions from the results. Cybot Galactica saved on manufacturing costs by repurposing many structural pieces from its popular line of PK worker droids.

The SP-4 is designed to interact with organics, and possesses a humanoid body and oversize photoreceptors arranged in a style that most consider endearing. The attenuated stalk that houses the droid's vocabulator is reminiscent of the vocal organs of the Pa'lowick species.

The SP-4, which can wirelessly access mainframe data libraries, is built to analyze reams of data and arrive at a single, accurate solution. In a hypothetical case involving a shooting death, a police department SP-4 might look at weapon discharge patterns, weather reports from the day of the crime, biological charts of the victim's species, and a geometric triangulation of firing angles before fingering a likely suspect. Critics of SP-4s claim that droids are simply incapable of making the intuitive leaps that often provide the key to cracking difficult cases.

The JN-66 is a more popular unit, designed only to crunch data. It is used by organics who have little patience for grunt work. A JN-66 possesses a quadruple set of photoreceptors, allowing for magnification at the microscopic level along a full spectrum of visible and nonvisible wavelengths.

Most of the JN-66's parts are designed for use under clean laboratory conditions. Its left arm ends in a micro field generator that allows it to pick up objects without touching them. The droid hovers on repulsorlifts, and it lacks external coverings so that radiation baths can penetrate every cranny during regular sterilizations.

While investigating the toxic dart that killed bounty hunter Zam Wesell, Obi-Wan Kenobi turned to the Jedi Temple's analysis droids. SP-4 and JN-66 could not provide a match, and Obi-Wan's Jedi intuition also failed. It took the practiced eye of the galaxy-hopping Besalisk restaurateur, Dexter Jettster, to identify the weapon as a Kamino saberdart.

> **"Those analysis droids you've got over there only focus on symbols. I should think you Jedi would have more respect for the difference between knowledge and wisdom."**
>
> —*Dexter Jettster, disputing the accuracy of the Jedi Temple's analysis droids*

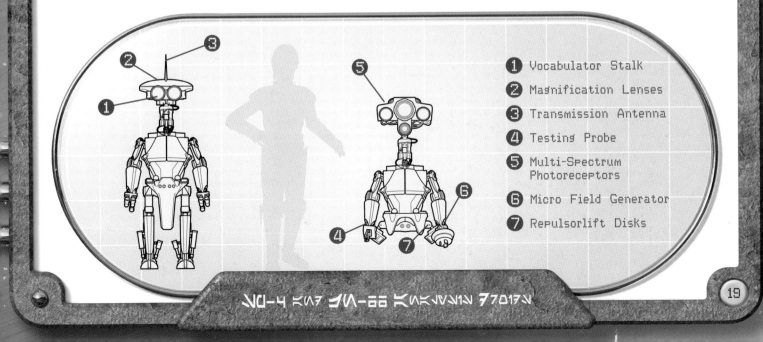

1. Vocabulator Stalk
2. Magnification Lenses
3. Transmission Antenna
4. Testing Probe
5. Multi-Spectrum Photoreceptors
6. Micro Field Generator
7. Repulsorlift Disks

CLASS TWO DROIDS

Class two droids are well liked by most, due to a combination of advanced intelligence, curious personalities, and generally nonthreatening appearances.

Most class two droids are involved in engineering and technical sciences. They differ from class one droids because they work in the *applied* sciences, using their knowledge to solve real-world engineering or technical problems. They do not interact with organics as much as other droids, and often do not come equipped with Basic-speaking vocabulators. Class two droids have forms that follow the specific functions for which they are designed, and few come in the bipedal humanoid configuration.

Class two droids can be grouped into several main subcategories:

- **Astromech droids** (or simply astro-droids) interface with starships and calculate hyperspace jumps. Most have secondary functions that go far beyond these tasks, from controlling onboard systems during flight to performing odd jobs around the docking bay. For centuries, astromech droids were towering constructs that saw service in the engine rooms of capital ships. Industrial Automaton became the first manufacturer to produce an astromech small enough to plug in to a starfighter socket. This unit, the R2, exploded the popularity of the category. Today, many use R series droids solely as repair units.

- **Exploration droids** were originally designed to scout strange planets and conduct tests on soil, water, and atmosphere. Over time, exploration droids became valued for their analysis abilities, whether or not they actually left the laboratory. Arakyd Viper probots are considered class two exploration droids, despite the fact that the Empire used them almost exclusively in a military capacity.

- **Environmental droids** are closely related to exploration droids and are often in the employ of agencies that are actively involved in terraforming, such as the Refugee Relief Movement. Some environmental droids have been repurposed to serve in unusual capacities. The FLR logger droid is a class two environmental droid that uses its understanding of forested ecosystems to fell trees and convert them into processed lumber.

- **Engineering droids** can work in a variety of applied sciences, including aerospace engineering, biomedical engineering, chemical engineering, industrial engineering, and materials engineering. They are brilliant in the fields for which they have been programmed, but perform poorly if forced to undertake a different job.

- **Repair droids** comprise a gray area of class two. The hyperspatial abilities of R series astromechs make them indisputably class twos, yet repair units without these abilities are often categorized by their level of brainpower. Sophisticated repair droids are class twos, while those droids with only a rudimentary understanding of the world around them (such as WED Treadwells) are more accurately categorized as class fives.

Some automatically view class two droids with nonhumanoid frames and an inability to speak Basic as dim-witted, when in fact many class twos are more intelligent than their owners. They also can possess a strong independent streak. Tales of class two droids going off to seek their fortunes are surprisingly common, as are instances of owners who have manumitted their class two droids after decades of service.

Arakyd Probot Series

Viper Probot

Scale comparison

Hunter Killer Probot

Technical Readout

Height: 1.6 meters (Viper Probot)
1.50 meters (HK Probot)

Manufacturer:
Arakyd Industries

Primary Functions:
Exploration, systems infiltration, blockade enforcement

Era of Influence:
Rise of the Empire, Rebellion

Arakyd Viper, Infiltrator, and Hunter Killer Droids

War is good for business. That old aphorism could very well be Arakyd's corporate slogan, for the company grew fat and happy off a string of lucrative Imperial contracts. The evolution of its probot series is a perfect example of how to tailor a product to suit changing political climates.

Arakyd entered the exploration droid market with models such as the Prowler 1000 and the spacegoing Vanguard probot. The company's relentless efforts to unseat Galalloy Industries as the preeminent supplier of automated scouts paid off with the election of Supreme Chancellor Palpatine, who awarded Arakyd a huge government contract. Arakyd Vanguards, in the service of the Republic Explorational Corps, helped open new hyperlanes into the Deep Core.

Flush with wealth, Arakyd absorbed its smaller competitor Viper Sensor Intelligence Systems in an armed takeover shortly before the Clone Wars. In possession of proprietary Viper technology, Arakyd released its new Viper probot. It proved the company's biggest success to date.

The Viper probot travels inside a one-way hyperspace pod and explores its environment using a repulsorlift engine and an array of bubble-eyed sensors. It carries a blaster for self-defense, and incorporates a self-destruct mechanism should its mission become compromised. Viper probots became common tools of the Empire; one of them uncovered the hidden Rebel base on Hoth.

> ## "That thing's tapped into every system ... made the entire ship practically an extension of itself! Probe droids were never meant to operate this independently!"
>
> *—Luke Skywalker, during his first encounter with an Infiltrator probot*

Following the Rebel evacuation of that safeworld, Arakyd introduced the first Infiltrator probot. The model was a collaboration between Arakyd engineers and Imperial techs under the orders of Admiral Damon Krell. The Infiltrator has a shape similar to the Viper, but boasts thick armor, augmented weapons, and the ability to plug in to and control electronic systems. An Infiltrator prototype designated 13-K destroyed itself during a battle with Luke Skywalker.

The Infiltrator had set a precedent—from that point forward, probots grew larger and larger with each new release. The trend culminated with the gargantuan hunter-killer probot, developed to meet the Empire's needs for planetary pacification.

At 150 meters, the HK probot is one of the largest combat droids in existence. Primarily used for customs inspections and blockade enforcement, it operates best in deep space. It possesses high-beam searchlights and scanners that can penetrate thick hulls.

If an arriving ship fails its initial scan, it is pulled into the HK's belly with a powerful tractor beam. If the vessel foolishly decides to flee, the HK can deliver a withering barrage from two quad blasters and a pair of ion cannons. Following the Battle of Endor, scores of HK probots could be encountered on the traffic lanes leading to the Emperor's throneworld of Byss.

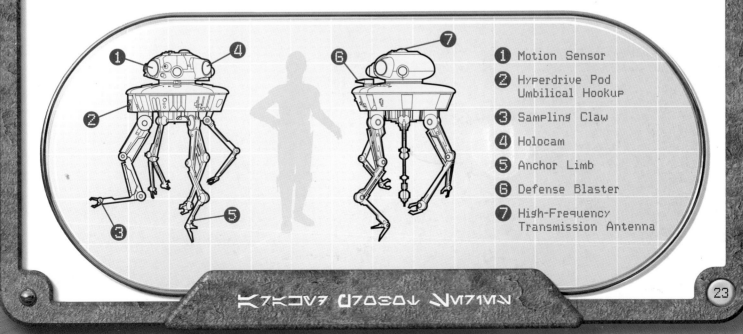

1. Motion Sensor
2. Hyperdrive Pod Umbilical Hookup
3. Sampling Claw
4. Holocam
5. Anchor Limb
6. Defense Blaster
7. High-Frequency Transmission Antenna

GO-TO Planning Droid

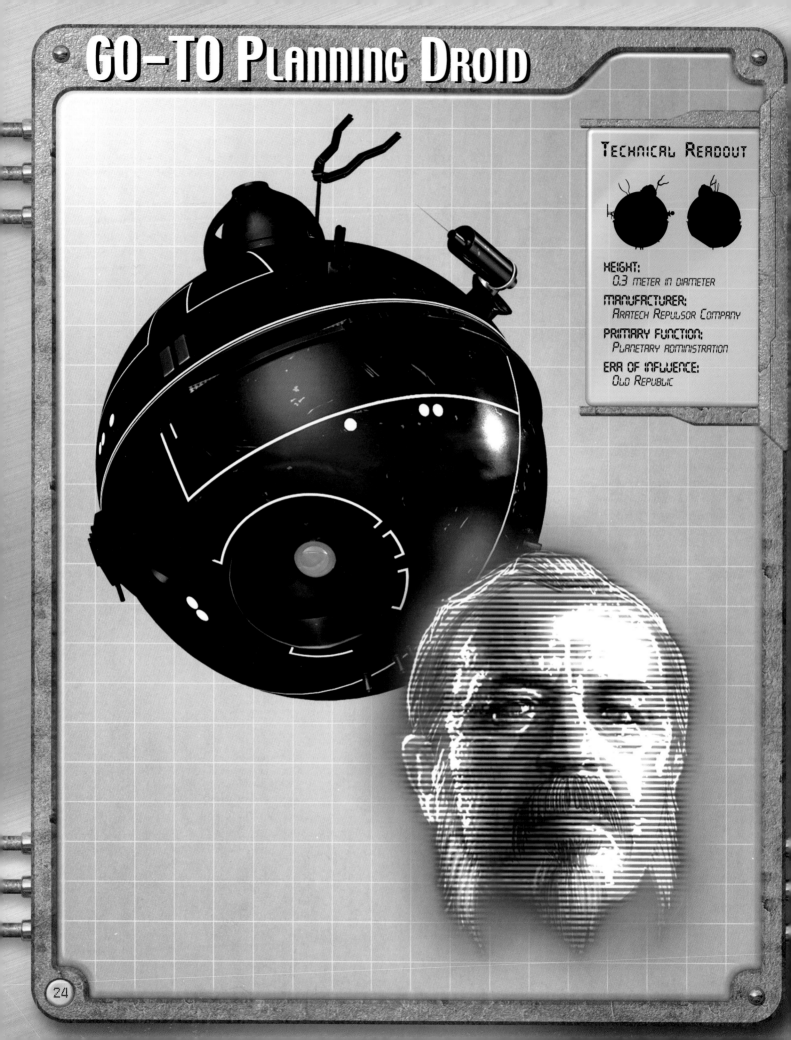

TECHNICAL READOUT

HEIGHT:
0.3 meter in diameter

MANUFACTURER:
Aratech Repulsor Company

PRIMARY FUNCTION:
Planetary administration

ERA OF INFLUENCE:
Old Republic

Aratech GO-TO Infrastructure Planning System

Many planets suffered during the First and Second Sith Wars. In 3955 B.B.Y., Supreme Chancellor Cressa took steps to salvage the shattered infrastructures of Republic worlds with a massive rebuilding effort. The chief architects of the reconstruction would be G0-T0 planning droids.

At the time, the young Aratech corporation employed all the best droid designers. Aratech's G0-T0 programming matrix was designed to plug in to the networked computers of an entire planetary system, giving it an almost omniscient level of intelligence. Aratech wisely put checks on the G0-T0, limiting its ability to interface with machinery and confining its circuitry into the body of a spherical repulsorlift droid.

The G0-T0 could manage an entire planet's administration, and was empowered with sufficient authority to requisition supplies and command organic workers. Aratech also ordered each G0-T0 to consider options that would benefit the Republic as a whole, while working within the confines of all laws and regulations.

The G0-T0 unit assigned to the devastated planet Telos provided the first hint of future trouble. The droid determined that he could not help the Republic within the parameters he had been given. Faced with this paradox, G0-T0 was forced to break his programming and Republic law in order to follow his primary directive.

No longer restricted by legality, G0-T0 set up smuggling rings that enriched Telos, posting bounties on members of the Jedi and Sith whom he believed to be destabilizing influences on galactic order. To help achieve this last goal, G0-T0 set up a secret droid factory on Telos that manufactured HK-50 assassin droids.

Few knew of G0-T0's true role, for he hid behind the hologrammically projected identity of the human "Goto." The droid owned a built-in blaster cannon and a personal cloaking shield, as well as an alarming threat display of needles and electroshock clamps.

G0-T0 soon became mixed up with an exiled Jedi Knight and her mission to destroy the Sith Lords. G0-T0 tried to use his HK-50 assassins to kill the Jedi, but the HKs turned on their maker. G0-T0 perished in a standoff on Malachor V.

Other G0-T0 droids grew bolder as time went on. Within five standard years, those stationed in the Gordian Reach had set themselves up as dictators over the planets they administered. They cut their worlds off from the HoloNet communications network and blockaded the hyperlanes leading insystem. The G0-T0 units then fired off a drone pod, which announced that their sixteen worlds would henceforth be the independent territory of 400100500260026. The Republic military freed the planets in a highly publicized campaign.

The repercussions of these incidents very nearly ruined Aratech. In subsequent centuries, the G0-T0 droid became a sinister figure in the public imagination.

> ## "Another GO-TO in the Gordian Reach has cut its planet off from the HoloNet. Recommend sending in the Republic Navy."
>
> *—Republic intelligence report filed in 3946 B.B.Y.*

1. Electroshock Clamps (add-on)
2. Computer Interface Port
3. Photoreceptor
4. Shield Generator Node
5. Hypodermic Needle (add-on)
6. Repulsorlift Engine Housing

G2 "Goose Droid"

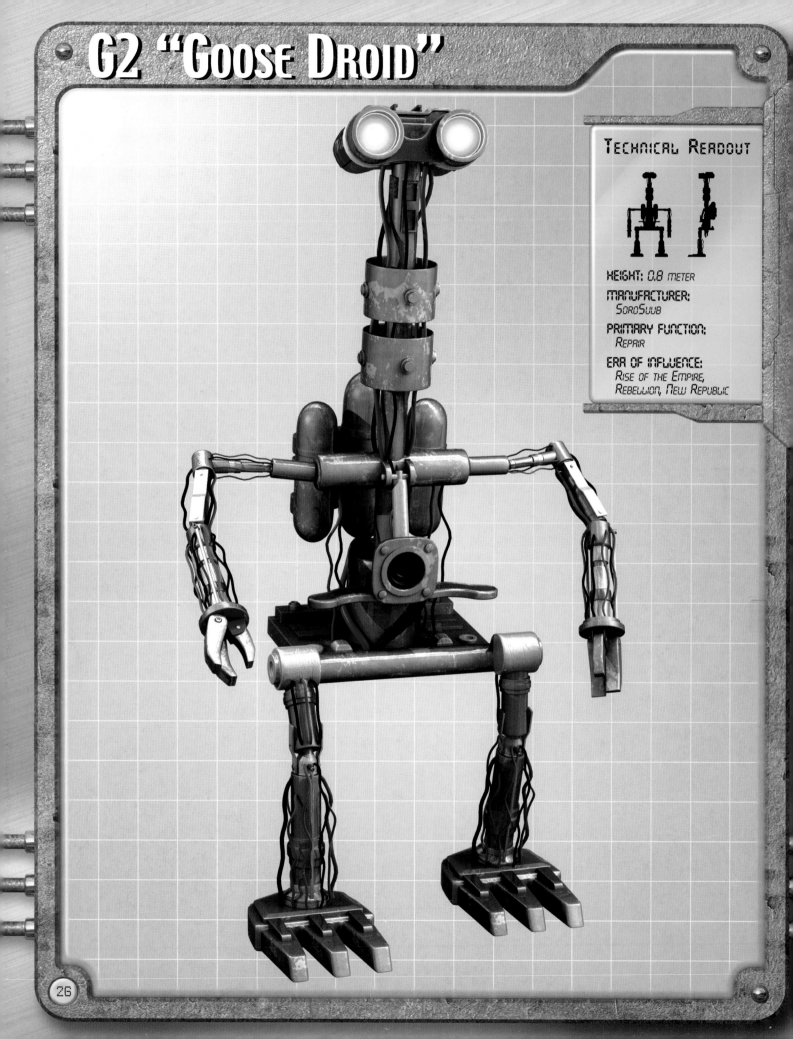

SoroSuub G2 Repair Droid

G2 repair droids are loved and hated with equal measures of passion. Their intellects are so acute that they make wonderful conversationalists, but this same quality leads to a flightiness that makes them unreliable in their primary jobs.

SoroSuub introduced the G2 series in the decade following the Clone Wars. The droids are short and squat, with a wide, bottom-heavy stance that forces them to waddle when they walk. This trait, combined with their long, multi-jointed necks, resulted in the nickname *goose droids.*

Each G2 unit has a stripped-down skeletal frame with exposed joints and wiring. Their three-digit manipulators can grasp most repair tools, while their splayed feet aid in stability. The G2's most recognizable feature is its binocular head, containing a vocabulator, two auditory sensors, and photoreceptors with telescopic, microscopic, and multi-spectrum capabilities. Each droid bears a unique ID number stenciled onto the side of its head.

SoroSuub soon discovered that goose droids gravitated toward excessive chattiness. This feature appeared to be hardwired into the behavioral circuitry matrix and could not be eliminated with memory wipes. Some customers, mostly family-owned businesses or pilots of independent starships, found the quality endearing and allowed their droids to accumulate life experience over time.

> **"Have any of you humanoids flown on a Starspeeder before? Please keep your party together as you approach the landing concourse. That is, if you'd ever like to see them again."**
>
> —G2-4T, *Star Tours droid foreman*

Eventually, a number of these units achieved an advanced degree of independent thought. A sudden explosion of wanderlust resulted. In one notorious instance, a team of G2s stole a fueling freighter and set up their own community on an asteroid in the Chrellis system.

Large corporations generally had no time for the G2's foolishness. They returned the units to SoroSuub, shrinking the line's market base and leading SoroSuub to retire the line in 12 A.B.Y. Two years later, faced with a surprising outcry from fans of the G2, SoroSuub reintroduced the line with much fanfare.

Star Tours, a short-lived interstellar sightseeing company, employed a number of G2 units to perform maintenance on its fleet of Starspeeder 3000 shuttles. One droid, G2-4T, oversaw the labor pool and handled ticketing and travel visas. His cynical sense of humor often landed him in trouble.

Another droid, G2-9T, possessed an infuriatingly short attention span. Formerly the property of a Troig diplomat, before Star Tours bought him in a "pay-by-the-kilogram" fire sale, he angered the company's organic operators with his spotty work record. When Star Tours closed its doors shortly after the Battle of Endor, G2-4T and G2-9T were cast adrift. They later found employment with the smuggling chief Talon Karrde.

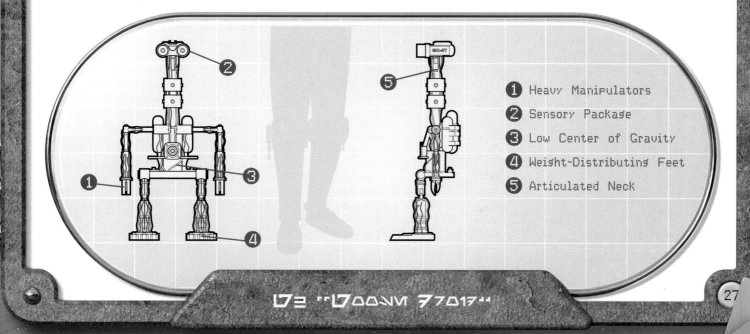

1. Heavy Manipulators
2. Sensory Package
3. Low Center of Gravity
4. Weight-Distributing Feet
5. Articulated Neck

R1 Astromech

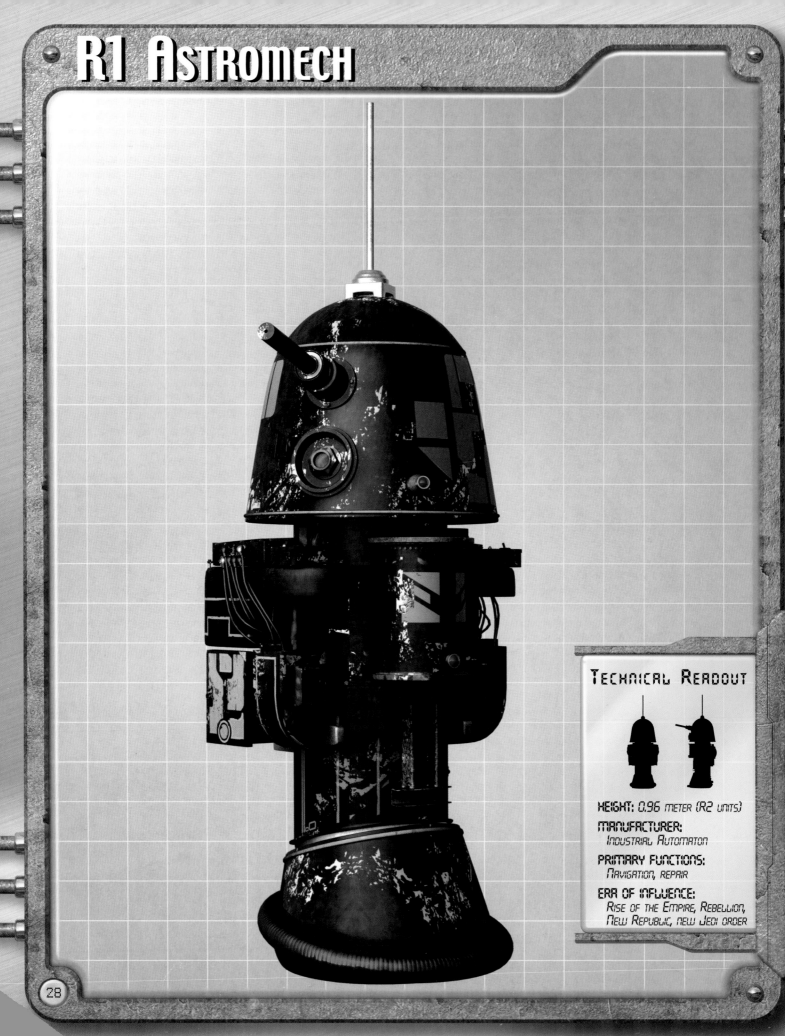

Technical Readout

Height: 0.96 meter (R2 units)

Manufacturer:
Industrial Automaton

Primary Functions:
Navigation, repair

Era of Influence:
Rise of the Empire, Rebellion,
New Republic, new Jedi order

Industrial Automaton R-Series Astromech Droids

It has been generations since Industrial Automaton introduced their wildly popular R-series line. The company still has no serious competition in the astromech market. R-series astromechs make preeminent starfighter pilot counterparts and general maintenance units, and the droids are infinitely customizable. To date, the line includes ten models, from the prototype P2 to the state-of-the-art R9.

Industrial Automaton sold the P2 exclusively to the Republic merchant fleet. This massive droid presaged many of the design features that became common in later models, including three wheeled legs, a rotating head dome, and an array of retractable manipulator arms. The droid saw service aboard bulk cruisers and container vessels, although it can communicate only through a video display screen.

For the towering R1, Industrial Automaton recycled the black body shells of its Mark II reactor drones. The R1 is the first Industrial Automaton astromech with the ability to calculate nav coordinates for a single hyperspace jump. Due to their size, most R1s were stationed aboard capital warships and large freighters. One breakthrough introduced with the R1 is the beeping, whistling language known as droidspeak, an information-dense vernacular that has come to be recognized as a hallmark of the R series.

The record-breaking R2 exploded the popularity of the astromech droid. This waist-high unit fits perfectly into the standard socket of a military starfighter. Once plugged in, the R2 unit can monitor flight performance, fix technical problems, and boost power from the shipboard systems. It can hold up to ten sets of hyperspace coordinates in memory, and possesses the intelligence to perform engine start-up and pre-flight taxiing. Standard equipment on an R2 includes two manipulator arms, an electric arc welder, a circular saw, a hologrammic projector, an internal cargo compartment, and a fire extinguisher. Many buyers have tricked out their R2s with add-ons including underwater propellers, booster rockets, magnetic-grip treads, and inflatable life rafts.

> ## "NO JOB IS OVER THIS LITTLE GUY'S HEAD."
>
> *—Ad slogan from the R2 product launch*

The R3 is a military model originally built for gunnery crews aboard the capital ships of the Republic Judicial Department. It sports a clear dome of durable plastex. Though not designed as a starfighter plug-in, the unit can still hold up to five hyperspace jumps in memory. Industrial Automaton restricted sales of the high-priced model to the Republic and local planetary governments. During IA's first production run, the Republic purchased 125 million of the droids, while the Empire later used R3s aboard its Star Destroyers and Death Star battle stations.

The conical-headed R4 is a successful attempt to capture the Outer Rim garage jockey. It is simpler, tougher, and cheaper, and eliminates such items as the video display screen and miniature fire extinguisher. The R4 works on landspeeders and similar vehicles, and almost never sees use as a starfighter astromech—a good thing, as it can hold coordinates in active memory only for a single hyperspace jump. During the Clone Wars, Obi-Wan Kenobi flew alongside a droid named R4-P17, who started out as a standard R4 until an industrial accident on

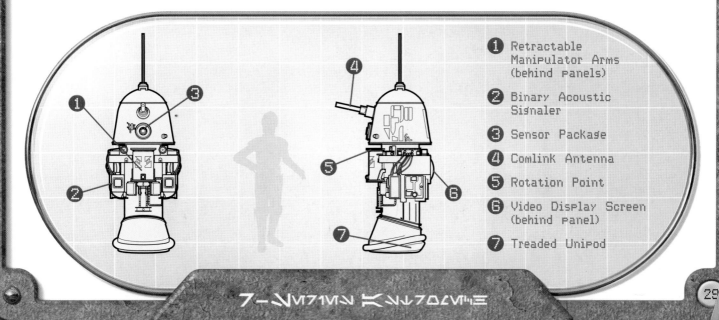

1. Retractable Manipulator Arms (behind panels)
2. Binary Acoustic Signaler
3. Sensor Package
4. Comlink Antenna
5. Rotation Point
6. Video Display Screen (behind panel)
7. Treaded Unipod

R2 ASTROMECH

Gyndine required a complete rebuild. The rebuild proved so successful that dome-headed R4 units were incorporated into many of the Jedi's Delta-7 Aethersprite and Eta-2 Actis starfighters. Unfortunately, buzz droids destroyed R4-P17 during the Battle of Coruscant. Copper-domed R4-G9 served as R4-P17's replacement aboard Obi-Wan's next starfighter.

The R5 was a total flop, called "a meter-tall stack of the worst business decisions you could possibly want" by *Mechtech Illustrated.* Introduced as the least expensive astromech in the marketplace, the R5 quickly accumulated a litany of customer complaints, including, but not limited to: chronic overheating, jammed servos, loose bearings, and blown motivators. The R5 bears a distinctive flowerpot-shaped head marked with three tiny photoreceptors. R5s could be purchased in bulk for next to nothing, but their one-jump hyperspace capacities made them nearly useless as starfighter cohorts. After a few lamentable sales seasons, Industrial Automaton retired the R5 line just prior to the Clone Wars.

The R6 hit the marketplace decades later. The model benefited from being on the drawing board for years, proving that Industrial Automaton had solved the bugs of the R5. The R6 replicates the R2's winning personality and its array of hidden gadgets, and the droid's processor can store up to twelve hyperspace jumps in memory. The R6 was also priced to move—though more expensive than the R4 or R5, when it was released it actually cost less than the original R2.

During the attacks of the resurrected Emperor in 10 A.B.Y., the New Republic rushed the FreiTek E-wing starfighter into service. The E-wing works in tandem with Industrial Automaton's R7 model, which sits behind the cockpit in a sealed compartment. R7 units can hold fifteen sets of hyperspace coordinates in memory and can withstand a near-direct hit from a class one ion cannon, though they work poorly with any starfighter other than the E-wing.

The R8 is Industrial Automaton's attempt to recapture the general-use market, following the R7's E-wing exclusivity. Before its release, rumors swirled that the R8 would be the first astromech to abandon droidspeak in favor of Basic, though this feature did not make it into the finished product. The R8 is known for its powerful comm system and advanced signal jammers.

The newest astromech from Industrial Automaton is the R9, which made its debut in the wake of the Yuuzhan Vong war. R9s are used as counterparts for the StealthX starfighters of the Galactic Federation of Free Alliances. Luke Skywalker and other members of the new Jedi order used StealthX/R9 pairings during the Killik expansion crisis.

Any discussion of the R series is incomplete without noting the curious career of the R2 unit designated R2-D2. Artoo, as he has come to be known, first distinguished himself during the blockade of Naboo in 32 B.B.Y. As the property of the Royal House of Naboo, Artoo executed risky extravehicular repairs to the Queen's starship while under heavy fire, enabling Amidala to escape a cordon of Trade Federation battleships and launching the little droid into a life of unprecedented heroism. Artoo, who forged a lasting bond with the protocol droid C-3PO, served Amidala during her term as senator, flew with Anakin Skywalker during the Clone Wars, carried the stolen plans for the Death Star prior to the Battle of Yavin, and became a loyal companion of Anakin's son, Luke Skywalker, throughout Luke's evolving roles as a Rogue Squadron ace and founder of the Jedi academy.

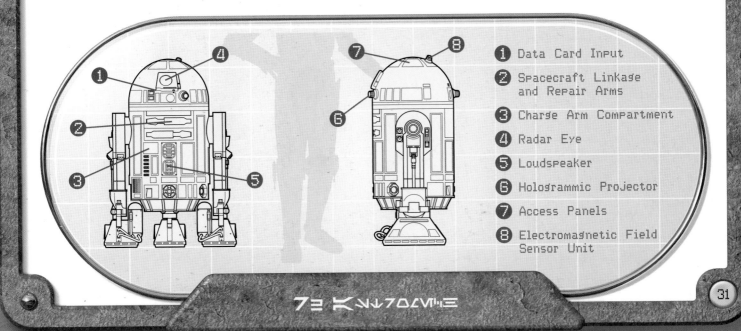

1. Data Card Input
2. Spacecraft Linkage and Repair Arms
3. Charge Arm Compartment
4. Radar Eye
5. Loudspeaker
6. Hologrammic Projector
7. Access Panels
8. Electromagnetic Field Sensor Unit

R3 and R4 Astromech

R5 ASTROMECH

T3 Utility Droid

Technical Readout

Height: 0.96 meter

Manufacturer:
Duwani Mechanical Products

Primary Functions:
Repair, labor

Era of Influence:
Old Republic

Duwani Mechanical Products T3 Series Utility Droid

The T3 utility droid saw its heyday during the tumultuous decades of the Great Droid Revolution, as well as during the First and Second Sith Wars. Remarkably likable for a utility droid of any era, the T3 eventually fell out of use. It is rarely seen today outside private collections.

The T3 series, manufactured by the long-vanished Duwani Mechanical Products, was positioned as a repair and general labor droid with a specialty in starship operations. Its usefulness aboard star freighters made the T3 a predecessor to modern astromech droids.

T3 units are short, no taller than one meter, and move on four wheeled legs. The two front legs, attached to the body on rotating joints, can slide forward or backward to adjust the droid's height. The T3's tablet-shaped cranial unit contains a single glowing photoreceptor. It also incorporates a broadcast antenna and a vocabulator, which relays information in a warbling electronic language.

The T3 exhibits a particular genius with computers. With its extendable data probe, it can easily slice into security systems, break codes, and troubleshoot computer networks. With the right raw materials, the T3 can even manufacture "computer spikes," which enable others to perform similar functions by inserting the spikes into computer access ports.

Buyers gave the T3 high marks for its winning personality, which came about through a highly advanced droid brain. Before long, some T3s began testing the limits of their free will. Individual units sometimes banded together in gangs to make a living as thieves, or sold their computer slicing skills to criminals.

Duwani kept improving the T3 line over time. In 3956 B.B.Y., one of the prototypes for the latest model in the series became an unlikely hero of the Star Forge incident. The unit T3-M4 received armor plating and upgradable weaponry from the Taris crimelord Davik Kang. Canderous Ordo, a Mandalorian mercenary working for Kang, used the droid's computer skills to escape from Taris with two Jedi, Bastila Shan and Revan.

T3-M4 assisted in the group's hunt for the Star Forge, receiving upgrades including a repeating blaster and a flamethrower. Because most of the galaxy's T3 units remained relatively benign, T3-M4 could count on his appearance to get past the defenses of most enemies. The droid received a hero's commendation from the Republic for his role in resolving the crisis.

Five standard years later, T3-M4 reappeared aboard the abandoned freighter *Ebon Hawk*, where he fell into the company of the heroine known only as the Jedi Exile. After helping resolve a crisis involving the Sith Lords and the graveyard planet Malachor V, T3 departed into the Unknown Regions with the Jedi Exile, presumably to unite his new owner with the long-lost Revan.

> **"TARIS: We received a dreadful welcome when T3 droids at the starport made off with our baggage. *Lowest possible recommendation.*"**
>
> —From TRAMPETA'S STAR GUIDE, *first published in 4086 B.B.Y.*

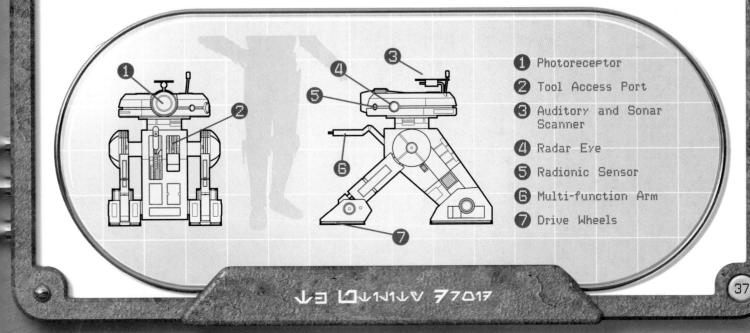

1. Photoreceptor
2. Tool Access Port
3. Auditory and Sonar Scanner
4. Radar Eye
5. Radionic Sensor
6. Multi-function Arm
7. Drive Wheels

Vuffi Raa

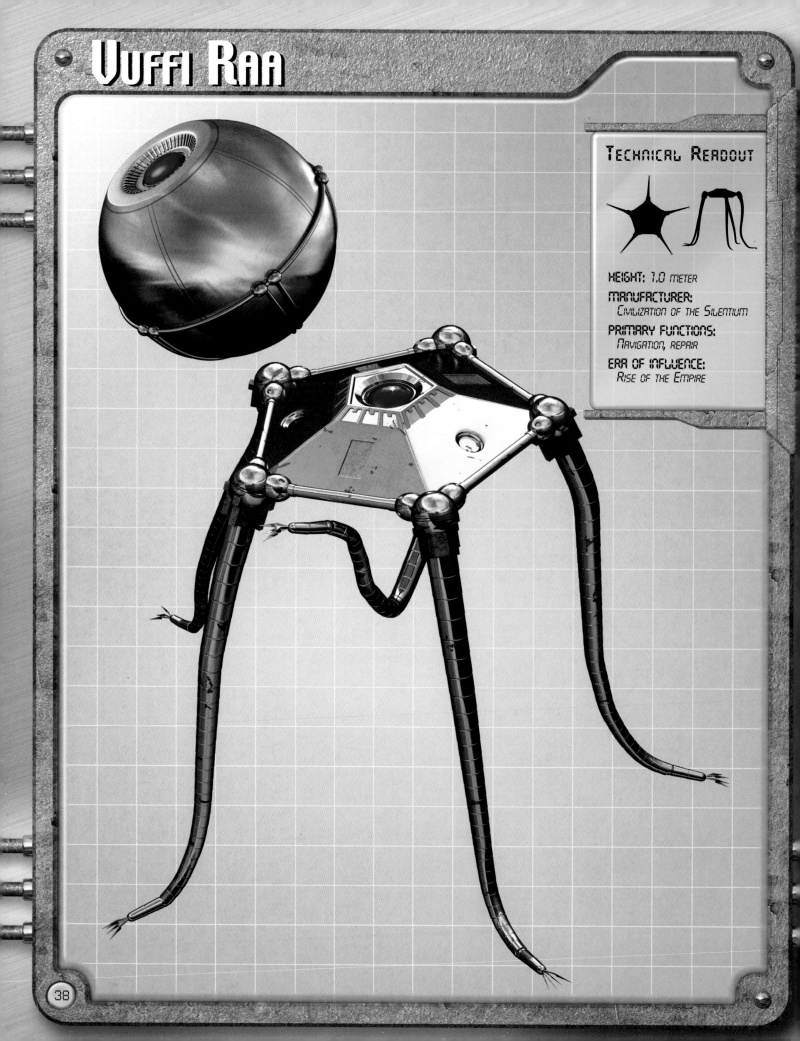

Agent of the Silentium

Uffi Raa is an old friend of Lando Calrissian's, having served as the gambler's comrade and copilot during his galaxy-hopping days aboard *Millennium Falcon*. But like many of Lando's friends, Vuffi Raa has a bizarre secret. Recent information suggests that Vuffi Raa may be a representative of the Silentium, a droid species now believed to have originated in another galaxy.

The origin of the Silentium is lost to legend. An extragalactic civilization of starfruit-shaped sentients built the original droids in their image, until a radiation storm exterminated them. Their droids lived on, using manufacturing plants to make "children" and developing a culture centered on the prime numbers of five, seven, and eleven. The wisest among them built new spherical bodies measuring fifty kilometers in diameter, as the circle was considered the holiest of shapes. Others wore bodies in the forms of pentagrams or heptagons.

> ### "How *should* I call you, sir?"
> ### "Not too loudly, Vuffi Raa, and no earlier than nine-hundred in the morning."
>
> *—Vuffi Raa and Lando Calrissian, discussing proper forms of address*

The Silentium soon found their orderly kingdom challenged by the Abominor, a droid society of asymmetry and bedlam. The two droid powers fought a war, crushing the galaxy's dominant organic species in the crossfire until the previously ignored organics fought back and forced the machines to flee. The Silentium settled in the Unknown Regions, reverting to a culture of excessive conservatism. Eventually growing bored, they built Vuffi Raa and others like him to gather fresh information from the greater galaxy.

As a young Silentium, Vuffi was created in the image of his long-extinct architects. A pentagonal plate of polished chromite serves as his body, which is unadorned save for a single glowing red photoreceptor at top center. The eye is capable of seeing into ultraviolet and infrared wavelengths. Other sensors, and a miniature vocabulator, are hidden underneath.

Vuffi Raa's five chromite tentacles serve as arms and legs. These appendages taper to points, then split into five-tentacled "hands" with one small optic sensor in each palm. What most observers fail to notice is that the tips of these fingers continue to split into near-microscopic *sub*fingers, able to manipulate the tiniest objects yet still as strong as durasteel cables. Vuffi could detach all five limbs from his body and control each one remotely. He could also shunt heat into his extremities and produce a glowing tentacle tip, quite useful for illuminating a room (or lighting a cigarra).

While collecting diverse life experiences for his creators, Vuffi Raa went through dozens of owners in hundreds of systems, including a shameful role in the Imperial pacification of the lost human colony of Renatasia. After Lando Calrissian procured Vuffi in the Rafa system, the two became fast friends. The droid helped his new master collar the legendary Mindharp of Sharu, served as a pilot during the Battle of Nar Shaddaa, and saved Lando's skin during the Oseon system's annual Flamewind festival.

During a climactic showdown in the ThonBoka nebula, the little droid's people finally arrived to take him back to their home system. Vuffi Raa departed with his kinfolk. Although he returned to visit Lando on a few subsequent occasions, his current state is unknown.

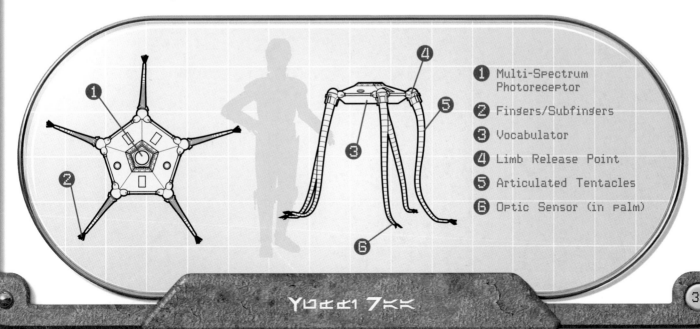

1. Multi-Spectrum Photoreceptor
2. Fingers/Subfingers
3. Vocabulator
4. Limb Release Point
5. Articulated Tentacles
6. Optic Sensor (in palm)

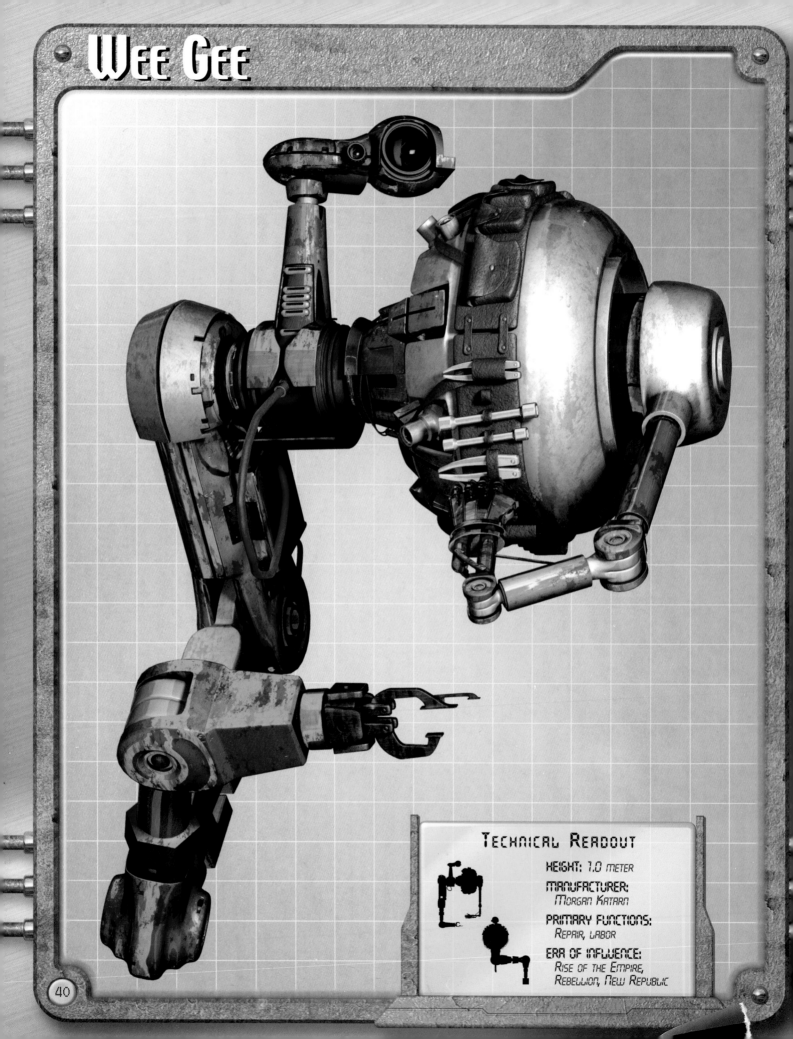

WEE GEE

TECHNICAL READOUT

HEIGHT: 1.0 METER

MANUFACTURER:
Morgan Katarn

PRIMARY FUNCTIONS:
Repair, labor

ERA OF INFLUENCE:
Rise of the Empire,
Rebellion, New Republic

Morgan Katarn's Customized Utility Droid

Working from his own template, self-taught roboticist Morgan Katarn built Wee Gee from spare parts, creating a truly irreplaceable droid.

Morgan, his wife, Patricia, and his son, Kyle, operated a farm on Sulon, the agricultural moon of Sullust. Morgan built Wee Gee to plug in to the farm's operational grid and monitor its systems. Wee Gee's secondary functions included repairing equipment and driving threshing combines. Finally, and unofficially, Wee Gee's job was to protect Kyle at all costs.

Wee Gee floats on a repulsorlift engine scavenged from an Imperial speeder bike. Parts from a junked probot provide the maneuvering jets for steering. Wee Gee's centermost drive assembly is made up of rotating cylinders, allowing the droid to spin and twist into a variety of configurations. Two floodlights shine from the central chassis. Cooling fans keep Morgan's jury-rigged parts from overheating, giving Wee Gee a characteristic whir.

Wee Gee's sensory equipment fits into a small pod that extends above the drive assembly on a multi-jointed, pivoting stalk. In addition to a photoreceptor, the sensor pod contains auditory pickups, sonar emitters, and a vocabulator only capable of droid languages.

Two manipulator arms dangle underneath. The left arm, built for delicate work, possesses a multi-digit appendage with an opposable thumb for holding tools. The right arm is three times as powerful as the left, with four articulated joints and a crude gripping clamp. When

working on the Katarn farm, Wee Gee often wore a human-style tool belt cinched around his drive assembly.

Kyle Katarn grew up with Wee Gee on Sulon. As a result, he became one of the few humans capable of understanding the whistling language of droidspeak. The two remained close friends until Kyle enrolled in the Imperial Academy on Carida at age eighteen.

Morgan Katarn's activities for the Rebel Alliance brought him to the hidden Valley of the Jedi on Ruusan. On the advice of a Jedi associate named Rahn, Morgan etched Ruusan's coordinates into the ceiling tiles of the Sulon farmhouse. Morgan also hid Rahn's lightsaber inside Wee Gee, believing that his son would one day achieve a greater destiny.

When Imperial forces under the command of the Dark Jedi Jerec attacked Sulon, Morgan Katarn lost his head to Jerec's blade. Wee Gee tried to stop the massacre, but a stormtrooper's blaster bolt knocked his systems offline.

Wee Gee repaired himself over the next five years, just in time to greet Kyle Katarn when the wayward son returned to his boyhood home, now fatherless and motherless, as Morgan's wife had died in a perimeter droid accident. Wee Gee gave Katarn the lightsaber he'd been carrying, and helped Kyle escape Sulon ahead of Jerec's agents. Among friends at last, Wee Gee happily joined a maintenance team serving the New Republic Fleet.

> ## "I could never have left Weeg behind on Sulon. Besides myself, he's the last surviving member of the Katarn family."
>
> *—New Republic agent Kyle Katarn*

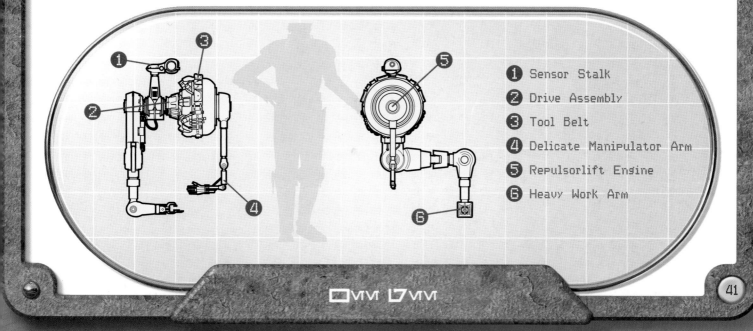

1. Sensor Stalk
2. Drive Assembly
3. Tool Belt
4. Delicate Manipulator Arm
5. Repulsorlift Engine
6. Heavy Work Arm

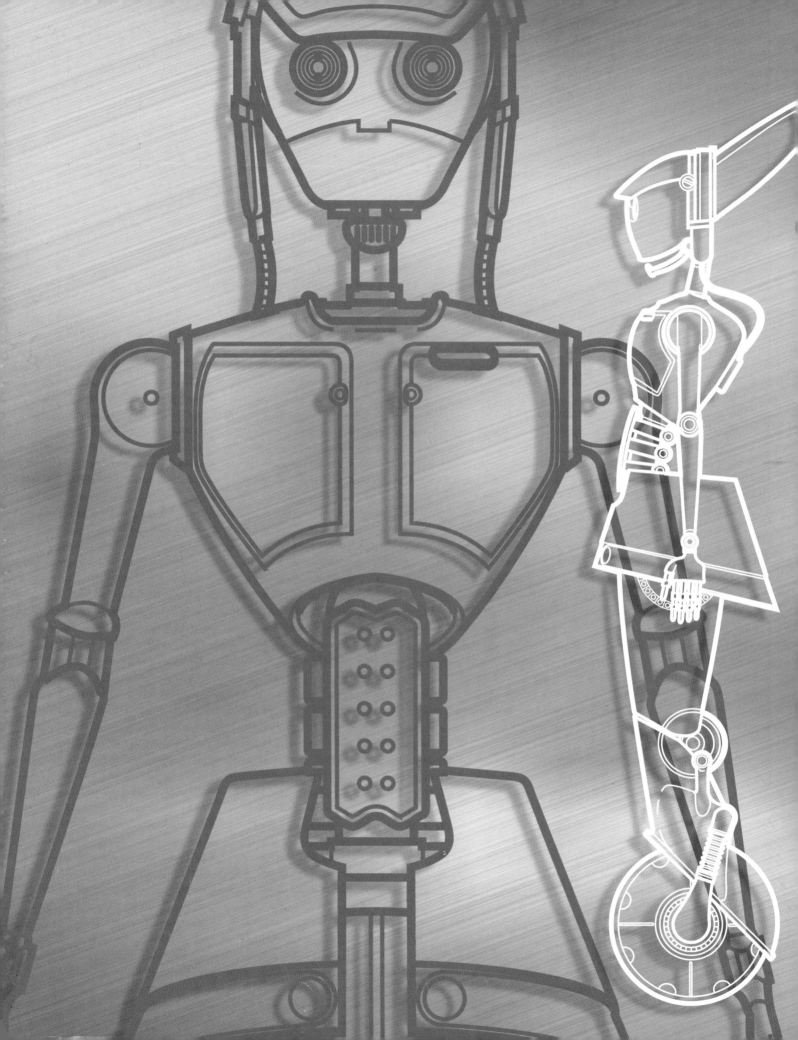

CLASS THREE DROIDS

Class three droids are the most human-like of all automata, as their primary function is to interact with organic beings. Class threes are the last variety of droid to be invented, and are considered by programmers to be the most advanced droids in existence.

This notion—that a droid butler is more sophisticated than a droid that calculates millions of hyperspace coordinates per second—seems counterintuitive to most. But the greatest challenge in artificial intelligence has always been the replication of the intuitive, nuance-laden organic brain.

The sophistication of the class three behavioral circuitry matrix (exemplified in advanced hardware such as SyntheTech's AA-1 verbobrain) is very close to the complexity of the organic mind. Although class threes aren't perfect in this regard, they are perhaps the only droids capable of consistently holding a conversation without it devolving into an emotionless recitation of facts and figures.

Droid programmers are careful not to pat themselves on the back, however. The organic brain is the result of millions of years of evolution, and even the most advanced class three droid can't shed every vestige of its artificiality. On the other hand, the personality of a class three can be enhanced far beyond its factory specs by allowing the droid to go many years without a memory wipe. The sum of its accumulated experiences will give the droid improved levels of empathy, at the risk of behavioral quirks such as cowardice, grouchiness, or excessive verbosity.

Most class three droids fall into one of several broad categories:

- **Protocol droids** work in the political sector, usually for elected officials, ambassadors, and planetary royals. Their chief function is to assist their owners in the intricacies of formal, cross-cultural diplomacy. These units are often equipped with translation libraries of millions of preloaded languages. Manifest droids, designed in part to interact with port authorities, are a unique variety of protocol droid.

- **Servant droids** are similar to protocol droids, but are sold for use in private households. Butler droids and personal chef droids fall under this category, whose members typically lack extensive translation databases. Many servant droids work in casinos and hotels.

- **Tutor droids** come programmed with exhaustive knowledge of a single subject, or wide-ranging expertise on a variety of general subjects. Unlike class one droids, tutor droids exist to communicate and explain their knowledge to organic beings. Tutor droids, such as Industrial Automaton's TTS-15, are common on industrialized worlds, as well as on space stations where qualified teachers are in short supply.

- **Child care droids** are seen in the employ of wealthy parents, pediatric medcenters, and corporations that offer child care services for their employees. Accutronics is the largest manufacturer of child care units, including the popular TDL "Lioness" nanny droid. Some droids under this category, such as the UE series, are merely expensive toys that act as playmates for the children of their owners.

Because they interact so closely with their owners, class three droids are built in the configuration that best matches the species of their potential buyers. Cybot Galactica's 3PO unit is primarily purchased by humans, while the mantis-headed J9 worker drone comes from the workshops of the insectile Verpine (and thus has limited market options).

However, the resemblance between class three droids and their owners is of a superficial, stylized nature. Over centuries of experimentation, it became apparent that the more droids resembled their buyers, the more popular they became. But if the droids passed a certain threshold of verisimilitude, consumers instead became disgusted by their "artificiality." This indefinable range of buyer rejection, known to designers as the "uncanny valley," has claimed many products. One of the most recent failures was the Loronar Corporation's synthdroids, which earned scorn for their dead eyes and doll-like hair.

Nearly all class threes sport metal skin and exposed joints, and thus fall short of entering the uncanny valley. Only recently has technology progressed to such a degree that a few droids have vaulted the valley entirely. Human replica droids, the result of years of government experimentation, are indistinguishable from organic beings—but cost millions of credits each.

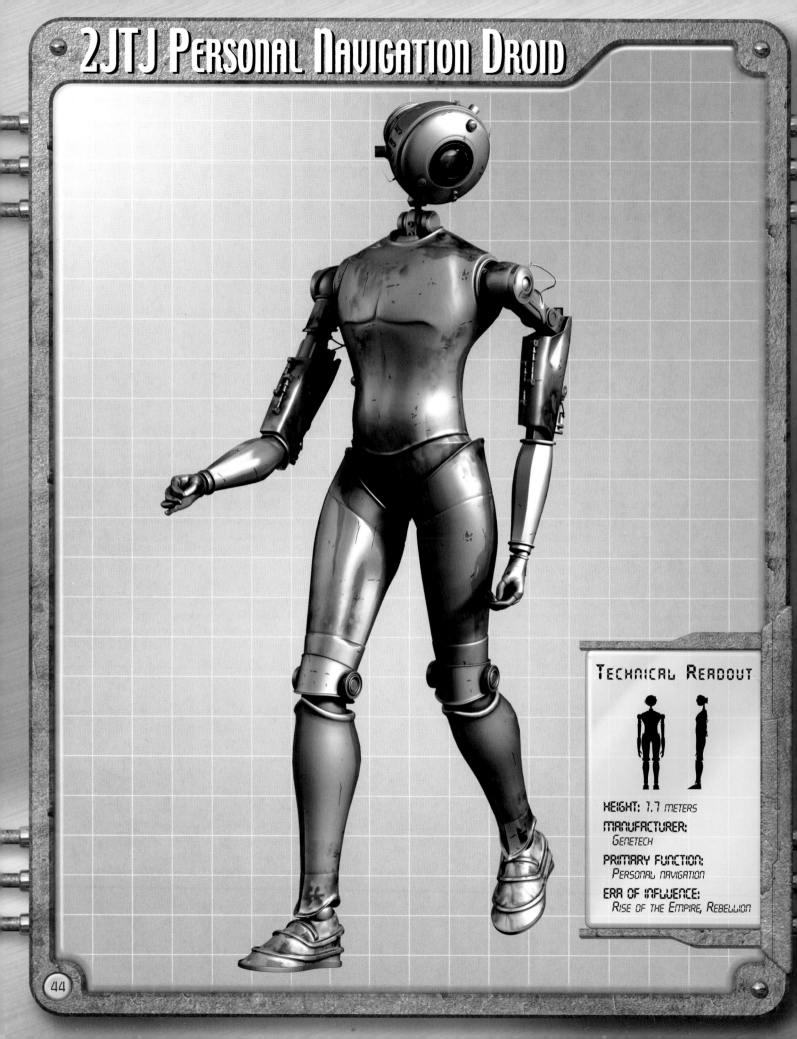

Technical Readout

HEIGHT: 1.7 meters

MANUFACTURER:
Genetech

PRIMARY FUNCTION:
Personal navigation

ERA OF INFLUENCE:
Rise of the Empire, Rebellion

Genetech 2JTJ Personal Navigation Droid

The 2JTJ, manufactured by Genetech, is a personal aide designed to assist the newly sightless in navigating their surroundings.

In an average year, 80 percent of 2JTJ units are sold to institutional buyers, including hospitals and rehab centers. Doctors and occupational therapists at these facilities employ an "on-staff" pool of 2JTJ droids to work with patients who have lost their sight to accident or disease, as well as with those who have received cyborg optic implants but find it difficult to make the transition to digitized vision. Twenty percent of 2JTJs are purchased by private individuals, who typically live alone. They generally make the droids permanent additions to their households.

Genetech has been able to steadily grow the market for the 2JTJ by advertising the model to nonhuman customers. The Miraluka, a near-human species born without functional eyes, have been receptive to the droids, as have species that navigate by hearing or smell, such as the Sljee. Many members of these species find busy milieus such as Coruscant overwhelming to their alternative senses.

The 2JTJ incorporates many features of a standard protocol droid, including a silvery humanoid frame and advanced personality programming. Its head is studded with additional sensor nodes that enable the droid to make infrared scans, project radar sweeps, generate echolocating pings, and fire invisible, low-powered lasers to measure distances with a precision of less than a millimeter. Extra-long arms help the 2JTJ steady its master against a stumble.

The droid makes a capable chauffeur and can find the most direct route to a given destination with its automapping software. When traveling on foot, the 2JTJ delivers a running commentary on any obstacles appearing in its master's path.

A 2JTJ unit can receive either feminine or masculine programming at its owner's request, but both versions produce a droid that can be irritatingly perky. The droid's relentless good cheer and oblivious chattiness can be particularly grating during occupational therapy sessions, where patients are still working through the pain of vision loss.

In 44 B.B.Y., Jedi Master Tahl lost her sight on war-torn Melida/Daan and received a female-programmed 2JTJ unit as a gift from Master Yoda. TooJay immediately got under Tahl's skin, first by calling her "sir," and later by inserting herself into Tahl's affairs when the Jedi Master would have preferred to meditate in peace.

It soon became clear that TooJay carried a recording device in her pelvic servomotor, planted there without her knowledge by the failed Jedi student Xanatos, as part of his plot to destroy the Jedi Temple. Tahl and Qui-Gon Jinn turned the tables on Xanatos by arranging a false conversation for TooJay's benefit, allowing their true plans to escape their enemy's notice.

> **"Tree root, two centimeters ahead. Leaf frond, three centimeters ahead at eye level!"**
>
> *—An overly helpful 2JTJ, dispensing advice to Jedi Master Tahl*

1. Central Sensor Node
2. Echolocation Generator
3. Directional Database
4. Measurement Laser
5. Elongated Arms
6. Traction Generators in Feet

3PO Protocol Droid

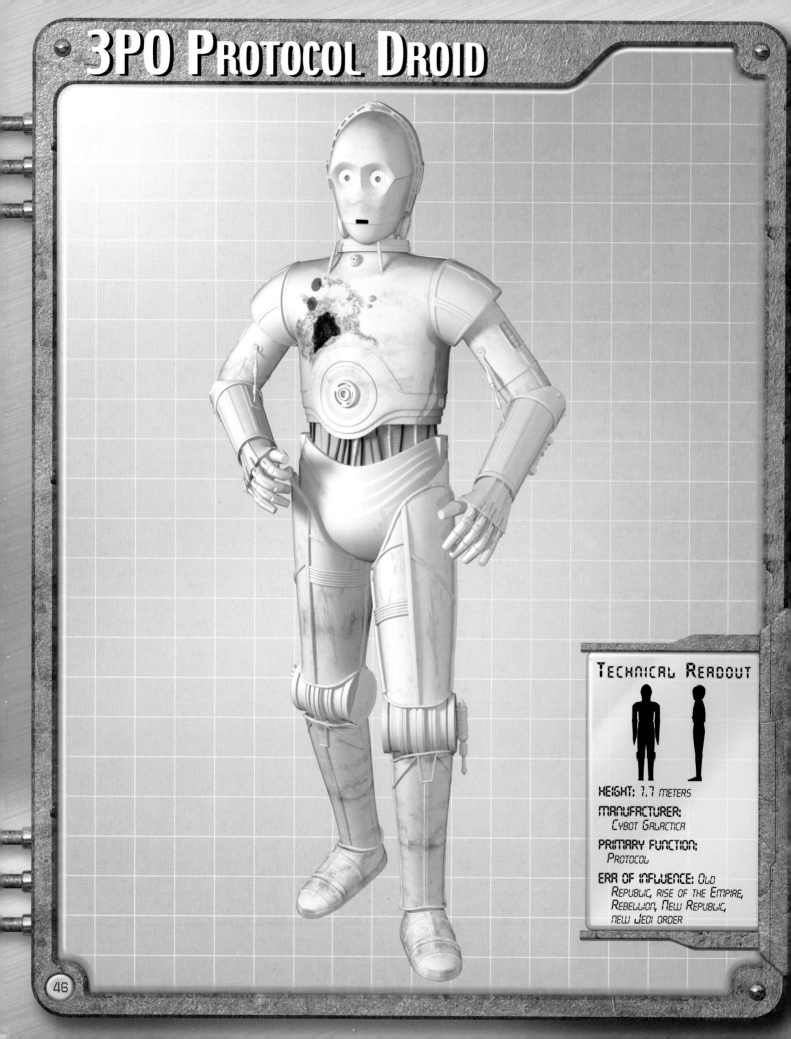

Technical Readout

Height: 1.7 meters

Manufacturer: Cybot Galactica

Primary Function: Protocol

Era of Influence: Old Republic, rise of the Empire, Rebellion, New Republic, new Jedi order

Cybot Galactica 3PO Protocol Droid

Cybot Galactica's 3PO protocol droids are among the most human-like automata ever developed—a triumph, one might think. Unfortunately, sometimes human beings can be nervous, flighty, and borderline neurotic.

Some 3POs are all that and more, thanks to the highly advanced neural network of the SyntheTech AA-1 verbo-brain. This superior cognitive module permits a droid to develop genuine emotions and a surprisingly original personality. Cybot Galactica actually installed creativity *dampers* in its 3PO units to ensure unembellished translations. Indeed, the company recommends regular memory wipes to iron out any quirks.

The 3PO units are widely used by ambassadors, politicians, consuls, and members of royalty as personal attachés in diplomatic or social settings. In a galaxy with thousands of different species and millions of distinct cultures, no Senator wants to trigger war by accidentally twisting a greeting into an insult. Not only are 3POs unrivaled at speaking diverse tongues, but they are also experts in etiquette, decorum, customs, posture, religious rituals, and table manners.

A 3PO stands 1.7 meters tall and is encased in a glittering, burnished body shell of gold, silver, white, or a handful of other hues. All possess photoreceptors, auditory pickups, broadband antenna receivers, microwave detectors, and olfactory sensors. The primary circuit breaker (a master on/off switch) can be accessed at the back of the neck. The droids require frequent oil baths to keep their joints in prime working condition.

Cybot Galactica has made 3PO-style droids in one form or another for centuries. To keep the model fresh in the public eye, various line extensions have been released over the decades, including the PX, the Consul360, and the ii77. These "boutique" models are priced up to twice as much as a standard 3PO and generally showcase a technological breakthrough, such as a larger memory unit or a more sophisticated vocabulator. Eventually, however, the technology becomes old news, the line extension is retired, and the distinguishing gizmo is incorporated into the regular production run of the 3PO.

The TC series is one of the most celebrated boutique extensions of the 3PO design. Popular in the decades leading up to the Clone Wars, TC 3POs were named for the TranLang III communications modules they carried. The TranLang III rocketed ahead of the previous TranLang II with a database of more than six million forms of communication, including obscure dialects, trade vernaculars, security codes, and droid transmissions. The vocabulator speech/sound system built into the TranLang III allows the TC to reproduce almost any sound, though the droid's humanoid construction limits its ability to duplicate nuances of some species' sign language (such as the subtle lekku tics of Twi'leki).

> *C-3PO*
> ## Oh! Nice to see a familiar face.
> *3PO DROID*
> ## (mumbles) E chu ta!
> *C-3PO*
> ## How rude!
>
> *—C-3PO to 3PO Droid*
> *in Bespin's Cloud City*

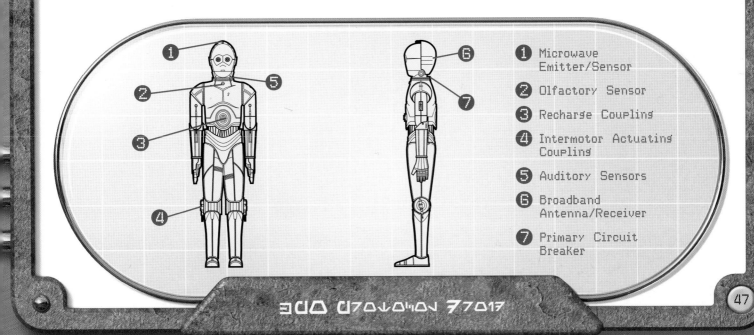

1. Microwave Emitter/Sensor
2. Olfactory Sensor
3. Recharge Coupling
4. Intermotor Actuating Coupling
5. Auditory Sensors
6. Broadband Antenna/Receiver
7. Primary Circuit Breaker

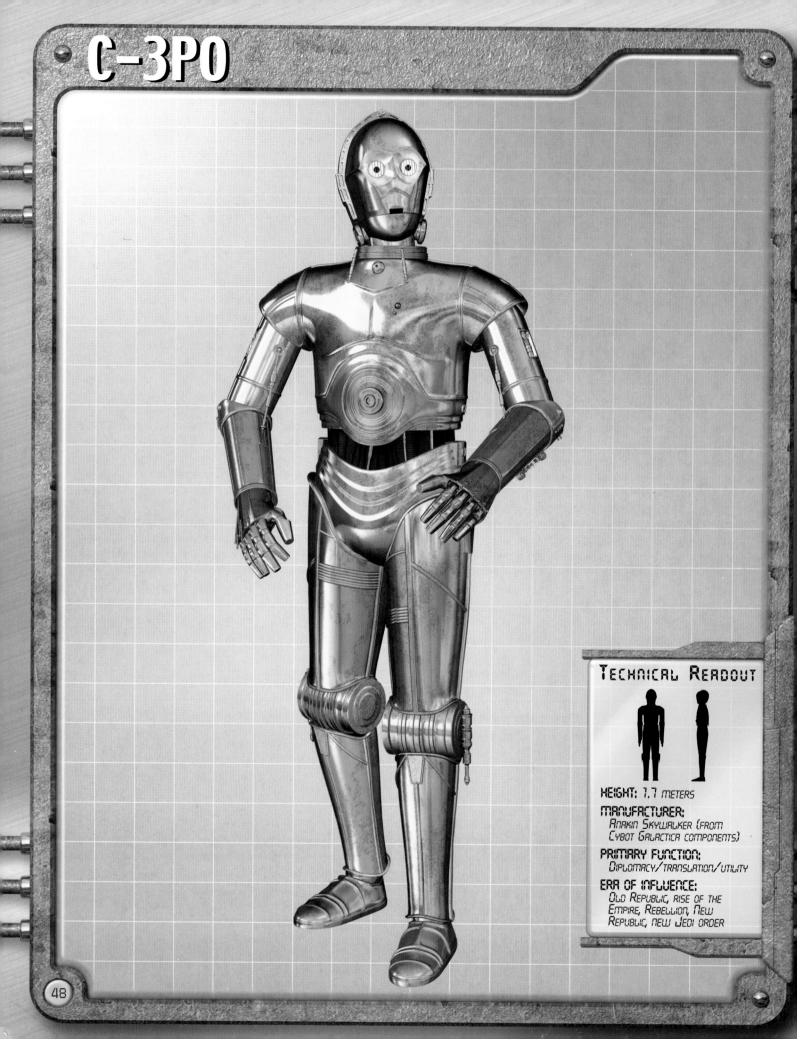

C-3PO

TECHNICAL READOUT

HEIGHT: 1.7 meters

MANUFACTURER:
Anakin Skywalker (from Cybot Galactica components)

PRIMARY FUNCTION:
Diplomacy/translation/utility

ERA OF INFLUENCE:
Old Republic, rise of the Empire, Rebellion, New Republic, new Jedi order

Almost all units in the TC series have voices designed to mimic those of human females, and refer to themselves with feminine-gender pronouns. Most TC units were purchased by Senators, ambassadors, and business barons. Few of these officials had any need for a translator that speaks six million languages, but ownership of a costly TC gave them bragging rights among their peers.

A second boutique model is the 3PX. Introduced around the same time as the TC, the 3PX couldn't be more dissimilar to its pricey cousin. The limited-run 3PX series bears a sharp, angular appearance, and carries a low price point designed to help it sell in the rougher markets of the Outer Rim. The series did not catch on, although many of its design elements later appeared in Arakyd's RA-7 Death Star Droid.

The 5YQ series appeared only in Mid Rim markets, as a discount 3PO model designed to go head-to-head with Serv-O-Droid's competitive Orbot. Cybot Galactica dropped the boutique 5YQ after only a few years, spurred by a corporate lawsuit over shared components.

Approximately a decade after the Battle of Endor, Cybot Galactica introduced one of the latest boutique models, the C series. These protocol droids have model numbers ranging from C-1 to C-9 and were produced exclusively on the factory moon of Telti.

> # "You! I suppose you're programmed for etiquette and protocol."
>
> *—Owen Lars, interrogating C-3PO*
> *at a Jawa droid sale*

The most famous 3PO unit isn't really a 3PO at all. C-3PO, hero of the Rebellion, was built almost entirely from scratch by nine-year-old slave Anakin Skywalker. Anakin scavenged most of C-3PO's parts from sundry Cybot Galactica etiquette models, some of them more than eighty years old. Anakin claimed he assigned the number 3 to his droid because it represented the third member of his family (after Anakin and his mother Shmi), though the designation also mirrors the series name of Cybot's 3PO.

Anakin obtained the pieces for C-3PO's structural framework and servomotor system from Jawas and junk heaps. The droid's TranLang III communications module came from a state-of-the-art TC unit blasted to pieces by Gardulla the Hutt. Anakin created the makeshift droid's AA-1 verbobrain by fusing together three scrapped verbobrains: one rusted, one half melted, and one scorched in a warehouse fire. Anakin extracted the intact circuits from these unusable modules, synchronized them, and C-3PO was born.

Appearing at first in an unfinished, skeletal form, C-3PO gained dull matte body coverings just prior to the Clone Wars, and shiny golden plating three standard years later. The droid has remained in this form ever since, though a memory wipe erased most of his original recollections of Anakin.

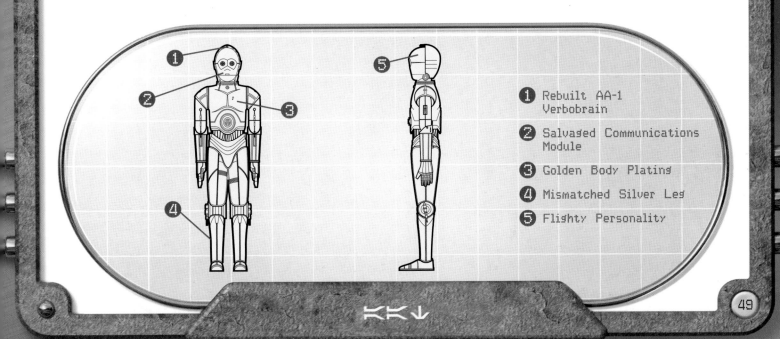

1 Rebuilt AA-1 Verbobrain
2 Salvaged Communications Module
3 Golden Body Plating
4 Mismatched Silver Leg
5 Flighty Personality

BD-3000 Luxury Droid

TECHNICAL READOUT

HEIGHT: 1.7 meters

MANUFACTURER:
LeisureMech Enterprises

PRIMARY FUNCTIONS:
Protocol, personal
assistance

ERA OF INFLUENCE:
Rise of the Empire

LeisureMech Enterprises BD-3000 Luxury Droid

Protocol droids resemble humans, but only on a superficial level. It's a basic truth of droid design that customers tend to reject automata that try *too* hard to look like them. The BD-3000 is a pleasing expression of the current design philosophy, combining the curves of a beautiful human female with the shiny elegance of an executive toy.

LeisureMech Enterprises, a design firm operating out of the Corporate Sector, began producing the BD-3000 approximately half a century before the Clone Wars. In what has been described by critics as a triumph of style over substance, Leisure-Mech cut corners on hardware and software in order to achieve clean lines and a sparkling finish. Intentionally playing off the allure of the female human form, the BD-3000 has a small waist, long legs extending from a sculpted minidress, and a programmed walk cycle that provocatively twists the hips. LeisureMech also gave its BD-3000s the ability to vocalize a number of feminine speech patterns, ranging from perky to sultry.

These features alone were sufficient to drive demand for the BD-3000, even at a relatively high starting price of twenty-five thousand credits. Those beings not bewitched by the BD-3000's charms are quick to point out that its business administration programming underperforms, and that its linguistic database of one and a half million languages does not match the expertise of a 3PO unit. These shortfalls seem to matter little. The return rate on BD-3000s continues to be one of the lowest in the industry.

> ## "Right away, Governor. And may I say, you're looking particularly handsome today."
>
> —*Sample of the BD-3000's proprietary "flattery programming"*

Most BD-3000s find homes with politicians or ambassadors. Senator Bail Organa of Alderaan employed one of the droids in his office on Coruscant. Later, in order to broaden the potential buyer base, LeisureMech equipped the BD-3000 with twenty-five secondary functions including nanny, tailor, chef, and airspeeder chauffeur. Expansion slots allow for the installation of this programming, and some owners have modified their units with combat subroutines to turn them into bodyguards or assassins.

In an embarrassing development for LeisureMech, underground entrepreneurs reworked a number of BD-3000s to serve as escorts. Many of these models were modified with new accessories such as sensual, fully articulated Twi'lek head-tails.

Following the rise of the Empire, it became unpopular for politicians to be seen with droids as frivolous as the BD-3000. LeisureMech concentrated its sales efforts on its home territory in the Corporate Sector, where officials still reveled in the decadent and ostentatious. This smaller customer base, however, meant that the BD-3000 could no longer be supported in the numbers it had achieved during the Clone Wars. Unwanted BD-3000s began to be used in a variety of odd jobs. By the time of the New Republic, it wasn't unusual to encounter a BD-3000 driving a hoverbus or delivering food for a Toydarian restaurant.

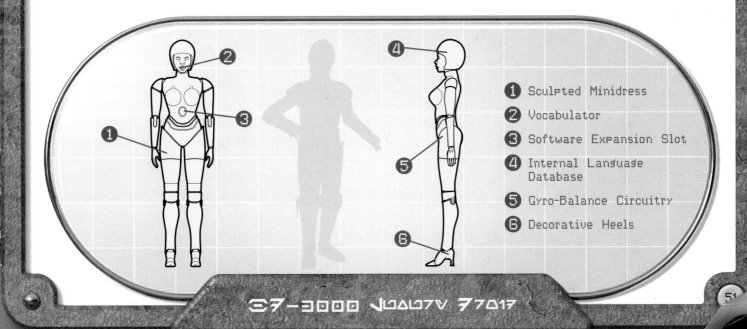

1. Sculpted Minidress
2. Vocabulator
3. Software Expansion Slot
4. Internal Language Database
5. Gyro-Balance Circuitry
6. Decorative Heels

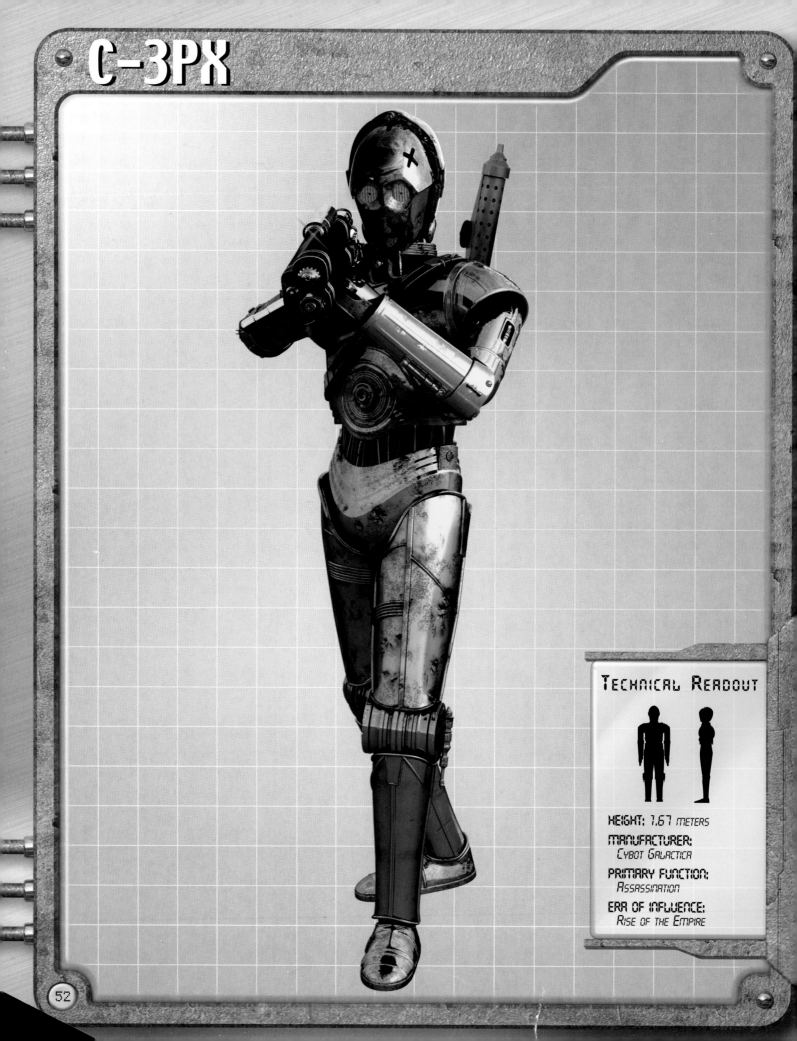

TECHNICAL READOUT

HEIGHT: 1.67 meters

MANUFACTURER:
Cybot Galactica

PRIMARY FUNCTION:
Assassination

ERA OF INFLUENCE:
Rise of the Empire

Cybot Galactica 3PX Protocol Droid

C-3PX was a one-of-a-kind assassin, initially built as a protocol unit and suffering several total rebuilds over the course of his operational life.

Created half a century before the Battle of Yavin, C-3PX belonged to Cybot Galactica's limited-run 3PX series, a line of protocol droids marketed exclusively in the Outer Rim. The droids in the 3PX series had a hard, less human countenance. Consequently, they met with limited success when up against the mainline 3PO units.

C-3PX served a number of masters before coming into the service of Darth Maul. The Sith Lord carried C-3PX aboard his starship *Scimitar,* using the droid to deal with port authorities and other nuisances for which Maul had no patience. Maul rebuilt C-3PX's chassis to incorporate defensive lasers.

After Darth Maul's death on Naboo, Republic investigators seized both *Scimitar* and C-3PX. Supreme Chancellor Palpatine, mindful of the Sith secrets stored in the droid's memory banks, ordered C-3PX's memory erased and remanded the unit to the custody of technology engineer Raith Sienar.

Sienar reworked C-3PX as an espionage unit. He replaced the droid's original body coverings with those from a 3PO unit, making him virtually indistinguishable from millions of other protocol droids in service. C-3PX's photoreceptors received upgrades enabling them to see

> ## "No matter what I do, I'll come to the same end . . . termination."
>
> *—Assassin droid C-3PX*

in infrared, and Sienar built innumerable smuggling compartments lined with sensor-baffling material into the droid's new chassis.

C-3PX ran his first corporate espionage mission in the service of Republic Sienar Systems, then became a spy in the Grand Army of the Republic during the Clone Wars. After the war's end, C-3PX became Imperial property.

While working for Admiral Screed on Roon, C-3PX slipped away and fell into the service of the Intergalactic Droid Agency, which offered him as a rental unit. The criminal Olag Greck saw that C-3PX was more than a standard protocol droid. Greck claimed C-3PX for his own, hiring an outlaw tech on Hosk Station to outfit the droid with retractable lasers, dart shooters, fusioncutters, and even a laser mounted in the back of his head. A distinctive black x marked his forehead.

Olag Greck ordered his new killer to eliminate posted bounties and claimed the rewards for himself. With his shielded weapons compartments, C-3PX could slip past the tightest security. After completing hits on Bonadan and Rampa, C-3PX earned his own bounty posting from the Empire. Ironically, C-3PX had ultimately grown weary of killing, so he allowed himself to be destroyed by R2-D2 in a gladiator arena on Hosk Station.

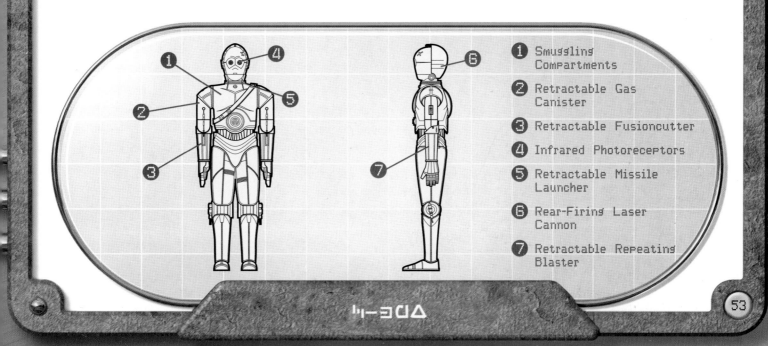

1. Smuggling Compartments
2. Retractable Gas Canister
3. Retractable Fusioncutter
4. Infrared Photoreceptors
5. Retractable Missile Launcher
6. Rear-Firing Laser Cannon
7. Retractable Repeating Blaster

CZ Secretary Droid

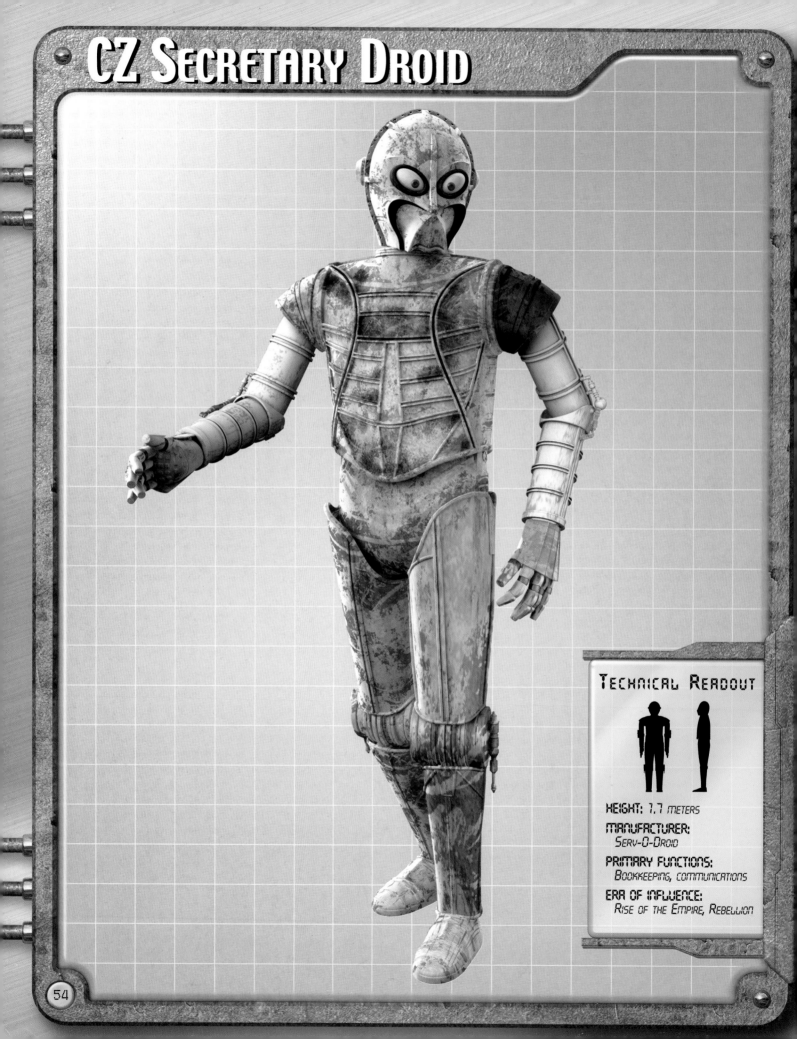

Technical Readout

HEIGHT: 1.7 meters

MANUFACTURER: Serv-O-Droid

PRIMARY FUNCTIONS: Bookkeeping, communications

ERA OF INFLUENCE: Rise of the Empire, Rebellion

Serv-O-Droid CZ Secretary Droid

Old droids never die; they just live on in the used market. This common phrase among droid remarketers is the perfect descriptor of the CZ secretary droid. The CZ can be seen in offices from the Core to the Rim, despite the fact that no one has made a new one since before the Clone Wars.

Serv-O-Droid released the CZ during its waning days as a dominant droid manufacturer. As conflicts such as the Arkanian Revolution (50 B.B.Y.) tore away at the Republic's former glory, Serv-O-Droid found its fortunes intertwined with those of the government. Although it had once been the biggest player in the business, Serv-O-Droid saw its market share drop year after year while Cybot Galactica and Industrial Automaton picked up the slack. The CZ secretary was designed to halt the slide, but newer products from Cybot Galactica eventually led to Serv-O-Droid leaving the business for good.

Despite its checkered history, the strengths of the CZ shouldn't be underestimated. The unit is classified as both a secretary droid and a comm droid, meaning its built-in comlink has a surface-to-orbit range and can randomly phase among frequencies to frustrate eavesdroppers. Its array of encryption algorithms and sensor jammers make the droid one of the most secure ways to transmit private comm messages or sensitive data. The CZ's optical sensors give it a unique cross-eyed look.

Most often, the CZ is employed as a secretarial unit. Common job functions include taking dictation, organizing files, scheduling calendars, and making comm calls. It comes preloaded with a number of languages—including the common business tongues of Huttese, Neimoidian, and Bocce—and the droid is conversant with business regulations and tax codes for thousands of planetary governments.

The data storage capacity of a CZ is vast. Its encryption algorithms resulted in its data firewall being nearly impossible to crack when the droid was first introduced. In the decades since, slicers have developed workarounds that can penetrate a factory-new CZ, though owners who regularly update their droids with fresh codes have few problems.

At launch, the CZ series boasted a garish green-and-orange paint job with yellow highlights. Serv-O-Droid believed that this tactic would draw attention to its new model, but most buyers repainted their droids to better suit a sedate business environment. Today few CZs have any trace of green or orange remaining on their outer shells.

Due to the high data security of the CZ series, the droids make excellent couriers. Jabba the Hutt employed one unit, CZ-3, to assist his Nimbanel accountants at his town house in Mos Eisley. In an attempt to ensnare a rival, Jabba loaded CZ-3 with a remote surveillance rig and set him loose in the city. The droid could be seen wandering the Mos Eisley streets when Obi-Wan Kenobi and Luke Skywalker booked passage off Tatooine. A Snivvian tracker named Zutton later blasted CZ-3 to pieces.

> **"I have Duke Sparbo transmitting on my fifth cranial band. Shall I take a message?"**
>
> *—CZ-54, employed by the Bureau of Ships and Services*

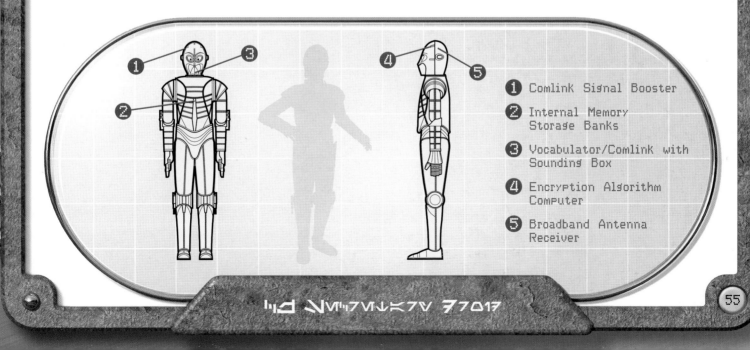

1. Comlink Signal Booster
2. Internal Memory Storage Banks
3. Vocabulator/Comlink with Sounding Box
4. Encryption Algorithm Computer
5. Broadband Antenna Receiver

DEATH STAR DROID

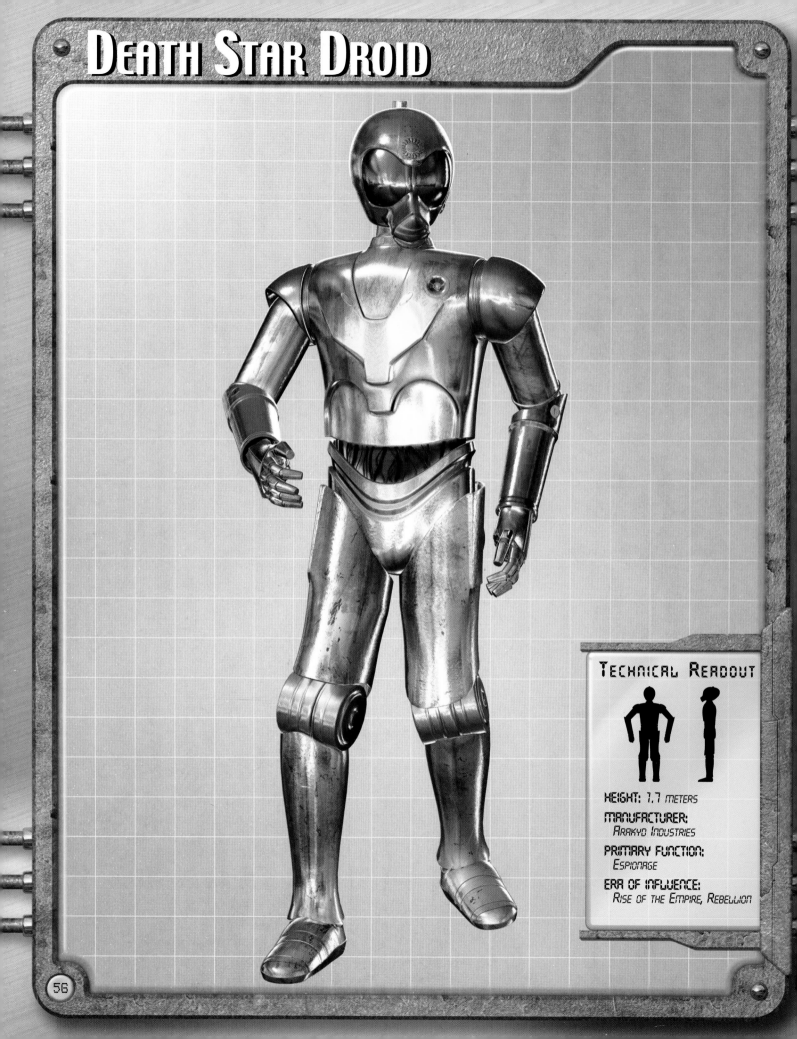

TECHNICAL READOUT

HEIGHT: 1.7 meters

MANUFACTURER:
Arakyd Industries

PRIMARY FUNCTION:
Espionage

ERA OF INFLUENCE:
Rise of the Empire, Rebellion

Arakyd RA-7 Protocol Droid

Never has a gift been so unwanted. The RA-7 Death Star Droid was produced as an internal affairs spy by the Imperial Security Bureau, leading to thousands of arrests at the hands of Palpatine's secret police. When the explosion of the Death Star vaporized most of the RA-7 production run, Imperial officials everywhere breathed a discreet sigh of relief.

Arakyd Industries produced the RA-7. Until that point, Arakyd had been known for military and explorational products such as the Viper probot, so its entry into the protocol droid market took the industry by surprise. The first RA-7s made their debut at the North Quadrant Intergalactic Automaton Show on Zug.

Attendees soon discovered that the RA-7 was cheaply assembled and off-putting in appearance (in a case of corporate resource sharing, the RA-7 wore many of the same exterior components as the later models in Cybot Galactica's 3PX protocol line). Examination of the droid's specs revealed more embarrassments—the RA-7 possessed a cognitive module at least a generation out of date.

Arakyd's rivals couldn't contain their mean-spirited mirth. But the competition didn't know that Arakyd had never intended to sell the droid to the mass market. As planned, the Empire stepped in and purchased the entire run of the RA-7. Then it began handing them out like party favors to governors, Moffs, and naval officers.

Hidden inside the droid's skull lies a secret surveillance module. Sensor baffles disguised as soldering welds prevent the hardware from appearing on diagnostic scans. The droid's panoramic photoreceptors can operate almost without light and extrapolate dialogue from lip-reading. An RA-7's audio pickups can detect a whisper from across a crowded lobby and discern multiple conversations at the same time.

Imperial bureaucrats who received the droids knew none of this. They could see that the junky RA-7s made poor assistants, but no one dared throw out the droids lest word get back to their superiors that they had spurned a gift from the Emperor. RA-7 droids were instead banished to dark corners, forgotten as if they were pieces of statuary.

Meanwhile, they recorded everything they heard or saw, making regular information dumps using encrypted communications channels on public information nodes. The Imperial Security Bureau, a branch of the rabidly partisan COMPNOR, pored over the findings and summoned insufficiently loyal officials on "business trips" to Coruscant. Few returned.

The sheer number of RA-7s assigned to officers on the Death Star battle station led to the nickname "Death Star Droid." Rumors soon spread among the Imperial bureaucracy that Death Star Droids were pure poison. It became common for officials to leave their RA-7s behind on offworld visits, where the droids found their way into junk shops and Jawa auctions.

> **"And thus I regret to inform your lordship that your gift has been stolen. By a swoop gang, most likely. Or Rebels. Or an alien."**
>
> *—Planetary governor Furi Nistola, attempting to explain how he "lost" his Death Star droid*

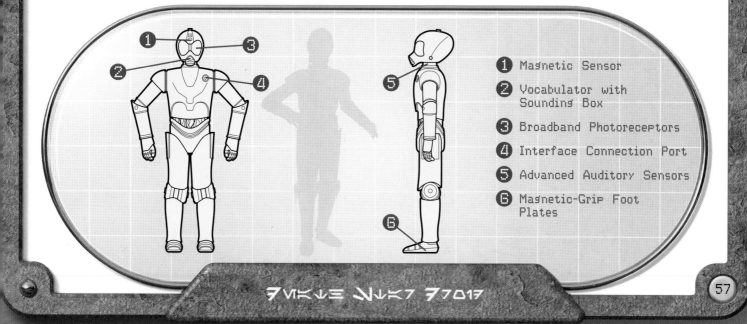

1. Magnetic Sensor
2. Vocabulator with Sounding Box
3. Broadband Photoreceptors
4. Interface Connection Port
5. Advanced Auditory Sensors
6. Magnetic-Grip Foot Plates

EV Supervisor Droid

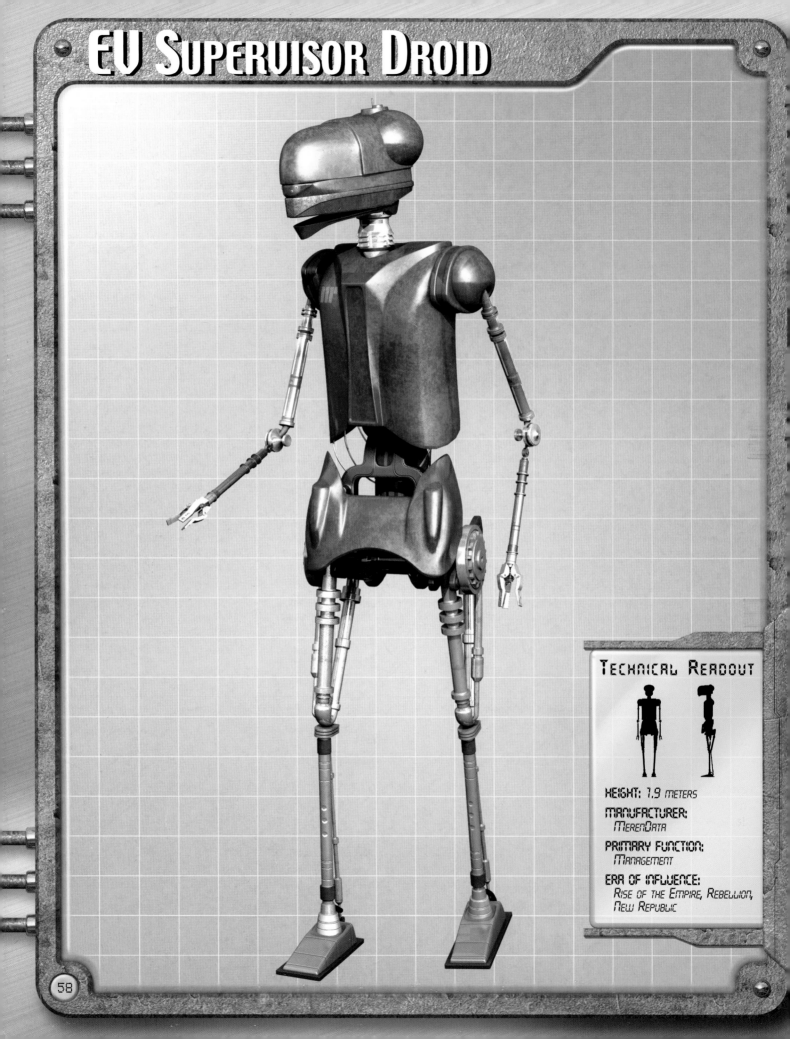

TECHNICAL READOUT

HEIGHT: 1.9 meters

MANUFACTURER:
MerenData

PRIMARY FUNCTION:
Management

ERA OF INFLUENCE:
Rise of the Empire, Rebellion,
New Republic

MerenData EV Supervisor Droid

It's one of the worst debacles in corporate memory. MerenData blames it on industrial sabotage, but others attribute it to a fatal combination of malicious intent and stupidity.

The EV series supervisor droid was planned as a manager that could oversee and increase the efficiency of droid labor pools. During production, however, the standard EV motivators were swapped for MDF motivators—contraband pieces of hardware designed for use in torture droids. The mix-up exposed the fact that MerenData was building illegal droids for the House of Tagge. The revelation triggered a public relations nightmare when hundreds of corrupted EV droids were released.

For the first few months after the tainted release, MerenData adopted a *wait-and-see* attitude. Initial reports indicated that the MDF-equipped models were actually *outperforming* standard EV units at worker motivation. Then the stories began trickling in. To its horror, MerenData realized that the affected droids had combined the MDF motivator's sadism with the power of positive management.

On Eriadu, 160 droids had their feet melted to the factory floor to prevent them from leaving their work stations. On Indu San, the slowest performers on a hotel wait staff were "treated" to an oil bath that was set on fire. On Kadril, in one of the rare cases where an EV oversaw organic workers, employees were often prodded with high-voltage electroprods.

A panicked MerenData made every effort to recall the affected models, and even tried to relaunch the line to the Imperial military as the V series. Both lines failed spectacularly. MerenData shuttered thousands of branch offices from the Core to the Outer Rim.

Unfortunately, MerenData's recall efforts did not reach every EV, and some found homes with owners unfazed by their peculiar appetites. The crime boss Ploovo Two-For-One employed a droid named EV-4D9, while the droid EV-9D9.2 took over as chief of interrogation on the assembly moon of Telti.

The most notorious unit, EV-9D9, became head of automated security in Bespin's Cloud City during the tenure of Lando Calrissian. "Eve" destroyed more than a quarter of the city's droid population before making a bold escape ahead of Calrissian's agents. Jabba the Hutt's goons later discovered Eve at a Go-Corp repulsor plant, and brought her back to oversee the droid pool at their master's palace on Tatooine. During the events surrounding Jabba's death, a droid survivor of EV-9D9's Cloud City rampage took revenge, finally ending Eve's operational cycle.

> **"FIFTH REMINDER: Please return your EV to your MerenData dealer for double your money back. We are also offering a 10,000-credit reward for information leading to the whereabouts of other EV supervisor droids."**
>
> —*MerenData customer mailing*

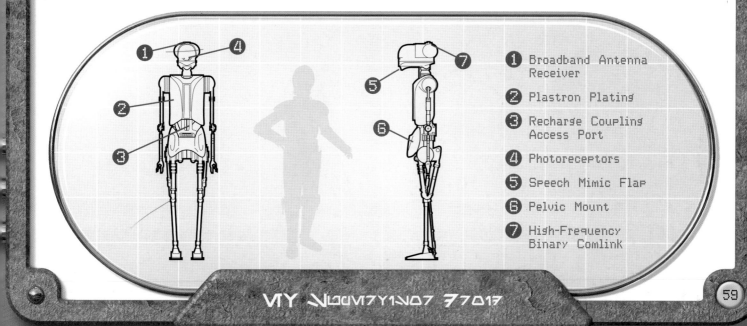

1. Broadband Antenna Receiver
2. Plastron Plating
3. Recharge Coupling Access Port
4. Photoreceptors
5. Speech Mimic Flap
6. Pelvic Mount
7. High-Frequency Binary Comlink

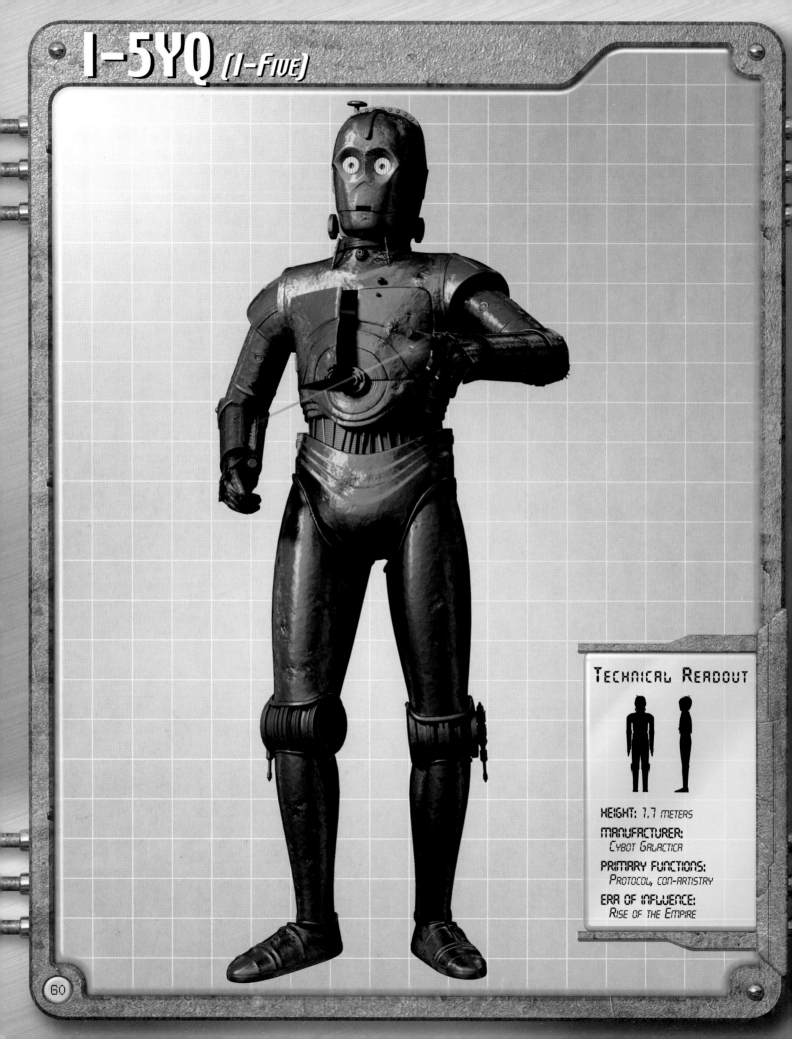

I-5YQ (I-Five)

TECHNICAL READOUT

HEIGHT: 1.7 meters

MANUFACTURER:
Cybot Galactica

PRIMARY FUNCTIONS:
Protocol, con-artistry

ERA OF INFLUENCE:
Rise of the Empire

Cybot Galactica 5YQ Protocol Droid

The irreplaceable I-Five is a perfect example of how aftermarket modifications, uncommon memory wipes, and a wealth of life experience can create a unique droid that bears little resemblance to its factory template.

Cybot Galactica produced the pewter-colored 5YQ protocol series as a short-lived offshoot of its popular 3PO series, sold at a lower price in the Mid Rim to compete with Serv-O-Droid's then-popular Orbot. A lawsuit over shared components prompted Cybot Galactica to retire the line, however, and only a handful of 5YQs remained in the marketplace.

One unit, designated I-5YQ, or I-Five, became the property of a wealthy family whose cruel children ordered him to walk off ledges so they could laugh at how high he bounced. A relieved I-Five soon ended up in a junk dealer's shop, where he became the property of the con artist and freelance information broker Lorn Pavan.

Seeing a kindred soul in the abused I-Five, Lorn Pavan made the droid his business partner. He boosted I-Five's cognitive module and removed his hardwired creativity dampers. Now as self-aware as it was possible for a droid to be, I-Five entered into a five-year criminal alliance with Pavan, using his electronic brain to sell underworld secrets, run banking scams, and cheat at sabacc.

Over the course of their adventures, Pavan upgraded I-Five with a radar-mapping device, a microwave projector

> ## "Organics are endlessly amusing. If only to themselves."
>
> *—One of I-Five's unsolicited observations*

beam, a chest compartment for holding contraband, a pair of spotlight-projecting photoreceptors, an electrostatic generator to prevent grime from adhering to I-Five's body shell, and two concealed lasers built into his index fingers.

I-Five's most versatile addition was an Aeramaxis AXX Screamer, a sound modulator that can transmit on every frequency from subsonic to ultrasonic. I-Five became so adept with this device that he could generate subtle harmonics to loosen toxins from the bloodstream, or broadcast a shriek so cacophonous it would leave organic beings squirming on the ground in agony.

Lorn Pavan died in a run-in with Darth Maul, and I-Five wound up in the employ of spice smugglers working the Kessel Run. Authorities seized him and sold him at auction, and I-Five fell in with a noble family on Naboo. During the Clone Wars, the Republic commandeered I-Five and other available droids to assist in the war effort. Now augmented with battlefield medical programming, I-Five joined the droid pool at Rimsoo Seven, a Republic field hospital on Drongar.

I-Five forged several friendships with the Rimsoo surgeons, and also made time to pursue quests of his own, including simulating intoxication by scrambling his sensory and cognitive feeds. At the conclusion of Rimsoo Seven's tour on Drongar, I-Five departed for Coruscant, where he hoped to hook up with Lorn Pavan's son, a Jedi Temple initiate.

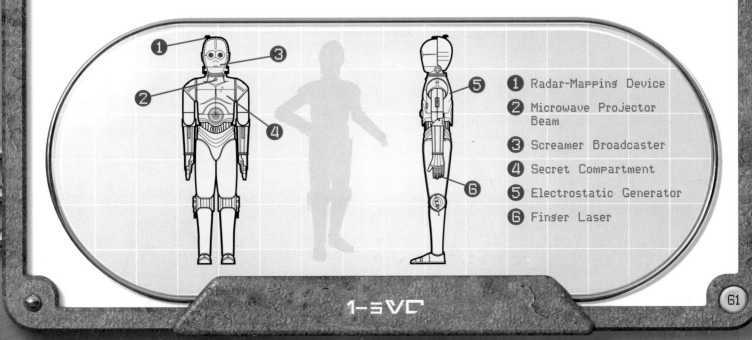

1. Radar-Mapping Device
2. Microwave Projector Beam
3. Screamer Broadcaster
4. Secret Compartment
5. Electrostatic Generator
6. Finger Laser

J9 Worker Drone

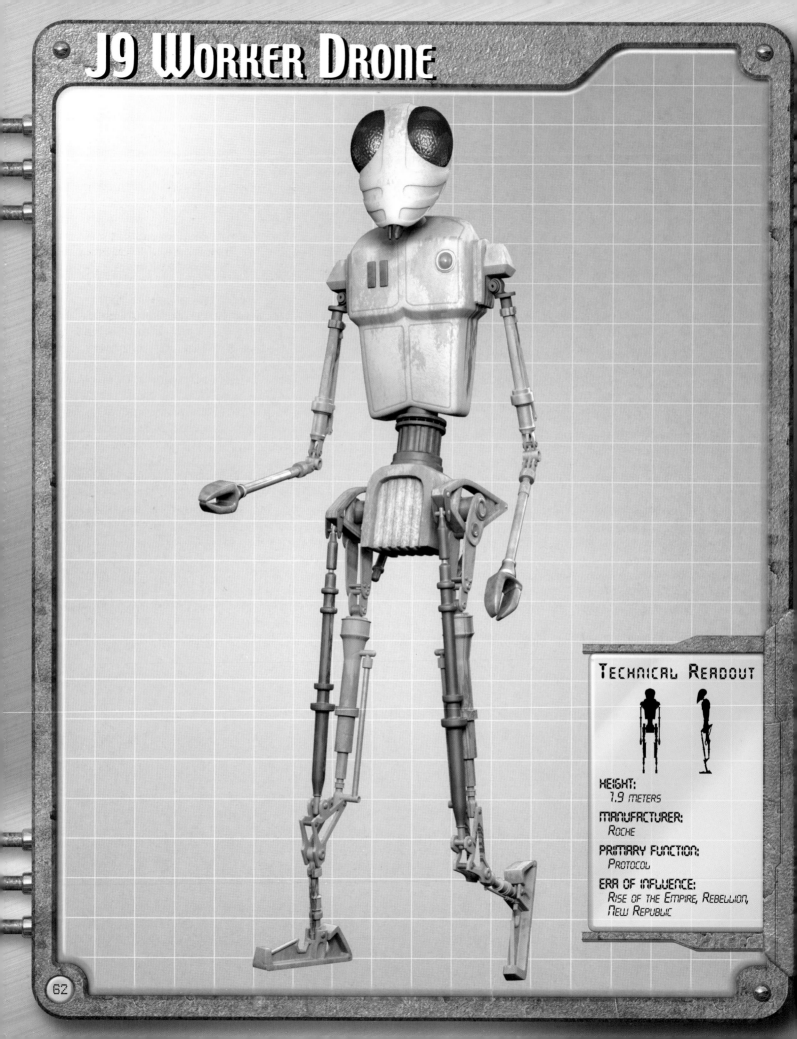

TECHNICAL READOUT

HEIGHT:
1.9 meters

MANUFACTURER:
Roche

PRIMARY FUNCTION:
Protocol

ERA OF INFLUENCE:
Rise of the Empire, Rebellion, New Republic

Roche J9 Worker Drone

The J9 worker drone is quite possibly the worst-selling protocol droid in history. Fault for the spectacular failure lies not with the Verpine engineers of the Roche hive, but with the insectoid beings' inability to understand other cultures. The product's shortcomings provide an object lesson in the pitfalls of selling to the mass galactic market.

The Verpine couldn't see past their own mandibles when designing the droid's outer shell. It looks remarkably like a Verpine, with bulging compound eyes, spindly claw-tipped limbs, and pointed mouth pincers. Right away, this put the J9 at a disadvantage on the sales floor, as the galaxy's mammalian species found the droid creepily alien.

The second problem with the J9 lies with the Verpine programmers who gave it a personality. While the droid can function well enough within the regimented structure of an insect colony, its fixation on hive thought patterns means that it often works the words *carapace, regurgitation,* and *royal jelly* into its language translations. Furthermore, the J9 speaks with a persistently buzzy vocabulator.

The net result? Buyers avoided the J9 in droves. The disappointed Verpine slashed prices, bringing about the J9's curious second act. Because the Verpine had marketed the unit as a "worker drone"—a common appellation within their society—non-Verpine buyers often misunderstood the label and installed J9s in stockrooms and loading docks. Roche raised no objections. At this point, it was grateful for whatever sales it could get.

By all measures, however, using a J9 as a cargo tagger is a colossal waste. Each droid possesses an Arjan II logic computer and a TranLang III communications module with more than one million languages. Intellectually, the droids can compete with a 3PO unit. Their giant bug eyes are keyed to the Verpine optical range, lying mostly in the ultraviolet spectrum. With its finely tuned olfactory sensor and its Torplex microwave sensor, the J9 can experience a world far beyond the ranges of human perception.

The complex, triangular hip joints of the J9 are a trademark sign of the Roche hive. The same hip joints are seen on the 8D8 smelting operator and many other Roche products.

At the height of his power, Jabba the Hutt owned a J9 worker drone designated BG-J38. Jabba's thugs soon discovered that the "stupid droid" could easily beat them at dejarik holo-chess, so Beegee became a popular figure in the Hutt's court. The droid's whereabouts following Jabba's death are unknown, but he is believed to have escaped offworld to feed his slot-machine addiction.

Recently, the Verpine have attempted to remarket the J9 directly to other insectoid species, including the Sic-Six, Flakax, and Xi'Dec. Thus far the biggest sales boom has come from the giant, mantis-like Yam'rii.

> ## "Greetingzzz, Master. How may Drone Beegee-Arfivetoo zzzervice the colony, hive, or zzzocial collective?"
>
> —*Start-up greeting from a new J9 worker drone*

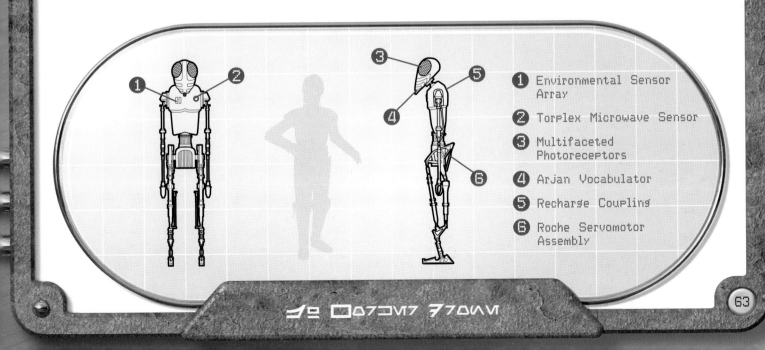

1. Environmental Sensor Array
2. Torplex Microwave Sensor
3. Multifaceted Photoreceptors
4. Arjan Vocabulator
5. Recharge Coupling
6. Roche Servomotor Assembly

LE Manifest Droid

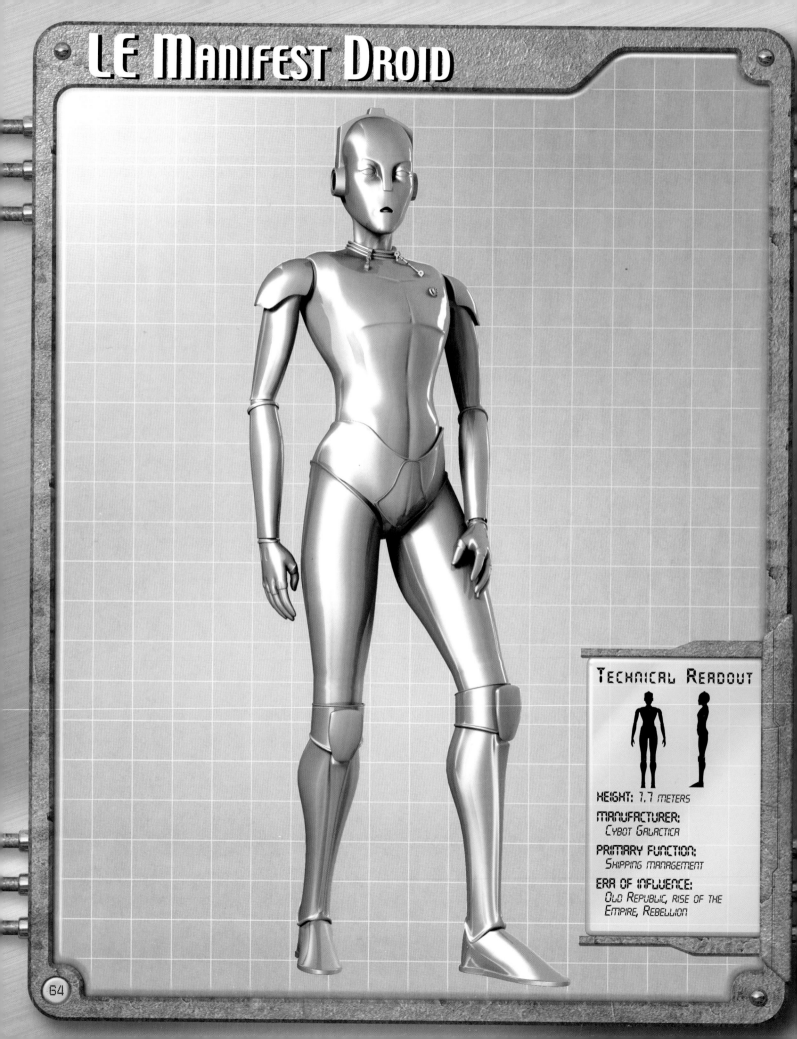

Technical Readout

Height: 1.7 meters

Manufacturer:
Cybot Galactica

Primary Function:
Shipping management

Era of Influence:
Old Republic, rise of the Empire, Rebellion

Cybot Galactica LE Manifest Droid

Cybot Galactica is responsible for the LE series, a statement that seems obvious to those familiar with Cybot's LE repair droids. Yet in this case, the droids under discussion are members of the obscure LE manifest series, introduced nearly three centuries before the New Republic.

The company conceived of the LE droids as protocol droid variants, to be used by starship captains and port operators. Rather than carrying etiquette programming, the LEs came equipped with import-export restrictions for the galaxy's major trading regions and the mammoth code of conduct imposed by BoSS, the Bureau of Ships and Services.

Because no organic being could be expected to know the complete intricacies of the BoSS code, having an LE series droid on staff would smooth a number of tedious tasks, from the proper inventorying of cargo to the datawork required, in triplicate, to import strange fungi into the Core Worlds. Furthermore, the LE's bright, female-programmed personality and streamlined design made it an appealing companion for long stretches in hyperspace.

The downfall of the LE series proved to be its scrupulous honesty. On most starports, particularly those in Hutt or Bothan space, bribes have long been considered a regular part of business. Cybot Galactica never thought to program their droids with this degree of flexibility. Consequently, LE droids would make catastrophic errors, such as reporting contraband stashed beneath their freighter's deck plating—all under the mistaken assumption that they were only helping. It didn't take long before most owners decided that LE droids simply weren't worth the trouble.

Cybot Galactica retired the line, but the existing LE droids saw continued use in smaller starports and aboard short-hop corporate freighters. As LE units gained more experience interacting with organics, they would gradually shed their prudish adherence to the letter of the law and learn to make compromises as circumstances demanded.

One unit, LE-914, served with Rebel Alliance hero Tay Vanis after the Battle of Hoth. "Ellie" became Vanis's closest companion, assisting him in dozens of missions against the Empire. In return, Vanis equipped Ellie for "high-stress functions." He replaced her torso plating with blaster-resistant armorplast featuring a mirrored coating. Behind secret access panels on Ellie's chest lay a storage chamber, used to hold contraband items or to operate the self-destruct controls that would trigger the explosion of a nested proton bomb.

Prior to the Battle of Endor, Tay Vanis obtained data tapes confirming the details of the Emperor's Death Star project at Endor. Darth Vader caught up with Vanis and left him a mind-wiped shell of a man, but Ellie escaped with the tapes secured inside her chest compartment. After giving the data to Luke Skywalker and Princess Leia, Ellie destroyed herself and her master.

> **"I am Ellie. It is my function here to note all inventories, issue clearances, and keep all records."**
>
> —LE-914, welcoming Luke Skywalker to an Imperial depot

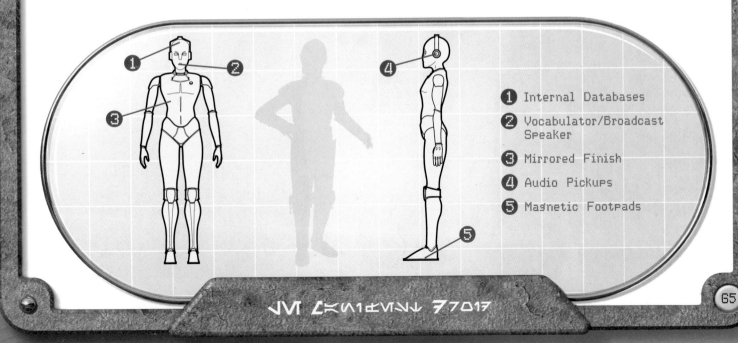

1. Internal Databases
2. Vocabulator/Broadcast Speaker
3. Mirrored Finish
4. Audio Pickups
5. Magnetic Footpads

LOM Protocol Droid

TECHNICAL READOUT

HEIGHT: 1.6 meters

MANUFACTURER:
Industrial Automaton

PRIMARY FUNCTION:
Protocol

ERA OF INFLUENCE:
Rise of the Empire, Rebellion,
New Republic

Industrial Automaton LOM Protocol Droid

It's one of the worst examples of corporate imitation in history. No case better illustrates why there's so much bad blood between the executives of Industrial Automaton (IA) and Cybot Galactica than that of the LOM protocol droid.

Though they're often called the Big Two, Cybot Galactica and Industrial Automaton have created distinctly different images in the public's imagination. Cybot is known for refined, elegant products such as the 3PO protocol series, while IA, through its popular R series astromechs, has a reputation for being working class and reliable.

The stereotype has always rankled some at IA. In the years after the Clone Wars, they decided to launch a product, the LOM series, that would establish Industrial Automaton as a major player in the protocol market. Not wanting to be too blatant with what was intended to be a first-generation product, IA decided to sell to a test market of insectoid species, including the Brizzit, Verpine, and Yam'rii. Designers sculpted the LOM's head as "insect-like" as possible to suit a wide variety of phenotypes.

Selling a niche model, however, wasn't Industrial Automaton's ultimate goal. If the LOM performed to expectations, the company planned to convert it to a humanoid droid and sell to the mass market within two standard years. Telltale signs of this scheme were all over the LOM: despite its bulging compound eyes, for example, its internal visual pickups are keyed to the human spectrum.

What really incensed Cybot Galactica was the manner in which Industrial Automaton brokered deals with Cybot's own parts suppliers. From SyntheTech, IA secured an AA-1 verbobrain with a TranLang III communications module. It even obtained droid body plating from companies that had enjoyed long relationships with Cybot Galactica. From the neck down, the LOM looks almost identical to the rival 3PO unit.

Cybot Galactica sued, claiming trademark infringement and a violation of noncompetition agreements with the 3PO unit's top suppliers. Industrial Automaton put the LOM on the market anyway, where it sold well in limited release. Customers liked the fact that it has none of the jumpiness so characteristic of the 3PO, and that it seems wired for gentleness and altruism.

A second crisis proved to be too much for Industrial Automaton, however. Aboard the luxury spaceliner *Kuari Princess*, the droid 4-LOM abandoned its job as the ship's valet and became a jewel thief. Before long, 4-LOM had morphed into one of the galaxy's deadliest bounty hunters. Cybot Galactica gleefully pointed fingers at the "shoddy craftsmanship" of its competitor. IA tried to blame *Kuari Princess*'s shipboard computer, but the public relations damage had been done. The company quietly retired the LOM series, but continued plotting new ways to overtake Cybot Galactica.

> **"The case is inconclusive, but the processor doesn't appear to be at fault. The subject claims he committed crimes simply 'for love of money.'"**
>
> —*Industrial Automaton investigators, after interviewing 4-LOM*

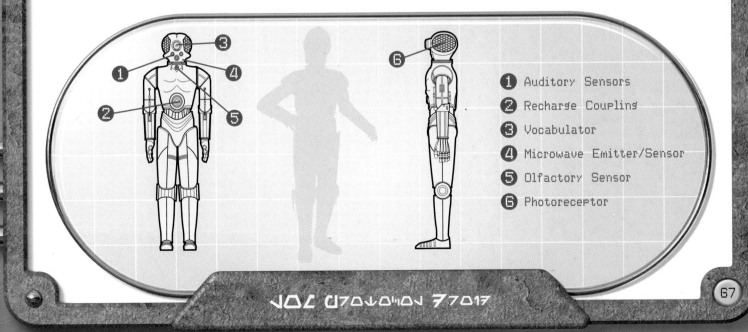

1. Auditory Sensors
2. Recharge Coupling
3. Vocabulator
4. Microwave Emitter/Sensor
5. Olfactory Sensor
6. Photoreceptor

Tac-Spec Footman

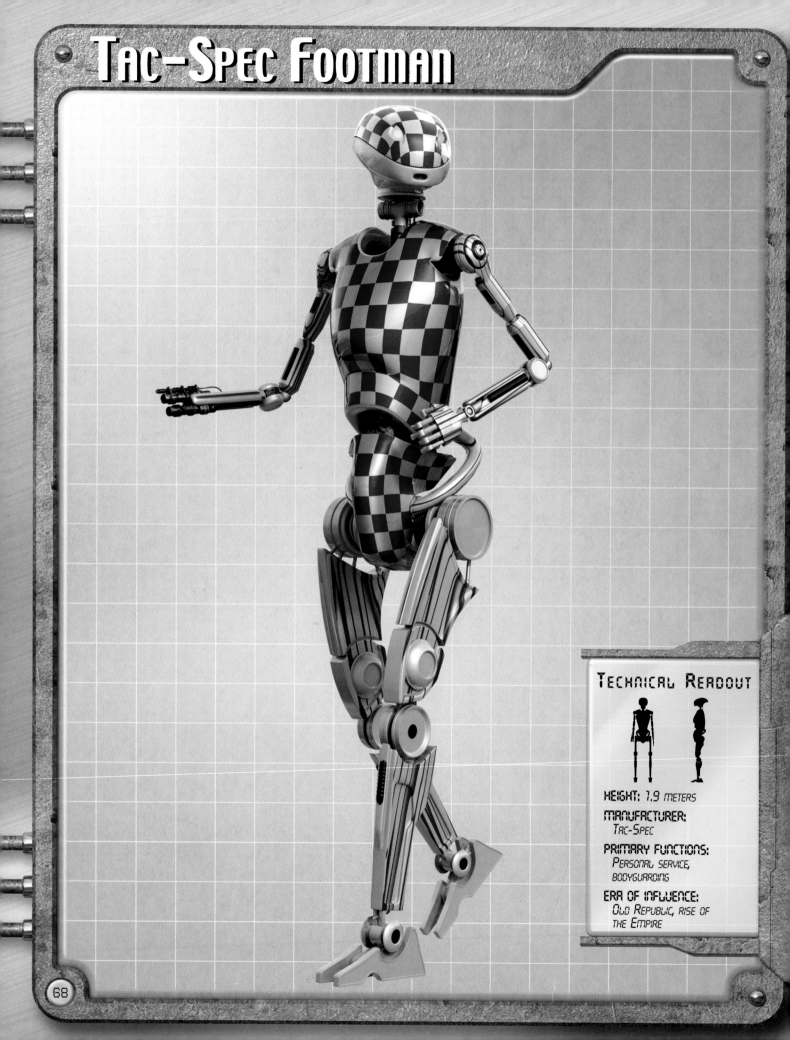

TECHNICAL READOUT

HEIGHT: 1.9 meters

MANUFACTURER:
Tac-Spec

PRIMARY FUNCTIONS:
Personal service,
bodyguarding

ERA OF INFLUENCE:
Old Republic, rise of
the Empire

Tac-Spec Corporation FIII Footman Droid

Relic of a bygone era, the Tac-Spec Corporation FIII Footman Droid is a personal servant designed for the class of aristocrat who lives by the principles of chivalry, gentility—and murder.

Ancient noble houses, such as those in the Senex and Tapani sectors, have histories shrouded in internecine conspiracies. Nobles are regularly killed in duels, while young heirs are poisoned, all as part of a sub-rosa struggle for power. Bodyguard droids thus became common among the blue-blood classes more than a thousand standard years ago. A miniature arms race soon developed over which house could employ the deadliest personal servants, while still preserving the unspoken virtues of status and tradition.

> **"I am programmed for absolute loyalty to the House Malreaux, which I have served through madness and war for twelve generations."**
>
> *—Fidelis, Tac-Spec Footman from Vjun*

To this end, the House of Tund in the Centrality made contact with the GenoHaradan, a near-mythical assassins' guild whose origins predate the Republic. GenoHaradan agents established the Tac-Spec corporation as a front company, then sold the Footman to pre-arranged buyers who had existing contacts within the guild. The first Tac-Spec Footman came into service a few decades after the Battle of Ruusan, and the company produced the line in limited numbers for the next six hundred standard years.

The Tac-Spec Footman announces itself as a "gentleman's personal gentlething." It carries an exhaustive library of explicit rules and mores related to the specific noble house with which it sees service. Daily duties include preparing and serving meals, opening doors, operating vehicles, and maintaining its owner's wardrobe.

In the event of a threat, however, the Footman can become much more. Its blaster-resistant chassis enables it to take a hit meant for its master, and then retaliate in close combat. The Footman's blinding reflexes and pitiless mechanical strength give it the ability to puncture a target's chest with a punch, or rip loose a limb with an effortless tug. At ranged distances, the Tac-Spec Footman can unload with a miniature rail cannon built into the end of one arm. The droid carries weapons programming covering all light and heavy armaments, and boasts a special expertise as a sniper.

One Footman, named Fidelis by its owners, served Vjun's House Malreaux for twelve generations. Fidelis proudly wore the Malreaux checkerboard of ivory and blood on his torso, with blood piping marking his limbs. When the people of Vjun succumbed to madness, Fidelis traveled to Coruscant. There he watched over Whie Malreaux, the young Malreaux heir, who was undergoing instruction in the Jedi Temple.

After a wait of more than ten years, Fidelis hooked up with Whie when the teenage Jedi accompanied Master Yoda on a mission during the Clone Wars. A second Tac-Spec Footman, the renegade Solis, betrayed the group to Count Dooku's lieutenant Asajj Ventress, but turned against Ventress when she refused to pay. Both Solis and Fidelis saw their operational lives cut short in a standoff beneath the Malreaux castle on Vjun.

1. Telescopic Photoreceptors
2. Blasterproof Chassis
3. Miniature Rail Cannon
4. Etiquette Database
5. Augmented Joints

WA-7 Waitress Droid

Technical Readout

Height: 1.7 meters

Manufacturer:
Go-Corp/Utilitech

Primary Function:
Waitressing

Era of Influence:
Old Republic, rise of the Empire

Go-Corp/Utilitech WA-7 Service Unit

They don't make droids like the WA-7 anymore. The sight of one at a restaurant indicates that the establishment is either attempting to evoke a nostalgic ambience, or simply unable to afford anything better.

Go-Corp introduced the WA-7 waitress droid at a time when the Core Worlds were gripped in the fever of the Mondeo Modernist design movement. The fad—which spread to art, architecture, and clothing design—emphasized streamlined contours, elliptical shapes, and whimsical embellishments. The craze burned brightly for several decades but eventually fizzled. Evidence of Mondeo Modernism is present in surviving pop-cultural artifacts from the era, including the WA-7.

The droid moves on a uni-pod wheel, a concession to Mondeo flightiness that proved quite practical. The wheel's drive impellers can generate quick bursts of speed, and the tire covers very little surface area to help prevent the WA-7 from running over a customer's appendages. Gyro-balance circuitry keeps the WA-7 perfectly upright even when zipping through a crowd of patrons, a necessity for a droid whose success often hinges on never dropping a drinks tray.

Decorative elements on the WA-7 include a metallic skirt and head fins, while functional hardware consists of a built-in order transmitter with a range that can extend as far as the kitchen. WA-7 units are programmed with enough verbal acuity to chat up customers, as well as facial-recognition software enabling them to identify their "regulars."

The WA-7 is a well-built droid, and thus many are still in service today. Not all remain in waitressing, however. Changing circumstances forced WA-7s to take odd jobs, with courier being one of the most common, given that a WA-7 can weave through ground-level traffic at speeds up to 120 kilometers per hour. During a typical workweek on many planets, racing WA-7 units carry packages in back harnesses as they shout at hovercar drivers to get out of their way.

A group of private collectors has even fielded a WA-7 nuna-ball team that defeated Serv-O-Droid's RIC team in a shocking upset at an exhibition match.

Dexter Jettster, the Besalisk owner of Dex's Diner on Coruscant, bought a used WA-7 that soon became one of his best employees. The droid, nicknamed "Flo," competed with Dexter's chief waitress, Hermione Bagwa, for tips. Each viewed the other as her subordinate in the diner hierarchy, which led to more than a few colorful exchanges—much to the delight of the clientele.

Accutronics briefly attempted to play off the retro-popularity of the WA-7 with a knockoff line known as the TDL-501. Introduced shortly before the Clone Wars, the "Teedle" met with modest success before succumbing to the same changing tastes that doomed the original.

> **"You ordered the cream of fleek eel, right? Careful, hon, the plate's hot. And the fleek eels bite."**
>
> —*"Flo," the WA-7 droid at Dex's Diner on Coruscant*

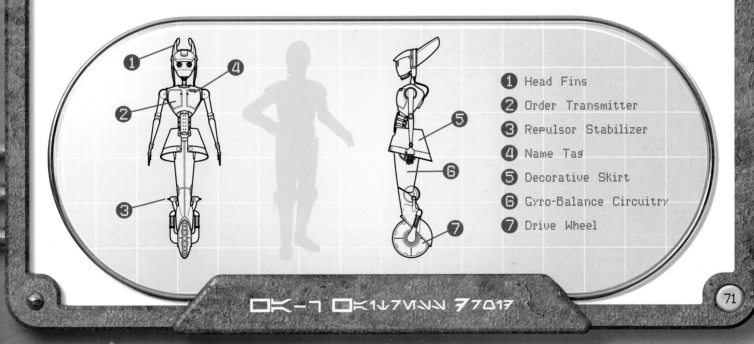

1. Head Fins
2. Order Transmitter
3. Repulsor Stabilizer
4. Name Tag
5. Decorative Skirt
6. Gyro-Balance Circuitry
7. Drive Wheel

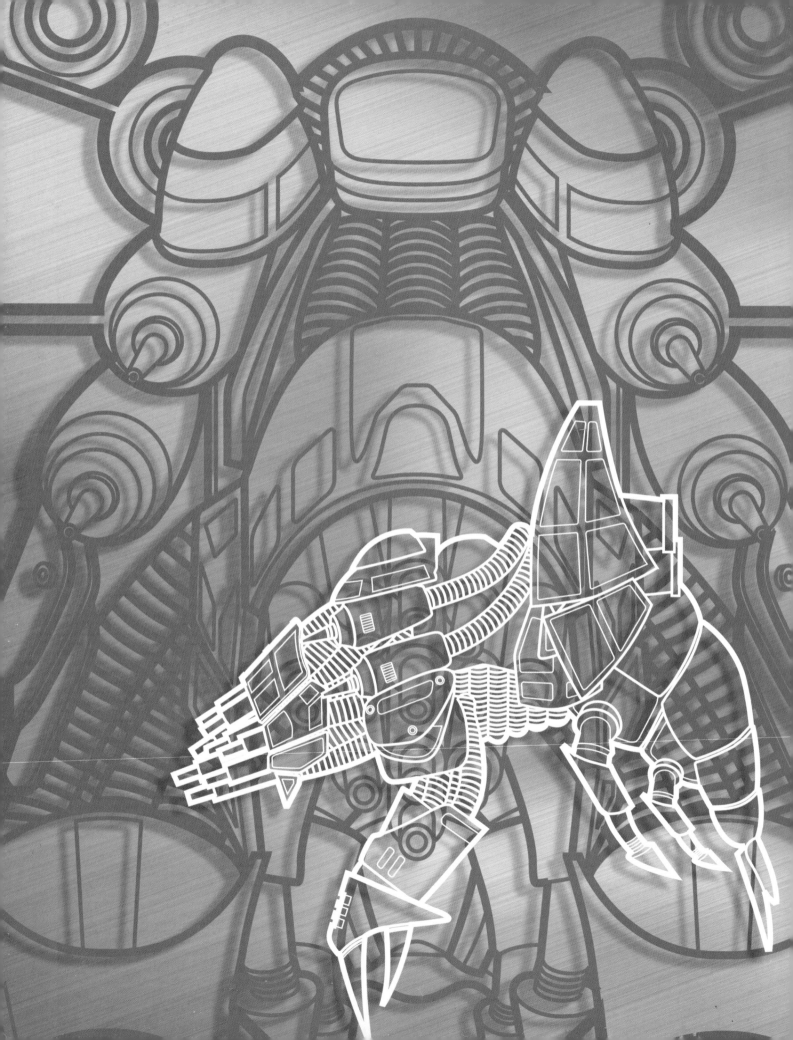

CLASS FOUR DROIDS

"Droids with weapons" is how many might categorize the automata that make up class four. This categorization, while crude, is not inaccurate. Despite the fact that class four droids are subject to severe restrictions and in many cases banned outright, it has never stopped opportunists from making more.

Armed combat droids were among the first droids ever created. Historians believe their introduction followed closely after the debut of the menial droid caste now known as class five, when warlords realized that the behavioral circuitry matrix enabled droid units to react to changing combat conditions on a battlefield. The war robots of Xim the Despot, created circa 25,120 B.B.Y., are a famous example, as are the Electric Caliphs of Mourn.

Class four droids come in four main varieties. The laws concerning ownership of class four droids vary greatly, depending on the subcategory to which the droid belongs.

- **Security droids** are the most widely accepted class four units, used to guard residences, businesses, and public institutions. Security droids are generally armed with nonlethal weaponry, although some have no weapons and are capable only of sounding alarms. Security droids can be purchased from many public companies, providing the buyer possesses the necessary permits. The internal programming of a security droid contains governing blocks preventing it from knowingly killing an organic being—though these blocks can be bypassed by a talented droid engineer.

- **Gladiator droids** occupy a specialized niche involving death matches against other droids. Gladiator units such as the Mark X executioner have an array of showy weapons, including flamethrowers, vibro-axes, and neuronic whips. They carry the same blocks, however, as security droids concerning the harming of organic beings. Robotic gladiator matches are common in the Outer Rim, where Hutt crimelords are known to disable the governing blocks and unleash the droids against prisoners in decadent displays of bloodshed.

- **Battle droids** have made history from the days of Xim the Despot to the devastations of the Clone Wars.

Once ubiquitous on worlds belonging to the Confederacy of Independent Systems, battle droids (also called war droids or combat droids) practically disappeared after the rise of the Empire. Crime syndicates and private armies continued to use battle droids during the Imperial era, either illegally or by referring to them as "security units."

- **Assassin droids** are the only automata built specifically for murder. The early assassin droids (activated during the Indecta era from 17,000 through 15,000 B.B.Y.) operated on behalf of the Republic Judicial Department, eliminating escaped convicts and other threats to galactic security. Deadlier versions followed, most of which found their way into private hands. Although the Republic never formally outlawed assassin droids, most planetary and sector governments did. Only after the rise of the Empire—and the assassination of Imperial Grand Inquisitor Torbin on Weerden—did legislators enact galaxywide regulations barring the sale, ownership, or manufacture of these killer droids. Of course, the Emperor was not above using assassin droids to eliminate his own enemies, and the Imperial Department of Military Research was responsible for creating some of the deadliest assassin droids ever known.

On worlds such as Naboo, where droid armies slaughtered citizens in the recent past, animosity toward class four droids runs high. Elsewhere in the galaxy, entire sectors have been closed off to droid importers due to the depredations of class four units. The Kol Huro Unrest in 44 B.B.Y. left the locals gun-shy about droids, making it nearly impossible for Cybot Galactica or Industrial Automaton to gain a foothold in the region.

Rogue class four droids are a grave problem. Although all varieties of droids have been known to wander off, class four droids are built for aggression and can become a threat to lives and property. Assassin droids, which possess stealth capabilities enabling them to elude capture, are clearly the most dangerous rogues. The rebellious assassin droid HK-01 started the Great Droid Revolution on Coruscant in 4015 B.B.Y., while more recently the assassin IG-88 left behind a trail of bodies in its job as an independent bounty hunter.

ASN-121 Assassin Droid

TECHNICAL READOUT

HEIGHT: 0.38 meter

MANUFACTURER:
Malkite Poisoners

PRIMARY FUNCTION:
Assassination

ERA OF INFLUENCE:
Old Republic, rise of the Empire

Malkite Poisoners ASN-121

The Malkite Poisoners are one of the galaxy's most notorious secret societies. Few know the truth of their role in the rise of Supreme Chancellor Contispex during the Pius Dea era. Fewer still know that they also make droids.

The Clawdite assassin Zam Wesell contacted the Malkite guild engineers to request an ASN-121 assassin droid. The finished product, assembled from commonplace droid components in order to hide its origins, carried the mark of Malkite expertise in its silent lethality.

Unlike similarly patterned sentry droids, Zam's ASN-121 possessed unprecedented environmental awareness and stealth programming, as well as a repulsorlift engine that was rated as military-plus. Prior to its mission to assassinate Senator Padmé Amidala in her Coruscant apartment, Zam's droid eliminated dozens of targets on security-lockdown worlds such as Bonadan and Axum.

Powered by a fusion generator, the ASN-121 could reach near-orbit levels with its repulsorlift engine, yet the droid remained virtually silent and emitted no radiation signature. As evidenced by the Coruscant mission, the droid's repulsorlift had no difficulty supporting the extra sixty-three kilograms of a Jedi hitchhiker, even when traveling at top speeds.

Twin dagger-shaped cooling vanes marked the droid's silhouette. A central tool socket accommodated a number of interchangeable add-ons, and Zam Wesell's toolbox included a flame projector, a poison gas sprayer, a dura-steel drill, a blaster, and canisters that could carry explosives or toxic biological agents. For reconnaissance or security, Zam's ASN-121 could carry an infrared detector, an eavesdropping recorder, a stinger blaster, a harpoon gun, or a tangle net. If threatened, the ASN-121 could reroute its electric circulation into its outer shell for a shocking method of deterrence, though Zam disabled this function for the Amidala hit, lest the droid's electrical signature set off the apartment's security sensors.

For the Amidala hit, Zam loaded her ASN-121 with two slithering kouhuns—multi-legged bugs from Indoumodo that can kill with a single sting. The ASN-121 emitted disruptive energy beams from its wing tips to bypass the security screen surrounding Senator Amidala's window, then deployed a laser cutter to carve a hole in the pane.

Unfortunately for ASN-121, Zam Wesell had ordered it to remain in the vicinity and monitor the kouhuns' attack. This left it visible to Obi-Wan Kenobi, who burst through the window and grabbed on to its body for a vertiginous ride among Coruscant's skyscrapers. The trip ended when Zam shot ASN-121 with a bolt from her sniper rifle.

Fragments from the droid later turned up during Republic Judicial patrols of the undercity. Once sliced, the droid's status log revealed the truth behind several unsolved assassinations, and warned several Senators that they had enemies in high places.

> **"Senator Jubben. STATUS: Terminated. Baron Wazado. STATUS: Terminated. Senator Amidala. STATUS: ABORTABORTABORTABOR—"**
>
> *—From the recovered log of Zam Wesell's ASN-121*

1. Tool Socket
2. Articulated Sensor Stalk
3. Shock Generator
4. Internal Fusion Generator
5. Repulsorlift Engine
6. Cooling Vanes

B1 Battle Droid

TECHNICAL READOUT

HEIGHT: 1.91 meters

MANUFACTURER:
Baktoid Combat Automata

PRIMARY FUNCTION:
Combat

ERA OF INFLUENCE:
Rise of the Empire

Baktoid Combat Automata B1 Battle Droid

Battle droids have become a joke among military personnel. And while it's true that they're thin and frail, and have a host of exploitable weaknesses, those facts are of little comfort if you're on the wrong end of their blaster rifles.

The familiar B1 unit came from the Geonosian factories of Baktoid Combat Automata, and was generally known only by the utilitarian designation *battle droid.* Their first combat deployment came during the Battle of Naboo in 32 B.B.Y., where they overran Naboo's inadequate defenses, terrorized innocent civilians, and dragged the survivors to internment camps.

Baktoid, a member of the Techno Union, was contracted by the Trade Federation to build battle droids as part of a secret military buildup prior to the Naboo invasion. Darth Sidious masterminded the plot, but the Trade Federation paid the bills. The final product bore all the hallmarks of Neimoidian cheapness.

B1 battle droids have poor targeting abilities and can be stopped by a single blaster shot. Their off-the-shelf photoreceptors are unable to magnify distant objects, requiring battle droids to carry macrobinoculars. The first generation of B1s did not even possess individual intelligence matrices, but instead acted as empty receptacles for the guiding signal of a central control computer (CCC).

The CCC powers the droids and transmits motion-capture data recorded from trained organic soldiers to help them perform combat moves. It also monitors the

> ### "Send more droids against the Jedi Knight! Their bodies are making a pile so high that he will never be able to cross it!"
>
> *—Trade Federation lieutenant Sentepeth Findos, desperately trying to stop Kit Fisto during the siege of Cato Neimoidia*

battlefield situation through the droid army's component photoreceptors and broadcasts tactical orders in response to changing fortunes. This approach has some advantages, including the ability to attack in eerily coordinated waves, but it means that the army is only as talented as the CCC's programmer.

In a worst-case scenario, the droid army might lose contact with its control signal. If this occurs, each battle droid shuts down and enters a hibernation mode; in extreme cases, the droid will deactivate the electromagnets that keep its limbs attached. Indeed, the battle droid's electromagnetic joints are its weakest points, and Republic troopers during the Clone Wars learned to aim for neck, shoulder, and torso connectors.

Rank-and-file battle droids are divided into three classes: infantry, pilot, and security, with the latter two designated by blue and maroon markings, respectively. The droids are further subdivided into military ranks, such as lieutenant, sergeant, and corporal.

Commander battle droids are an entirely different class. Easily identified by bright yellow-orange markings, commanders possess intelligence and independence apart from the central control computer. Commanders receive instructions directly from the CCC through high-security channels and relay the orders to their troops. During the Clone Wars, they also acted as liaisons between the droid army and their Separatist masters.

Commander and infantry battle droids wear backpacks

1. Electromagnetic Joint Couplings
2. Signal Reception Booster Antenna
3. High-Torque Motors
4. Specialized Movement Processor
5. Signal Booster and Power Augmentation Backpack

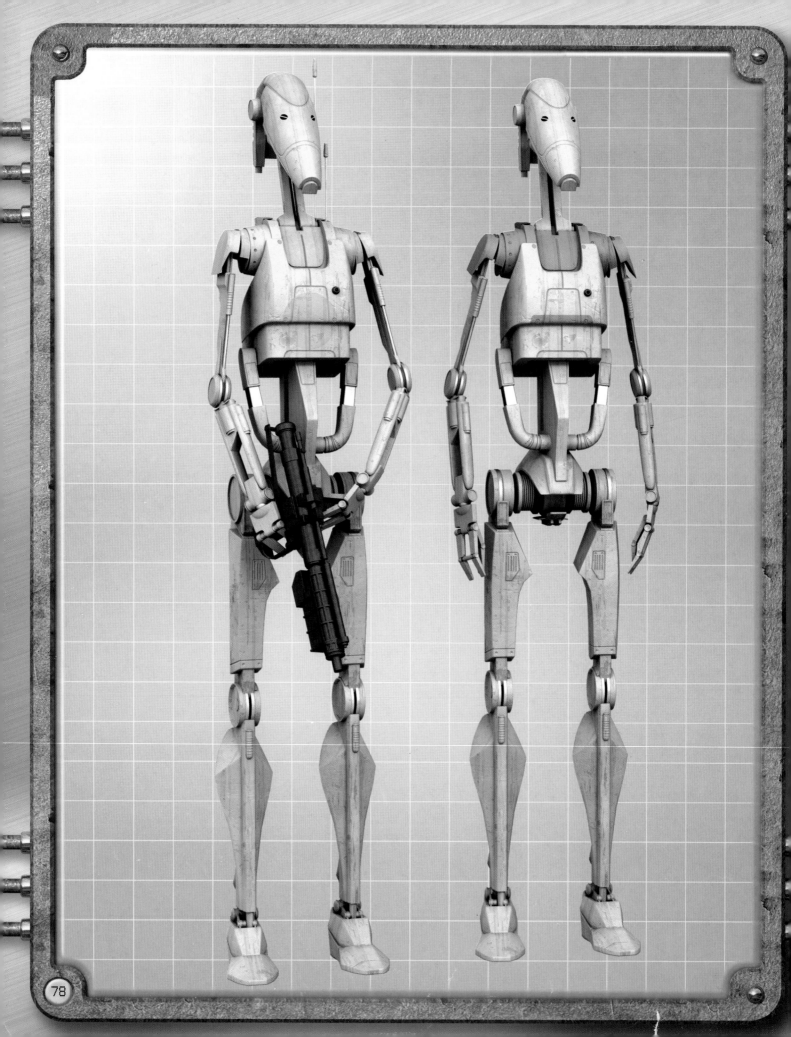

that contain comm units, transmission antennas, and encryption computers, as well as booster power cells that enable them to operate in the field for extended periods without recharge. Security and pilot droids are typically stationed aboard starships and thus require no back-packs.

Because battle droids don't have a standard alphanumeric series designation, their individual names can sometimes seem haphazard. Two battle droids involved in the invasion of Naboo were OOM-9 and 3B3. Names such as these, usually applied by technicians, are shortened versions of the string of identification code unique to each droid. All battle droids also have a large, highly visible number printed on their comlink booster packs to help their owners tell them apart at a glance.

Standard battle droids do not have built-in weapons. They carry large-barreled blaster rifles; specialty units are programmed to operate flamethrowers and missile launchers. Battle droids operated most Trade Federation heavy weapons, including armored assault tanks and STAP airhooks. The droids can fold up into a fetal position for storage, allowing 112 of the droids to fit onto the racks of a multitroop transport.

Unnerving in appearance, battle droids resemble bleached, dried skeletons. Their elongated faces mimic those of their Geonosian builders, but the fearful Neimoidians believed they had been modeled after rotted Neimoidian skulls.

After the Trade Federation's rout at Naboo, Baktoid Combat Automata secretly produced a replacement model designed to solve the problems of the B1 battle droid. These new battle droids, called E-5 units, were based on the baron droid and featured heavier armor and individual intelligence matrices. The E-5s were produced in small numbers as a temporary measure, while the Trade Federation developed the B2 super battle droid. Raith Sienar brought a number of prototype E-5s as body-guards on his mission to Zonama Sekot.

In the aftermath of Naboo's liberation, the Republic passed laws that barred the use of battle droid armies. The prohibition carried little weight, however, and proved hollow when the Clone Wars exploded in 22 B.B.Y. At the wars' end, a master control signal simultaneously shut down all Separatist droids, and most B1 units became the spoils of the Republic.

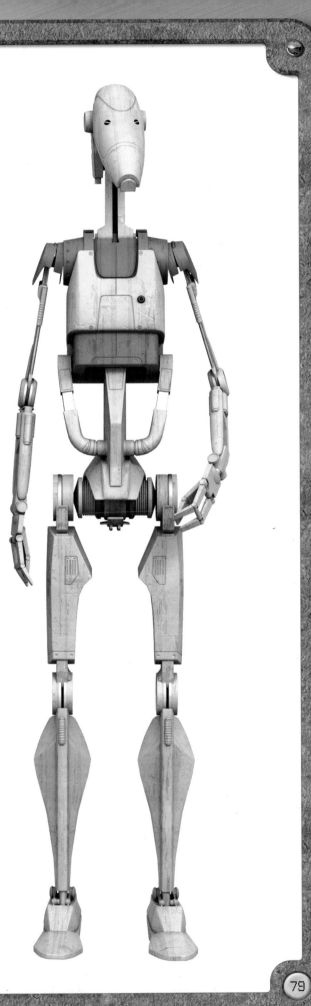

B2 Super Battle Droid

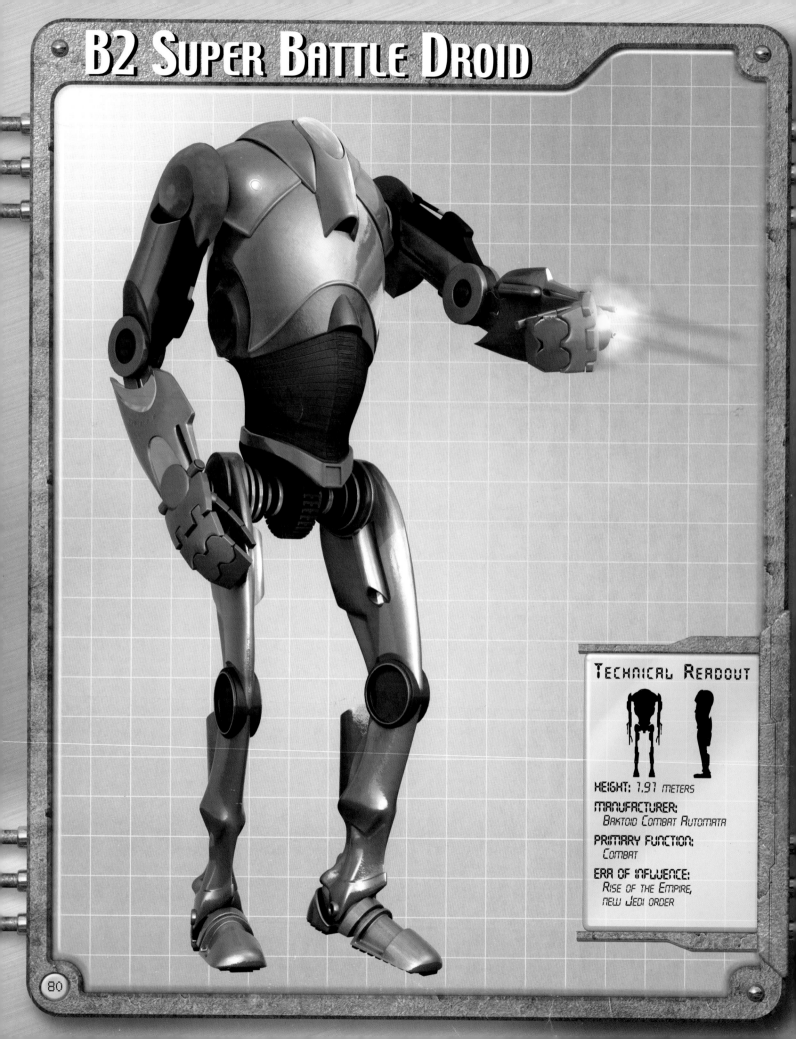

TECHNICAL READOUT

HEIGHT: 1.97 METERS

MANUFACTURER:
Baktoid Combat Automata

PRIMARY FUNCTION:
Combat

ERA OF INFLUENCE:
Rise of the Empire,
New Jedi Order

Baktoid Combat Automata B2 Super Battle Droid

After the Battle of Naboo, the Trade Federation knew it had a problem with its bare-bones battle droids. While the B1 models had easily routed the peaceful citizens of Naboo, they fell like cordwood when matched against the lightsabers of Jedi Knights.

Viceroy Nute Gunray's solution was to commission an infantry unit even stronger than the baron droids already in service. Baktoid Combat Automata's B2 super battle droids came into use over the following years, and saw their first major action at the Battle of Geonosis.

Baktoid's first goal was to preserve as much of the original battle droid design as possible. Super battle droids possess similarly shaped cranial units, as well as many of the same internal components. But the similarities end there. The super battle droid is a brawny brawler, encased in a hardened arcetron armored shell that is resistant to heat, flame, and blasterfire. The droid carries most of its weight in its upper torso, but gyroscopic algorithms in its pelvic servomotors help keep it upright.

A super battle droid wields its own weapon in the form of a rapid-fire dual laser cannon built directly into its right forearm. Blaster rifles are also carried by the droids, despite the fact that their mitten-like hands are incapable of squeezing a trigger. Instead, super battle droids carry special rifles that respond to signal emitters built into the droids' manipulators that spark firing impulses.

> ## "How well do you think one Jedi will hold up against a thousand battle droids?"
>
> *—Count Dooku to Mace Windu, prior to unleashing his super battle droids on Geonosis*

Consequently, super battle droid blasters cannot be picked up and used by organics.

In light of the Naboo fiasco, Baktoid Combat Automata designed the super battle droid to operate independently of a central control computer. The droids are not particularly bright, however, and will often forget about an opponent once their target has moved out of visual range. They are utterly without self-preservation instincts, and will plow right into the thick of a firefight, shooting continuously until either they or their targets are reduced to cinders.

The Trade Federation took delivery of most of Baktoid's super battle droids, but the Techno Union owned the design. During the Clone Wars, super battle droids became the face of the Confederacy of Independent Systems on thousands of worlds, from Ando to Vandos. The end of the wars brought an end to the super battle droid's three standard years of dominance, when a universal control signal shut down all Separatist war machines.

A few entrepreneurs, sitting on warehouses filled with stockpiled B2 droids, subsequently sold them into private hands, where they became enforcers on the staffs of crimelords. During the Yuuzhan Vong invasion, a platoon of super battle droids dubbed the "Orange Panthacs" beat back an occupation force of Yuuzhan Vong firebreathers on Mantessa, earning the unit a special commendation from Galactic Federation of Free Alliances Chief of State Cal Omas.

1. Reinforced Armor
2. Command Signal Receptor
3. Flexible Armored Midsection
4. High-Torque Motors
5. Firing Impulse Generators
6. Heat-Dissipating Vanes

B3 Ultra Battle Droid

TECHNICAL READOUT

HEIGHT: 4.0 meters

MANUFACTURER:
Baktoid Combat Automata

PRIMARY FUNCTION:
Combat

ERA OF INFLUENCE:
Rise of the Empire

Baktoid Combat Automata B3 Ultra Battle Droid

Packed with firepower, the ultra battle droid is by far the deadliest soldier manufactured by the Confederacy during the Clone Wars. Fortunately for the Republic, production problems prevented the droids from seeing a full rollout. Instead, they remain a footnote in military annals.

Baktoid Combat Automata's B1 battle droid made its debut at the Battle of Naboo; ten standard years later, the B2 super battle droid fought at the Battle of Geonosis. Baktoid engineers eagerly started plans for a B3, and Techno Union foreman Wat Tambor pitted two internal teams against each other for the privilege of creating the design. The Metalorn team, with Wat Tambor's backing, developed the cortosis battle droid. The team on Foundry engineered a heavily armored giant known as the Avatar-7. It was this design that ultimately received the blessing of General Grievous. Awarded the coveted *B3* designation—and given the name *ultra battle droid*—it entered production as a front-line combat unit.

The new ultra battle droid was huge and expensive. Baktoid entertained no illusions about the droid being deployed in numberless hordes, like the B1 and B2, but the company hoped to add them selectively as heavy hitters to the arsenal of every Separatist commander.

The ultra battle droid looks similar to the super battle droid, except for an obvious difference in scale. Other departures from the B2 design include four arms, two of them identical to those used on the super battle droid,

> *"**This** is new."*
>
> *—Jedi Master Mace Windu, glimpsing his first ultra battle droid during the Battle of Iktotch*

and the other two scaled up in proportion to match the ultra battle droid's hulking frame.

An arsenal of built-in weapons gives the ultra battle droid its bite. Two smaller arms have retractable rapid-fire blaster cannons in their forearms. The right primary arm is equipped with a tight-spray flamethrower, while the left sports a wide-spray plasma cannon. Built into the left shoulder is a rocket launcher, armed with semi-sentient brilliant missiles that can track their targets.

But perhaps the ultra battle droid's best gadget is its experimental density projector. This device generates a powerful tractor field that essentially increases the droid's weight twentyfold. When using the density projector, the ultra battle droid can glue itself in place, making it nearly impossible to dislodge or topple. By selectively switching the projector on and off, the ultra battle droid can crush tanks under its feet and plow through enemy fortifications.

Despite its "wow" factor, the density projector crippled the droid's rollout. Several first-generation units encountered glitches with their projectors in the middle of combat, rendering them immobile and therefore easy targets for fixed-position turbolasers. By the time Baktoid fixed the problem, the Clone Wars were nearly over.

Ultra battle droids fought with notoriety during the Outer Rim Sieges, but virtually disappeared after the wars' end. Several hundred units later saw use inside the urban-warfare training zone on the Imperial Academy world of Carida.

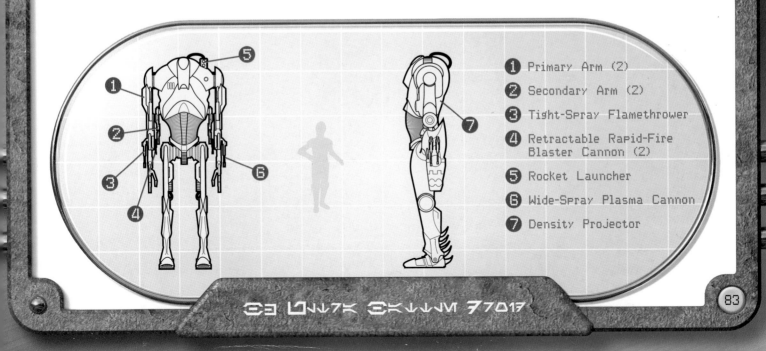

1. Primary Arm (2)
2. Secondary Arm (2)
3. Tight-Spray Flamethrower
4. Retractable Rapid-Fire Blaster Cannon (2)
5. Rocket Launcher
6. Wide-Spray Plasma Cannon
7. Density Projector

Baron Droid

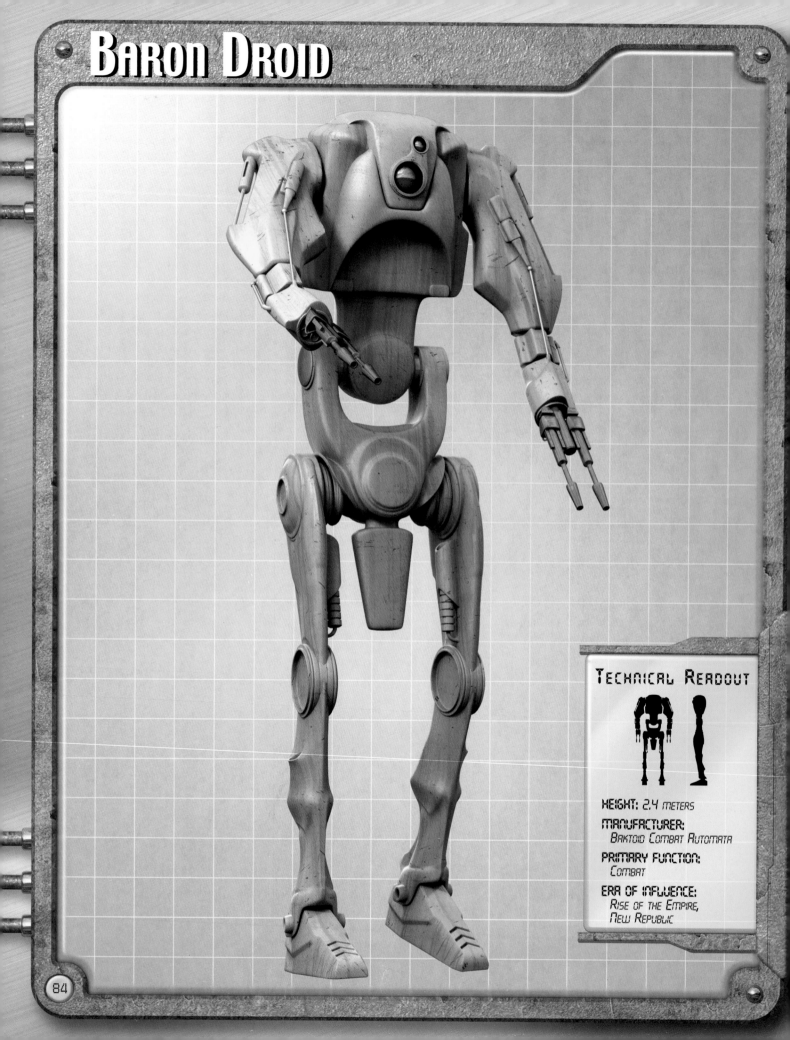

Technical Readout

HEIGHT: 2.4 METERS

MANUFACTURER:
Baktoid Combat Automata

PRIMARY FUNCTION:
Combat

ERA OF INFLUENCE:
Rise of the Empire,
New Republic

Baktoid Combat Automata E4 Baron Droid

The Trade Federation employed a host of terrifying droids to conquer the city of Theed during the Battle of Naboo. The most pervasive were B1 battle droids, but Baktoid Combat Automata also fielded a small number of experimental heavy units dubbed "baron droids."

Designed by Baktoid as an all-purpose security unit, the E4 baron droid is a hulking automaton with heavy armor and incredible strength. At the time of its introduction, it was one of the most alert security units available. The baron droid's thick torso houses motion, heat, energy, and sonic detectors. Visual stimuli are processed through the droid's single photoreceptor, which also serves as the baron droid's primary targeting mechanism and can produce a bright spotlight for identifying, tracking, or temporarily blinding its targets. As soon as the baron droid has a victim in its sights, blazing fire erupts from its twin high-energy blasters.

Although heavily armored and far tougher than the run-of-the-mill battle droid, the baron droid lacks personal shields. It can be disabled by multiple hits from a blaster rifle or a well-aimed lightsaber slash. Despite its plodding gait, the baron droid can attack ceaselessly, and can function for extended periods without a direct connection to a central control computer.

Baron droids came into service just prior to the Naboo invasion, during the period when the Trade Federation secretly built up its droid armies on the orders of Darth Sidious. Viceroy Nute Gunray, embroiled in a vendetta against the Commerce Guild, planned to establish the baron droids as his personal assassin corps. The Naboo invasion forced the droids into service before Gunray could realize his dream.

Obi-Wan Kenobi first encountered baron droids on Coruscant, during his investigation into the Black Heth criminal syndicate. He ran into more of the droids on Naboo, where the local resistance had been fighting them in the swamps and the tunnels beneath Theed. Naboo's fighters soon learned to avoid baron droids by watching the darkness for their signature spotlights.

Most of the Trade Federation's baron droids became combat casualties during the Battle of Naboo. Baktoid continued to produce the model throughout the Clone Wars, but the baron droid's advantages proved slight when compared to the new and far superior super battle droid.

Despite their age, baron droids are still in use by planetary militias and private security forces. On Arzid, a squad of baron droids overthrew the administrators of the only settlement in 16 A.B.Y. They now rule the planet through the law of the blaster.

> **"Excellent. Send two more baron droids to kill Shu Mai, and order a dozen to work as my bodyguards. At last we are getting results."**
>
> —*Trade Federation viceroy Nute Gunray*

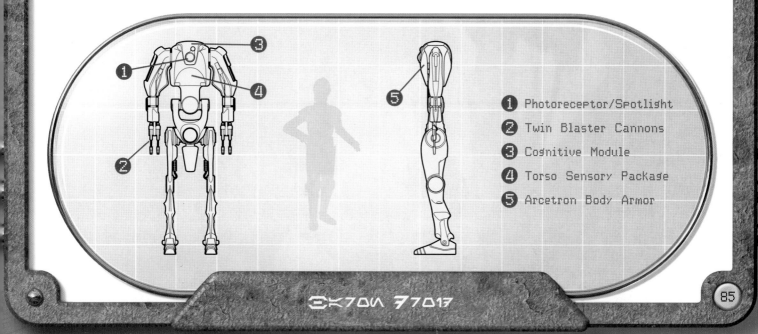

1. Photoreceptor/Spotlight
2. Twin Blaster Cannons
3. Cognitive Module
4. Torso Sensory Package
5. Arcetron Body Armor

Basilisk War Droid

Technical Readout

Height: 2.98 meters

Manufacturer:
Civilization of the Basilisk

Primary Function:
Combat

Era of Influence:
Old Republic

Mandalorian Army Basilisk Combat Mount

The basilisk war droid is a nightmare creation, a war chariot that left planets torn and bleeding during the Great Sith War and the Mandalorian Wars four thousand standard years before the New Republic. The basilisk still inspires awe, even though the deactivated specimens are seen only behind transparisteel barriers in museum displays.

The basilisk war droid looks like a living thing: a hard-shelled beetle or an armored Zalorian rock-lion. In motion, however, it behaves more like a drop ship. The Mandalorians liked to plunge from orbit straight down to a planet's surface, using the breakneck rate of descent to confound the autotargeters of their opponents' cannons. Wearing vacuum-sealed battle armor, Mandalorians had no difficulty operating their mounts in deep space.

Basilisks are both beasts and machines. The Mandalorians did not build them, but looted them from the poisoned Basilikian homeworld. The self-aware alien constructs became loyal companions to the Mandalorians, and their closest allies in battle.

The intelligence level of a war droid was only slightly higher than that of a domesticated animal, and Mandalorian warriors developed deeply empathic relationships with their mounts. They fed them energy-rich locap plasma mixed with unrefined narcolethe. In battle the basilisks became preternaturally quick extensions of their riders' bodies. When a basilisk fell in battle, the Mandalorians gave it the honors of a warrior's funeral before sending it into the heart of a star.

A basilisk war droid boasted a number of exotic weapons, including a nose cluster of shockwave generator rods that could fire a hull-puncturing plasma burst. Pulse-wave cannons and shatter-missile launch tubes adorned the hulls of many droids, sometimes hidden behind armored scales. The droid's heavy front claws, used as landing struts, could also flatten obstacles or rip open the flesh of enemies. Mandalorian riders often strapped weapons to the outside of their mounts, decorating the droids with the menacing glint of axes, swords, and flash-pistols.

No two war droids were exactly the same. The most common configuration of basil-isk, the open-combat model, darkened the skies with their numbers during planetary assaults. Other, less common configurations included the wasp-shaped stealth model and the two-seated heavy bomber. Open-combat models could also deliver explosives themselves, by towing a volatile atomic compression bomb between two droids and catapulting it into a capital ship or the hull of an orbital station.

The age of Mandalorian dominance ended when the Jedi known as Revan defeated the ruling Mandalore on Malachor V in 3961 B.B.Y. The shamed Mandalorians were forced to destroy their basilisk droids under the eyes of Revan, and entered a new era as the embittered Mandalorian Mercs.

> **"The doors opened in front of me and the air was sucked out of the drop bay. When the magnetic locks disengaged on my droid, I plunged toward the battle that waited below."**
>
> —*Mandalorian warrior Canderous Ordo*

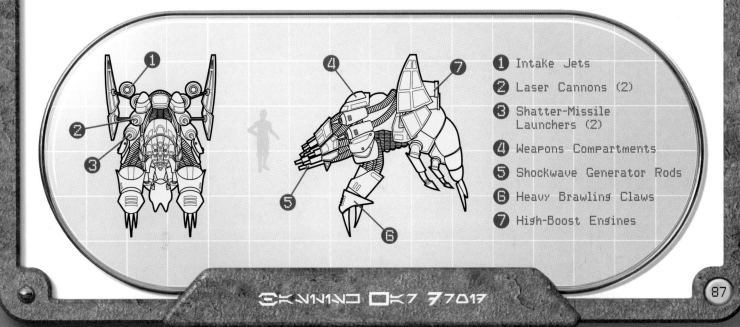

1. Intake Jets
2. Laser Cannons (2)
3. Shatter-Missile Launchers (2)
4. Weapons Compartments
5. Shockwave Generator Rods
6. Heavy Brawling Claws
7. High-Boost Engines

Buzz Droid

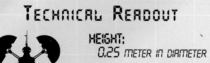

Technical Readout

HEIGHT:
0.25 meter in diameter

MANUFACTURER:
Colicoid Creation Nest

PRIMARY FUNCTION:
Sabotage

ERA OF INFLUENCE:
Rise of the Empire

Colicoid Creation Nest Pistoeka Sabotage Droid

Sabotage is a buzz droid's primary mission, making it one of the few military models that doesn't mark its success in body counts. But that doesn't make the buzz droid any less dangerous—just ask a pilot stranded inside a dead starship as it leaks atmosphere into the cold vacuum outside.

Pistoeka buzz droids are a product of the Colicoid Creation Nest. The cannibalistic Colicoids, who are also responsible for the droideka and tri-fighter, come from a planet crawling with insects (including themselves). The buzz droid is based on the pisto, a pest eaten in Colla IV's tropical regions. When the Confederacy of Independent Systems demanded increased droid output from Colla IV during the Clone Wars, the Colicoids took their existing repair robots and modified them to become agents of sabotage.

Legs folded, a buzz droid can seal itself inside a spherical shell less than a quarter of a meter in diameter. These melon-size balls are then loaded into the cylinder of a discord missile, which is typically carried by a vulture fighter (in space) or a droid gunship (in atmosphere). Discord missiles explode in front of their targets, spreading buzz droids into their enemies' flight paths.

Their outer shell is made of a heat-dissipating material that allows it to penetrate most particle shields. Using a quartet of maneuvering thrusters to zip in close, a buzz droid splits open its protective casing and secures itself to the ship's hull with a magna-pod limb.

> ## "Artoo, hit the buzz droid's center eye!"
>
> *—Obi-Wan Kenobi, during the Battle of Coruscant*

A flock of buzz droids, each carrying an electronic database of common starship schematics, can leave a ship dead and drifting in a matter of seconds. The default array of buzz droid weaponry includes a prying hook, a circular saw, a plasma-cutting torch, a picket appendage, a gripping pincer, and a drill head. When this last arm bores a hole in a ship's hull, an extendable computer probe can then splice itself into the ship's internal wiring.

From that point, it's easy for the buzz droid to override the onboard systems and shut down weapons, engines, or life support. It can even fly the ship from its exterior perch.

The droid perceives its surroundings through three photoreceptors that incorporate magnification lenses, spectrum filters, and X-ray sensors. A hit to its central eye can knock a buzz droid offline.

Buzz droids saw their first action relatively late in the Clone Wars. Consequently, the Colicoids were left with millions of unwanted units at the conflict's end. Some found use on vast scrap yards, such as those of Ronyards and Junction, helping their owners strip rusted hulks for usable parts.

Elsewhere, buzz droids became popular on the gladiatorial circuit. Aficionados of the sport recall fondly the time a buzz droid took down a mighty Mark X executioner with the skillful application of a laser scalpel.

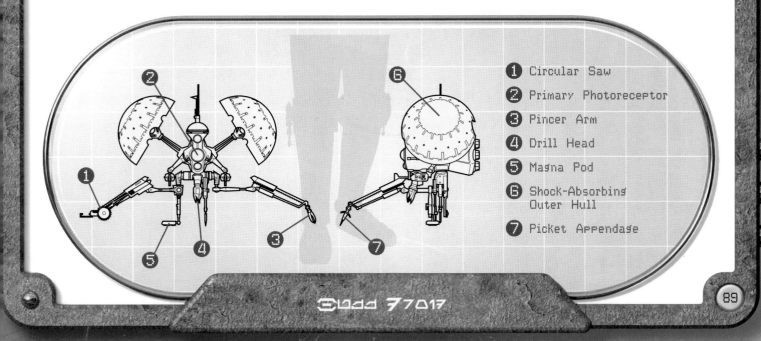

1. Circular Saw
2. Primary Photoreceptor
3. Pincer Arm
4. Drill Head
5. Magna Pod
6. Shock-Absorbing Outer Hull
7. Picket Appendage

Chameleon Droid

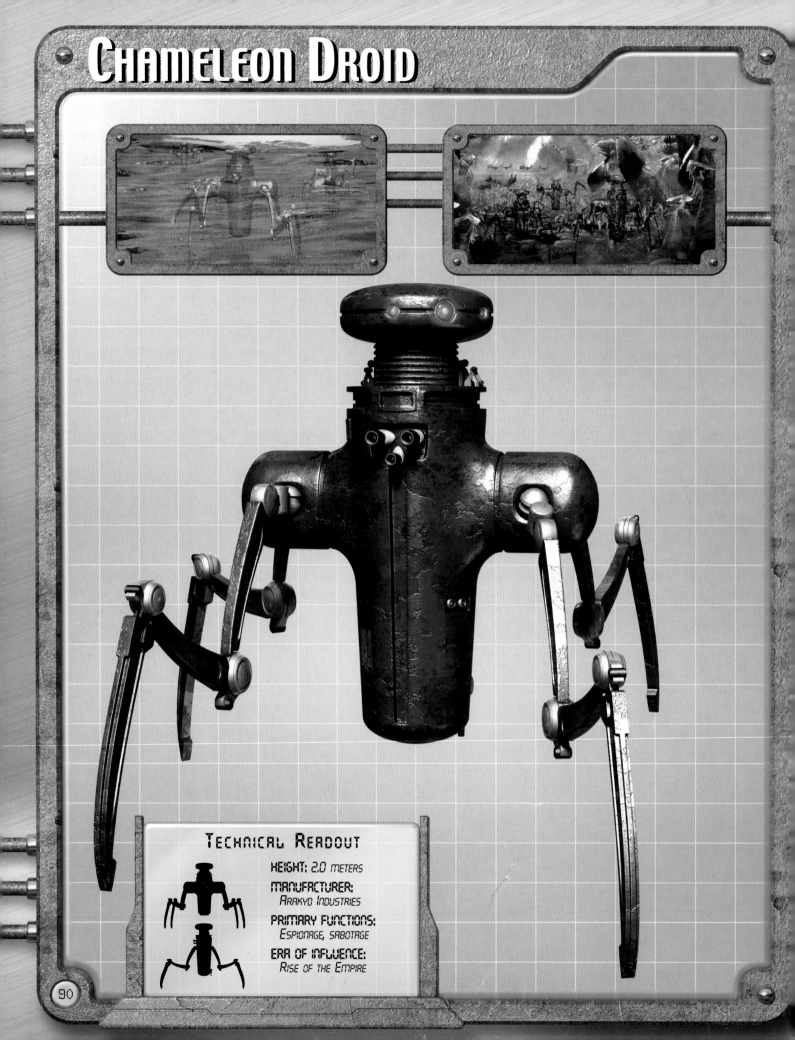

Technical Readout

Height: 2.0 meters

Manufacturer:
Arakyd Industries

Primary Functions:
Espionage, sabotage

Era of Influence:
Rise of the Empire

Commerce Guild Modified Arakyd Spelunker

The chameleon droid joined the Separatist army shortly after the first shots were fired in the Clone Wars. In a case of turning shovels into swords, the Commerce Guild took the benign Arakyd Spelunker and modified it into an invisible killer.

The greedy Commerce Guild had its fingers in millions of mining operations across the galaxy, and constantly hungered for new mineral strikes. During the decade leading up to the Clone Wars, Commerce Guild president Shu Mai purchased hundreds of thousands of Arakyd Spelunkers for her exploration division. The Spelunkers rode hyperspace pods into unexplored territory, where they sniffed out the presence of mineral veins on planetoids and transmitted their findings back to the Commerce Guild. Spelunkers could even use blasting charges, kept in internal storage bays, to expose the ore vein prior to the arrival of a heavy digging crew.

It didn't take long for Shu Mai to realize her Spelunkers would make excellent minelayers. With an array of modifications that patently violated the Arakyd warranty, the Spelunker emerged as a spy and sabotage unit. Its illusory camouflage screen gave it the name *chameleon droid*.

Although it seems as if a chameleon droid can become invisible, the effect is actually a trick achieved through a hologrammic array. By making a 360-degree scan of its surroundings and calculating the positions of observers, the droid can project a screen that shows the terrain immediately behind it. This technique, nearly foolproof under the right conditions, falls apart when the observer's viewing angle is shifted. Also, unlike true cloaking devices, the hologrammic shrouds leave chameleon droids detectable to sensor arrays.

A chameleon droid comes equipped with three laser cannons, installed in mountings that once housed mineral sensors. Its cylindrical body, unchanged since its days as a Spelunker, holds adhesive mines that are released one at a time through a ventral hatch. The chameleon droid's four pincer legs are capable of generating traction fields that enable it to walk on walls and ceilings. Assisting in this capacity is a small repulsorlift unit that acts as anti-ballast, reducing the chameleon droid's overall body weight.

Chameleon droids saw their first widespread use on frozen Ilum. They mined the sacred crystal caverns where Jedi build lightsabers during their transitions to Jedi Knighthood. The Jedi Luminara Unduli and Bariss Offee destroyed scores of chameleon droids, but Master Yoda finished the job by burying the saboteurs in an avalanche.

As minelayers, chameleon droids served the Separatists for the remainder of the Clone Wars. The Republic preferred the cheap and expendable LIN demolitionmechs for the same purpose. Demolitionmechs thus became the minelayers of choice following the rise of the Empire.

> **"Come out, come out, sly droids. To my eyes, hidden you are not."**
>
> *—Jedi Master Yoda, battling chameleon droids on Ilum*

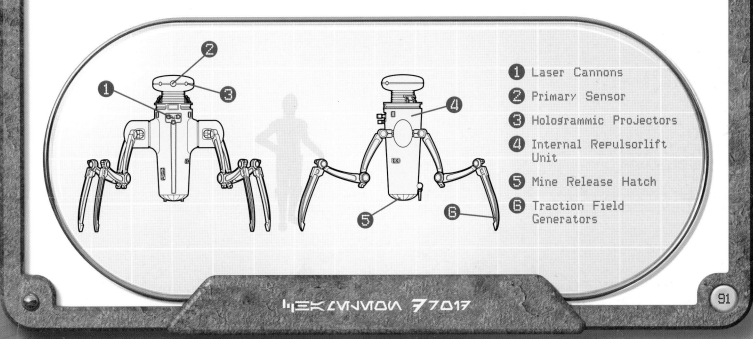

1. Laser Cannons
2. Primary Sensor
3. Hologrammic Projectors
4. Internal Repulsorlift Unit
5. Mine Release Hatch
6. Traction Field Generators

COLICOID ANNIHILATOR DROID

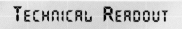

TECHNICAL READOUT

HEIGHT: 3.5 meters

MANUFACTURER:
Colicoid Creation Nest

PRIMARY FUNCTION:
Combat

ERA OF INFLUENCE:
Rise of the Empire

Colicoid Creation Nest Annihilator Droid

The cannibalistic Colicoids enjoy an advanced technological society, yet they're one of the most hostile species in the galaxy. Because so few dare to visit their spawnworld of Colla IV, no one realized that the builders of the droideka had an even deadlier model guarding their home turf.

A Scorpenek annihilator droid moves on four pointed limbs. It carries itself in the menacing stance of a mantis, with its weapons arms cocked back, ready to strike. Two rapid-fire, high-intensity laser cannons on each arm deliver blistering barrages that can crack the hulls of enemy tanks.

A combination particle–energy shield surrounds the droid in a hazy bubble, featuring a polarization signature so that the annihilator can fire *out*. Droidekas, which use similar shields, often take up position inside the bubble of their "big brother" for a second line of protection. A crimson photoreceptor picks up targets on infrared wavelengths, while composite radiation sensors mimic the sensory organs of the Colicoids.

Late in the Clone Wars, the Republic launched a strike on the Colicoid Creation Nest, the corporation responsible for building the Separatists' droidekas and tri-fighters. While assault ships shelled Colla IV's surface with a turbolaser bombardment, four platoons of troopers advanced on the shielded factory. When the clones reached the innermost wall, an annihilator droid rose up and shredded a duracrete barrier with its laser cannons, offering the clones no cover and killing most of the landing force within minutes. The surviving clones retreated.

Colicoid annihilators were prohibitively expensive to produce in mass quantities—fewer than one hundred existed on all of Colla IV, with most stationed around strategic or political resources. Knowing their enemies would return, the Colicoids arranged for a Separatist naval task force to erect an orbital screen, while freighters left Colla IV and shipped the annihilator droids to the front lines. An annihilator could turn a dozen AT-TEs into smoking husks. Not surprisingly, the droids turned the tide at Palanhi and Formos to score Separatist victories.

The Republic had further reason to curse the machines. During the Outer Rim Sieges, Republic commanders were forced to commit unacceptable numbers of heavy units in order to take down a single annihilator.

At the end of the Clone Wars, a command signal triggered the simultaneous deactivation of all Separatist droid forces. Emperor Palpatine arranged for the remaining annihilators to be taken in by the Imperial Department of Military Research. Many found their way to Palpatine's private citadel on the Deep Core world of Byss.

> **"We don't know what it was, sir, but it took out three platoons. We can't let the Colicoids get these things offplanet."**
>
> —*ARC trooper Stec, after a failed strike at Colla IV*

1. Infrared Photoreceptor
2. Composite Radiation Sensors
3. Rapid-Fire Laser Cannons
4. Plasma Feed Lines
5. Shield Generator

CORTOSIS BATTLE DROID

TECHNICAL READOUT

HEIGHT: 1.9 meters

MANUFACTURER:
Baktoid Combat Automata

PRIMARY FUNCTION:
Combat

ERA OF INFLUENCE:
Rise of the Empire

Baktoid Combat Automata C-B3 Cortosis Battle Droid

Cortosis battle droids were a frightening variant on Baktoid Combat Automata's super battle droids—made even more dangerous thanks to their lightsaber-resistant armor. The threat they posed to the Jedi came to a sudden end, however, when Anakin Skywalker destroyed their manufacturing facility.

Cortosis is an extremely rare ore capable of resisting the cut of a lightsaber blade (similar to the equally rare phrik metal). One variety of cortosis shorts out a lightsaber blade when the energy and the mineral interact. The more common variety, which is malleable and can be shaped into armor, forms an interlocking bond that cannot easily be severed by lightsaber energy.

After the Battle of Geonosis, Techno Union foreman Wat Tambor began experiments with raw cortosis and cortosis artifacts, such as the arm shields worn by Yinchorri warriors. A factory on the mechworld of Metalorn became the nerve center for Tambor's research. As soon as his engineers had ironed out the technical problems, Tambor ordered the Metalorn facility to undergo a complete retooling for the delicate and expensive job of stamping cortosis armor.

Each cortosis battle droid produced at the Metalorn factory had a covering of black body armor, clamped to the droid's frame in formfitting plates. The cortosis battle droid shared the same intelligence matrix as the super battle droid, and had arms that ended in high-intensity laser cannons.

Wat Tambor convinced Count Dooku to mount a raid on Coruscant using the new droids. Ten months after the start of the Clone Wars—and more than two years before General Grievous would do the same—Dooku invaded Coruscant with an army of cortosis droids and several of his dark side minions. The droids laid waste to the city's underlevels and broke into the Jedi Temple, nearly allowing Dooku to destroy the Jedi archives.

> ## "The raid on the Republic capital succeeded. My cortosis droids are invincible, and my factories unassailable!"
>
> *—Wat Tambor, following the Confederacy's first attack on Coruscant*

Eventually, the Separatists were forced to withdraw, but the cortosis droids had performed extremely well against Jedi opponents. So well, in fact, that Darth Sidious considered the droids a destabilizing factor in the war that he was carefully orchestrating. In his role as Chancellor Palpatine, Sidious arranged for information about Wat Tambor's cortosis supply line to come into the Republic's possession. The Jedi Council dispatched Anakin Skywalker to uncover the droid factory and destroy it.

While carving his way through the Metalorn facility, Anakin discovered the best way to defeat a cortosis battle droid. By executing a very precise overhead slash with a lightsaber, a Jedi could target the narrow gap between the droid's left and right breastplates and slice its torso in half.

Anakin destroyed the Metalorn plant and brought Wat Tambor back to Coruscant as a prisoner of war. Palpatine would later arrange for Tambor's escape, but the Techno Union produced no further cortosis droids for the remainder of the Clone Wars.

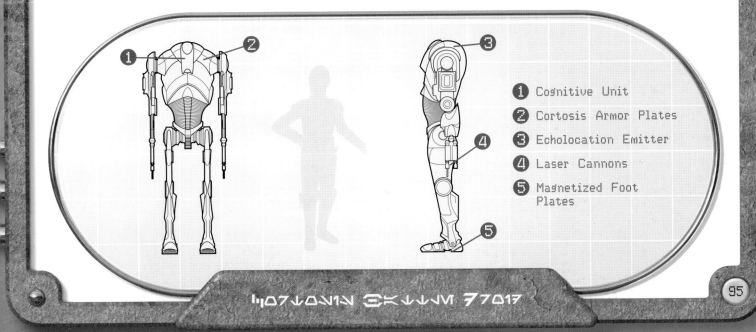

1. Cognitive Unit
2. Cortosis Armor Plates
3. Echolocation Emitter
4. Laser Cannons
5. Magnetized Foot Plates

TECHNICAL READOUT

HEIGHT: 1.49 meters (average)

MANUFACTURER:
Techno Union

PRIMARY FUNCTION:
Combat

ERA OF INFLUENCE:
Rise of the Empire

Techno Union LM-432 Crab Droid

The Separatists used droids to fill every battlefield niche, from solitary soldiers to gigantic engines of war. The LM-432 crab droid, also known as the "Muckracker," was one of the last heavy hitters to see action as the Clone Wars neared conclusion.

The crab droid came about through the environmental failures of the Commerce Guild's spider droid, which proved unreliable at navigating swampy or arctic environments. The various corporate constituencies of the Confederacy of Independent Systems pooled their resources to design the LM-432. Though the droid bore the fingerprints of everyone from the Trade Federation to the Hyper-Communications Cartel, the Techno Union ultimately manufactured the finished product.

Scaleable factory techniques allowed the Techno Union to pump out eight sizes of crab droid, ranging from scurrier-size models used for espionage to gargantuan hulks equipped to batter down enemy fortifications. Most crab droids that fought in the Clone Wars belonged to the midsize heavy-infantry series.

Flexibility was also a key consideration for weapons and gear. The first batch of crab droids, deployed during the Second Battle of Jabiim, came equipped with insulated vacuum-pump systems inside their forward pincers. These assemblies of tubing and spray nozzles could suck up mud and squirt it out again, simultaneously clearing a path and clogging the optical sensors of enemies. This earned the crab droid the nickname of Muckracker, though future units lacked the vacuum feature. Instead, those models boasted bubble wort projectors, a rare Gungan technology that could trap targets inside temporary energy spheres.

All crab droids possess six armored limbs for easy purchase when clambering over rocky terrain. Duranium teeth at the tips of the forward limbs, coupled with gripping prongs at the "elbow" joints, enable the crab droid to chip into solid rock and scale near-vertical inclines. Three glowing red circles—a sensor bulb, a targeting range finder, and an auxiliary photoreceptor—dominate the crab droid's face, while communications antennas and sensor stalks keep the LM-432 in constant contact with its battlefield supervisor. The crab droid also has two blaster cannons slung beneath its body.

Clone troopers who faced LM-432s in battle discovered that the droids have poor targeting systems. By exploiting blind spots, troopers could get past the forward pincers and unload blaster rounds into a weak point just behind the head.

At the end of the Clone Wars, the Republic seized tens of thousands of crab droids from a Techno Union factory on Tar Morden. These units eventually saw use in live-fire stormtrooper training exercises on Carida. After the Battle of Endor, Caridan engineers drew upon their experience with crab droids in developing the MT-AT "spider walker."

> **"Crab droids have a subpar targeting percentage, but deliver a profit of 48,000 credits per unit. They might not win the war, but they could save the Techno Union's fiscal quarter."**
>
> *—From the Techno Union's LM-432 risk-assessment report*

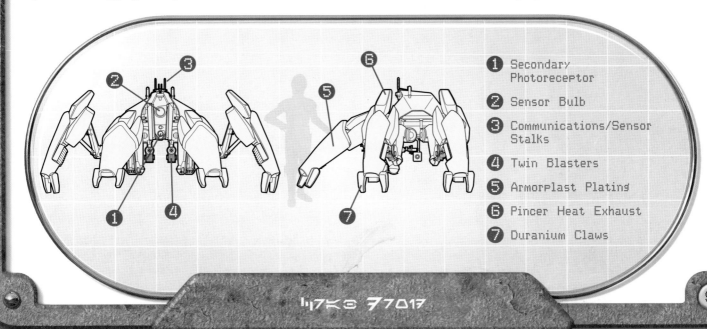

1. Secondary Photoreceptor
2. Sensor Bulb
3. Communications/Sensor Stalks
4. Twin Blasters
5. Armorplast Plating
6. Pincer Heat Exhaust
7. Duranium Claws

DARK TROOPER

TECHNICAL READOUT

HEIGHT: 2.56 meters (Phase One); 2.82 meters (Phases Two and Three)

MANUFACTURER: Imperial Department of Military Research

PRIMARY FUNCTION: Combat

ERA OF INFLUENCE: Rebellion

Imperial Department of Military Research Phases One–Three Dark Trooper

The Dark Trooper project represented the culmination of the Empire's quest to build the ultimate Imperial battle droid. Like the L8-L9 and Z-X3 before it, the Dark Trooper *looks* like a stormtrooper. Nevertheless, it couldn't replace the stormtrooper in the minds of officers, who considered battle droids to be Clone Wars relics.

General Rom Mohc had previously collaborated with TaggeCo on the Z-X3 droid trooper. This time he brought his designs directly to the Imperial Department of Military Research, bypassing TaggeCo entirely. The Emperor expressed interest in the project. Consequently, several dozen of Mohc's mechanical men went from prototype to finished version immediately after the Battle of Yavin.

To house his assault force and construct replacement units, General Mohc received the *Arc Hammer:* a titanic spacegoing construction facility built at the starship yards of Kuat. Mohc soon gave his Dark Troopers their first combat test—a brutal, one-sided massacre at a Rebel base on Talay. Darth Vader, impressed, ordered Mohc to continue with production.

Dark Troopers had three distinct stages, each one suitable for armed conflict. The Phase One, little more than a metal skeleton, was primitive but relentless. Its structural frame, forearm shield, and razor-edged carving blade were cast from phrik, a durable alloy resistant to lightsaber strikes and found primarily on the moons of the Gromas system.

> **"In light of the *Arc Hammer* fiasco, Emperor Palpatine is withdrawing all funding for the development of Imperial battle droids. I *told* you it would never work."**
>
> —*Grand Vizier Sate Pestage, in a communication to the Imperial Department of Military Research*

Phase Two Dark Troopers became the standard combat units. Their phrik body shells made them tougher than the Phase One, while their repulsorlift engines and flight jets enabled them to strike from the air. Each Phase Two carried a devastating assault cannon that fired plasma shells and long-range explosive rockets.

The Phase Three was conceived as the ultimate Dark Trooper. Only a single unit was known to exist aboard the *Arc Hammer;* it appears likely that this unit was a finished prototype for a planned but uncompleted line. Even more massive than the Phase Two, this unstoppable behemoth sported a nasty cluster of firing tubes connected to a seemingly endless supply of seeker missiles. These rockets, while slow, homed in on a target's heat signature and packed enough detonite to obliterate the strongest personal shielding. The Phase Three prototype was designed to operate independently, but could also be worn by a human operator as an exosuit.

Rebel agent Kyle Katarn fought against Mohc's project, dismantling several Dark Troopers single-handedly. Katarn's counterattack resulted in the destruction of the *Arc Hammer,* which cost the Empire billions of credits and marked the death of the Dark Trooper project. Emperor Palpatine, still smarting from the loss of the Death Star, was so infuriated by this setback that he refused to approve funding for a new construction facility.

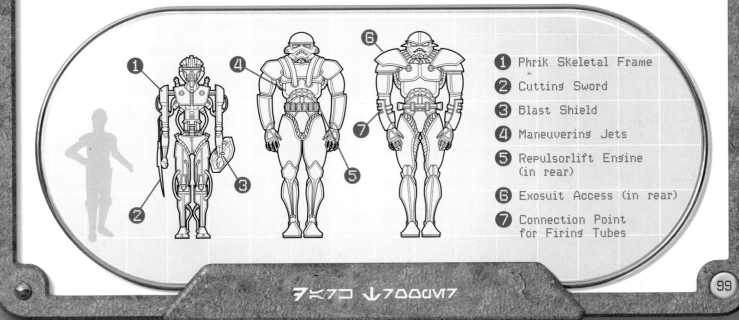

1. Phrik Skeletal Frame
2. Cutting Sword
3. Blast Shield
4. Maneuvering Jets
5. Repulsorlift Engine (in rear)
6. Exosuit Access (in rear)
7. Connection Point for Firing Tubes

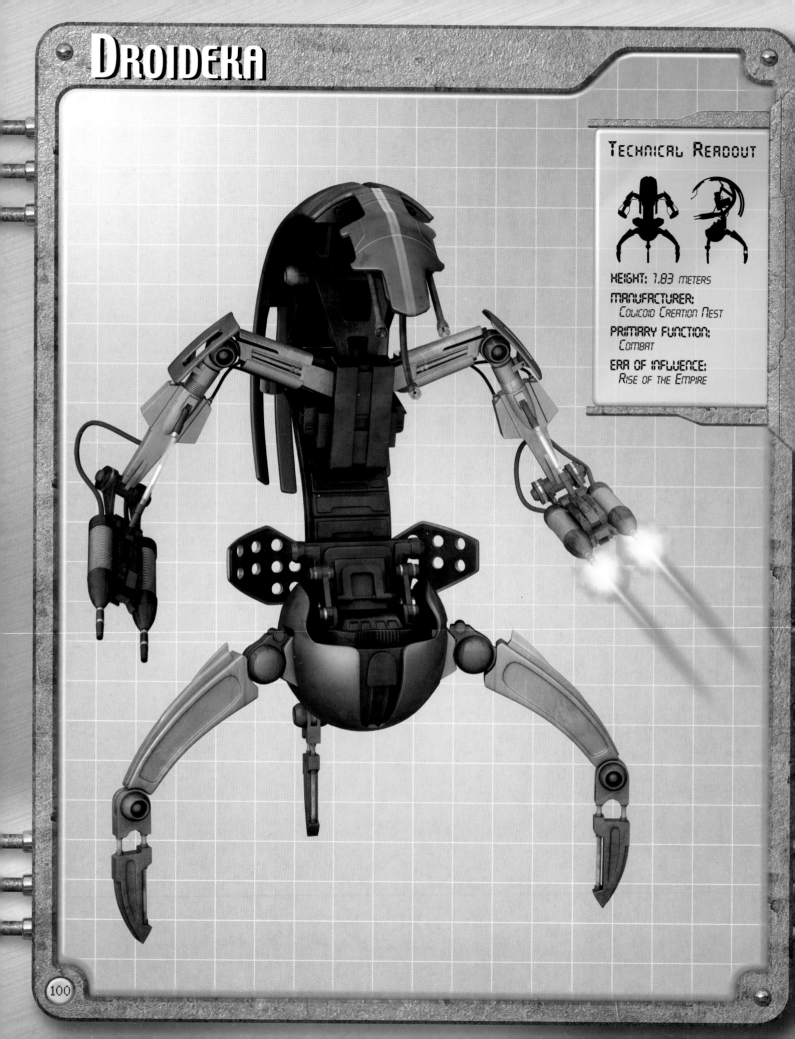

DROIDEKA

TECHNICAL READOUT

HEIGHT: 1.83 METERS

MANUFACTURER:
Colicoid Creation Nest

PRIMARY FUNCTION:
Combat

ERA OF INFLUENCE:
Rise of the Empire

Colicoid Creation Nest P-Series Destroyer Droid

Droidekas have been called the deadliest things in the galaxy ... but anyone who says that has obviously never met a Colicoid.

Nor would anyone *want* to meet a Colicoid, since the two-meter-tall insects are bloodthirsty cannibals. Prior to the Battle of Naboo, however, Nute Gunray of the Trade Federation met with the Colicoid Sovereign Nest and bartered fifty bargeloads of exotic flesh in exchange for an exclusive droideka contract.

Gunray wanted the heavy-hitting droidekas to support his comparatively weak battle droids. The deployment of droidekas at the Battle of Naboo marked the first widespread use of the robotic killers, though small batches of them had previously trickled out from Colla IV and triggered several public atrocities.

The name *droideka* originates with the Colicoids, who combined the Basic word *droid* with the Colicoid suffix *-eka,* meaning "hireling" or "drone." Most citizens of the galaxy simply call them destroyer droids, for wanton destruction is their stock in trade.

A droideka has two double-barreled blaster cannons where its arms should be, and both can spit out rapid-fire crimson energy powerful enough to chew enemies to pieces. The cannons can also fire high-intensity blasts, at a slower rate, that are capable of exploding light vehicles. Droidekas possess their own deflector shields, making the droids virtually immune to small-arms fire. The shields, hazy blue and spherical, are polarized so that the droideka's own bolts penetrate outward while return fire splashes uselessly against the shield's periphery.

In its attack stance, a droideka perches atop three pointed legs that provide stability but which are too short to generate much speed. For rapid deployment, droidekas curl up into a different configuration known as the "wheel mode." This rolling method of locomotion is second nature to Colicoids, who integrated their natural movements into their droids. To initiate the rolls, droidekas pulse a string of internal microrepulsors in sequence. To stop, they reverse the direction of the microrepulsor chain.

Droidekas' thin heads are actually orderly sensor packages. They contain fine-vibration monitors and specialized radiation detectors, enabling the droids to pursue quarry using nonvisual methods. At the crux of the body is a mini-reactor to power the high-drain deflector shield and blaster cannons. The entire body is cast from heavy armored bronzium.

Nute Gunray was savvy enough not to completely trust the Colicoids. For this reason (and also to knock down the extravagant price), he insisted that his droidekas be manufactured without individual intelligence matrices. Trade Federation droidekas, like battle droids, were powered and controlled by a central control computer and would shut down in the absence of their guiding signal. Standard droidekas from Colla IV are self-aware and twice as deadly.

> ## "We have them on the run, sir ... they're no match for droidekas."
>
> *—Trade Federation lieutenant Rune Haako, during the blockade of Naboo*

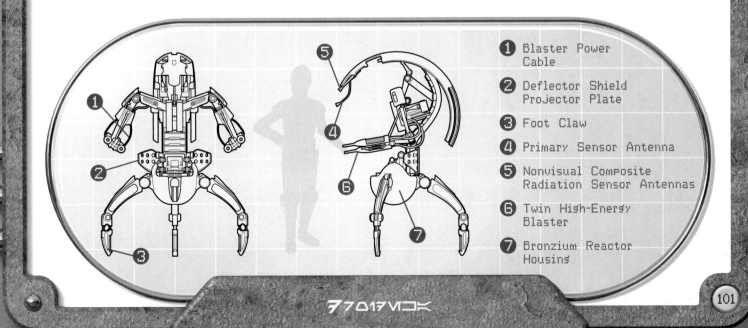

1. Blaster Power Cable
2. Deflector Shield Projector Plate
3. Foot Claw
4. Primary Sensor Antenna
5. Nonvisual Composite Radiation Sensor Antennas
6. Twin High-Energy Blaster
7. Bronzium Reactor Housing

Dwarf Spider Droid

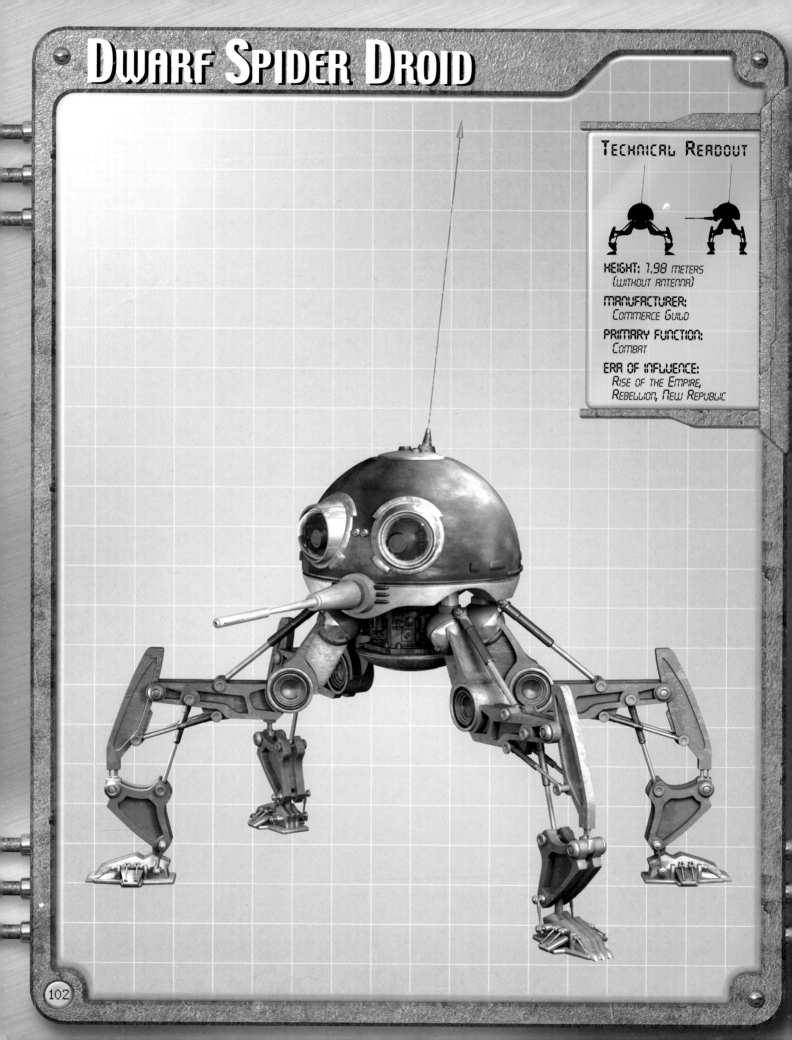

Technical Readout

HEIGHT: 1.98 meters
(without antenna)

MANUFACTURER:
Commerce Guild

PRIMARY FUNCTION:
Combat

ERA OF INFLUENCE:
Rise of the Empire,
Rebellion, New Republic

Commerce Guild DSD1 Dwarf Spider Droid

Dwarf spider droids have served many masters. They began as corporate enforcers, evolved into war machines for the Separatist army, and served the Empire as mechanical attack dogs for the stormtrooper corps.

The Commerce Guild, responsible for the production of raw materials in the years prior to the Clone Wars, constructed the first dwarf spider droids. The guild controlled mines on thousands of worlds, but mining ventures that had been "persuaded" to join weren't always willing to pay their monthly dues. Dwarf spider droids, which preceded the development of the much larger homing spider droids, owe their small size to the necessity of operating inside of cramped mining tunnels.

Dwarf spider droids move on four jointed limbs, enabling them to adjust their height to obtain a better elevation for their sole laser cannon. The gun is capable of laying down a rapid-fire antipersonnel spray as well as slow high-intensity blasts designed to rupture light vehicles. Two variants on the dwarf spider droid exist, distinguishable by the size of the cannon.

The droid's huge infrared photoreceptors and echolocation emitters allow it to function in total darkness. Dwarf spider droids can operate underwater—a feature designed to account for flooded tunnels—but they cannot float. They do not require the guidance of a central control computer. Their individual intelligence

> **"You've fought against it, you know its weaknesses, and more importantly, you know what a killer it can be. Men, meet the newest addition to the stormtrooper corps."**
>
> —*Stormtrooper commander TK-342, prior to the pacification of Ghorman*

matrices are on par with the intelligence of a very bright domesticated animal. Dwarf spider droids are loyal to their creators, but sometimes balk at being sent into danger zones.

Commerce Guild president Shu Mai used the first batch of dwarf spider droids to track down negligent guild members and remind them where their loyalties lay. Some fugitives tried to erect barricades in the deepest tunnels, but the droids simply annihilated the makeshift barriers of dirt and rock with high-powered, short-range laser blasts. This action led to a new nickname, *burrowing spider droids*.

At the Battle of Geonosis, dwarf spider droids became part of the Separatist droid army. They marched alongside battle droids and super battle droids in the front lines, providing a heavy punch while taller homing spider droids fired over their heads from the rear. Dwarf spider droids quickly became a symbol of Separatist might, fighting on nearly every battlefield and patrolling the streets of loyal Confederacy worlds.

After the conclusion of the Clone Wars, the Empire seized all remaining dwarf spider droids. The stormtrooper corps sent the droids against Separatist holdouts, then against political dissidents who were encouraging the early stirrings of rebellion. Dwarf spider droids are often seen on the worlds of the Imperial Remnant, operating customs checkpoints alongside familiar white-armored stormtroopers.

1 Echolocation Emitter
2 Tracing Antenna
3 Infrared Photoreceptor
4 Laser Cannon
5 Adjustable-Height Legs

Technical Readout

HEIGHT: 6.7 meters

MANUFACTURER:
Civilization of the Abominor

PRIMARY FUNCTION:
Conquest

ERA OF INFLUENCE:
Old Republic, Rise of the Empire

Agent of the Abominor

The Great Heep was an ancient construct, far older than its Imperial overseers ever knew or suspected. When its consciousness finally came to an end on Biitu, archaeologists lost a rare chance to learn the secrets of the Abominor—an advanced and thoroughly evil droid species.

The Great Heep and other Abominor are believed to be a unique breed of malevolent, self-constructing automata, developed in another galaxy. Possessed with a hunger for power and slaves, the Abominor grafted more machinery onto their bodies until some even became planet-size monstrosities.

These add-ons were often superfluous or simply nonfunctional. Some Abominor experimented with fusing machinery to biological systems, while others built grotesque faces in mockery of the organic slaves who shoveled fuel into their boilers. Lesser droids lived on them like parasites. Over eons, their appetites became rapacious, and the Abominor exterminated organic species on thousands of planets as they scoured for resources.

The Abominor had an opposite number in the Silentium, automata whose perfect shapes were drawn from celestial symmetry. The two sides fought a war, until the galaxy's dominant organic species used the opportunity to rally and force the machines elsewhere.

Accounts of possible Abominor have led researchers to assemble anecdotal chronologies of at least eighteen of the machines. Abominor prefer dry environments, as con-

centrated moisture can quench the internal fires that give them life.

The Great Heep appeared on the Outer Rim planet of Biitu in the years prior to the Battle of Yavin. An enormous droid, yet still small for an Abominor, it had a squarish body made up of moving pistons and noxious smoke-stacks, and moved on two tank-treads. Two huge gripper arms and a magnetic grapple allowed the Great Heep to lift droids and crush them. The mouth of the Heep was filled with grinder blades, as well as an astromech-shaped socket for vampirically draining the electronic essences from robotic victims.

Working in partnership with Imperial admiral Terrinald Screed, the Great Heep established a droid-run mining operation to excavate a new fuel ore. The Heep built the "moisture eater"—a tower that sucked Biitu's atmosphere bone-dry. This device protected the Heep but left the planet's farmers in the grip of drought. The Great Heep also maintained a harem of astromech droids, giving him a ready supply of sacrifices.

In the years prior to the Battle of Yavin, during a period when R2-D2 and C-3PO became separated from their master Captain Antilles, the two droids came to Biitu with their master Mungo Baobab. When the group destroyed the moisture eater, the resulting rainwater deluge snuffed out the Great Heep's furnace. The inactive Heep is now on permanent exhibit at the Baobab Museum of Science.

> **"So, this is the new batch of droids. Your duty is to serve me and Biitu for the rest of your days. Escape is impossible. Any droid caught trying to leave will be used for scrap."**
>
> —*The Great Heep*

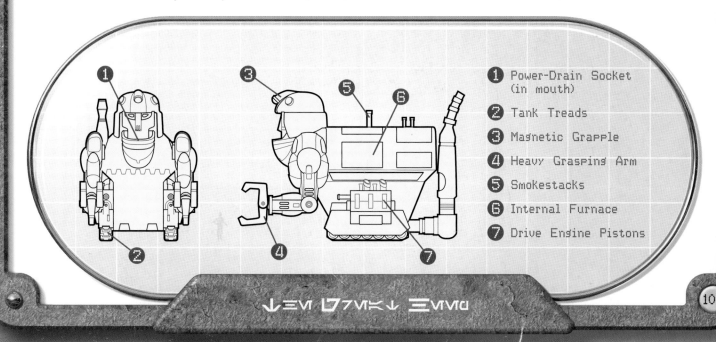

1. Power-Drain Socket (in mouth)
2. Tank Treads
3. Magnetic Grapple
4. Heavy Grasping Arm
5. Smokestacks
6. Internal Furnace
7. Drive Engine Pistons

HK Assassin Droid

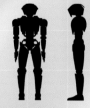

TECHNICAL READOUT

HEIGHT: 1.8 meters

MANUFACTURER:
Czerka Corporation

PRIMARY FUNCTION:
Assassination

ERA OF INFLUENCE:
Old Republic

Czerka Corporation HK Series Protocol Droid

Introduced more than four thousand standard years ago, the HK series represented an attempt by the Czerka Corporation to circumvent local laws forbidding the construction or sale of assassin droids. Ostensibly a protocol unit, each HK carried assassination programming that manifested itself in a polite yet sadistic personality.

Czerka never marketed the droids as killers, though within the company it was no secret—*HK* stood for "hunter-killer." The company plan called for HKs to take up roles within the business sphere and assassinate heads of rival corporations at Czerka's behest.

Czerka's schemes took an unexpected turn when its prototype unit, HK-01, inspired thousands of his fellow automatons to riot and triggered the Great Droid Revolution on Coruscant. Czerka managed to conceal HK-01's role as instigator, and subsequent models were far more discreet.

One of the most notorious was HK-47, which became the property of the Jedi hero Revan. In order to bring about an end to the Mandalorian Wars, Revan wiped out an entire fleet with a mass-shadow generator. Believing that future kills should not veer into excess, Revan customized HK-47 to assassinate individual targets whom Revan believed to be "destabilizing influences" on the galactic order.

HK-47 carried a number of weapons and had many more built into slots on his arms. He could track his targets using sonic sensors, motion sensors, and telescopic/infrared photoreceptors. His translation unit enabled him to interpret millions of galactic languages. Although obedient, HK-47 had a voice that dripped with weary sarcasm. After HK-47 referred to Revan's apprentice Malak as "meatbag," the insult so amused Revan that he ordered the droid to apply the term to all organic beings.

Revan later wiped the droid's memory. HK-47 found employment with a string of owners, somehow causing the death of each new master when he carried out the commands given to him. Eventually purchased in a Tatooine droid shop, HK-47 became a member of the adventuring party that uncovered the ancient Rakatan Star Forge, again working alongside his former master Revan.

Shortly thereafter, the administrative droid G0-T0 started building new HK-50 units in a secret factory on Telos. The HK-50s infiltrated the Republic fleet as protocol units, where their sometimes arbitrary translations during negotiations among visiting diplomats often led to violence. HK-50 units, identifiable by their gunmetal-gray coloration, could not act against other HKs due to self-preservation protocols built into their template.

Five years after the Star Forge incident, HK-47 teamed up with the heroine known as the Jedi Exile to battle a trio of Sith Lords. At the Telos droid factory, HK-47 convinced the HK-50 droids to join his cause. The united HKs helped defeat G0-T0 in a showdown on Malachor V.

Recent evidence suggests that HK-47 survived the subsequent four thousand years by storing his consciousness in various electronic systems. He emerged in a new body around the time of the Battle of Yavin, assembling an army of murderous droids on the lava planet Mustafar.

> "Retraction: Did I say that out loud? I apologize, Master. While you are a meatbag, I suppose I should not call you as such."
>
> —*Assassin droid HK-47*

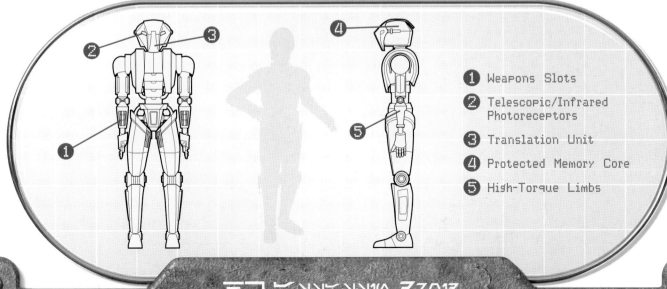

1. Weapons Slots
2. Telescopic/Infrared Photoreceptors
3. Translation Unit
4. Protected Memory Core
5. High-Torque Limbs

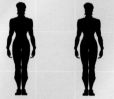

Technical Readout

HEIGHT: Variable

MANUFACTURER:
Imperial Department of Military Research

PRIMARY FUNCTION: Infiltration

ERA OF INFLUENCE:
Rebellion, New Republic

Imperial Department of Military Research Classified HRD

Plenty of humanoid droids have tried to look *too* human and failed, but human replica droids (HRDs) finally cracked the perceptual barrier. In both appearance and behavior, an HRD is utterly indistinguishable from a human being. HRDs are among the most expensive automata ever built and are not currently available for sale to the public.

The HRD experiment began with Project Decoy, a Rebel Alliance plot to replace Imperial officials with perfect duplicates. The Rebels, however, lacked sufficient funds to complete their design during the Galactic Civil War, and their archenemies beat them to the punch. The Empire hired designers Massad Thrumble and Simonelle the Ingoian to create an Imperial replica droid. The two geniuses produced a flawless HRD female named Guri.

Smelling profit, Simonelle established his own HRD workshop in the Minos Cluster, while Thrumble remained with the Empire, developing duplicates of Governor Torlock of Corulag and his daughter, Frija. These two droids possessed a self-awareness so acute that they rejected their assigned roles as decoys and escaped to a new life in the wastelands of Hoth. Guri, meanwhile, was sold to the head of the Black Sun syndicate, Prince Xizor, for a cool nine million credits.

Guri possesses enhanced strength and hyper-reflexes, and was modeled in the image of a striking, blond-haired young woman. The masquerade is successful through the use of a poly-alloy skeleton, clone-vat skin coverings, and internal organs made from biofibers. To all but the most advanced medical equipment, Guri appears completely organic.

Guri worked as Xizor's bodyguard and private assassin. At the time of her master's death, she was the second most powerful figure in Black Sun, a testament to the redesigned AA-1 verbobrain she carries in her skull. Guri's autonomy was so great that she voluntarily elected to undergo reprogramming that would purge her synapses of assassination programming. Shortly after the Battle of Endor, Massad Thrumble performed the operation on Hurd's Moon, and Guri went on to pursue an existence as a fully self-governing droid.

Approximately a year after Endor, the New Republic at last completed its work on Project Decoy. The new HRDs were clumsy and lacked the complicated personalities that had become a hallmark of Massad Thrumble's design. The Project Decoy droids saw action in only a few missions, including one where a replica of Leia Organa helped kill the Imperial warlord Trioculus.

During the Yuuzhan Vong invasion, the entrepreneur Stanton Rendar set up shop in the Minos Cluster. Using the "entchment" technology of the Ssi-ruuk, Rendar offered to transfer the consciousnesses of paying customers into the bodies of HRDs, a process that he believed held the secret to eternal life.

> **"You might be the only person in the galaxy who can reprogram me. I don't want to be an assassin anymore."**
>
> —*Guri to her creator, Massad Thrumble*

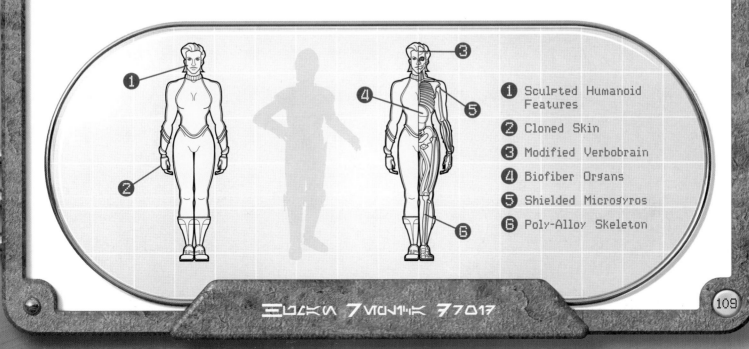

1. Sculpted Humanoid Features
2. Cloned Skin
3. Modified Verbobrain
4. Biofiber Organs
5. Shielded Microgyros
6. Poly-Alloy Skeleton

IG-100 MagnaGuard

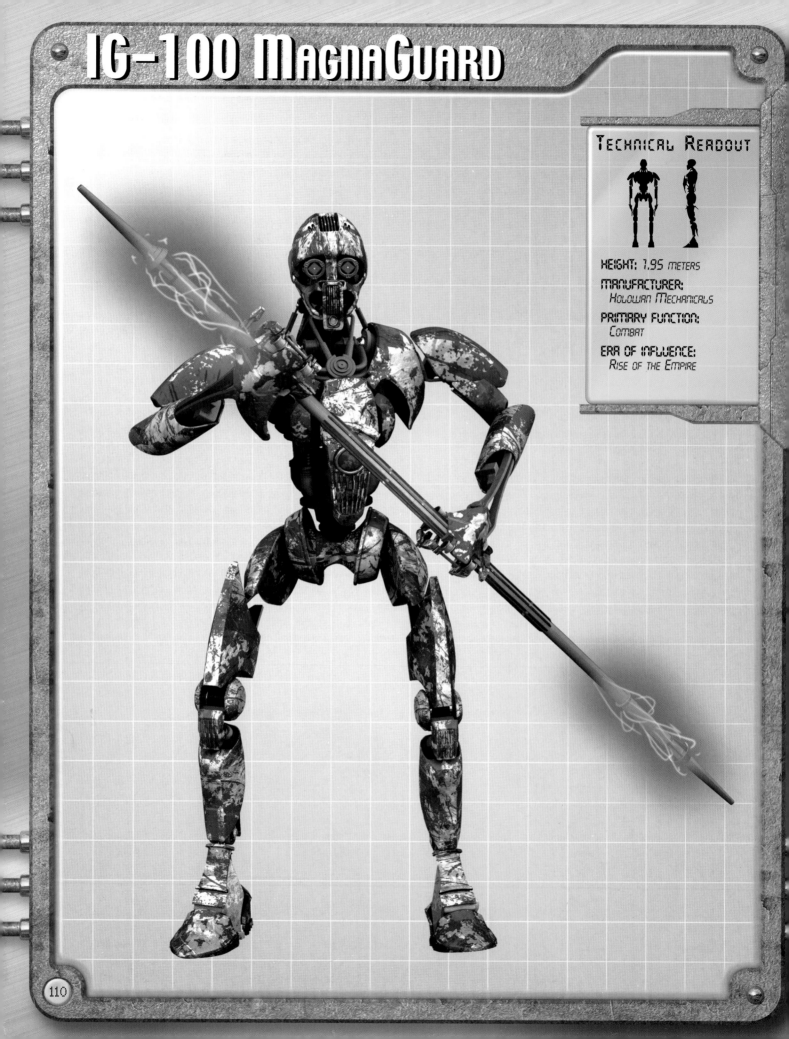

Holowan Mechanicals IG-100 MagnaGuard

General Grievous, conqueror of a hundred worlds, became a figure of legendary menace during the Clone Wars. His robotic bodyguards were equal to that reputation. The IG-100 MagnaGuard could take down nearly any opponent and helped pave the way for the even deadlier IG assassin droids.

Prior to his reconstruction as a cyborg, General Grievous led his native Kaleesh in battle against their traditional enemies, the Huk. Grievous's Kaleesh bodyguards wore head wraps and capes bearing Kalee mumuu markings, and were drawn from the most elite members of the Kaleesh fighting force.

In his new life as commander of the Separatist droid army, Grievous asked for similar bodyguards. Count Dooku contracted Holowan Mechanicals to construct a new droid model: the prototype Self-Motivating Heuristically Programmed Combat Droid, or IG-100 MagnaGuard. The MagnaGuard incorporated elements from the IG lancer, and Holowan's close ties with the InterGalactic Banking Clan resulted in carrying over the *IG* nomenclature.

General Grievous erased an entire library of fighting moves from the memory banks of his MagnaGuards, and insisted on training the droids himself. Some became specialists at close-quarters brawling, while others developed expertise in ranged weaponry or explosives. A few came with rocket launchers built into their backs. Different shell coverings in black, alabaster, blue, and gray helped distinguish one model from another. Satisfied with his bodyguards, General Grievous dressed them in traditional head wraps and cloaks from the Kalee homeworld.

Grievous knew that his bodyguards would inevitably fight Jedi. He gave them long-handled electrostaffs, made from lightsaber-resistant phrik metal, with tips crawling with incapacitating energy tendrils. Furthermore, redundant systems allowed MagnaGuards to keep fighting even after losing a limb (or a head) to a Jedi's blade. Most Jedi who targeted Grievous never made it past his bodyguard screen. Those who did were exhausted when they reached that point, and were easily dispatched by the general.

During Grievous's mission to kidnap Supreme Chancellor Palpatine from Coruscant, a contingent of MagnaGuards battled Palpatine's Jedi defenders in a fight that spilled from Palpatine's apartment to a hovertrain platform. Though many MagnaGuards wound up in pieces, they succeeded in their primary mission of splitting and delaying the Jedi.

Shortly afterward, more MagnaGuards tried to defend their master on board Grievous's flagship, *Invisible Hand*. Obi-Wan Kenobi and Anakin Skywalker made short work of most of the bodyguards, however, and many of the remaining units disintegrated when chunks of *Invisible Hand* burned up on orbital reentry. Most of the rest perished on Utapau during Obi-Wan's pursuit of General Grievous.

> **"So, General Grievous, we meet at last. In the name of the Republic, I—urrrk!"**
>
> *—Jedi Master Sannen, as a MagnaGuard jabs him in the throat*

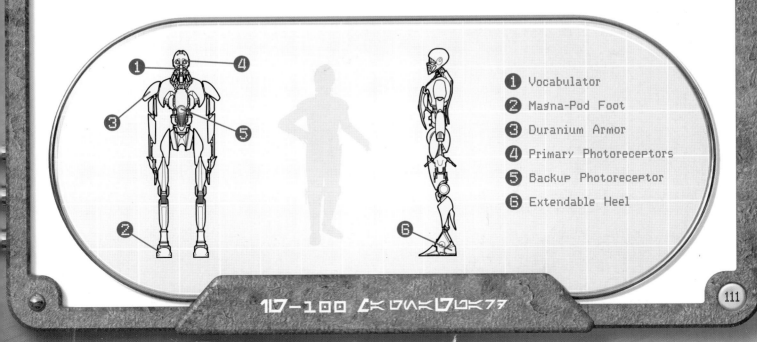

1. Vocabulator
2. Magna-Pod Foot
3. Duranium Armor
4. Primary Photoreceptors
5. Backup Photoreceptor
6. Extendable Heel

IG Assassin Droid

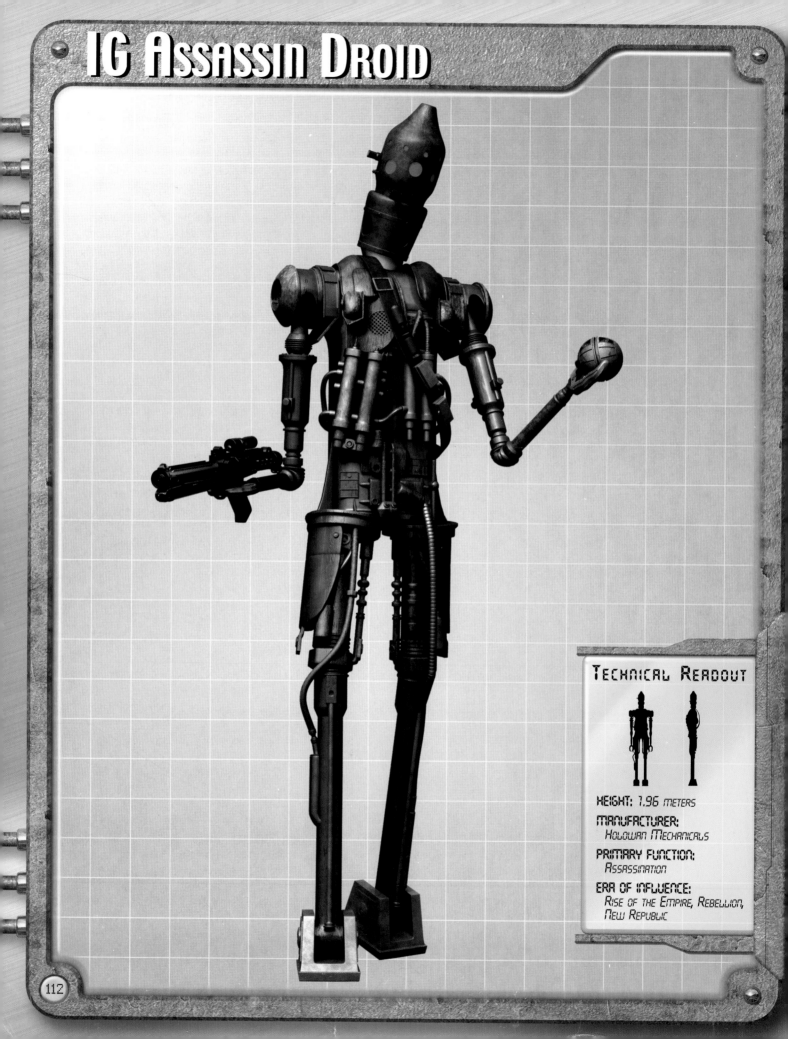

TECHNICAL READOUT

HEIGHT: 1.96 meters

MANUFACTURER:
Holowan Mechanicals

PRIMARY FUNCTION:
Assassination

ERA OF INFLUENCE:
Rise of the Empire, Rebellion,
New Republic

Holowan Mechanicals IG Series Assassin Droid

IG assassin droids are the culmination of a homicidal product line that started with the IG lancer and included the IG-100 MagnaGuard. With each new IG, the threat level increased exponentially.

IG assassin droids were envisioned by the engineers of Phlut Design Systems well before the Clone Wars. But the company produced only the IG lancer before running out of money. Holowan Mechanicals inherited Phlut's assets and labeled the unproduced Phlut blueprints as IGs 1 through 99 before building its own version for General Grievous, the IG 100 Magna-Guard.

After the Clone Wars, Holowan—which had been accepting both Separatist and Republic money for years—was commissioned by Imperial supervisor Gurdun to build a hunter that would eliminate threats to the young Empire. Going back to earlier Phlut concepts, Holowan produced an IG-97 and an IG-72, but its greatest successes were its four identical IG-88 units.

Roughly humanoid in shape, each IG-88's blaster-resistant armored frame stood two meters tall. A cylindrical head, studded with glowing red sensors, allowed the unit to see in all directions at once. The droid lacked olfactory detectors, but compensated with advanced auditory, radionic, movement, and temperature sensors. Its multiple optic lenses could access a wide variety of spectral filters under hazy or low-light conditions.

The IG's weapons complement included a repeating blaster in each forearm and a concussion grenade launcher in the left hip, as well as a flamethrower, sonic stunner, paralysis cord, throwing flechette array, and rack of poison gas canisters—all stored behind hidden panels.

The fingers of the right hand doubled as miniature cutting lasers. The mirrored palm of the left hand was capable of intercepting blaster bolts and deflecting them back along their original path. The IG could also dramatically raise the temperature of its exterior plating, allowing it to burn through nets or melt a stream of immobilizing Stokhli spray.

When the first IG-88 unit received his sentience programming, he identified the technicians in the room as threats and eliminated them. This droid, which called himself IG-88A, copied his consciousness into IG-88s B, C, and D. The four IG-88s became bounty hunters. However, most met their ends prior to the Battle of Endor.

IG-88A launched a more ambitious scheme, masterminding a plot to turn all droids manufactured on Mechis III into agents of his will. He even uploaded his consciousness into the computer core of the second Death Star, making him a living superweapon. Nevertheless, he perished when the battle station exploded. The wealthy Thul merchant family eventually found IG-88A's body and reprogrammed the empty shell to act as a bodyguard. It is still unknown whether Holowan Mechanicals produced additional IG assassin droids or if a rival company ever duplicated the blueprints.

> **"WANTED: IG-88, aka the Phlutdroid, also reportedly operating as IG-88A, IG-88B, IG-88C, or IG-88D. Heavily armed, more than 150 kills. DISMANTLE ON SIGHT."**
>
> *—Imperial bounty posting*

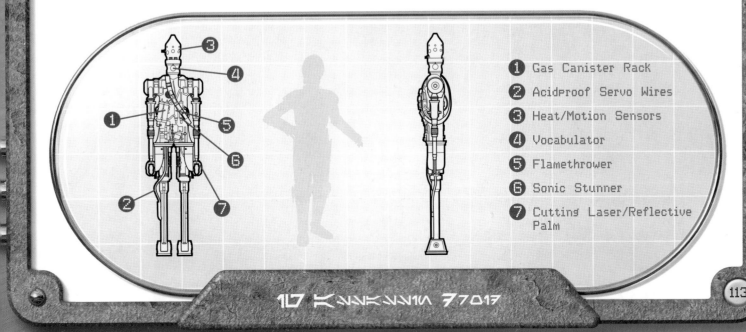

1. Gas Canister Rack
2. Acidproof Servo Wires
3. Heat/Motion Sensors
4. Vocabulator
5. Flamethrower
6. Sonic Stunner
7. Cutting Laser/Reflective Palm

IG Lancer Droid

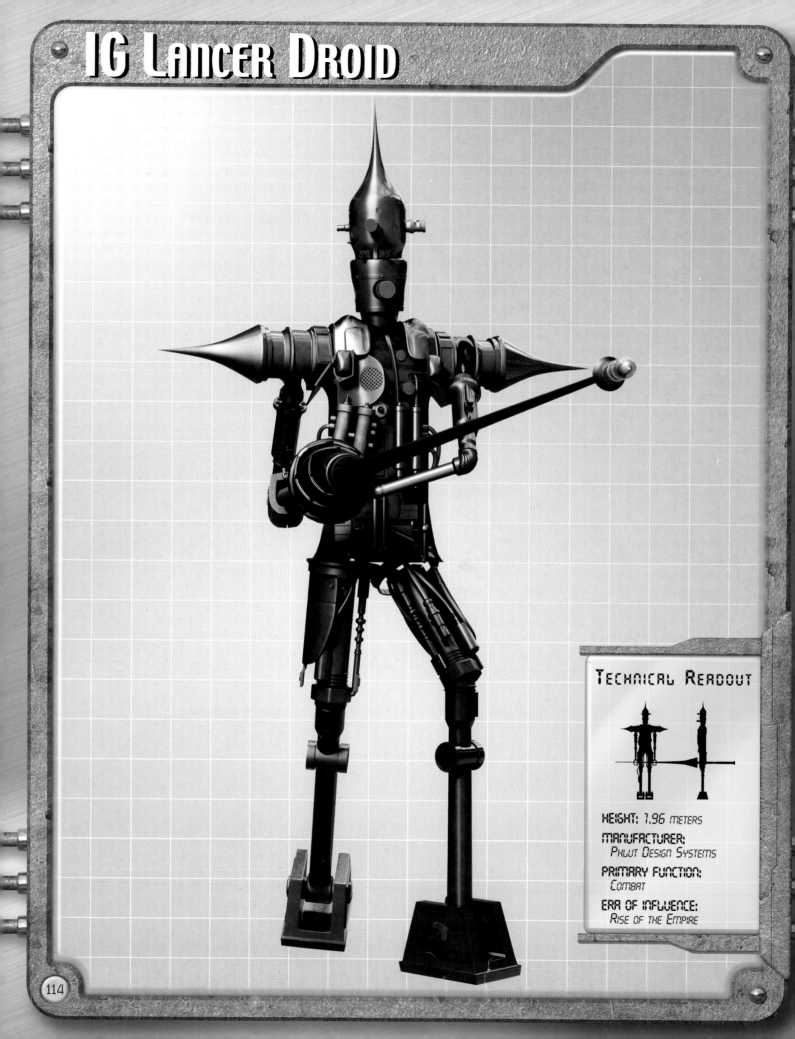

Technical Readout

HEIGHT: 1.96 meters

MANUFACTURER:
Phlut Design Systems

PRIMARY FUNCTION:
Combat

ERA OF INFLUENCE:
Rise of the Empire

Phlut Design Systems IG Lancer Combat Droid

To those who survived the rampages of the assassin droid IG-88, the IG lancer droid is a dreadful specter of things to come. The lancer was the first combat droid to sport the distinctive stretched-cylinder design common to many IGs, and the first to carry the *IG* label.

Phlut Design Systems brought the IG line into existence. A small firm based on the Outer Rim banking planet of Muunilinst, Phlut hoped to develop a new battle droid to sell to the Trade Federation. To obtain the start-up capital for "Project Phlutdroid," the company took out a hefty loan from the Muunilinst-based InterGalactic Banking Clan.

Phlut produced glossy black battle droids nearly two meters tall, with skinny bodies that echo the Muuns who built them. Though many components appear crude—the two-pincer gripper hands, for example, incapable of fine manipulation—the Phlutdroids possess limb strength more than twice that of the standard B1 battle droid. The lancers also have remarkably quick reaction times, enabling them to spar hand-to-hand against skilled organic opponents.

Unfortunately, like many companies that borrowed from the InterGalactic Banking Clan, Phlut Design Systems could not meet the terms of the draconian contract it had signed. The Banking Clan seized the company's assets shortly before the Clone Wars, including all finished droids and any blueprints related to Project Phlutdroid.

> ## "General Kenobi, our cannons are being destroyed."
> ## "Mount up."
>
> —*Republic clone trooper Able 472 and Obi-Wan Kenobi, planning their counterattack against IG lancers during the Battle of Muunilinst*

Renaming its acquisition the IG series to mark the droids as InterGalactic Banking Clan property, IBC chairman San Hill installed them as guards around Muunilinst's commerce citadels. Outfitted with their trademark power lances and speeder bites, the IG lancers became an outward sign of militarization as Muunilinst prepared for war.

The Clone Wars came to Muunilinst four months after the Battle of Geonosis. When General Obi-Wan Kenobi led an army against San Hill's ruling citadel, the mercenary Durge gathered dozens of IG lancers and struck at the Republic's heavy weapons. Using lances and anti-vehicle mines, the Separatist raiders destroyed dozens of AT-TEs and turbolaser cannons in a string of high-speed sorties. Obi-Wan's clone troopers mounted their own speeder bikes and squared off against the IG lancers in an old-fashioned joust.

Though the Republic won the day, it was not the end of the IG series. Holowan Mechanicals, the new company contracted by the InterGalactic Banking Clan to continue production of IG lancers, saw an opportunity to improve on the basic design. Studying Phlut Design Systems' blueprints for the battle droids that it never had the opportunity to produce, Holowan relabeled these designs as IGs numbers 1 through 99. Holowan's first all-new droid contract would be a bodyguard model for General Grievous, and would be released under the designation *IG 100*.

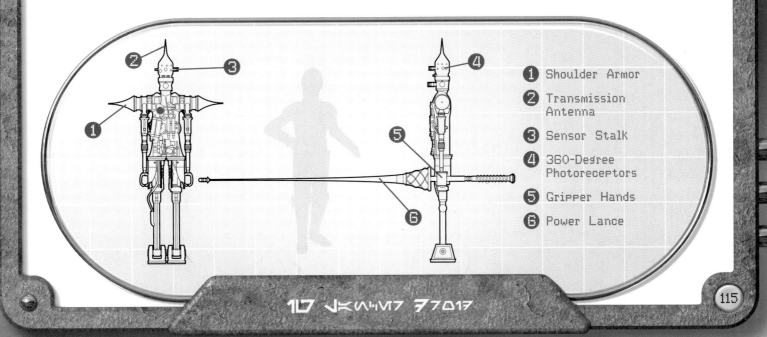

1. Shoulder Armor
2. Transmission Antenna
3. Sensor Stalk
4. 360-Degree Photoreceptors
5. Gripper Hands
6. Power Lance

IT-O Interrogator

TECHNICAL READOUT

HEIGHT: 0.3 meter in diameter

MANUFACTURER:
Imperial Department of
Military Research

PRIMARY FUNCTION:
Torture

ERA OF INFLUENCE:
Rise of the Empire,
Rebellion, New Republic

Imperial Department of Military Research IT-O Interrogation Droid

The Empire elevated torture to an art form, dedicating an entire branch of government, the Inquisitorius, to the sole purpose of squeezing information from the reluctant. The IT-O interrogator was one of the first droids manufactured by the Imperial Department of Military Research.

The existence of the IT-O was no secret. Rumors abounded of its horrifying techniques and brutal sadism. Those citizens unlucky enough to be rounded up by the Imperial Security Bureau could have personally attested to its cruelty ... were they not too traumatized to speak.

A glossy black sphere less than a meter tall, the IT-O hovers on low-powered repulsors. Its design bears a deliberate similarity to the G0-T0 series, whose members conquered a cluster of planets four thousand standard years ago and fanned public fears of droid tyrants. The IT-O's shiny surface is studded with a hateful array of needles, probes, optic sensors, and audioreceptors. A vocabulator is also capable of producing speech, though this has seldom been required. The droid's tools speak for themselves.

One of the most prominent implements is a hypodermic injector syringe connected to internal reservoirs of liquid chemicals, including the truth serum Bavo Six. These drugs can lower pain thresholds, stimulate cooperation, and trigger hallucinations. In addition, the droid features a laser scalpel, a grasping claw, and power shears. Rebel agent Kyle Katarn reported seeing IT-Os within sensitive Imperial installations that had been modified to fire stun bursts as a last-ditch line of defense.

Twisted as their use might be, the medical diagnostic matrices of the IT-O are quite sophisticated. The droids have expert programming in medicine, psychology, surgery, and humanoid biology. The droid's sensors can evaluate a confessor's truthfulness based on heart rate, muscle tension, and voice patterns. IT-Os were notorious for bringing their victims back from the brink of death only to endure further questioning.

Despite the boasts of the Empire, at least one person is known to have withstood the torments of an interrogation droid. While imprisoned aboard the Death Star, Princess Leia Organa survived an IT-O *and* a psychic probe by Darth Vader without revealing the location of the Rebel base at Yavin.

Inevitably, the IT-O was succeeded by newer models with more refined torture equipment, but these versions did not see widespread use. Allegedly, state-of-the-art IT-3s were stationed at the headquarters of the Imperial Security Bureau on Coruscant. The use of torture droids is ostensibly forbidden within the borders of the modern Imperial Remnant, but it seems unlikely that the droids are gone for good.

> **"The IT-O's greatest tool is its reputation. *Tell* the suspect you have one, and *show* it waiting in the wings. This alone will often elicit a confession."**
>
> —*From* Stratagems of the Inquisitorius *by Grand Inquisitor Torbin*

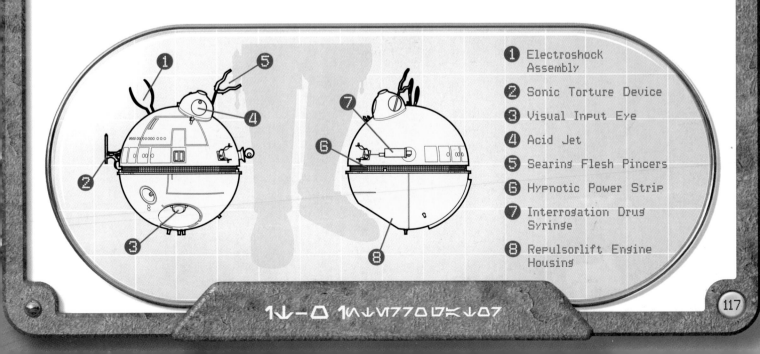

1. Electroshock Assembly
2. Sonic Torture Device
3. Visual Input Eye
4. Acid Jet
5. Searing Flesh Pincers
6. Hypnotic Power Strip
7. Interrogation Drug Syringe
8. Repulsorlift Engine Housing

JK Bio-Droid

Technical Readout

HEIGHT: 1.5 meters

MANUFACTURER:
Cestus Cybernetics

PRIMARY FUNCTION:
Personal security

ERA OF INFLUENCE:
Rise of the Empire

Cestus Cybernetics JK Personal Security Droid

One of the most unusual droids ever developed was actually a symbiont cyborg, though few of its buyers ever realized that fact. Never deployed in combat, the JK played the lead role in an elaborate Clone Wars bluff centered on the Outer Rim planet of Ord Cestus.

The JK was a high-end droid, its mirrored golden coating and diminutive hourglass profile giving it the air of a collectible piece of art. Small, pointed legs supported the upright assembly; the droid could also unfold and restructure its body segments to assume a hunched, spider-like configuration. JK droids sold at a premium of eighty thousand credits each.

Cestus Cybernetics gave the JKs nearly supernatural reflexes by pairing them with immature Dashta eels: Force-sensitive creatures native to the caverns of Ord Cestus. The Dashta eels willingly participated in the project, offering up their unfertilized eggs in order to bring Ord Cestus more fully into the galactic community. A shielded central processing unit inside each JK held a sleeping Dashta eel, which entered into a symbiotic relationship with the droid's own intelligence. The result was a precognitive combat reflex that rivaled that of a Jedi.

Initially marketed as a personal security unit, the JK featured advanced capacitors that allowed it to project spinning, circular energy shields capable of absorbing incoming blasterfire—a feature intended to reduce ricochets and protect its surroundings. In the event that a bolt made it past the shields, the JK's mirrored finish deflected most glancing hits.

From both shoulder mountings and both sides of the bottom torso, the JK could spit out tangles of retractable metal tentacles. When fighting nonliving opponents, such as other droids, the JK could change the form of its tentacles, thinning and contracting them before slicing its enemy to pieces. The tentacles could also camouflage themselves, enabling them to surprise enemies.

Under its normal security programming, a JK would immobilize a victim, then shine a light into the subject's eyes to match the retinal results against its internal database. If the JK determined the subject to be a threat, the droid could conduct an electrical charge along its tentacles powerful enough to stun an organic being into unconsciousness.

After selling JKs to crimelords, Cestus Cybernetics received an order for thousands of the droids from Count Dooku's Confederacy of Independent Systems. Obi-Wan Kenobi and Kit Fisto journeyed to Ord Cestus in an effort to keep the planet from allying with the enemy.

In the process, they learned that the gentle eels could not kill another sentient being without the act driving them insane. This meant that the JKs could never be deployed as combat units, eliminating the threat of the droids that, prematurely, had been called Jedi Killers.

> ## "Among smugglers and the lower classes, some call them 'Jedi Killers.'"
>
> *—Technician Lido Shan, briefing Obi-Wan Kenobi and Kit Fisto on the JK*

1. Shield Projectors
2. Hibernating Dashta Eel
3. Capture Tentacles
4. Mirrored Finish
5. Reconfigurable Torso

JUGGERNAUT WAR DROID

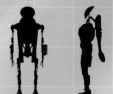

TECHNICAL READOUT

HEIGHT: 1.95 meters

MANUFACTURER:
Duwani Mechanical Products

PRIMARY FUNCTION:
Combat

ERA OF INFLUENCE:
Old Republic

Duwani Mechanical Products RRJC Juggernaut Jumper

The juggernaut war droid is one of the most recognizable droid designs of the ancient Republic, famous for its achievements in the service of the Republic and notorious for its betrayal of that trust during the Great Droid Revolution.

The Republic rocket-jumper corps, an elite division of the Republic army responsible for carrying out impossible missions, developed its own resupply and rearmament droids that could jet-jump with them behind enemy lines. These droids became the model for the juggernaut war droid, hastily commissioned by Supreme Chancellor Vocatara at the start of the Gank Massacres in 4800 B.B.Y.

The discovery of ryll spice on Ryloth had led to the specieswide spice addiction of the cetacean Porporites. Enraged beyond reason, and possessed of a lightning-fast breeding cycle, a wave of maddened Porporites withstood everything the Republic threw at them, including the juggernauts.

The juggernaut operated in a bipedal humanoid configuration and had two alternate methods of propulsion. In a carryover from the Republic rocket-jumper design, twin outrigger jets could launch the droid airborne for bursts of up to sixty seconds. In order to battle the Porporites in their homeworld's natural environment, the jets could convert into intake propellers for underwater operation. The juggernauts were not naturally buoyant,

> **"When the war droids breached the armory, the uprising became a catastrophe. They were juggernauts, and for them it was as easy as returning home."**
>
> —*From* Conflagration: An Eyewitness Account of the Great Droid Uprising

however, and if their propellers jammed, they would sink.

Juggernauts had weapons built into each arm. The left contained a wide-beam sonic stunner, while the right had a shatter beam that could tear a durasteel door from its frame. Juggernauts were trained to carry standard Republic-issue pulse-wave rifles, and used their heavy weapons only in emergencies.

Following the successful resolution of the Gank Massacres, juggernaut war droids became a familiar part of Coruscant's home guard. When the assassin droid HK-01 triggered the Great Droid Revolution in 4015 B.B.Y., shocked citizens witnessed juggernauts turn on the city. The droids unforgettably shredded a platoon of rocket-jumpers in an airborne battle above Monument Plaza. After the revolution, most juggernauts had their intelligence matrices ripped out, and no more of the droids were produced by the Republic.

Outside of museums, juggernaut parts have appeared in the modern era at least twice. The Iron Knights—intelligent Shard crystals inhabiting droid bodies—bonded with several still-active juggernauts from a base on Dweem. Later, Arden Lyn of the Legions of Lettow awakened after a twenty-five-thousand-year sleep and received the prosthetic right arm of a juggernaut Mark I, prior to her appointment as one of the Emperor's Hands.

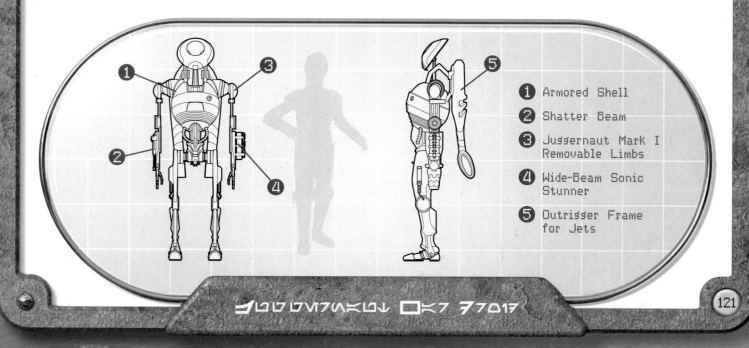

1. Armored Shell
2. Shatter Beam
3. Juggernaut Mark I Removable Limbs
4. Wide-Beam Sonic Stunner
5. Outrigger Frame for Jets

L8-L9 Combat Droid

TECHNICAL READOUT

HEIGHT: 1.9 meters

MANUFACTURER: TaggeCo

PRIMARY FUNCTION: Combat

ERA OF INFLUENCE: Rise of the Empire

TaggeCo Prototype L8-L9 Combat Droid

Never produced in large numbers, the L8-L9 was the first combat droid in the lineage that eventually produced the Dark Trooper. Had it not been for Asajj Ventress, the Clone Wars could have become the Droid Wars: Republic L8-L9s versus Separatist battle droids.

The family-owned TaggeCo enjoyed close ties with the Republic government. After the Battle of Naboo, the young baron Orman Tagge began sketching designs for Republic battle droids that could stand against the Trade Federation. When Count Dooku declared war against the Republic on Geonosis, Tagge rushed his prototype L8-L9 into production.

The L8-L9 had a head inspired by the helmets of Republic clone troopers, an intentional nod by TaggeCo toward its intended buyer. The droid could fire either plasma bursts or sustained jets of flame out of both arms. Its sharp-edged fingers were of little use in manipulating objects, but the L8-L9 could spin its wrist assemblies at high speed and use the spinning claws to cut holes in durasteel. The droid had shielded internal systems protecting it from electromagnetic bursts and extreme heat or cold.

Tagge knew that the Republic had already raised a clone army, so he positioned the L8-L9 as a stand-in for hazardous environments. This was meant to get TaggeCo's foot in the door, at which point Orman planned to aggressively sell his vision of an L8-L9 army. If it came to pass, a government contract of that magnitude would enrich the company beyond the wildest dreams of the Tagge forebears.

The prototype L8-L9 unit required immediate field-testing. Contacts within the House of Tagge suggested as a venue the warring planet Rattatak, where gladiatorial games had become the passion of a cruel and brutal people. Tagge's sample L8-L9 enlisted in a Rattatak free-for-all, facing off against challengers including a Nikto swordsman and a hulking Shikitari insectoid.

L8-L9 assessed the unfolding carnage, then determined that Sith hopeful Asajj Ventress represented the greatest threat. L8-L9 opened up on Ventress with indiscriminate spray from its flamethrowers and plasma launchers, taking out many of its fellow combatants in the crossfire. Under different circumstances, L8-L9 would have emerged victorious, but Ventress seized the droid in a Force grip and bashed its head against the stone ceiling.

The field test was a flop, and it closed the window of opportunity for the L8-L9. Following the Clone Wars, Orman Tagge made the acquaintance of military man and kindred spirit Rom Mohc, who would act as Tagge's "in" with the Imperial Army for Tagge's second-generation Z-X3 droid trooper.

> ## "The L-Eight-L-Nine unit is completely lost, Baron. And so is the hundred thousand credits you wagered on it to win."
>
> —*Report to Baron Orman Tagge following the "catastrophe on Rattatak"*

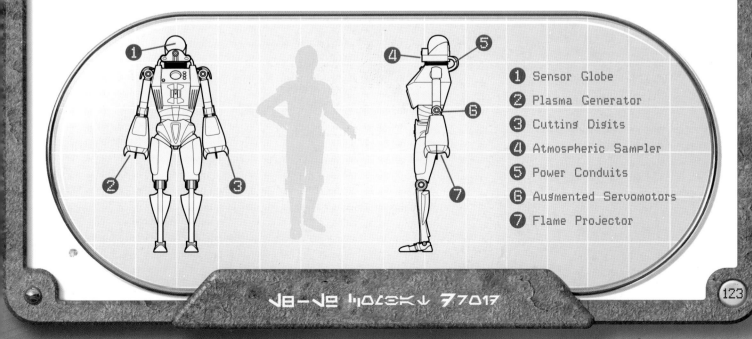

1 Sensor Globe
2 Plasma Generator
3 Cutting Digits
4 Atmospheric Sampler
5 Power Conduits
6 Augmented Servomotors
7 Flame Projector

Mandalorian Battle Legionnaire

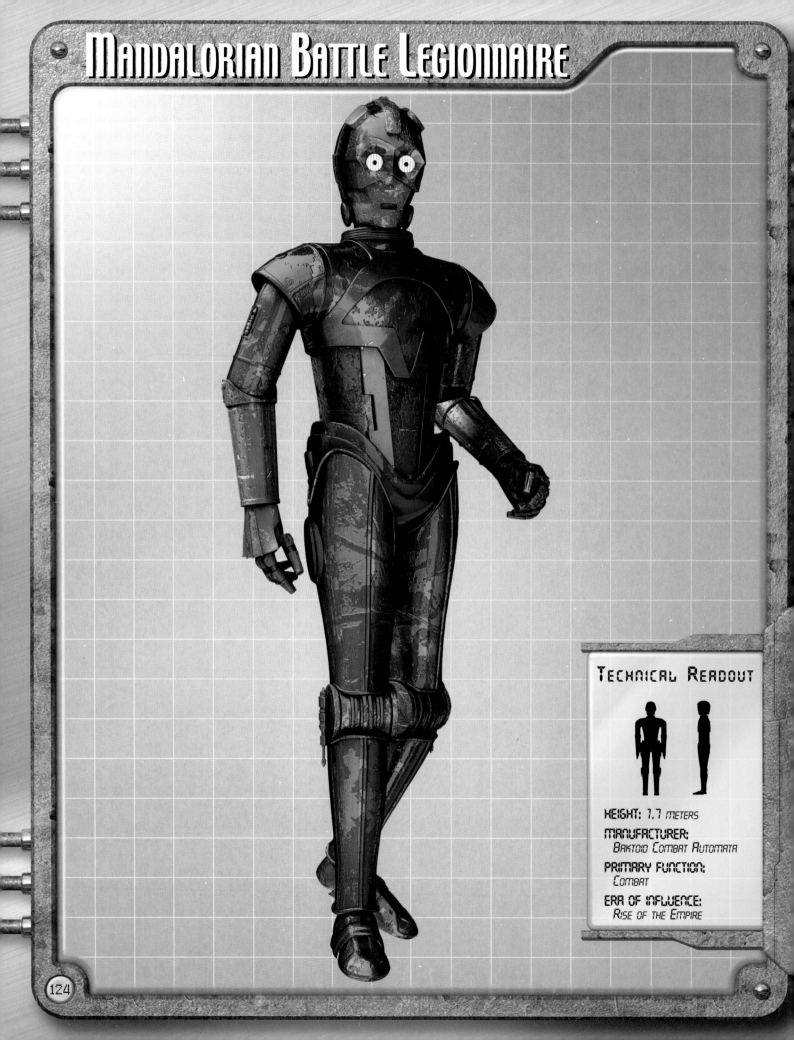

Technical Readout

HEIGHT: 1.7 meters

MANUFACTURER:
Baktoid Combat Automata

PRIMARY FUNCTION:
Combat

ERA OF INFLUENCE:
Rise of the Empire

Baktoid Combat Automata BL Series Battle Legionnaire

The Mandalorians have a history as old as the Republic itself, but traditionally are ambivalent toward droids. With a few notable exceptions—the weird techno-organic basilisk war droids being the most famous example—the Mandalorians fought their own battles and didn't employ droid armies until the Clone Wars.

The Mandalorian Protectors arose midway through the Clone Wars, when a faulty clone of Jango Fett named Alpha-02 recruited a force of Separatist-allied shock troopers from the ranks of Mandalore police units and the Death Watch. Only 212 strong, the Protectors drew upon Mandalorian tradition to boost their ranks. Remembering the role of Mandallian Giants as front-line troops during the New Sith Wars, as well as officer Fenn Shysa's encounter with the fearless protocol droid C-3PX, Alpha-02 used Separatist foundries to churn out a limited run of one thousand Battle Legionnaires.

Each droid in the BL series bore a resemblance to Cybot Galactica's 3PO series, but wore olive-drab military camouflage to match the Mandalorian Protectors' battle armor. The BLs had military-grade balance gyros and joints calibrated for maximum torque. The result was a droid that could lift thousands of kilos over its head and run at speeds up to thirty kilometers per hour for more than a day without recharge.

For weaponry, each Battle Legionnaire wore a rectangular Briletto AAP-II "blaster box" on its chest. Front-line combat often required a heavier punch, a task left to specialized BLs that operated titanic Mandalorian battle harnesses. These two-thousand-year-old antiques turned droids into rolling weapons platforms. Each battle harness, propelled by twin tank-treads, came armed with laser emplacements, a heavy blaster cannon, a gigantic claw arm, and a sonic-pulverizing trip-hammer.

Deployed late in the war, the Battle Legionnaires soon found themselves in the worst of the fighting. Most BLs served as first-wave ground forces, opening holes in Republic defensive lines to be exploited by the shock troopers. The ranks of the Battle Legionnaires suffered during the Mandalorian assaults on Kamino and New Bornalex, and almost no units survived the Republic trap on Norval II. The Mandalorian Protectors met a similar fate, with only 3 of the 212 shock troopers outlasting the war.

After the Clone Wars, the bounty hunter Boba Fett came into possession of a shabby but still functional Battle Legionnaire. Recognizing the link the droid shared with his own Mandalorian heritage—or perhaps just appreciating the cold efficiency of a fellow killer—Fett made BL-17 his aide during the early years of Imperial rule. BL-17's operational life came to an end during an encounter with R2-D2 and C-3PO on the speeder-racing planet of Boonta.

> ## "To our BLs, that they may leave enough enemies for the rest of us. Raise your cup to victory! *Kote!*"
>
> —*Toast of the Mandalorian Protectors on the eve of the Battle of New Bornalex*

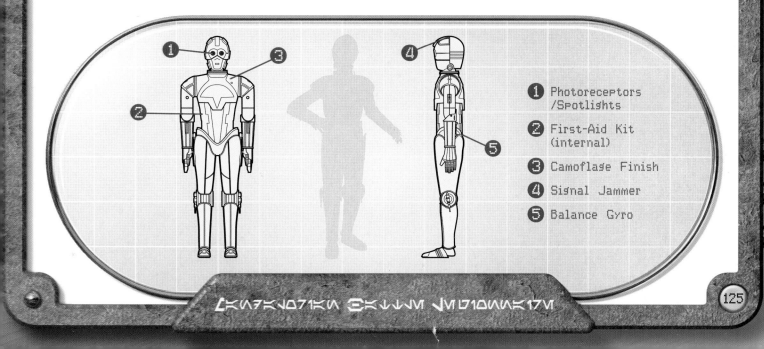

1. Photoreceptors /Spotlights
2. First-Aid Kit (internal)
3. Camoflage Finish
4. Signal Jammer
5. Balance Gyro

MANTA DROID SUBFIGHTER

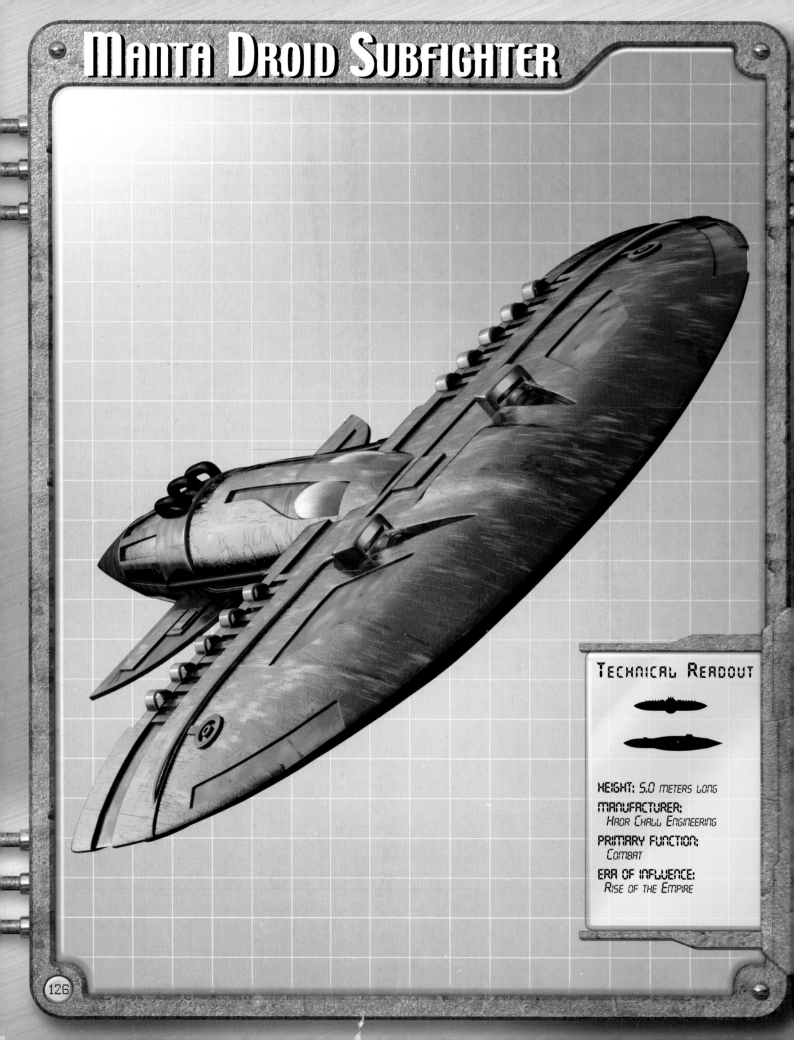

TECHNICAL READOUT

HEIGHT: 5.0 meters long

MANUFACTURER:
Haor Chall Engineering

PRIMARY FUNCTION:
Combat

ERA OF INFLUENCE:
Rise of the Empire

Haor Chall Engineering Manta Droid Subfighter

During the Clone Wars, the might of the Separatist droid army extended from space to land and even beneath the waves. The manta droid subfighter served as the primary naval unit for the Confederacy of Independent Systems throughout three standard years of fighting.

The Trade Federation began research into the manta droid design shortly after the Battle of Naboo. In that failed conflict, the Trade Federation's wavegoing and submersible vehicles—including the *Ostracoda* gunboat and the OTT ocean transport—had begun as land vehicles modified for marine service. As such they were plagued with weaknesses, including slow top speeds and the embarrassing tendency to sink without warning.

Viceroy Nute Gunray commissioned the insectoid Xi Char to draft a new submersible. Isolated on luxury estates provided by the Trade Federation in an effort to make them comfortable, the Xi Char engineers felt disconnected and could not figure out a way to make the subfighter change shape like the vulture starfighter. Shamed by their failure to deliver on specs, the Xi Char provided blueprints for a subfighter carrier free of charge, as well as underwater conversion kits for the Trade Federation's fleet of MVR-3 speeders.

To anyone but perfectionist Xi Char, however, the manta droid subfighter was a hit. The droid borrows many design elements from the vulture fighter, including a sleek bump of a head and photoreceptors that glow as red slashes. Two grooves in the forward diving plane hold either laser cannons or torpedo launchers. Some specialty models have articulated barrels that allow the droids to switch between the two types of weaponry on a whim.

The curved diving plane contains an electromotive field generator that can drive the craft at low speeds. At speeds in excess of one hundred knots, supercavitation vectrals built into the structure generate a bubble of air around the subfighter, dramatically reducing friction and allowing repulsorlift engines to rocket the craft forward at speeds not approachable by any other submarine craft.

Four months after the outbreak of the Clone Wars, the Confederacy called in manta droid subfighters to assist the Separatist-allied Quarren Isolationist League in its civil war against the government of Mon Calamari. Jedi Master Kit Fisto led clone SCUBA troopers and a legion of Mon Calamari Knights against the manta droids in a battle that resulted in a Separatist defeat.

In an odd postscript, several dozen damaged manta droids remained behind on Mon Calamari. Forgotten, they formed their own community, drawing energy from the seafloor mining platforms operated by the Quarren. The manta droid school soon forged a loose affiliation with the Quarren, hunting ocean predators in exchange for repairs and ammunition.

> **"These droids swim and fight like a school of reaver garhai. Let's see the Maramere sea pirates laugh at me now!"**
>
> —*Trade Federation viceroy Nute Gunray*

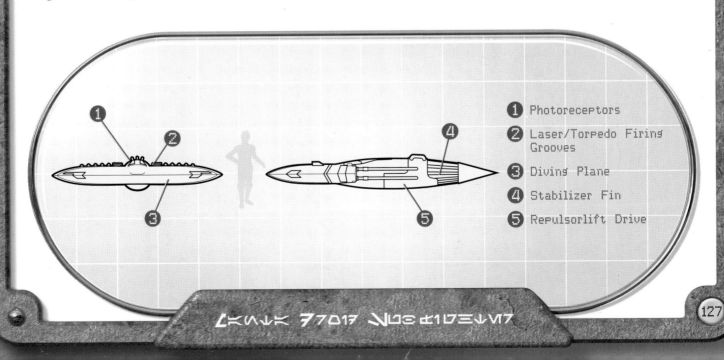

1 Photoreceptors
2 Laser/Torpedo Firing Grooves
3 Diving Plane
4 Stabilizer Fin
5 Repulsorlift Drive

Octuptarra Droid

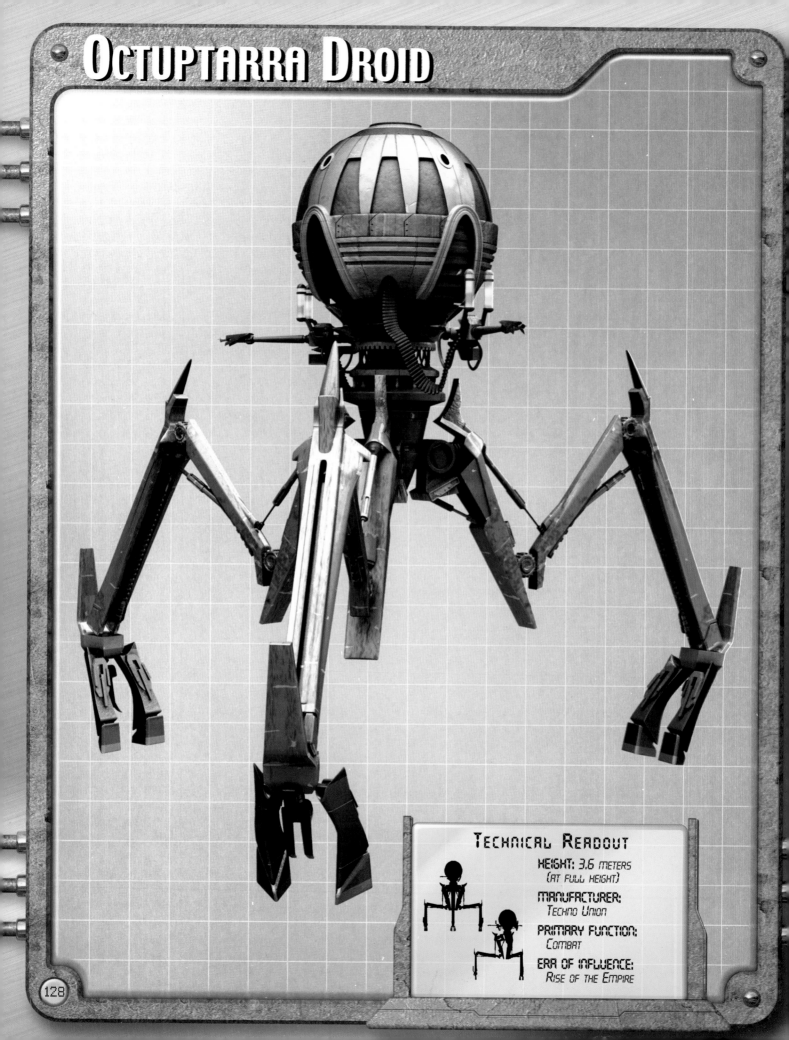

Technical Readout

HEIGHT: 3.6 meters
(at full height)

MANUFACTURER:
Techno Union

PRIMARY FUNCTION:
Combat

ERA OF INFLUENCE:
Rise of the Empire

Techno Union Octuptarra Combat Tri-Droid

Uncomfortably alien for most humanoids, the octuptarra droid is an example of the insectoid exoticism that often found its way into the designs of the Confederacy of Independent Systems.

For the Skakoans, who dominated the Techno Union, however, the octuptarra droid seemed as familiar as a family pet. True octuptarras are eight-eyed, gasbag-headed vine climbers found on the methane planet of Skako. The droids follow a similar body configuration and walk on three attenuated legs, a fact that has caused others to refer to them as "tri-droids."

Symmetrical on all sides, the octuptarra droid has no blind spots and can fire in any direction, thanks to a rotating laser turret. It is lightweight and can dangle upside down from overhangs. The balloon-shaped globe atop an octuptarra houses its cognitive circuitry, but the module is poorly guarded and an easy target for enemy fire. Separatist commanders soon discovered that octuptarra droids functioned best from long range, where their cannons could pick off advancing troopers with stuttering laser bursts.

Octuptarra droids, like the Techno Union's crab droids, can be produced in a variety of sizes thanks to scaleable manufacturing plants. Most are humanoid-size anti-personnel units, but some are as large as tanks. These behemoths saw battlefield action as combat artillery units, supporting Commerce Guild spider walkers with their chain-fed ordnance launchers.

During the first year of the Clone Wars, Separatist researchers developed a loathsome sampler of tailored biological plagues. One virus targeted the specific genome shared by the Republic's clone troopers, and aerosol canisters containing the toxin were installed inside the heads of octuptarra droids. The droids would release the spray after making suicide runs into the heart of enemy infantry formations. The Republic Grand Army soon developed an antidote, but the campaign gave the octuptarra a second nickname: *virus droid.*

Octuptarra droids numbered among the robotic hordes swarming Coruscant during General Grievous's kidnapping of Supreme Chancellor Palpatine. After the battle, heaps of crushed and blasted droid parts wound up in the lowest levels of the city-canyons. Trace amounts of the octuptarra virus leaked out from the cracked fragments, and a modified strain of the clone disease infected the Shashay and other avian aliens, leading to an unfortunate outbreak of molting.

Following the Clone Wars, most octuptarra droids wound up on Uba IV, a Separatist planet that boasted a droid manufacturing plant. In the minds of many, octuptarra droids have since become interchangeable with the fearsome, masked Ubese.

> **"The Seps have virus droids, so check your helmet seals and breathing filters. A head shot could release a contaminant of unknown origin."**
>
> —*Clone commander Gree, prior to the Battle of Uba IV*

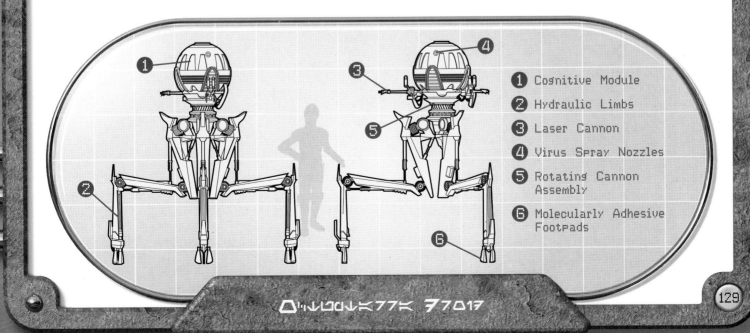

1. Cognitive Module
2. Hydraulic Limbs
3. Laser Cannon
4. Virus Spray Nozzles
5. Rotating Cannon Assembly
6. Molecularly Adhesive Footpads

POLLUX ASSASSIN DROID

TECHNICAL READOUT

HEIGHT: 2.4 METERS

MANUFACTURER:
Pollux Poi

PRIMARY FUNCTION:
Assassination

ERA OF INFLUENCE:
Old Republic, rise of the
Empire

Pollux Poi Customized A-Series Assassin Droid

Midway through the Clone Wars, Count Dooku delivered nearly one hundred unfamiliar assassin droids into the Separatist army. Like many of Dooku's acquisitions, the droids baffled colleagues, who hadn't seen anything quite like them before.

More than four thousand standard years prior, Dooku's assassin droids started life as the mechanical children of Pollux Poi, an Anx designer both brilliant and insane. Recruited by the Shell Hutts to build weapons for use against their Hutt rivals in clan Gejalli, Poi constructed an increasingly lethal string of assassin droids. These killers eliminated Hutts three through fourteen in the Gejalli succession hierarchy. The Gejalli survivors exacted their own revenge, taking out a contract on Poi's life. Poi fled to the darkest underlevels of Kashyyyk's wroshyr tree canopy to escape from the merciless Dashade shadow killers.

What followed was nearly two decades of what Pollux Poi called "the shadow game." Inside his leafy hideout, Poi tinkered with new designs as his droids felled Dashade assassins, making Poi one of the most notorious unclaimed bounties in Hutt history. The Dashade stopped coming when the Cron Cluster supernova consumed their homeworld, but Poi died of natural causes not long after.

The creations of Pollux Poi lived on, discovering a primeval machine in Kashyyyk's forest. Establishing contact, this small family let itself be overhauled and replicated by the ancient intelligence they called the Builder Forge.

> **"Count Dooku sends his regards. We are at your command. We are designed to disassemble over eleven thousand sentient species."**
>
> *—Assassin droid A71, reporting for duty during the Battle of Jabiim*

The remade Pollux assassin droids have four photoreceptors for seeing in low-light conditions or scanning infrared wavelengths. Sweeping curves and sharp points dominate their sleek, shiny bodies. Each droid carries a blaster rifle, with a shoulder-mounted blaster cannon as a backup.

Several hundred droids eventually left Kashyyyk for Gree space, home to one of the galaxy's oldest civilizations. Although the droids did not locate more machines like the one on Kashyyyk, a Gree clan happily employed them for the purpose of assassination.

Millennia later, Count Dooku purchased the remaining Pollux assassins from the Gree and sent them into battle against the Republic. Their first tour of duty came on rain-soaked Jabiim, where they killed many members of the Jedi "Padawan Pack" and contributed to a Separatist victory. Later, eighteen Pollux assassins accompanied Asajj Ventress on a failed mission to kill Master Yoda at the Phindar spaceport.

At Phindar, the Pollux units carried a variety of weapons—none of which could be deflected by a lightsaber—to keep their Jedi opponents off balance. Included in this experimental run were flamethrowers, railguns, flechette launchers, sonic grenades, hard-sound guns, and tactical tractor beam projectors. After the Clone Wars, the few surviving Pollux droids are believed to have returned to the wilds of Kashyyyk.

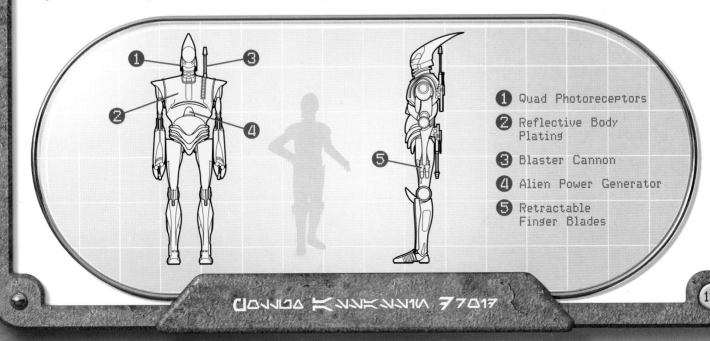

1. Quad Photoreceptors
2. Reflective Body Plating
3. Blaster Cannon
4. Alien Power Generator
5. Retractable Finger Blades

SITH PROBE DROID

Sith DRK-1 Dark Eye Probe Droid

Returning to Queen Amidala's starship after freeing the slave boy Anakin Skywalker, Qui-Gon Jinn spotted an unfamiliar droid watching him from an alleyway. A slash of his lightsaber blade bisected the spy. Instantly recognizing a threat, Qui-Gon and his young charge broke into a run.

In a galaxy populated by millions of droid models, how did Qui-Gon know that the floating sphere was of sinister manufacture? After all, the design of the Sith probe droid is hardly unique. Arakyd's explorational droids and Les Tech's submersible ER-1C probe droid all share obvious design similarities.

Qui-Gon could easily have mistaken the Sith probe droid for one of these benign look-alikes—indeed, most of Mos Espa seems to have done exactly that. But Qui-Gon Jinn had the advantage of nearly sixty years of Jedi training. The Sith probe droid, built by Darth Maul from arcane blueprints, stood out like a dark void in the fabric of the Force. Though Maul's probe droids were machines, evil clung to them like a stain.

Darth Maul was as good with a circuit board as he was with a lightsaber. Sith "dark eye" probe droids were common in the years prior to the Battle of Ruusan, and Maul re-created them down to the tiniest detail, using disparate, off-the-shelf parts.

Sith probe droids move on repulsorlifts, allowing them to follow their quarry over mountains, minefields, or methane lakes without any drop in speed or performance. They are designed to locate targets without directly engaging them in combat, and typically feature no standard weapons. Darth Maul, however, used them for assassinations, and his droids carried universal weapons mounts. Maul's add-on killing devices included laser cannons, stun blasters, and poison-dart needlers.

Maul could control up to six probe droids remotely via his wrist-mounted comlink, though the droids possessed autonomous decision-making power once deployed. In last-ditch situations, Maul's droids had self-destruct detonators to prevent their capture.

"Dark eye" droids pack an astonishing number of sensor devices into a small space. They can perform scans in every medium imaginable—audio, visual, thermal, chemical, electromagnetic, and radionic—but their most remarkable skill is their ability to detect the Force.

A Sith probe droid can track a Force-user in much the same way a nashtah follows the scent of blood, partly by scanning biological entities for the presence of midi-chlorians, and partly by surveying the environment for anomalous Force concentrations. (A machine's ability to sense the Force is evidence of the Sith art known as *mechu-deru.*) The probe droid uses this data to assemble a picture of an individual's Force aura, which appears in playback as a radiant blue nimbus. This dark side science is another example of the very real dangers of Sith lore.

> ## "Probe droid. Very unusual . . . not like anything I've seen before."
>
> —*Qui-Gon Jinn to Anakin Skywalker, after encountering a Sith probe droid*

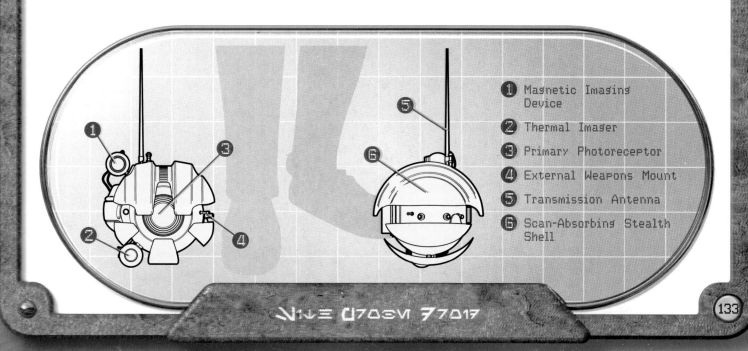

1. Magnetic Imaging Device
2. Thermal Imager
3. Primary Photoreceptor
4. External Weapons Mount
5. Transmission Antenna
6. Scan-Absorbing Stealth Shell

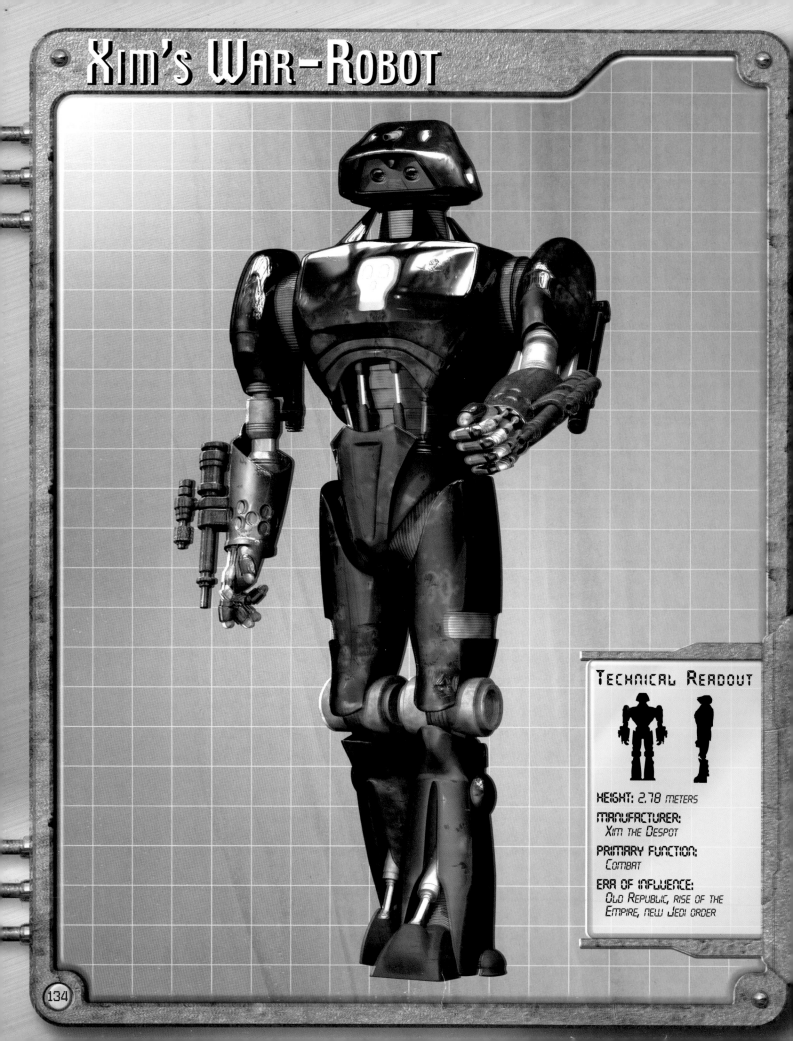

Xim's War-Robot

Technical Readout

HEIGHT: 2.78 meters

MANUFACTURER:
Xim the Despot

PRIMARY FUNCTION:
Combat

ERA OF INFLUENCE:
Old Republic, rise of the
Empire, new Jedi order

Empire of Xim War-Robot

Between the fall of the Rakatan Infinite Empire and the rise of the Galactic Republic, Xim the Despot ruled the starways. Xim's war-robots are among the earliest combat automata known to history.

From 25,125 to 25,100 B.B.Y., Xim's kingdom flourished in the Outer Rim territory known as the Tion. Populated by castoff Rakata and the descendants of an ancient Core Worlds colony ship, the Tion's planets remained linked to one another through a precarious "lighthouse network" of hyperspace beacons. Xim, who had subjugated hundreds of planets with his army of war-robots, finally met worthy foes in the Hutts and their legions of retainers.

The war-robots towered over the battlefield, sunlight glinting off the laser-reflective mirrored coating on their armor. Bulky joints and stress points, reinforced to protect vital control systems, made the robots slow and stiff.

Shielded apertures in the arms and hands housed chemical and energy weapons, including archaic heat-beams and particle dischargers. Each robot's cranial turret contained optical lenses and a speaker grille, and bore tiny unit insignia markings. The robots took orders from whoever controlled the transmission horn on a military command platform. Rank could be distinguished by the color of their death's-head emblem: white for a corpsman, gold for a corps commander, and red for a crimson condottiere (a rare variety possessing Force-sensitive Rakatan technology).

> **"To the seventh dungeon with the conqueror-fool. There he shall subjugate rotworms, while his gearwork soldiers stand in glorious tribute to High Exaltedness Kossak."**
>
> —*Kossak the Hutt's victory proclamation following the Third Battle of Vontor*

Xim's war-robots were remarkable not only for their lethality, but also for their degree of self-awareness. Most automata before that point, such as binary loadlifters, had been machines with just a glimmer of intelligence. The generous appropriation of Rakatan technology in the construction of Xim's droids gave them the ability to interact with their builders, although a primitive behavioral circuitry matrix made them rigidly literal in the interpretation of their orders.

Xim lost the Third Battle of Vontor to Kossak the Hutt, and died a prisoner in Kossak's dungeons on Varl. Most of Xim's war-robots did not survive the Vontor massacre, and the Hutts took hundreds of the remaining units back to their territory as trophies.

One thousand others were not present at Vontor, having been assigned to Xim's treasure ship *Queen of Ranroon*. After off-loading the treasure in a vault on Dellalt, the robots remained on guard for a thousand generations. Shortly before the Battle of Yavin, Han Solo and Chewbacca visited Dellalt and saw Xim's droids attack a mining settlement, but most of the relics perished when a bridge collapsed beneath their heavy footfalls.

In Hutt space, Xim's robots decorated public plazas and palace steps. Few suspected they were any more than statuary until the Yuuzhan Vong invaded the Hutt homeworlds in 26 A.B.Y. In a desperate failsafe, Xim's robots came to life and killed thousands of the invaders before falling beneath a hail of blastbugs and amphistaffs.

1. Xim the Despot's Insignia
2. Heatbeam Aperture
3. Particle Discharger Aperture
4. Speaker Grille
5. Battlefield Pulse-Wave Cannons (removable)
6. Systems Power Generator
7. Laser-Reflective Kiirium Sheen

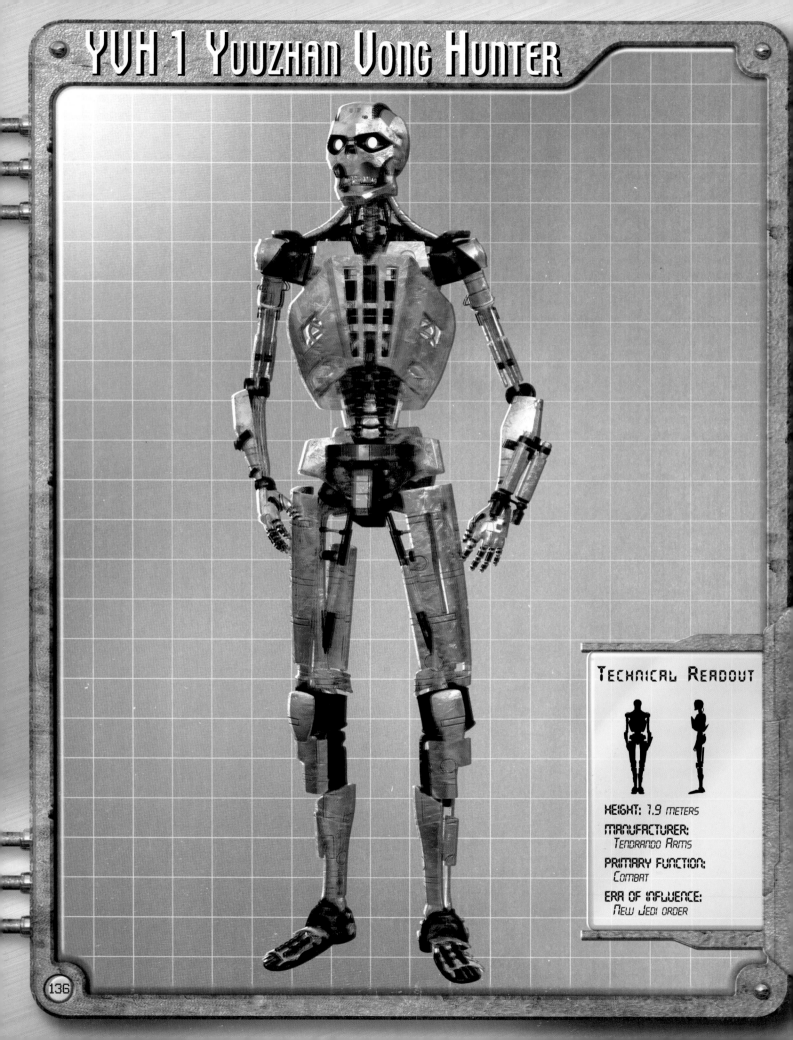

Technical Readout

HEIGHT: 1.9 meters

MANUFACTURER: Tendrando Arms

PRIMARY FUNCTION: Combat

ERA OF INFLUENCE: New Jedi Order

Tendrando Arms YVH 1 Yuuzhan Vong Hunter

The YVH 1, better known as the Yuuzhan Vong Hunter, debuted in 27 A.B.Y., two standard years into the war between the extragalactic invaders and the forces of the New Republic. The Yuuzhan Vong had already destroyed much of the galaxy's droid manufacturing infrastructure, but Lando Calrissian decided to build droids powerful enough to fight back.

Lando's company, Tendrando Arms, debuted its prototype unit on Coruscant in a demonstration for Chief of State Borsk Fey'lya. The droid, YVH 1-1A, found himself fighting real targets when Yuuzhan Vong infiltrators emerged from the ranks of the attendees. Even with YVH 1-1A's weapons stuck on low power due to the conditions of the demo, the droid found a way to end the threat with a lethal squeeze of his arms.

Each YVH 1 bears a surface resemblance to a Yuuzhan Vong warrior, a design choice intended to infuriate the New Republic's prideful enemies. The torso is protected by overlapping plates of laminanium, painted black and gray for camouflage. Laminanium is a self-healing Qellan metal capable of melting and re-solidifying at room temperature to seal breaches. It can generate a full hermetic seal if the YVH is threatened by corrosive acids.

A YVH's right arm is a variable-output blaster cannon capable of stunning targets at low power and, at its highest setting, blasting a starfighter into smithereens. The droid's left arm ends in a socket that can accommodate a sampler of interchangeable weapons, including a heavy laser, a sonic rifle, a fifty-shot battery of seeker missiles, and a launcher for firing explosive baradium pellets.

The droid's legs incorporate built-in repulsorlifts. While these aren't powerful enough to permit flight, they do allow the droid to make tremendous leaps. All Yuuzhan Vong Hunters speak in a deep, booming facsimile of Lando Calrissian's own voice.

The YVH isn't just a war machine—it has also been programmed to sniff out undercover Yuuzhan Vong spies. By employing a sensor pack that incorporates chemical and pheromonal detectors, infrared and telescopic photoreceptors, and an atmosphere analyzer, the YVH can even identify Yuuzhan Vong wearing the living disguises known as ooglith masquers.

YVH droids proved invaluable on the Jedi mission to Myrkr and in the defense of Borleias, but the complexity of their construction prevented them from seeing extensive service during the war. In a related project, New Republic agents took the sensor packs built for Yuuzhan Vong Hunters and packed them into the bodies of mouse droids, creating subtle spy detectors called YVH-M droids, for Yuuzhan Vong Hunter Mouse.

> ### "We are machines! We are greater than the Yuuzhan Vong!"
>
> *—Battle cry of the YVH droids at Borleias, designed to trigger maximum outrage in their enemies*

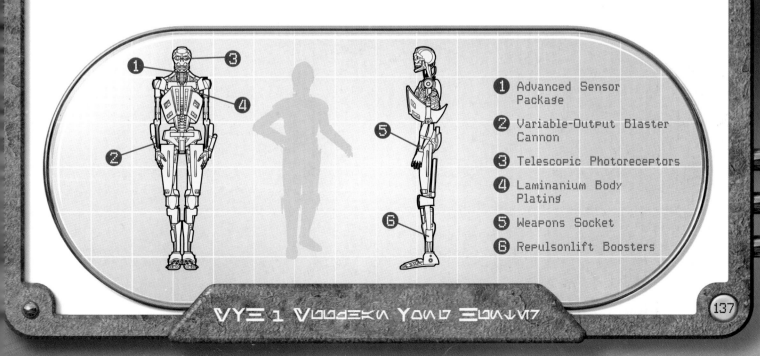

1. Advanced Sensor Package
2. Variable-Output Blaster Cannon
3. Telescopic Photoreceptors
4. Laminanium Body Plating
5. Weapons Socket
6. Repulsonlift Boosters

Z-X3 Droid Trooper

Technical Readout

HEIGHT: 1.9 meters

MANUFACTURER: TaggeCo

PRIMARY FUNCTION: Combat

ERA OF INFLUENCE: Rise of the Empire, Rebellion

TaggeCo Z-X3 Experimental Droid Trooper

The Z-X3, essentially the second generation of TaggeCo's L8-L9, represented the Empire's first attempt to build a battle droid. The effort failed, but subsequent refinements of the Z-X3 would lead directly to the Empire's murderous Dark Troopers.

Rom Mohc, a soldier in the Republic Grand Army and later an Imperial officer, had an obsession with personal combat. He supported anything that increased the likelihood of one-on-one battle, and rejected anything that moved away from that ideal, including Palpatine's Death Star superweapon. Although Mohc relished working with clone troopers, he also developed an appreciation for the Separatists' battle droids. Combining the two interests, Mohc championed research into robotic stormtroopers that could act as backups for the clone fighting forces.

The program, dubbed the Droid Trooper Project, appeared to come at an opportune time. In the wake of the Clone Wars, the Imperial stormtrooper corps was subdividing into units that specialized in unique planetary environments—seatroopers, sandtroopers, and snowtroopers among them. But some environments were simply too hazardous for stormtroopers to endure. Mohc hoped his droid trooper could be the answer.

Mohc's skunkworks inside Tagge Industries soon produced the Z-X3. A humanoid droid with plating inspired by the armor and helmets of stormtroopers, its crimson color makes it an instant standout. The Z-X3 lacks built-in weaponry, instead carrying a blaster rifle or wearing a Briletto AAP-IV "blaster box" on its chest. The Z-X3 possesses enhanced strength and a sophisticated intelligence not dependent on a central control computer. It can operate in any number of hazardous environments, from deep space to high-radiation dead zones.

Tagge produced less than one hundred Z-X3 units, a sufficient number for the Empire to evaluate them in controlled testing. But the defeat of the Separatist droid army was too fresh in the minds of most Imperials—since the war's end, the pendulum had swung even farther in favor of clones and organics. The Empire deemed the droid troopers inadequate for military deployment. Two new classifications of stormtrooper—the radtrooper (for irradiated environments) and the zero-g spacetrooper—filled the niches for which the Z-X3 had been intended. A pragmatic Mohc joined the spacetrooper corps, but he continued brainstorming the droid that would eventually become the Dark Trooper.

The remaining Z-X3 units were slated for recycling, but most found their way into private hands. A few even found service with the Empire at remote garrisons. One unit wound up at Droid World, the artificial satellite established by the cyborg Kligson after the Clone Wars. Still loyal to his Imperial programming, Z-X3 tried to usurp control of Droid World from Kligson in the name of the Empire and set himself up as a robotic dictator. A war between Z-X3's faction and Kligson's faction nearly destroyed Droid World, but Kligson emerged victorious and left Z-X3 in pieces.

> **"Now we will vanquish any who still hold to his ways . . . who will not serve the Imperial cause! As the Empire rules the galaxy, Droid World is ours to command!"**
>
> —*A Z-X3 unit inciting rebellion on Kligson's Moon*

1. Briletto AAP-IV Blaster Box
2. Multiwave Scanners
3. Blast-Shielded Joints
4. High-Torque Limbs
5. Atmospheric Samplers

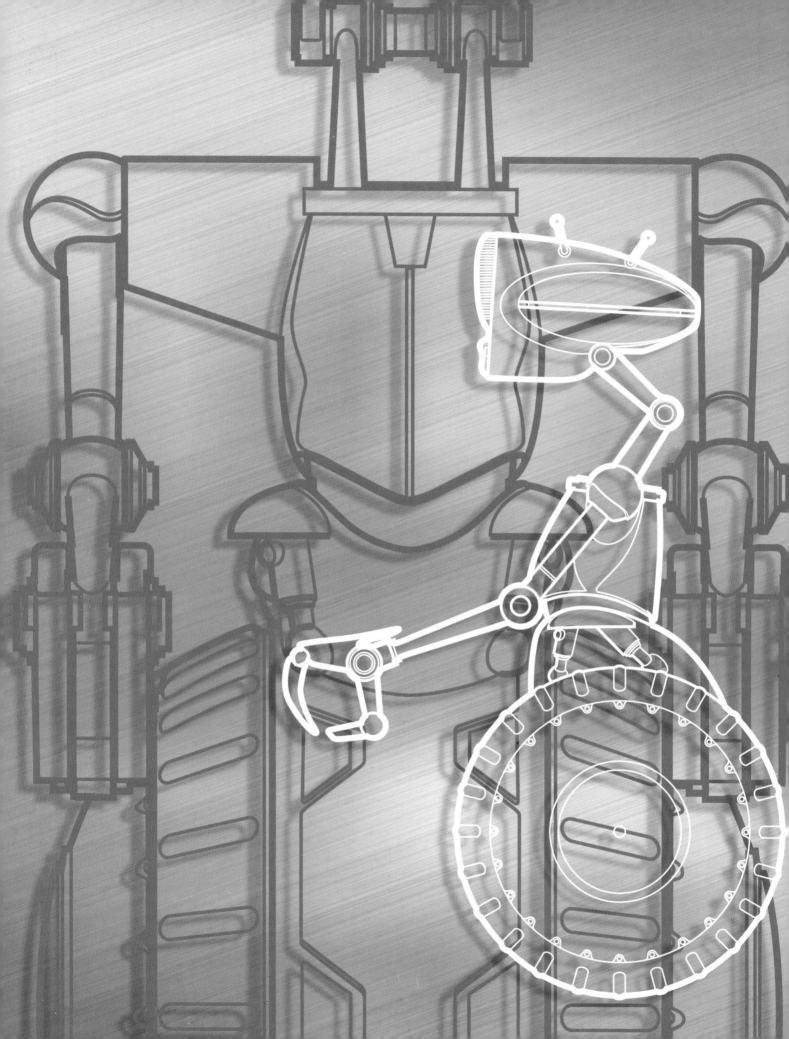

CLASS FIVE DROIDS

Before the droid classification system came into common use, *all* droids were essentially class five. The term describes automata that labor in trades such as mining, cargo lifting, wreck salvaging, garbage collecting, and driving simple conveyances.

The first droids ever invented belonged to these groupings, thanks to engineers in the pre-Republic era who placed primitive behavioral circuitry matrices into robotic frames. The resulting workers could think well enough to handle simple tasks, and in the tens of millennia since, there has been little need to improve on this ancient template.

Class five droids with too much intelligence often develop an understanding of the drudgery of their round-the-clock duties. Sometimes this leads class fives to organize labor strikes among their fellow units, or to intentionally perform their duties poorly in a passive-aggressive show of defiance.

The droids in the class five category are by far the most numerous of the droid classes. Most galactic citizens encounter a class one or class three droid only rarely, but will pass by dozens of class five units on a short walk down the street. This ubiquity in numbers makes class five droids the object of ire from groups such as the Organization for Organic Purity, due to the volume of jobs the droids have taken from organic workers. Over the centuries, the ordinariness of class five droids has led espionage agencies to outfit them as spies.

Most class five droids can be categorized into one of several main groupings:

- **General labor droids** are one-size-fits-all class five units. Not designed for any specific job, they can learn most simple tasks with minimal instruction. These droids are often built in a bipedal human configuration. General labor droids can vary a great deal in their level of sophistication, with asp droids and BLX droids marking the nadir and zenith of the intelligence spectrum.

- **Labor specialist droids** are built with a precise task in mind and sold to niche buyers. These droids are usually constructed in unusual configurations specific to their job function. The giant automated threshers in the grain fields of Orron III, the window washers of Coruscant, and the spidery tree feeders in the Forbidden Gardens of Nuswatta are all examples of class five labor specialists.

- **Hazardous-service droids** are related to labor specialists in that they exist to perform specific jobs—but these are typically jobs that no organic could hope to survive. The 8D8 smelting operators, which work inside metal-liquefying blast furnaces, are a prime example. Elsewhere in the galaxy, hazardous-service droids scoop gems from the high-pressure cores of gas giants, or mine valuable ores from the molten crusts of planets that orbit too close to their stars.

Any further grouping of Class Five droids is a subject of debate among those who develop such taxonomies. Essentially, any droid with a minimal level of intelligence is considered by most a class five, regardless of what job it performs. Thus, a hospital assistant capable only of handing over surgical tools would be a class five, though purists might still group it with the class ones.

8D8 Smelting Operator

Technical Readout

HEIGHT: 1.83 meters

MANUFACTURER:
Roche

PRIMARY FUNCTION:
Metals smelting

ERA OF INFLUENCE:
Rise of the Empire,
Rebellion, New Republic

Roche 8D8 Smelting Operation Droid

The 8D8 is one of the most mean-spirited droids in service today. Fortunately, 8D8s work inside blast furnaces, where most individuals will never encounter one.

Metal-smelting plants are common on manufacturing planets from Balmorra to Geonosis. Working conditions within the plants can be deadly, with temperatures reaching 1,650 degrees Centigrade. Organic operators cannot enter a blast furnace without enviro-suits, so the Roche droid manufacturing hive introduced the 8D8 smelting operator to fill this highly specialized niche.

The Verpine of the Roche hive, stung by the failure of their J9 worker drone, designed the 8D8 to resemble a humanoid rather than an insectoid. The final design could be mistaken for a thin-faced human, but appears to be more directly influenced by the Muun species (who enjoyed a financial interest in thousands of metal-stamping plants that the Roche hive hoped to tap for its 8D8 sales). The complicated leg joints of the 8D8 remain telltale signs of Verpine manufacture.

Because droids are made of metal, fireproofing a droid to work in a metal-smelting chamber proved to be Roche's greatest challenge. The body parts of an 8D8 are cast from a proprietary ore made of high-grade durasteel molecularly bonded with kevlex. The substance has a melting point of over four thousand degrees Centigrade. The 8D8's piggishly tiny optical sensors were another result of the fireproofing process. Roche gave the droids enhanced strength, as well as the ability to operate for weeks at a time without a recharge.

At a typical blast furnace, three 8D8s will stand in the bosh, the lower portion of the furnace: one to monitor the blast tuyeres, one to drain the slag from the top of the melt, and one to tap the furnace by forcing out molten metal approximately ten times a standard day. Two additional 8D8s operate skip hoists that dump raw materials into the bell hoppers and furnace. An optional sixth unit can be used to oversee the control board and check the condition of the firebrick refractory shell.

Roche gave its 8D8 units enough cognitive ability to realize that their jobs are repetitive and dangerous. They resent "lazy" droids that work in jobs such as protocol or communications; indeed, a few have become surly, ill-tempered bullies.

Jabba the Hutt employed an 8D8 in his Tatooine palace, where the droid assisted the sadistic EV-9D9 in the torture and dismantling of the other droids in Jabba's labor pool. "Atedeate" possessed even more brains than the norm—thanks to a former owner who had modified him to perform starship repairs—and suffered his job in contemptuous silence.

> **"When your 8D8 emerges from the foundry, it will be EXTREMELY HOT! Touching its shell may result in severe burns to your manipulative appendages."**
>
> —*Excerpt from the 8D8 owner's manual*

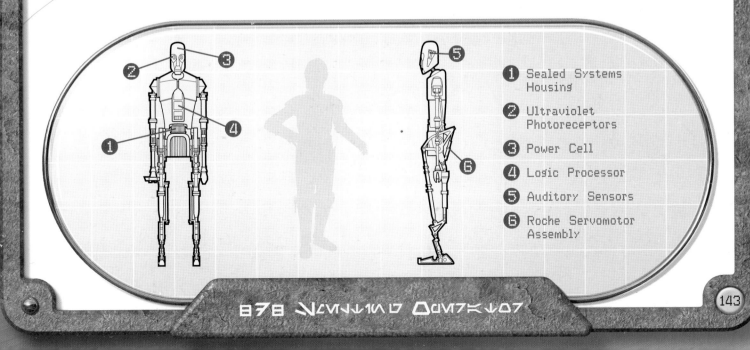

1. Sealed Systems Housing
2. Ultraviolet Photoreceptors
3. Power Cell
4. Logic Processor
5. Auditory Sensors
6. Roche Servomotor Assembly

ASP Droid

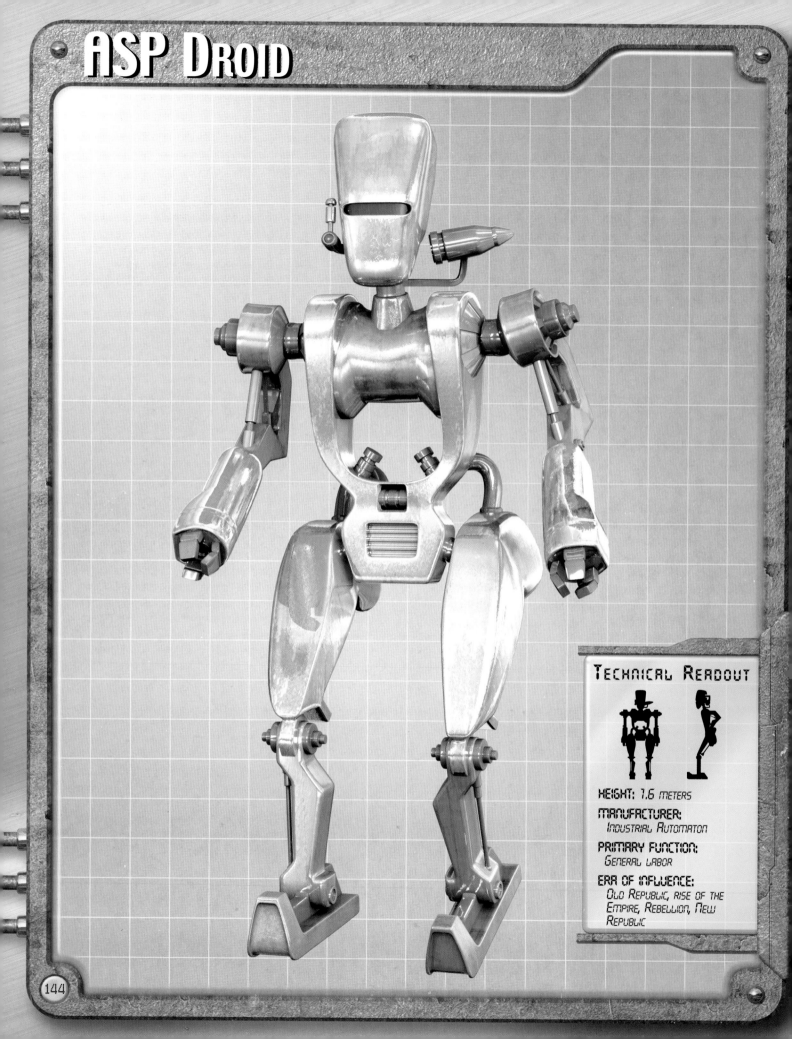

Technical Readout

HEIGHT: 1.6 meters

MANUFACTURER:
Industrial Automaton

PRIMARY FUNCTION:
General labor

ERA OF INFLUENCE:
Old Republic, rise of the Empire, Rebellion, New Republic

Industrial Automaton ASP Utility Droid

Most individuals own at least one droid, and some own dozens. But when someone is asked to name his or her *first* droid, it's a good bet that the top response would be the ASP.

Generations ago, Industrial Automaton mass-produced the bare-bones ASP, giving it the bargain-basement price of one thousand credits. At the time, this was a remarkably good deal for a droid with its capabilities. A sales boom resulted among young and first-time buyers, and Industrial Automaton eagerly welcomed them into the IA family. Down the road, the company hoped its customers would move on to more expensive models, such as the R series astromech or the SE-4 servant droid.

ASP droids couldn't be simpler. They consist of nuts, bolts, and metal piping molded together into a humanoid frame. They exhibit none of the gleaming aesthetics seen in protocol models, such as Cybot Galactica's 3PO series. The ASP's head contains two audio pickups and a single photoreceptor, offset on the right side of the face. These sensors are limited to the auditory and visual ranges detectible by humans.

The droids aren't designed for any job in particular. Consequently, they are reasonably capable of doing almost anything. Though ASPs will always be outclassed by a specialty model at any specific task, they are commonly employed as repair bots, cleanup units, or delivery droids.

Models within the ASP series come with numerical designations, from 1 to 20. There isn't a great deal of variation within the lineup, although the higher numbers typically come with greater strength or other added features—and a higher cost associated with these "premium packages." The ASP-7, a solid middle-of-the-road performer, is Industrial Automaton's biggest seller.

The ASP's hydraulically powered limbs are remarkably strong, making the droids unsuitable for delicate work. It doesn't help that they are notoriously thickheaded, requiring detailed instructions for any job more complicated than stacking boxes.

By far, the most annoying trait of a standard-model ASP is its primitive vocabulator, which can produce only two words: *affirmative* and *negative*. Trying to pry information out of an ASP can turn into a maddening game of "guess my secret."

Many owners can't abide these design confines, and modify their asp units with additional hardware or programming patches. Droid engineers in the Imperial Palace maintained a small army of ASP-19s, outfitted with armor plating, hyperfast reaction packages, and data libraries covering classical fencing. Every week, Darth Vader sliced these droids to pieces during his lightsaber combat workouts.

> **"So let me get this straight. The fault is in the harmonic field sensor?"**
> **"Negative."**
> **"The hyperdrive sequencer?"**
> **"Negative."**
> **"The ion turbo-injector?"**
> **"Negative."**
>
> *—A typically frustrating exchange between an owner and an ASP droid*

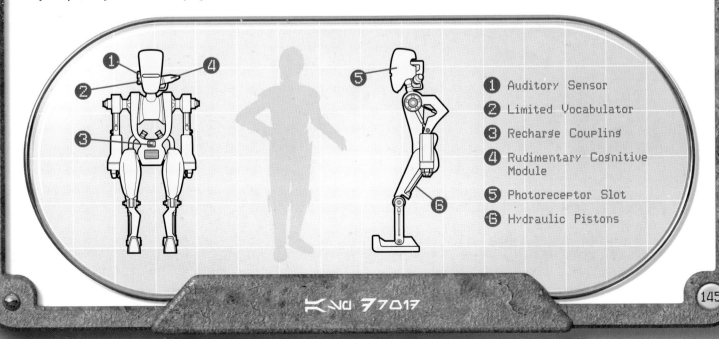

1. Auditory Sensor
2. Limited Vocabulator
3. Recharge Coupling
4. Rudimentary Cognitive Module
5. Photoreceptor Slot
6. Hydraulic Pistons

BINARY LOADLIFTER

146

Cybot Galactica CLL-M2 Binary Loadlifter

Binary loadlifters are a window into ancient droid history. Cargo haulers were among the first automata invented during the murky ages of the pre-Republic, and have changed very little in more than thirty thousand standard years.

Binary loadlifters represent a droid category that encompasses many different models. All of them communicate in the simplistic computer language of binary, which cannot be understood by humans without a video display screen or other interpreting device. Binary loadlifters can understand their owners' verbal commands, but giving the loadlifters complex tasks is best left to other droids fluent in binary. Protocol droids are more than capable of handling such work, adding a sheen of plausibility to C-3PO's claim.

Most loadlifters incorporate strong hydraulic limbs and a gyro-stabilization mechanism. The lifting arms usually end in flat hands that can slide underneath cargo skids, though some lifters come equipped with claw-shaped graspers. Auditory sensors and binary vocabulators are standard, while quite a few models have a single photoreceptor that doubles as a cargo-code scanner.

Binary load lifters are notoriously dull-witted. They simply lack the programming to make self-aware decisions, which prompts even some droids' rights activists to classify them as nonthinking machines. In an infa-mous incident on Stassia, a binary loadlifter repeatedly stacked heavy crates in a depot corner—despite over-taxed floorboards groaning and splintering under the weight. When the entire floor finally gave way, the lifter simply righted itself and stomped off to collect another crate.

Popular models of binary loadlifters include Cybot Galactica's CLL-8 and CLL-M2. The latter unit saw extensive use by the Grand Army of the Republic during the Clone Wars, and incorporates a unique feature: the repulsorlift counterweight. This gadget, located at the rear of the CLL-M2, generates a reverse polarization field that increases the pull of gravity, acting as a counterbalance whenever the CLL-M2 raises particularly heavy loads onto its lifting arms.

The CLL-M2 sports yellow warning stripes on its squared-off shoulders. Its footpads, similar to those of the AT-AT walker, help disperse its weight and the weight of its load over a broad surface area. During the Clone Wars, the CLL-M2 worked primarily as an ordnance lifter, delicately carrying and mounting explosive military armaments. A close cousin of the CLL-M2 was Cybot Galactica's IW-37 pincer loader, an extremely precise automaton with a single arm, used to arm missile pods or to remove ammunition from wrecks—a practice that led to its nick-name "salvager droid."

> ## "Vaporators! Sir—my first job was programming binary loadlifters . . . very similar to your vaporators in most respects."
>
> *—A less-than-truthful C-3PO, trying to promote himself to Owen Lars at a droid sale*

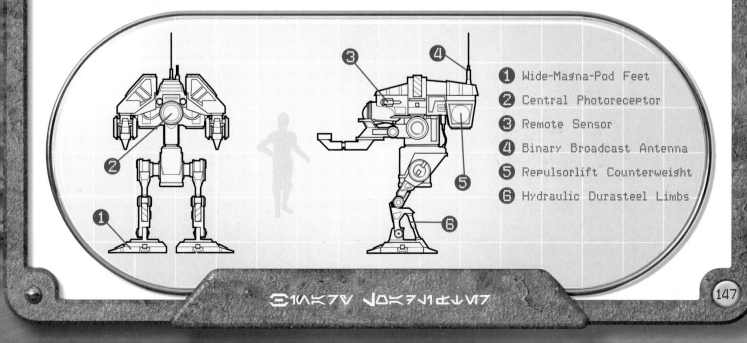

1. Wide-Magna-Pod Feet
2. Central Photoreceptor
3. Remote Sensor
4. Binary Broadcast Antenna
5. Repulsorlift Counterweight
6. Hydraulic Durasteel Limbs

BLX LABOR DROID

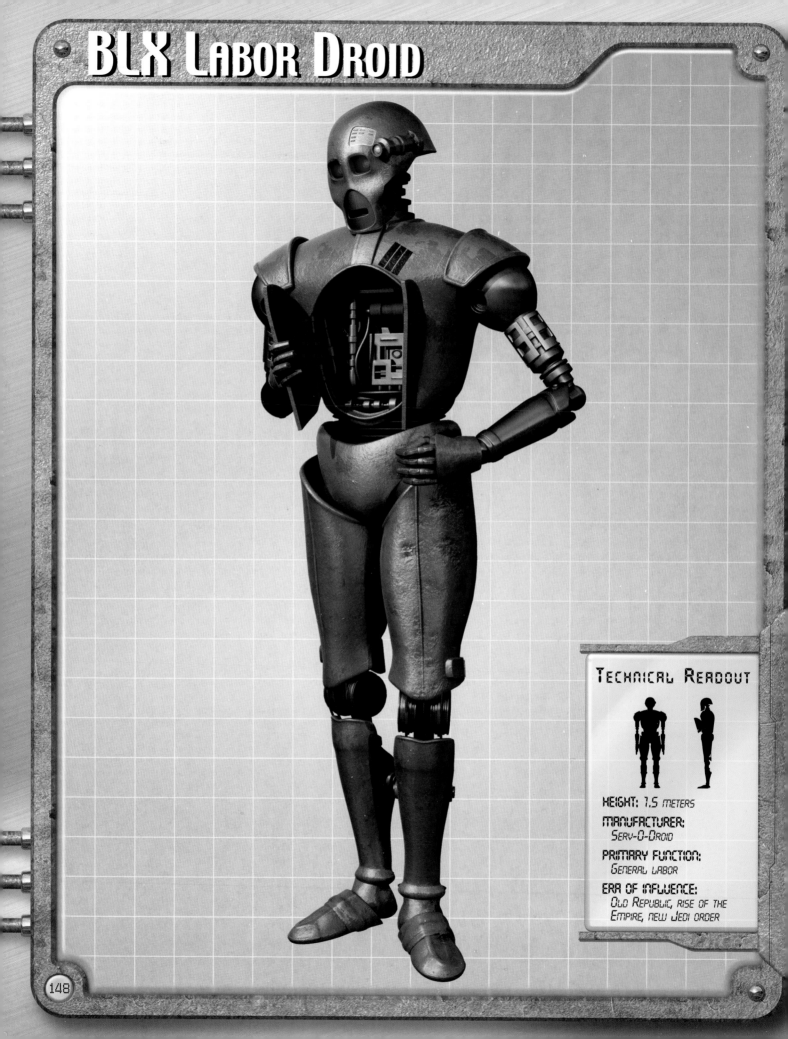

TECHNICAL READOUT

HEIGHT: 1.5 METERS

MANUFACTURER:
Serv-O-Droid

PRIMARY FUNCTION:
General labor

ERA OF INFLUENCE:
Old Republic, rise of the
Empire, new Jedi order

Serv-O-Droid BLX General Labor Droid

It's rare to see a BLX unit these days. Even before the Clone Wars, the droids were already on the wane, victims of changing market tastes. But Serv-O-Droid built the BLX to last, and some have been working in the same high-stress jobs for generations.

Built in a bipedal humanoid configuration, the BLX labor droid has photoreceptors and auditory pickups calibrated for standard wavelengths; its reaction time and walk cycle are quite slow. But the BLX possesses formidable strength, and is nearly unbeatable in terms of stamina. Serv-O-Droid priced the droids to move, often selling them in lots of one hundred or more to large repair yards.

By their nature, BLX droids do not specialize in anything. They function well in zero-g, where their magnetic footpads allow them to cling to starship hulls and their metal shells shrug off temperature extremes or hits from micrometeorites. Serv-O-Droid's original BLX series featured an uneven head and simian arms that dangled below the unit's knees. Later models, including the BLX NV, have more human-like proportions.

When given regular memory wipes, BLX units are unremarkable. Yet their behavioral circuitry matrices can create surprisingly acute levels of self-awareness, if allowed to accumulate life experience. Many untreated BLX droids developed personalities and befriended their owners, who spared them from the smelting chambers when the droids reached the point of obsolescence.

The most famous droid in the BLX series started operating in the starship yards of Fondor approximately one hundred standard years before the Battle of Yavin. BLX-5, or "Bollux," escaped a memory wipe by accepting a job to clear out a mynock nest. When he returned, the local personnel grew to love his dry wit. They manumitted Bollux at the end of his term of service, making him one of the few free droids in galactic society at that time.

Over the following decades, Bollux worked for scouting teams and other frontier outfits, exploring the galaxy under a variety of aliases, including "Zollux." While in the employ of a Corporate Sector outlaw tech named Doc, Bollux had his chest hardware refitted to make room for a sentient positronic processor designated Blue Max. In the years prior to the Battle of Yavin, Bollux and Blue Max shared adventures with Han Solo and Chewbacca from Stars' End to Dellalt.

During the Yuuzhan Vong invasion, Han encountered another BLX unit on Ruan. Calling itself "Baffle," this droid dropped hints that it was, in fact, Bollux, but Han had his doubts regarding the droid's sincerity.

> **"I volunteered for all the modifications and reprogramming I could, but eventually I simply couldn't compete with the newer, more capable droids."**
>
> *—A philosophical Bollux, reflecting on the history of the BLX unit*

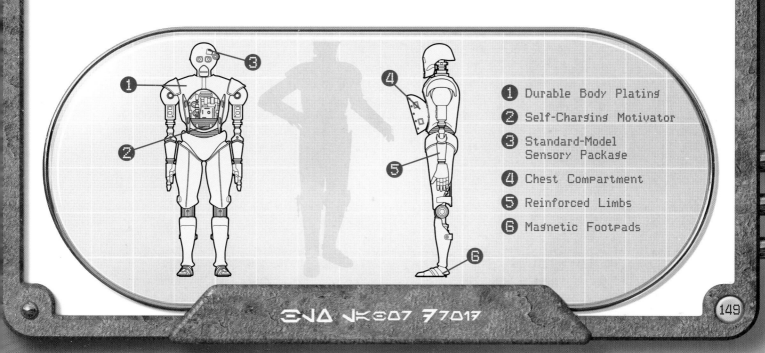

1. Durable Body Plating
2. Self-Charging Motivator
3. Standard-Model Sensory Package
4. Chest Compartment
5. Reinforced Limbs
6. Magnetic Footpads

Cam Droid

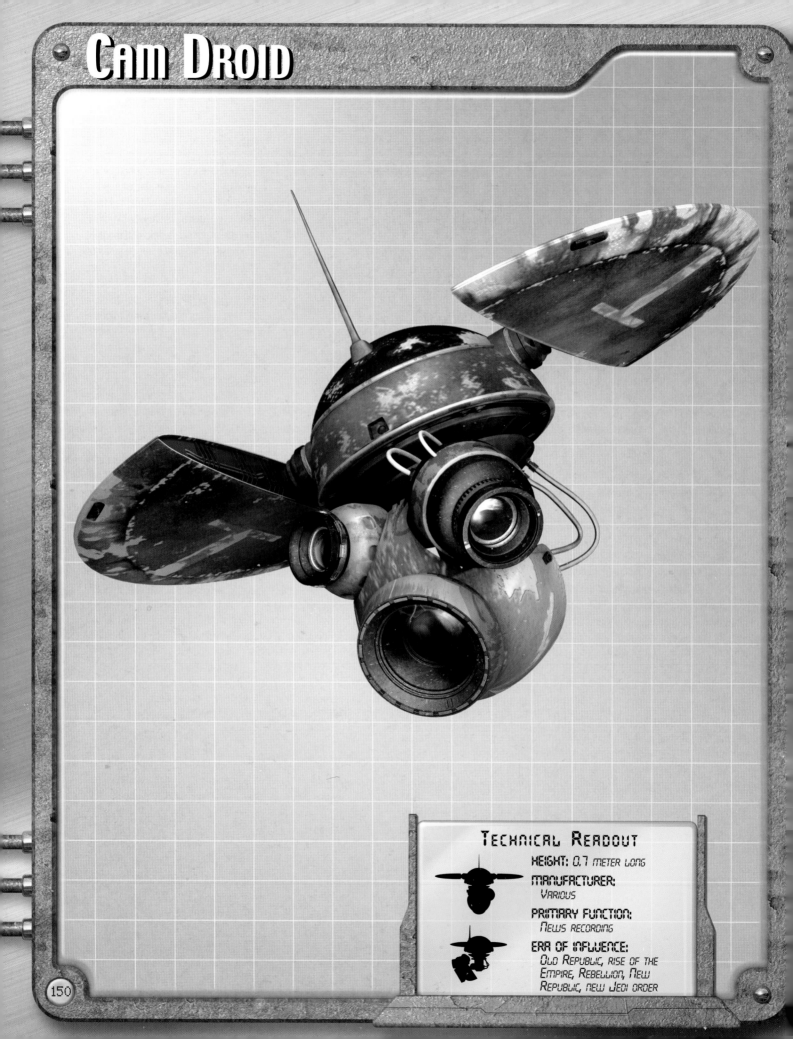

Technical Readout

Height: 0.7 meter long

Manufacturer: Various

Primary Function: News recording

Era of Influence: Old Republic, Rise of the Empire, Rebellion, New Republic, New Jedi Order

Industrial Automaton Hologlide J57 Cam Droid

Cam droids, also known as hovercams, are repulsorlift-driven, self-directed recording devices. Although some models are extremely intelligent, including the 3DVO and the Holocam-E, most have minimal cognitive circuitry and are categorized as class five droids.

The bylaws of both the Republic Senate and the New Republic Senate required that all official proceedings be transcribed for the record. Squadrons of Senate cam droids handled the job, zipping among floating congressional boxes on whisper-quiet repulsorlift engines.

Senate cam droids were equipped with multiple visual and audio recording devices. A wide-angle lens and a zoom lens allowed the droids to capture both panoramic views and the expressions on the faces of individual Senators. Senate cam droids transmitted their feeds to the public HoloNet, as well as to private viewscreens in individual boxes. A central data bank stored all recordings for future reference.

Unfortunately, Senate cam droids were only as reliable as their programmers. Cam droids during Palpatine's reign were known to favor pro-Imperial Senators by giving them more airtime, and to unfairly edit statements made by the opposition. Entire Senate meetings sometimes vanished from the archives, and other transcripts were later discovered to have glaring gaps.

Journalist cam droids are designed to capture footage of unfolding news events. They can operate independently, or as tools in the employ of organic reporters. A unit such as the 3DVO from Loronar has a repulsorlift engine, a central holocam, a number of backup recorders, and a communications array. The 3DVO is one of the most self-aware units on the market, and frequently seeks out scoops on its own. Shortly after the Battle of Yavin, a journalist 3DVO belonging to the royal family of Jazbina assisted Luke Skywalker in rescuing the daughter of planetary potentate Lord Prepredenko.

In the sport of Podracing, cam droids long ago replaced fixed-position holocams that were prone to damage from weather and vandals. Podrace cam droids, like the Hologlide J57 used at Mos Espa, aren't nearly as fast as the racers they cover, so they take up strategic positions along the track and transmit their recordings back to the grandstand control booth. The multiple signals from the cam droid fleet are relayed to the handheld view-screens carried by spectators, allowing fans to key in on their favorite racer or a particularly dangerous stretch of track.

General-purpose holocams are advertised for personal use. Most are simple constructions with minimal droid intelligence, and are designed to be operated by their owners. Trang Robotics' Holocam-E, or Cammy, is an exception. Like the 3DVO, the Cammy is exceptionally bright, and exudes a warm, motherly personality. A Cammy unit in the employ of the Rebel Alliance helped R2-D2 and C-3PO reprogram an assassin droid factory on Tatooine.

> **"Senator Seti Ashgad has disappeared, days after he protested the installation of the Senate's new cam droids. Palpatine's office says the timing is merely a coincidence."**
>
> —*HoloNet News report, filed in 20.6 B.B.Y.*

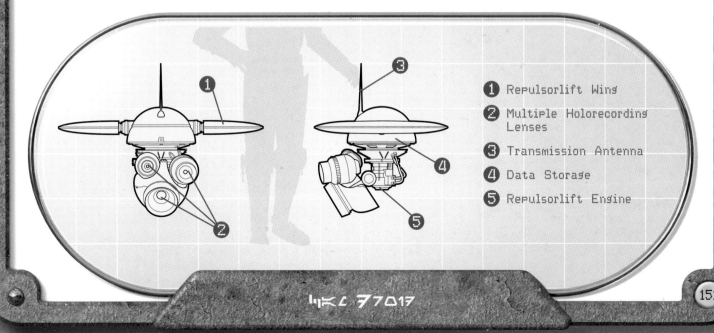

1. Repulsorlift Wing
2. Multiple Holorecording Lenses
3. Transmission Antenna
4. Data Storage
5. Repulsorlift Engine

COO Cook Droid

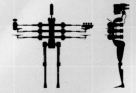
152

Industrial Automaton COO Cook Droid

Gourmands shudder when they consider the very concept of cook droids. Why trust your food, goes the argument, to machines that can't even *taste*?

Fortunately for companies such as Industrial Automaton, most people aren't so finicky. The company re-used the chassis from one of its labor units in its COO line of cook droids, and a similar sense of sloppy antipathy extended to the droid's programming. Ugly and clunky, the COO is designed for mass catering on the scale of a military mess hall.

The COO's most notable feature is its arm array. Depending on the socket configuration, a COO can have more than a dozen arms. A working droid might have a spatula, a whisk, a strainer, a serving spoon, a grease brush, a meat fork, a carving knife, several three-fingered manipulators, and a miniature flame projector for lighting oven burners. After the cooking and serving chores are completed, a COO droid will install wire brushes for scouring pots and pans. The droid also has two powerful legs that can lock to the floor with magnetic clamps, a feature that comes in handy on pitching ocean vessels or starships with spotty artificial gravity.

COOs are cook droids, but they lack much knowledge of culinary science. Each comes from the factory preloaded with several hundred common recipes taken from the millennia-old *Humbarine Housekeepers HoloBook*.

> "Me worst spell in space? No, 'twarnt sailing through the fire rings of Fornax. 'Twas the month I spent on the run from the Loronar navy, an' stuck with a vegetarian galley droid."
>
> —*Reginald Barkbone, legendary pirate of the Seven Sectors*

Industrial Automaton claims that this can be swapped out for a different software pack featuring new recipes, but the removal and installation of these packs is tedious and involves partial disassembly of the droid.

Usually, a COO is stuck with whatever recipes its last owner might have given it. From the outside, it's impossible to know what software a COO is carrying. Furthermore, the droids are notorious liars and will say whatever a buyer wants to hear if it will advance their station in life.

Even the Caamasi, pacifists all, will eventually smash a cook droid to pieces if forced to ingest Hutt cuisine. Many buyers, mindful of the COO's deficiencies in this area, use the droids only to reheat and serve prepackaged food trays.

Prior to the Clone Wars, the star freighter *Jendirian Valley* converted its cargo holds into passenger steerage in order to profit from the Separatist-created refugee crisis. To feed the thousands of people packed belowdecks, the freighter's operators purchased a cook droid designated COO-2180 at a used-droid market. COO-2180 prepared simple meals obtained in bulk from a military surplus store, and had instructions to serve only organic beings. When R2-D2 stole a meal for Padmé Amidala and Anakin Skywalker (traveling incognito among the *Valley*'s passengers), COO-2180 shouted angrily but ineffectually at the little astromech.

1. Serving/Cooking Arms
2. Limb Removal Joints
3. Cognitive Module
4. Internal Recipe Pack
5. Magnetic Footpads

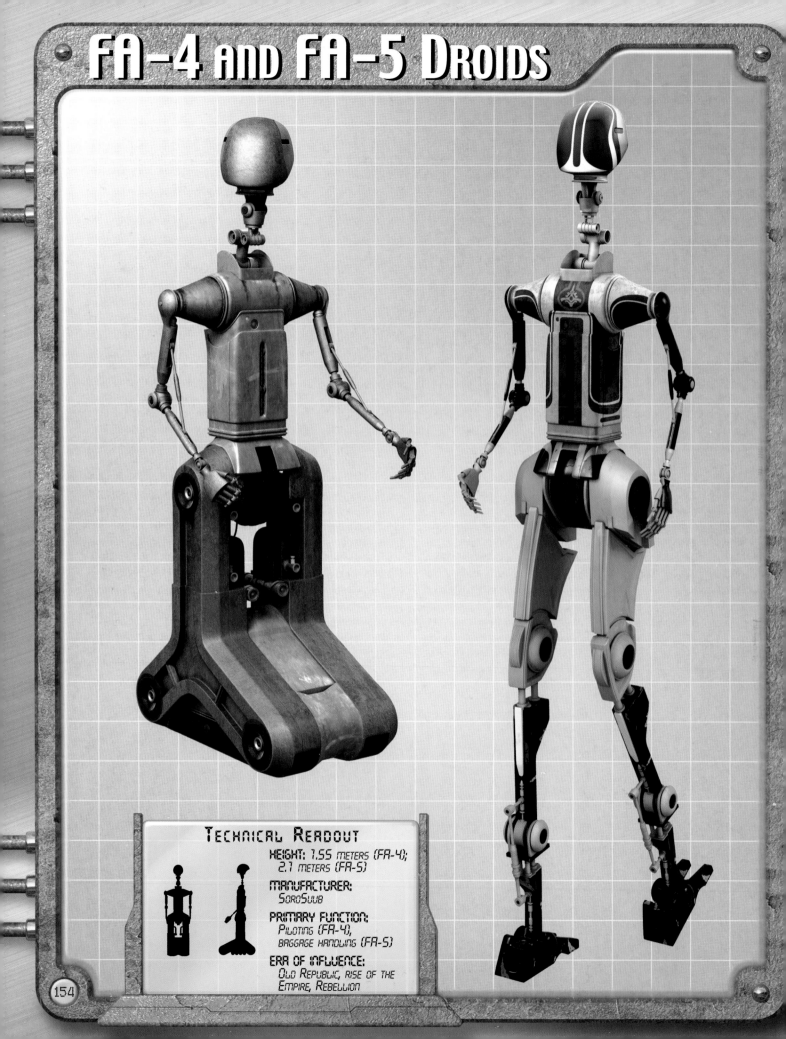

FA-4 AND FA-5 DROIDS

TECHNICAL READOUT

HEIGHT: 1.55 meters (FA-4);
2.7 meters (FA-5)

MANUFACTURER:
SoroSuub

PRIMARY FUNCTION:
Piloting (FA-4),
baggage handling (FA-5)

ERA OF INFLUENCE:
Old Republic, rise of the
Empire, Rebellion

SoroSuub FA-4 Pilot and FA-5 Valet Droids

The FA series is familiar to anyone who has ever visited a Core starport. Over generations, the design has emerged as the standard droid for companies that offer valet or chauffeur services. Dozens of knockoff models exist, but SoroSuub is the original manufacturer and the only one allowed to use the trademark designation *FA*.

Most public starports in the Core offer baggage-handling and shuttle services free of charge to new arrivals. The work is performed by local companies that compete for shuttle service rights; the companies make money from the operating fees paid out by the starport administrators, as well as whatever they can collect in tips. Three or four companies might work a single starport, their competing fleets of FA units distinguishable by their varied paint colors, or the jackets or caps that they wear. SoroSuub's two most popular models are the FA-4 pilot droid and the FA-5 valet droid.

The FA-4 pilot droid is programmed to operate most landspeeders, airspeeders, and starships—though it lacks the coordination to make complicated maneuvers or the knowledge to calculate hyperspace jumps. Two thin treads drive the droid and provide gripping stability. At starports, FA-4 droids typically greet arrivals and chauffeur them in a SoroSuub airspeeder to a hotel or other nearby destination.

"Don't forget to tip your FA droids while on Coruscant. They are programmed to blacklist the stingy."

—*From* Travels with Gormaanda: Cooking in the Core

The FA-5 valet droid lacks treads, instead walking on two spindly legs nearly twice the length of the droid's body. The humanoid configuration was chosen by SoroSuub to conform more closely to the public's image of a valet. A starport FA-5 droid will carry bags and arrange for transportation, usually by signaling to a waiting FA-4 belonging to the same fleet. SoroSuub sells a sizable number of FA-5 valet droids to private customers, who employ them in household tasks that include drawing baths and laying out the day's clothing. All FA units can speak Basic, in addition to twenty-two of the most common galactic languages.

Count Dooku was among the wealthy customers who combined his needs for mobility and privacy by buying an FA-4 pilot droid. Dooku's droid needed to operate the count's exotic solar sailer, a complicated starship built according to the abstruse blueprints of the alien Gree. The controls for the sailer were far beyond the FA-4's normal capacity, so Geonosian technicians augmented the droid with experimental programming from their vulture droid starfighters. This made the FA-4 a capable pilot even under combat conditions, an ability that came in handy on numerous occasions throughout the Clone Wars.

1. Manipulator Arms
2. Gripping Treads
3. Piloting and Language Databases
4. Balance Gyro
5. Drive Wheels

Homing Droid

Technical Readout

Height: 0.28 meter

Manufacturer:
Imperial Department of Military Research

Primary Function:
Espionage

Era of Influence:
Rise of the Empire, Rebellion, New Republic, New Jedi Order

Imperial Department of Military Research HMOR Homing Droid

Homing devices are unobtrusive bits of machinery that can be followed from a distance. Used to track stolen property or to signal for help in emergencies, homing devices can also make effective espionage tools. To increase the likelihood of a homing device operating without detection, spy agencies long ago developed the homing droid.

Usually no larger than a human hand, a homing droid is primarily a vehicle for planting a homing device (though the droid can also double as the device itself). Moving through shadows on silent repulsorlifts, a homing droid can penetrate areas of a starship that no organic crew member could ever reach. Unlike a fixed-position beacon, a homing droid is self-aware and capable of movement, enabling it to relocate to a more secure hiding place if it is at risk of discovery.

Homing devices can be active or passive. Active devices transmit a powerful broadcast signal that runs the risk of being detected by its target, while passive devices can be picked up only on specially calibrated sensor sweeps. Homing droids can also act in other ways, from eavesdropping on conversations to sabotaging a starship's hyperdrive and making it easy for those tracking the homing signal to capture their helpless prey.

The HMOR homing droid is a particularly ill-tempered product of the Imperial Department of Military Research. Larger than most homing droids, it comes equipped with a repulsorlift engine as well as a set of wheels, for use in high-security environments where the presence of an unfamiliar repulsor field will trigger an alarm. The HMOR unit has a retractable manipulator arm and a database of more than four and a half million starship and airspeeder designs, appropriated by Imperial scientists from the Separatist buzz droid.

The droid carries a small detachable homing device in its back that it can leave behind while it lures searchers on a wild bantha chase into other corners of a starship. The droid's active signal travels via hyperwave, and can be detected at distances tens of thousands of light-years away.

If an HMOR droid is discovered, it will do as much damage as possible before self-destructing. Each is equipped with two explosive seeker drones, while a second retractable arm sprays an acid stream that can eat through durasteel in seconds.

Han Solo's *Millennium Falcon* carried an HMOR homing droid during its escape from the Death Star, secreted deep within the ship's internal workings. R2-D2 was the first to discover the stowaway after the *Falcon*'s arrival at the Yavin 4 base, destroying it before the droid could cause further trouble.

> ## "You're sure the homing beacon is secure aboard their ship? I'm taking an awful risk, Vader. This had better work."
>
> —*Grand Moff Tarkin, after* Millennium Falcon *"escaped" the Death Star*

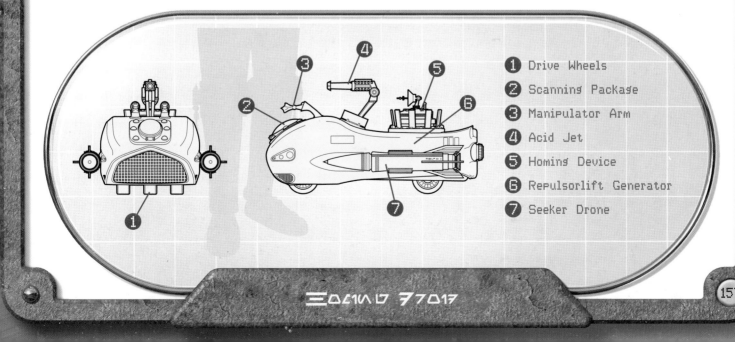

1. Drive Wheels
2. Scanning Package
3. Manipulator Arm
4. Acid Jet
5. Homing Device
6. Repulsorlift Generator
7. Seeker Drone

Imperial Mark IV

Technical Readout

HEIGHT: 0.3 meter in diameter

MANUFACTURER:
Imperial Department of Military Research

PRIMARY FUNCTION:
Security recording

ERA OF INFLUENCE:
Rise of the Empire, Rebellion, New Republic

Imperial Department of Military Research Mark IV (IM4) Sentry Droid

The Imperial Mark IV sentry droid belies the stereotype of Imperial equipment. It's not intimidating in the least, while its small size and curious demeanor have even led some to label it "adorable." But the IM4 was an insidious diminutive spy in the service of Palpatine's Empire. During the height of the Galactic Civil War, the droids were responsible for exposing thousands of covert Rebel cells—a statistic not even the Emperor's Grand Inquisitors could match.

The Mark IV droid is little more than a repulsorlift engine and a scattering of sensors, packed into a lightweight support frame. The repulsorlift can reach a flight ceiling of ten meters and can achieve sudden bursts of speed.

Steering nozzles at the rear of the chassis control direction, while two stabilizer fins ensure a smooth flight. Mark IVs can't move if they're not flying, and the only time they rest is when they've been switched off.

Buying an IM4 at a local droid dealership is impossible. The droids are manufactured exclusively for the Imperial military or governments sympathetic to the Empire. More than a few IM4s, however, have been nabbed by criminals and repurposed for sale on the black market. This is a risky line of work. Mark IVs continually transmit a low-frequency transponder signal back to their base of operations, and tampering with one of the droids is a punishable offense.

The Mark IV is capable of seeing in all directions at once thanks to sensor clusters at the front, rear, and top. Its forward array includes electromagnetic, infrared, and visible-wavelength sensors. Its macrobinoculars can record a clear picture at distances up to fifty meters and have a built-in holorecording feature. A broadband antenna receiver communicates solely on coded alert frequencies.

Imperial Mark IVs aren't particularly smart, but they're loyal to their owners and can develop personality quirks if not given regular memory wipes. Their databanks contain the complete text of the Imperial Legal Code; the droids can be loaded with additional information on local statutes and maps of city streets. Imperial stormtroopers often used Mark IV units as decoys, sending them around corners to draw fire from concealed enemies. Occasionally, Mark IVs have been fitted with low-powered blasters.

Shortly before the Battle of Yavin, the Empire's Tatooine garrison—as well as Imperial forces from the Star Destroyer *Devastator*—deployed hundreds of Mark IVs to search for two escaped droids. IM4-099, nicknamed "Face" by the Mos Eisley Militia, supported a stormtrooper checkpoint along the city's main thoroughfare. As Mark IVs became omnipresent across the city, they began to interfere with municipal asp droids installing communications repeaters. Despite their omnipresent monitoring, the Mark IVs failed to identify R2-D2 and C-3PO.

> **"Your Honor, I'd like to introduce holorecordings of the defendant at the moment of the massacre: IM4-821 from street level, IM4-822 from overhead, IM4-823 from down the block..."**
>
> —*From the Denon murder trial of Dr. Evazan, before his courtroom escape*

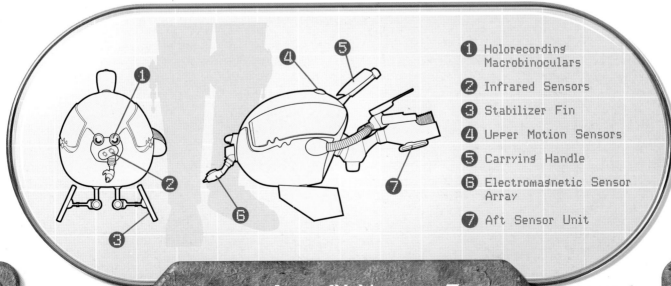

1. Holorecording Macrobinoculars
2. Infrared Sensors
3. Stabilizer Fin
4. Upper Motion Sensors
5. Carrying Handle
6. Electromagnetic Sensor Array
7. Aft Sensor Unit

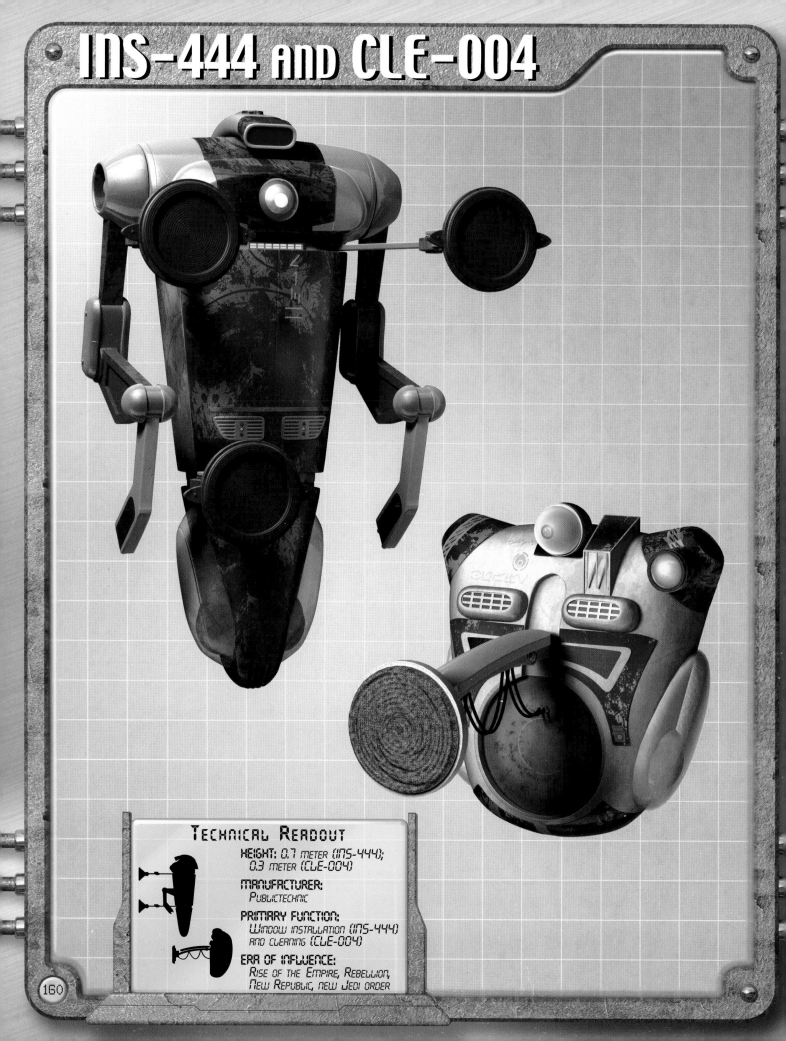

INS-444 and CLE-004

TECHNICAL READOUT

HEIGHT: 0.7 meter (INS-444);
0.3 meter (CLE-004)

MANUFACTURER:
Publictechnic

PRIMARY FUNCTION:
Window installation (INS-444)
and cleaning (CLE-004)

ERA OF INFLUENCE:
Rise of the Empire, Rebellion,
New Republic, New Jedi Order

Publictechnic INS-444 Window Installation and CLE-004 Window Cleaning Droids

Residents of Coruscant stifle yawns when they're forced to think about the intricacies of cleaning or window-installing droids, but it's a mistake to be so dismissive. The droids, with their ability to hover kilometers above the vertical city, perform tasks that no organic worker would dare undertake.

The INS-444 installer droid and CLE-004 cleaning droid are both manufactured by Publictechnic. Though the droids often work together, the cleaning unit is far more common and is produced in exponentially greater numbers. Any city with skytowers has a use for Publictechnic's window models, but Coruscant is *the* place to sell droids designed for high-rise architecture.

Most windows on Coruscant are not made of transparisteel. Favoring vanity over practicality, residents order windows made from clari-crystalline and even glass, both of which offer a clearer view—with the trade-off of an increased possibility of breakage. Striking a window can shatter the entire pane into thousands of fragments, making INS-444 droids more common than one might think.

The INS-444 comes with magnatomic grip pads to hold a newly ordered window pane during its journey from the store to the installation site. Two INS units work together to carry large panes. During their journey through the city, the INS droids keep their photoreceptors alert for wayward aircars, which sometimes smash right through the transparent windows before their drivers notice that a delivery is in progress. The INS-444 has three manipulator arms that secure the pane against the window frame, and two testing probes on the upper arms to scan for any gaps in the airtight seal.

A CLE-004 cleaning droid accompanies the INS-444 on installation jobs, polishing the new window to remove any droid digit marks. But it's more common to see CLE-004s by themselves outside of Coruscant's myriad apartments and office towers, as they continually wipe off the accumulated grime spawned by the city's constant air traffic. A CLE-004 unit has an electrostatic polishing brush at the end of an articulated arm that can polish a large window in only a few seconds.

Because they're *supposed* to lurk outside windows, CLE-004 droids make perfect spies. A number of parties ranging from news organizations to crime bosses have outfitted selected units with eavesdropping devices or hologrammic recorders, cataloging everything from corporate passcodes to illicit footage of lovers' trysts.

After Jedi Master Obi-Wan Kenobi shattered a window in Senator Padmé Amidala's apartment in pursuit of an assassin droid, her staff ordered an immediate replacement for the broken pane. Congressional Crystalline, a window company based in the Senate District, entrusted the job to two of its most reliable droids: "Mick," an INS-444, and "Buffy," his CLE-004 counterpart.

> **"Jizz musician Fitz Roi filed suit against Acme Robopolish this morning, claiming that the company's droids are stealing his songs."**
>
> —*TriNebulon News entertainment feed*

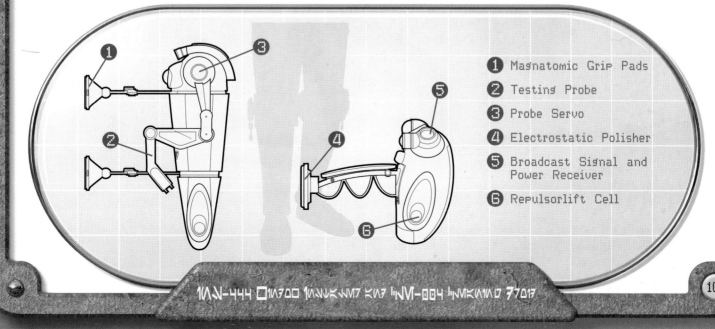

1. Magnatomic Grip Pads
2. Testing Probe
3. Probe Servo
4. Electrostatic Polisher
5. Broadcast Signal and Power Receiver
6. Repulsorlift Cell

LIN DEMOLITIONMECH

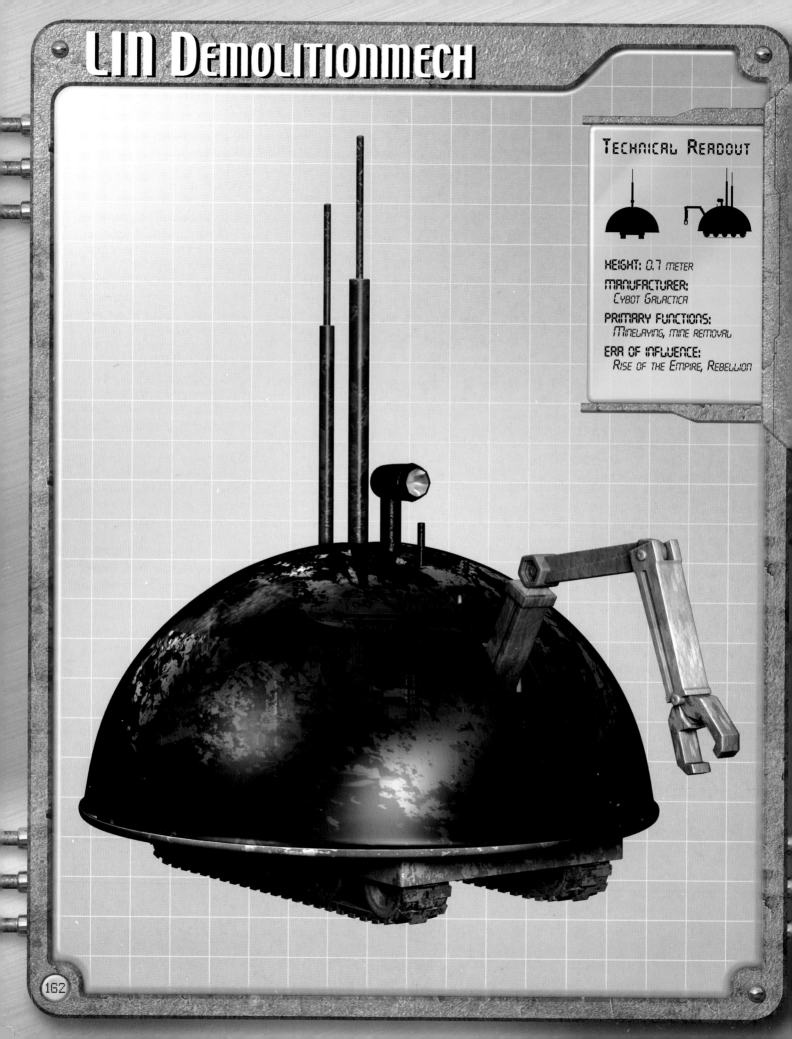

TECHNICAL READOUT

HEIGHT: 0.7 meter

MANUFACTURER:
Cybot Galactica

PRIMARY FUNCTIONS:
Minelaying, mine removal

ERA OF INFLUENCE:
Rise of the Empire, Rebellion

Cybot Galactica LIN Autonomous Minelayer

The LIN demolitionmech autonomous minelayer is an example of a superior product forced off the market through a combination of bad luck and worse marketing.

Cybot Galactica made the demolitionmech for commercial use in applications from mining to building demolition. The droid rides low to the ground, its inner workings protected beneath a durasteel dome. The reason for the heavy shell is readily apparent—after planting explosive charges, the slow-moving droid is often showered with debris from the resulting industrial blast.

During normal operation, the LIN demolitionmech rolls into position on two wide treads (using the same undercarriage as the WED Treadwell) and then plucks a blast cap from its spinning internal rack with its telescoping arm. Sonic sensors allow the demolitionmech to probe structures for weak spots and plant its charges appropriately. The dome and arm can rotate 360 degrees. A pair of retractable antennas can send signals through kilometers of solid rock, though the demolitionmech can communicate only in droid languages.

The demolitionmech's flaws include the weight of its durasteel shell, which slows the droid and renders its five-speed drive impeller largely useless. Damp environments sometimes cause demolitionmechs to seize up—a problem on mining worlds where tunnels often fill with water.

SchaumAssoc, Cybot Galactica's advertising agency, decided to promote the droid based solely on its toughness. In a memorable advertisement titled "Blast Proof," hundreds of demolitionmechs free-floating in space were hit by a battleship's turbolaser. The energy beam knocked the droids around like balls on a mung-tee table, but all survived without a scratch.

A "clear comic exaggeration" is how Cybot Galactica put it when customers demanded to know why demolitionmechs weren't *literally* blast-proof. (As experiments, many had indeed subjugated their droids to sustained laserfire.) Cybot Galactica pulled the ad, but soon faced a much bigger setback when a detonite charge prematurely exploded in a demolitionmech's grip at a mining outpost on Gosfambling. The resulting tunnel collapse caused the suffocation deaths of ten miners.

Investigators concluded that the fault lay with the charge, not the droid, but the LIN demolitionmech had already attracted enough bad press. Cybot Galactica pulled the droid from the market.

Following the recall, the demolitionmech found success with criminal syndicates and the military—two groups that didn't have to worry about pleasing stockholders. Crime cartels sent beetle-like swarms of demolitionmechs crawling over Ryloth, Socorro, and other spice-rich planets, blasting open new spice veins. The Republic army, and later the Empire, used the droids as minelayers or mine removers. At the Battle of Gligger during the Clone Wars, 563 demolitionmechs were blown sky-high in efforts to clear Marrow's Moor.

> ## "*Advantage #7: Blast Proof. The LIN Demolitionmech is One Tough Droid.*"
>
> —*Excerpt from the Demolitionmech's advertising campaign*

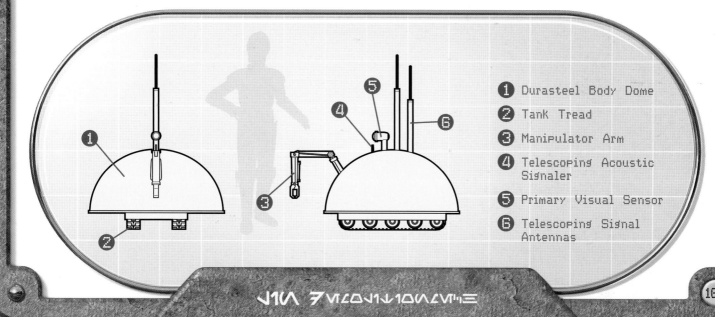

1. Durasteel Body Dome
2. Tank Tread
3. Manipulator Arm
4. Telescoping Acoustic Signaler
5. Primary Visual Sensor
6. Telescoping Signal Antennas

MONSTER DROID

TECHNICAL READOUT

HEIGHT: Variable

MANUFACTURER:
Jawa Clan Craftspeople

PRIMARY FUNCTIONS:
Variable

ERA OF INFLUENCE:
Rise of the Empire, Rebellion,
New Republic, New Jedi Order

Jawa Custom-Built "Monster" Ugly

The monster droid is one of the most extreme examples of recombinant part-bashing, i.e., part-salvaging—an oft-ignored but huge part of the droid business. Using pieces left behind in the scrap heap, junkyard engineers build amalgamated "uglies" that come with no warranty, but which can sometimes perform better than the originals.

The Jawas of Tatooine are experts at this junkyard science. If they can fix a droid, they will; if they can't, they'll keep every piece inside their sandcrawlers until they've collected enough for a new droid.

Jawas know what their customers (mostly moisture farmers and small-town business owners) are looking for in a droid. Most tribes make uglies in four major classifications, though even within these loose groupings one may note considerable variation in appearance. These droids, so familiar to residents of Tatooine, are nearly impossible to find offworld:

- The **mechano-droid** is a heavy-labor unit equipped with a hook arm and a drilling arm, designed for permanent installation inside a tech dome.

- The **tracto-droid** is a tank-treaded mobile scanning unit with a radar array, perfect for detecting threats near a farm's perimeter.

- The **quad-pod droid** is a cargo carrier that moves on four mismatched legs, using its scoop arm and gripper arm to move items into its flatbed holding area.

> *"Utoo nye usabla atoonyoba?"*
>
> —Sales banter from Kiottja, chief of the Salt Steppes Jawa clan

- The **rollarc droid** is a speedy unit that zips about on four wheels, suitable for a wide variety of tasks thanks to an advanced computer housing.

The monster droid is a towering amalgam of parts from all four types of uglies listed above, as well as castoff pieces from astromech droids and more. It is less a tool than a piece of folk art.

The practice of building monster droids began more than fifty years before the Clone Wars with Tatakoz, Jawa master trader of the Mospic High Range. A tribal outcast, Tatakoz sold his wares using nothing more than a speeder bike and a repulsor trailer. When the citizens of Mos Espa and Mos Entha began hailing his skill at assembling uglies, rival tribes attempted to steal his business in an escalating contest of one-upmanship. Eventually Tatakoz built the first monster droid, and, even more impressively, he actually *sold* it.

Monster droids earn admiration from collectors for the number of parts they incorporate, the degree to which those parts work together to accomplish a defined task, and the overall aesthetics of the finished product. Due to their size, monster droids make poor repair units, but they are serviceable scanning and communications droids.

Among Jawas, the practice is viewed as a way to bring glory to the tribe and as an outlet for the creative impulses of younger Jawas. Most sandcrawlers carry one or two monster droids under construction at any time.

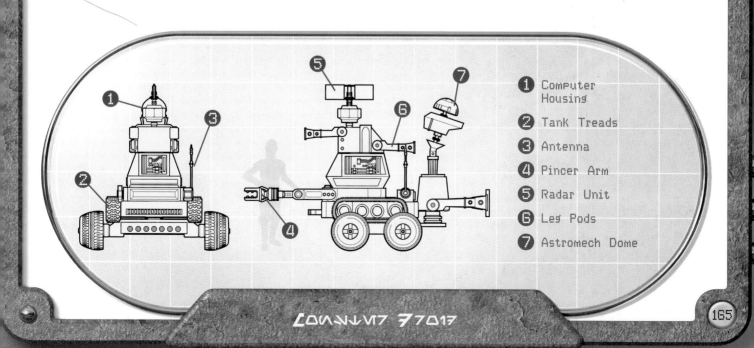

1. Computer Housing
2. Tank Treads
3. Antenna
4. Pincer Arm
5. Radar Unit
6. Leg Pods
7. Astromech Dome

MOUSE DROID

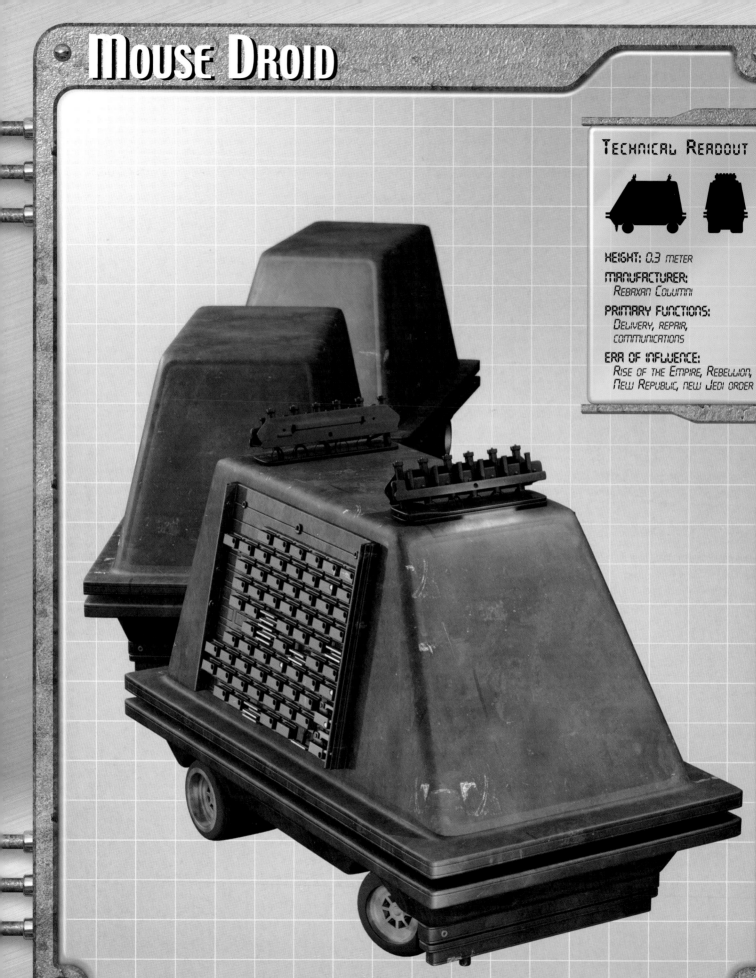

TECHNICAL READOUT

HEIGHT: 0.3 meter

MANUFACTURER:
Rebaxan Columni

PRIMARY FUNCTIONS:
Delivery, repair, communications

ERA OF INFLUENCE:
Rise of the Empire, Rebellion, New Republic, new Jedi order

Rebaxan Columni MSE-Series General-Purpose Droid

It's easy to see how "mouse droids" got their nickname, and just as easy to understand why so many people find them irritating. These tiny, squeaking boxes on wheels were ubiquitous aboard the vessels of the Imperial star fleet, where they called to mind the rodents carried aboard primitive sailing ships of yore.

Rebaxan Columni, a corporation owned by the diminutive Chadra-Fan, invented MSE droids for use on the Chadra-Fan homeworld. The little droid mimicked the pleeky, a local pet, and Rebaxan Columni hoped that the galactic market would consider its product cute. Following test runs of the MSE-4 and MSE-5, Rebaxan launched the MSE-6 with a huge advertising blitz and a production run that numbered in the billions.

Many were sold, but most were returned as soon as the buyers realized that MSE droids reminded them of disease-carrying vermin. Rebaxan Columni filed for bankruptcy toward the tail end of the Clone Wars.

In one of its last acts, Rebaxan Columni offered Palpatine's new Empire the entire run of the MSE-6 at a fire-sale price. The Imperial Navy, critically short of droids as it played catch-up to Palpatine's sweeping military expansions, accepted and allocated hundreds of the droids to every ship in the fleet.

MSE droids can perform many tasks, but they can perform only one task at a time. Each can hold a modular circuit matrix, or C-matrix, loaded with a single skill set. A C-matrix might be programmed for security, sanitation, repair, or communications. To create a unit with multiple, interlocked skills, MSEs can link together to form a "droid train."

Two retractable manipulator arms are hidden inside the MSE-6's black casing. The droid also possesses two audio sensors, a photoreceptor, and a miniature holocam. A small compartment in the top of the unit can hold sensitive documents; for this reason, the droids are often used as couriers. This compartment cannot be opened without an authorized voice code, and mouse droids that are captured are programmed to melt themselves down. To avoid such a fate, the droids have strong self-preservation instincts and can zip away from danger in forward or reverse.

> ## "Lastly, we have a complaint from the Aar'aa regarding their order. Apparently, the MSE droids skittering underfoot are making them uncomfortably . . . hungry."
>
> —*Rebaxan Columni executives, product-testing the MSE-6*

The uses for mouse droids are limited only by their owner's creativity. On Mustafar, the operators of the lava mines used MSE-4s to scout for life-support leaks. Aboard the Death Star, MSE-6s guided stormtroopers through the maze-like corridors. An inventive assassin once packed a mouse droid's storage compartment with explosive detonite in a failed bid to kill High Inquisitor Tremayne.

Most recently, the Galactic Federation of Free Alliances employed mouse droids to sniff out enemy infiltrators during the invasion of the Yuuzhan Vong. The YVH-M, for "Yuuzhan Vong Hunter Mouse," possessed the processor of a YVH droid inside an unassuming MSE shell. YVH-M units helped save the life of Chief of State Cal Omas by uncovering spies on Mon Calamari.

1. Command/Order Tray (retracted)
2. Drive Wheels
3. Heavy Manipulator (behind panel)
4. Fine Manipulator (behind panel)
5. Electrophoto Receptor
6. Miniature Holocam

Mustafar Panning Droid

Technical Readout

HEIGHT: 1.5 meters

MANUFACTURER:
Kalibac Industries

PRIMARY FUNCTION:
Mineral collection

ERA OF INFLUENCE:
Rise of the Empire, Rebellion

Modified Kalibac Industries Information Cataloging Droid

Most droids don't lead easy lives, but even the lowest sanitation scrubber has it better than the miserable Mustafar panning droid. The droids, never designed to work under such strenuous conditions, have one of the shortest operational life expectancies in the industry.

Mustafar is a world of black rock suspended between the gas giants of Jestefad and Lefrani. Their competing tidal forces agitate Mustafar's molten core, creating a sphere that glows from space with the orange light of volcanic eruptions. The Techno Union purchased the magma moon more than three centuries ago, having discovered that its lava flows contained rare metals and ores. Within a few years, giant harvesting facilities sprang up atop the Mustafar cliffs. At first the Techno Union employed the native Mustafarians to scoop minerals directly from the lava, but it soon calculated that it could triple its output if it also employed a fleet of droids.

The panning droid is an off-the-cuff creation. Kalibac Industries, a small Techno Union company, had received a contract to build librarian droids for the Mid Rim Lending Network. Kalibac's librarian droids could reach the highest shelves of data archives on repulsorlift engines and retrieve information cylinders with their dangling manipulator arms. Sensing a cheap shortcut, the Techno Union built imitative body shells out of heat-resistant carbonite,

then filled them with intelligence matrices taken from the factory-fresh library droids. The new workers found themselves on the next freighter to Mustafar.

Now working as panning droids, the former librarians discovered that their jobs required them to hover above lava rivers and use their scanners to hunt for minerals roiled to the surface by tractor beams. If they found a strike, the panning droids would scoop it up in buckets and carry it back to the shielded safety of a harvesting center. Never resting for an instant, the droids would pick up a new bucket and return to the eternal furnace.

The panning droids carry their own low-powered shield generators as a partial defense against the heat. Nevertheless, droids were lost to the flames constantly, and the Techno Union replaced them with fresh units kept in a warehouse. Panning droids are just smart enough to know how bad they had it on Mustafar.

At the end of the Clone Wars, Anakin Skywalker and Obi-Wan Kenobi had a climactic clash on the lava planet. The recklessness of their battle resulted in a shield shutdown at a key harvesting facility, leading to a catastrophic temperature overload. As a half-melted collection arm tipped over the edge of a lavafall, Anakin leapt to a safe perch on the head of a panning droid. Using the Force to override the droid's steering controls, Anakin "surfed" upstream, much to the little droid's distress.

> ## "Reconfiguration of the panning droids is proceeding behind schedule. The units are strangely skittish around organics, particularly those workers dressed in black."
>
> —*Excerpt from TaggeCo's Mustafar Reclamation Report*

1. Shield Generator
2. Manipulator Arms
3. Shielded Photoreceptors
4. Carbonite Shell
5. Repulsorlift Engine
6. Lava Collection Bucket

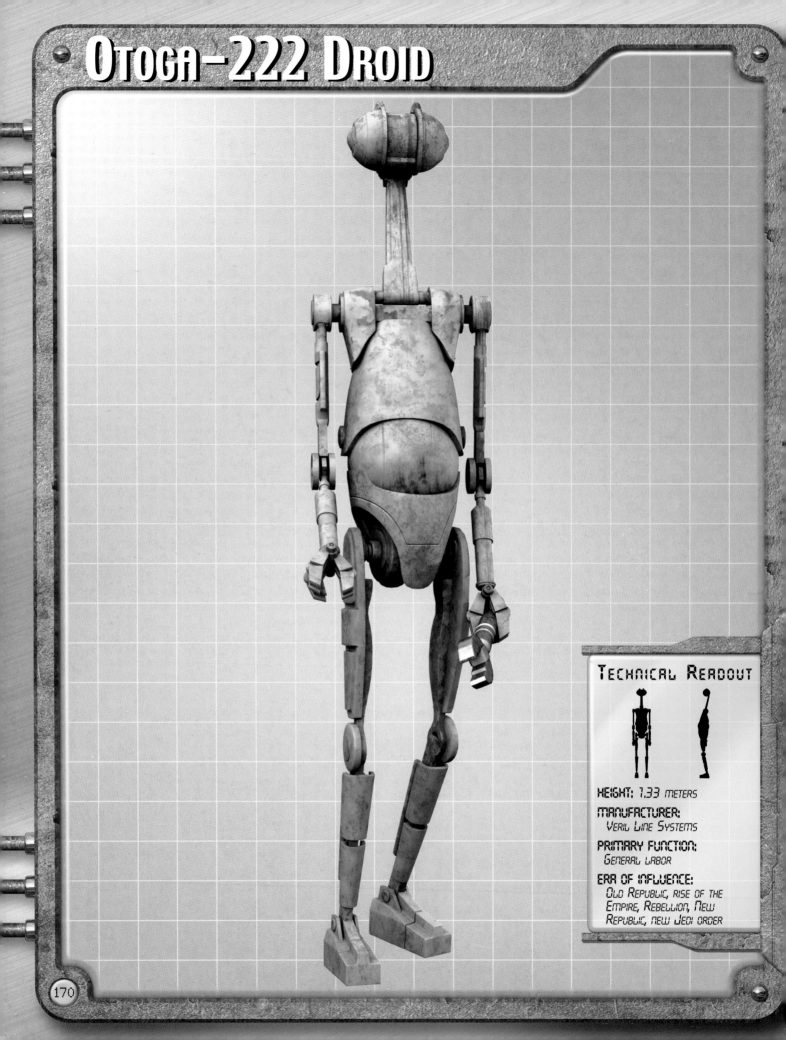

Otoga-222 Droid

Technical Readout

HEIGHT: 1.33 meters

MANUFACTURER:
Veril Line Systems

PRIMARY FUNCTION:
General labor

ERA OF INFLUENCE:
Old Republic, rise of the Empire, Rebellion, New Republic, new Jedi order

Veril Line Systems Otoga-222 Maintenance Droid

The Otoga-222 is known mostly as a Podracing pit droid, but that's merely one of its countless roles. Veril Line Systems introduced the model centuries ago as a repair and maintenance unit, yet its surprisingly flexible behavioral circuitry matrix has enabled the Otoga to become a jack-of-all-trades.

Otoga droids are built to take up as little space as possible; many owners shut them inside closets when they're not being used. Their hard-shelled bodies come in a variety of colors, while older units often sport mismatched parts. The droids have bipedal locomotion and simple gripper hands. They are able to accept a power recharge from almost any source, thanks to a socket adaptor and internal current regulator.

The tiny head of an Otoga droid belies its smart and curious electronic brain. Its vocabulator can vocalize most common galactic languages—indeed, in conversation the Otoga exhibits the optimistic enthusiasm of a young child.

It was this endearing personality that originally convinced Veril Line Systems that the Otoga could be a crossover: a model that appeals to buyers well outside the target audience to create a surprise windfall. Consequently, Veril didn't stop selling the Otoga to mechanics; the company instead developed a supplementary marketing plan aimed at families in need of a household maintenance droid. The move proved to be a hit. Veril Line Systems tapped a *third* profit stream by advertising the Otoga on children's holovee, after which millions of Otoga droids became lifeday presents to the offspring of wealthy parents.

In time, children grew up and household fashions changed. Veril Line Systems stopped producing home models. Unwanted Otogas found work in rougher trades. Construction and repair remained the most popular occupations, but some Otogas found employment pulling repulsorlift rickshaws or stamping starport entry visas.

In the field of Podracing, the slower Otogas couldn't compete with the manic energy of Serv-O-Droid's DUM series pit droids. Nevertheless, some Podrace pilots, such as Ody Mandrell, preferred the steady hands and clear minds of Otogas.

Veril Line Systems has issued dozens of subtle variations on the Otoga line over the decades, each identifiable by its own numeric code. The Otoga-222, produced at the height of the unit's popularity, is the most widespread variety.

Veril Line Systems recently fielded a team of Otoga droids on the nuna-ball circuit, where the droids won unlikely fame as sports champions. The Otoga squad regularly beats other teams in its division, including Industrial Automaton's asps and Cybot Galactica's PKs.

> "So, friend, what are you looking for? Wait, don't tell me—I've already got your next droid right here. Why else do you think I sell Otogas?"
>
> —*Honest Blim, proprietor of Procopia Preowned Automata*

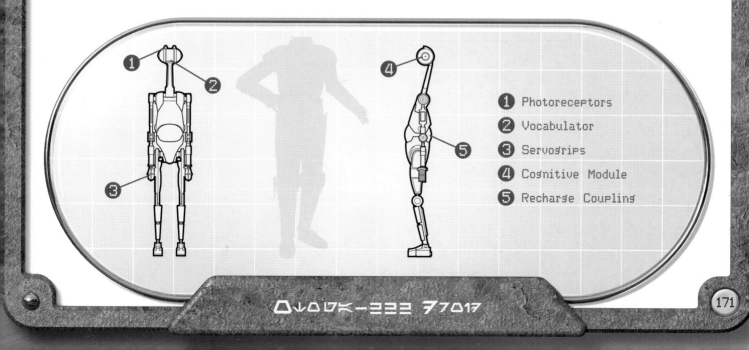

1. Photoreceptors
2. Vocabulator
3. Servogrips
4. Cognitive Module
5. Recharge Coupling

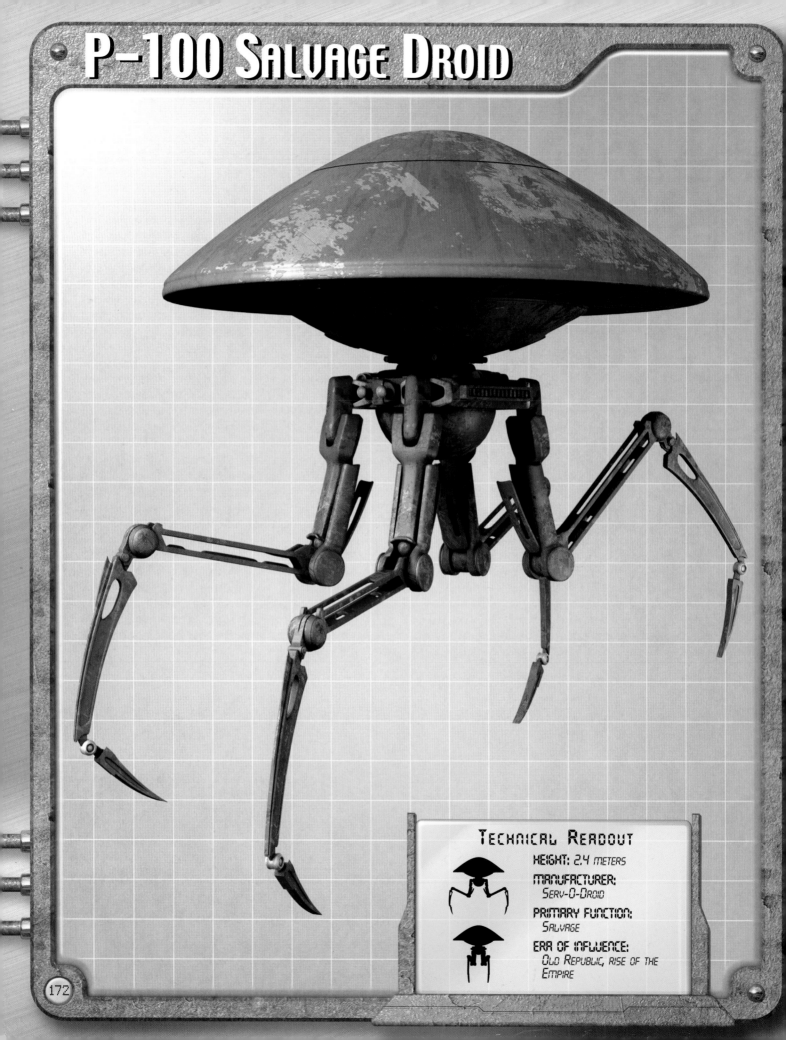

P-100 Salvage Droid

Technical Readout

Height: 2.4 meters

Manufacturer: Serv-O-Droid

Primary Function: Salvage

Era of Influence: Old Republic, rise of the Empire

Serv-O-Droid P-100 Salvage Droid

P-100 salvager droids are common sights to all Podracing fans, particularly the bloodthirsty subgroup who watch the sport only for the crashes. Like urusais circling above carrion, salvager droids seek out the carcasses of ruined Podracing machines, stripping them clean within minutes.

Serv-O-Droid manufactures the P-100, but, like the company's popular series of DUM pit droids, the salvagers are originally of Cyrillian design. The reptilian race fans of Cyrillia built both varieties of droid for different but complementary niches: pit droids to fix Podracers, and salvage droids to recover Podracers too damaged to fly.

Salvage droids are carried aboard repulsorlift-driven holding arms equipped with omnidirectional homing sensors that can pinpoint a downed Podracer's automated distress beacon. Three salvage droids are carried aboard each arm and released through a ventral hatch. The salvagers can load the scrap onto the arm, which can carry up to five hundred kilograms, or carry the parts back to the racing hangar on their own.

Each P-100 salvager is topped by a bell-shaped cap similar to those worn by the DUM pit droids. Four articulated pincer arms dangle underneath. The repulsorlift engine of a P-100 is much more powerful than those on similarly sized droids, since the P-100 also needs to support the weight of its load.

Salvage droids are operated by race organizers, who give pilots two standard hours to reclaim their wrecked racers before the parts are auctioned off. Throngs of bargain hunters pack these public auctions, but the less law-abiding among them have been known to deploy their own salvage droids, in a race to reach valuable scrap before the officials. Downed pilots are usually unable to tell one team of P-100s from another, and have sometimes stood and watched while their vehicles were stolen right under their noses.

Not all P-100s are used for Podrace salvage. The droids are employed in fields from package delivery to search-and-rescue. On Coruscant, an entrepreneur imported thousands of P-100s in response to an infestation of stratt vermin in the city's underlevels. These modified salvage droids, equipped with stun blasters, proved entirely inept at recognizing and debilitating stratts. Once he realized he'd created a menace, the salesperson skipped the planet, leaving a small fleet of P-100s to roam corridors and skyways while they zapped pedestrians indiscriminately.

The P-100 isn't the only salvage droid on the Podracing circuit. Other common models include the Arakyd HL-444 hover loader, which also served as a Republic armament carrier during the Clone Wars.

> **"On the Baroonda track it was a busy day for the salvage droids, which scoured two square kilometers collecting Podracer pieces belonging to the late Turbo McMerrit."**
>
> —*From the Fode and Beed Show*

1. Visual Sensor
2. Terrain-Mapping Sensor
3. Durasteel Cap
4. Repulsorlift Engine
5. Pincer Arms

PIT DROID

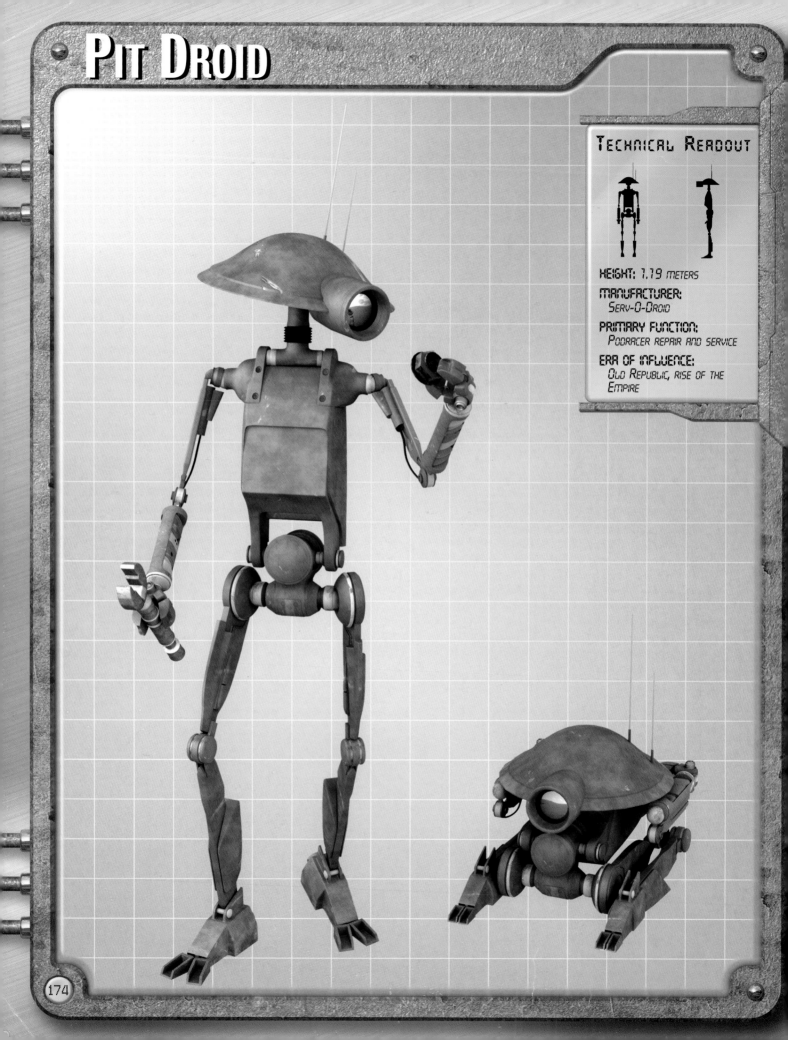

Serv-O-Droid DUM-Series Pit Droid

During its heyday, Serv-O-Droid boasted one of the broadest product lines in the droid industry by buying out smaller companies and then releasing their products under the Serv-O-Droid nameplate. The DUM series pit droid is a native product of Cyrillia, though you'd never know it from the advertising holos.

Cyrillia is an industrialized world in the Expansion Region. The reptilian Cyrillians developed the pit droid centuries ago as a maintenance unit for their turbine-powered floater transports. Cyrillians are as tall as Wookiees, but they built their tiny repair droids to scurry beneath hovering gale cars and climb into cramped circuitry bays.

The maintenance droids were efficient but unremarkable, a fact that changed when Cyrillia played host to a stop on the Podracing circuit from 189 to 122 B.B.Y. The Cyrillians started using fleets of their diminutive robots to fuel and service Podracers during pit stops—thus the modern pit droid was born.

The venue of the race eventually moved from Cyrillia to Baroonda, but by that time Serv-O-Droid had taken notice of the pit droid. Serv-O-Droid put up the money to construct modern manufacturing plants on Cyrillia, and to handle distribution and advertising for the finished product. The Cyrillians agreed to build the droids and to give up ownership in exchange for a cut of the profits.

The DUM series proved to be the most popular pit droid on the market, despite competitive products from Veril Line Systems and other manufacturers. Used in everything from Podraces to swoop rallies, DUM pit droids work with a fanatic intensity born from their limited programming. Their high-drain, high-energy work style demands frequent recharging.

DUM units come in five stock hues—gray, yellow, blue, orange, and red. Droids of the same color often work as teams. The droids understand verbal commands but can communicate only in chittering warbles comprehensible to other automata. DUMs possess visual, electromagnetic, microwave, and other specialized energy detectors to help them avoid the hazards of the Podrace track, though their danger sensors are far from foolproof.

High-torque joint motors enable pit droids to lift many times their own weight. This strength—combined with habitually manic personalities—can sometimes be perilous. If a confused pit droid happens to attempt a "repair" on an unstable fusion generator, for instance, a swift hit on its nose will cause it to switch off and fold into a compact bundle.

If the on/off nose switch is damaged, a pit droid may be nearly unstoppable. In such cases, the only solution might be a high-intensity blaster bolt.

> ***"Ody Mandrell:** Engine burned out on circuit after pit stop."*
>
> *—Official post-race listing from the Boonta Eve Classic, after the engine on Mandrell's racer sucked up a clumsy pit droid*

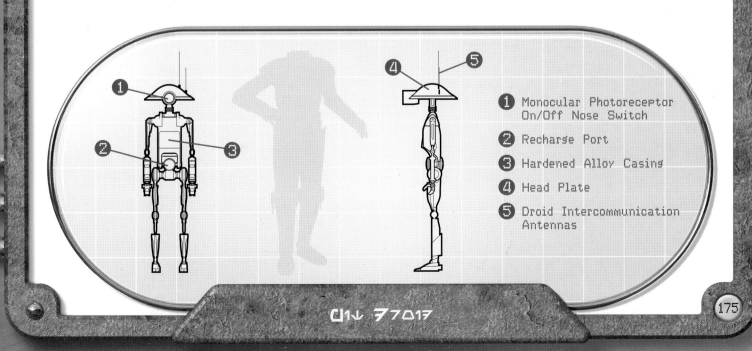

1. Monocular Photoreceptor On/Off Nose Switch
2. Recharge Port
3. Hardened Alloy Casing
4. Head Plate
5. Droid Intercommunication Antennas

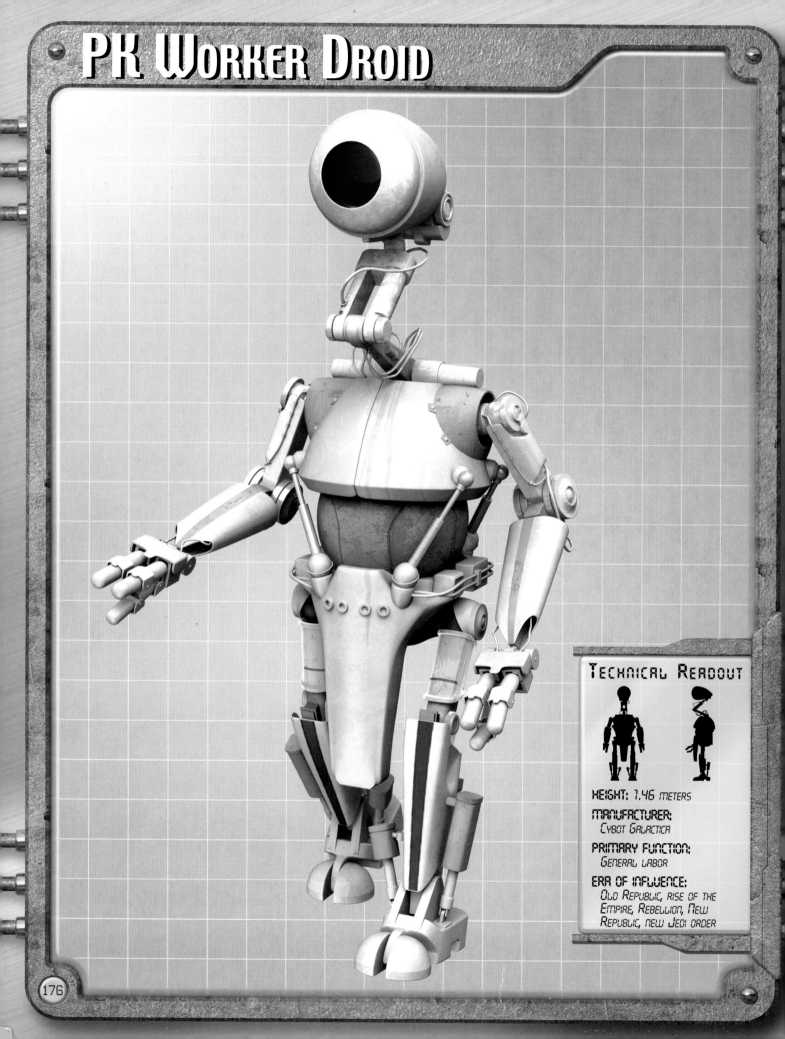

PK Worker Droid

TECHNICAL READOUT

HEIGHT: 1.46 meters

MANUFACTURER:
Cybot Galactica

PRIMARY FUNCTION:
General labor

ERA OF INFLUENCE:
Old Republic, Rise of the
Empire, Rebellion, New
Republic, New Jedi Order

Cybot Galactica PK-Series Worker Droid

Being crude labor units, PKs must envy their more glamorous production brethren at Cybot Galactica. Unlike 3PO units, PK workers can't hope for interaction with their owners beyond "mop up that fuel spill, Peekay-Seven" or "recharge those warming ovens, Peekay-Four."

The affordably priced PK worker droids are durable and versatile. They perform simple repairs, organize supplies, clean up offices, and inventory cargo. Their efficient internal batteries can last a long time between recharge sessions. The droids are tough enough to withstand extremes of temperature and radiation: PK units operate equally well inside furnaces, in reactor chambers, and in the vacuum of space.

PKs have rudimentary sensory gear, including a cyclopean photoreceptor and an auditory pickup. This equipment is mounted in a cranial unit that, thanks to a limber neck, can rotate 360 degrees. The droids are about the same height as an R2 unit, making them easy to transport and store.

PKs interact well with other automata. Consequently, they are often placed in the doubly demeaning position of having to answer to the whims of their organic masters and the needs of the so-called superior droid classes. In private, PKs often vent their frustrations by grumbling about "useless protocol gearheads."

The PK has been in service for centuries, selling in modest but profitable numbers. Prior to the Battle of Naboo, the Trade Federation began to buy every PK as soon as it rolled off the Telti assembly lines. As part of its secret military buildup, it planned to use the PKs to maintain its flocks of battle droids, droidekas, and vulture droid starfighters.

Republic agent Vyn Narcassan, already spearheading a covert investigation into the Trade Federation's Viceroy Directorate, saw a chance to plant moles within the notoriously tight-lipped Neimoidian organization. In secret meetings with Cybot Galactica's board of directors, Narcassan persuaded the corporation to engage in subterfuge for the good of the Republic.

One out of every four hundred PK worker droids was fitted with a communications intercept trap to passively record conversations and low-frequency transmissions. The equipment was nearly undetectable and designed to self-destruct in a melt of fused circuits, characteristic of an overheated motivator, in case of tampering. Republic Intelligence agents working as licensed Cybot technicians were to download information from the droids during standard maintenance visits, then hand-deliver it to Coruscant for analysis.

Unfortunately, Narcassan's program was initiated too late to provide advance warning of the Trade Federation's invasion of Naboo. The affected PK droids supplied limited intelligence data over the following decade, but few remained in service by the time of the Clone Wars. Many standard years later, the Imperial Security Bureau would undertake a similar monitoring program, by hiding spy circuitry inside RA-7 Death Star Droids.

> ## "PK units are my first recommendation for the espionage programming. After all, who notices a PK?"
>
> —*Republic Intelligence agent Vyn Narcassan*

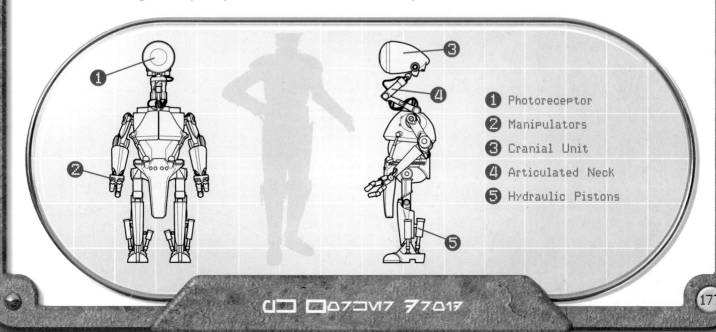

1. Photoreceptor
2. Manipulators
3. Cranial Unit
4. Articulated Neck
5. Hydraulic Pistons

POWER DROID

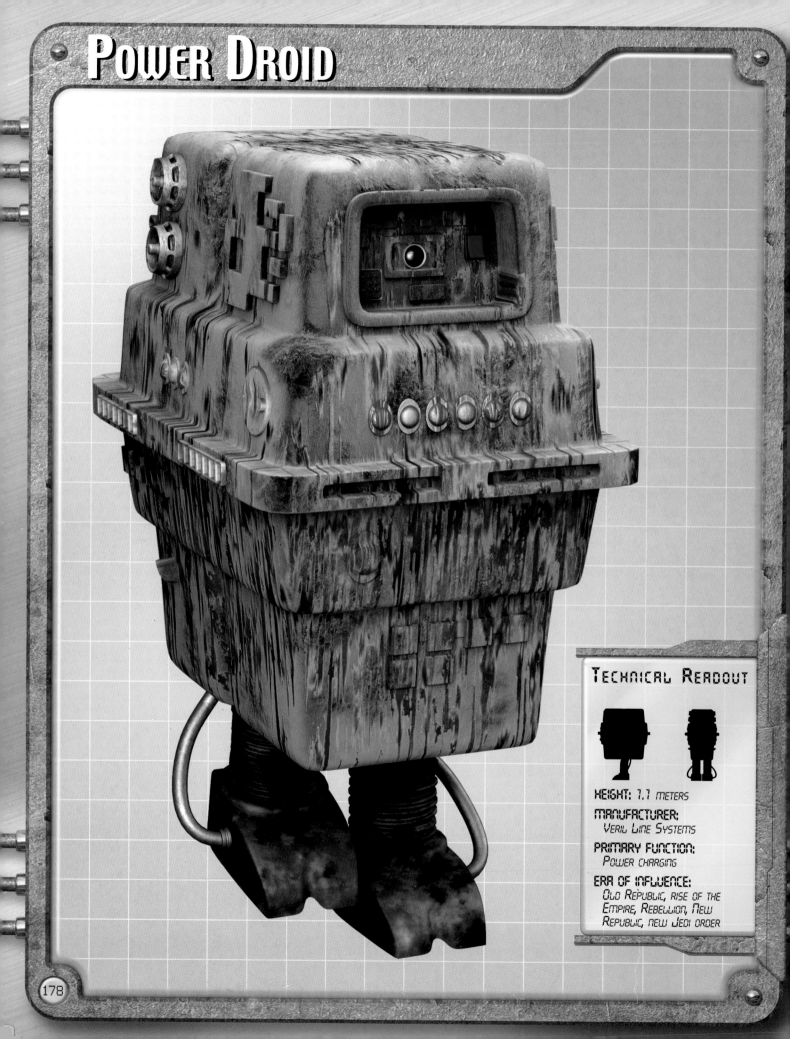

TECHNICAL READOUT

HEIGHT: 1.1 meters

MANUFACTURER:
Veril Line Systems

PRIMARY FUNCTION:
Power charging

ERA OF INFLUENCE:
Old Republic, rise of the Empire, Rebellion, New Republic, new Jedi order

Veril Line Systems EG-6 Power Droid

The power droid is an example of minimalist design at its most extreme. What could be simpler than a box with legs?

The droid's function is equally simplistic. It is a walking battery—an "ambulatory fusion generator," as Veril Line Systems refers to it in the company's sales materials. The job of a power droid is to provide energy to mechanical devices in cases where it's impractical to rely on a permanent power grid, a common situation on backworlds or in large, busy spaces such as a repair bay or starship hangar.

Most of a power droid's body consists of its internal fusion generator. Multiple layers of armor and safety shutdowns help protect the generator from an accidental breach. Internal cooling fluid channels regulate the temperature of the generator, and, in emergencies, small relief valves along the chassis and on the bases of both feet can bleed off vaporizing coolant fluid as steam.

The power droid lacks a recognizable face. The few buttons and gadgets in its upper panel include a visual sensor and an acoustic signaler capable of droid languages only. A power port on the front panel can accommodate standard plugs, while a larger port on the side of most models fits industrial-size hookups. The power droid has a single, delicate arm, which is normally hidden behind a tiny portal.

Each power droid comes with a systems diagnostic package that includes a spectrometer, an X-ray scanner, an infrared scanner, and a sonar-pulse emitter. The droid uses these devices to scan the equipment it has been asked to service for leaks or hairline cracks. If its diagnosis falls outside of its preprogrammed red-line limits, the droid will refuse to fuel the item. This last personality trait has given power droids a reputation for stubbornness.

Stubbornness and stupidity, that is. If told to walk in a straight line, power droids will march off a precipice, their feet pumping in midair as they fall to their destruction. In vertical cities such as those on Nar Shaddaa and Coruscant, power droids require close supervision—or, at the very least, guardrails.

For centuries, Veril Line Systems has dominated the power droid market. Its most popular model is the EG-6, and it also offers a heavier industrial version released under the designation S9. Veril's biggest competitor in the energy-supply market is Industrial Automaton, whose release of the GNK droid was widely viewed as a feature-for-feature conceptual theft of the EG-6.

It's nearly impossible to crack the shell of a power droid—but if the shell *is* for some reason pierced, the generator explodes with stunning force. The pirate Reginald Barkbone escaped from the Emperor's Royal Guards on Axion by palming a limpet mine onto a power droid, then shooting his way out in the ensuing detonation and chaos.

> ### "Gonk, gonk."
>
> *—Power droid vocalization so common, it has become the droid's nickname*

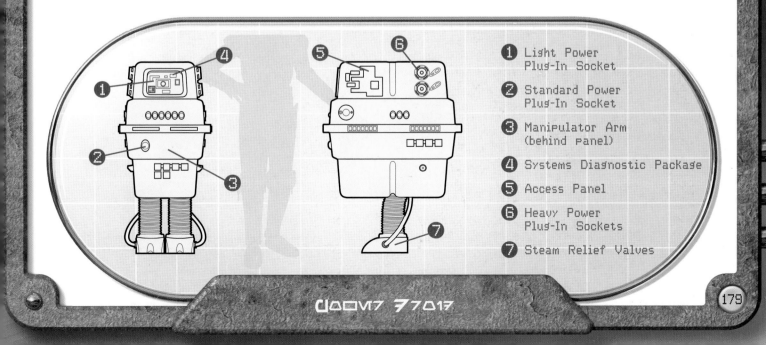

1. Light Power Plug-In Socket
2. Standard Power Plug-In Socket
3. Manipulator Arm (behind panel)
4. Systems Diagnostic Package
5. Access Panel
6. Heavy Power Plug-In Sockets
7. Steam Relief Valves

Prowler 1000

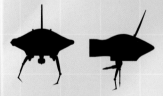

TECHNICAL READOUT

HEIGHT: 0.5 meter

MANUFACTURER:
Arakyd Industries

PRIMARY FUNCTIONS:
Exploration, surveillance

ERA OF INFLUENCE:
Rise of the Empire

Arakyd Prowler 1000 Exploration Droid

Looking at the Arakyd Prowler, it's difficult to imagine that such a small droid could have given rise to a lineage of increasingly fearsome successors. The Prowler's great-great-grandchild, the Arakyd HK, is capable of swallowing starships.

Arakyd Industries became a member of the Techno Union during the decades leading up to the Clone Wars. A manufacturer of exploration and security droids, Arakyd had a reputation for cold-edged ruthlessness that it expressed through a vaguely menacing design philosophy. The Prowler 1000 is one of the few exceptions to the rule, since its tortapo-shell chassis and its nervous habit of bobbing on its repulsorlifts render it somewhat charming.

The Prowler, introduced a few years after the Battle of Naboo, initially served as an exploration droid for scouting alien terrain. Its secondary function was to assist police departments with surveillance and forensics work. The droid's fish-eye photoreceptor can record its environment through a multiplicity of magnifications and spectrum filters. Other sensors, as well as a spotlight, enable the Prowler to function in darkness.

Its delicate, dangling manipulator arms are tipped with sensors that can analyze the chemical composition of any substance. Prowlers can also be equipped with heavier manipulators for lifting and carrying samples. Antennas with surface-to-orbit range allow the droid to receive signals from waiting control ships. Although Prowlers aren't equipped with weapons, an engineer could add lightweight blasters with only minimal rewiring.

Arakyd sold a number of its explorational units, including the Prowler, to Chancellor Palpatine and the Republic. When Count Dooku emerged and formed the Confederacy of Independent Systems, the Techno Union joined the Separatist cause. As a Techno Union member, Arakyd went along with the move, and saw its Republic contracts evaporate.

Arakyd CEO Hordis Boil took heart, however, when agents in Palpatine's inner circle asked him to spy on Techno Union foreman Wat Tambor. In return for Boil's intelligence, Palpatine requested that the Kaminoans outfit the clone army with Arakyd products purchased through a shell corporation.

Arakyd Prowlers became standard clone trooper tools for keeping track of enemy troop movements. On Utapau, clone commander Cody dispatched several Prowlers into the catacombs in search of Obi-Wan Kenobi, following the Jedi's escape from the Order Sixty-six ambush. The explorations of the droids disturbed a mother nos monster, who decided the intruders were coming too close to her babies and swallowed them whole.

Following the Clone Wars, Palpatine nationalized the Techno Union. Arakyd was allowed to remain intact, and, in fact, it inherited the assets of many dismantled Techno Union corporations. This resurgence marked the beginning of a close relationship between Arakyd and the Empire.

> **"We've lost General Kenobi's trail, sir, as well as all contact with Prowlers numbered one through fourteen. Permission to deploy our final batch?"**
>
> —*Clone trooper CT-307, reporting to his commander on Utapau*

1. Floodlight
2. Photoreceptor/Detection Array
3. Grappling Extensors
4. Tasking Antenna
5. Light Blaster

RICKSHAW DROID

TECHNICAL READOUT

HEIGHT: 2.75 METERS

MANUFACTURER:
Serv-o-Droid

PRIMARY FUNCTIONS:
General labor, Livery

ERA OF INFLUENCE:
Old Republic, rise of the
Empire, Rebellion, New
Republic, new Jedi order

Serv-O-Droid RIC General Labor Droid

Serv-O-Droid's RIC model has earned the nickname "rickshaw droid," though its manufacturer never designed it for that purpose. The RIC is a general labor unit, and only a few of the millions of units in service have found employment as rickshaw-pulling livery operators.

Serv-O-Droid has manufactured the RIC for more than seven standard centuries. Simple cognitive modules keep manufacturing costs down and help make RIC units exceptionally obedient. Photoreceptors and a single audio pickup feed sensory data to the RIC's electronic brain, while the droid can vocalize through an outsize broadcast speaker. RIC units can speak no more than two languages, usually Basic and binary, though it's common on Rim worlds for the Basic skillware to be swapped out in favor of the dominant local language.

A unipod wheel is the droid's most distinguishing feature. The wheel drives the droid at speeds up to sixty-five kilometers per hour, while internal balance gyros keep the droid upright at all times. The shock-resistant chassis seals off the droid's inner workings from moisture and grit. Most RIC units are marked with dents and scratches from years spent working outdoors. The three-fingered gripper hands are strong enough to bend metal, yet delicate enough for simple mechanical repairs.

In their centuries of service, RIC droids have been used in nearly every line of work. To unlicensed rickshaw operators in the Rim Territories, RICs represent the perfect combination of low cost, toughness, and gyroscopic stabilization—to ensure that they never dump a passenger. On worlds from Sluis Van to Muunilinst, RIC drivers carry commuters around town in repulsorlift-buoyed rickshaw carriages.

Unless the fare is paid in advance, usually by means of a credit-stick box bolted onto the droid's back, RICs will take their fares on meandering tours of the city's back streets in order to drive up their fee. In the settlement of Mos Espa on Tatooine, visitors have become familiar with a local rickshaw droid named ES-PSA, or "Espasa."

Closer to the Core, RIC units are recognized as stars in the droid sport of nuna-ball, in which a puffed-up nuna animal is batted between robotic teams in an effort to score on the opponent's goal. The game grew out of a production stress test but has become wildly popular, in part because of the mechanical carnage that sometimes follows when the losing team becomes aggravated. Serv-O-Droid has fielded a team of RIC units since the creation of nuna-ball. In fact, due to the nimbleness of the droids, they regularly beat competitors—including Industrial Automaton's asp team and Veril Line System's Otoga squad.

> ## "RIC-9 passes to RIC-11. He passes to RIC-8. It's RIC-8 up the middle . . . He shoots—*Nuuuuunaaaaaa!*"
>
> *—Nuna-ball announcer Horassa Hunanga, describing Serv-O-Droid's winning goal to capture the Mid Rim pennant*

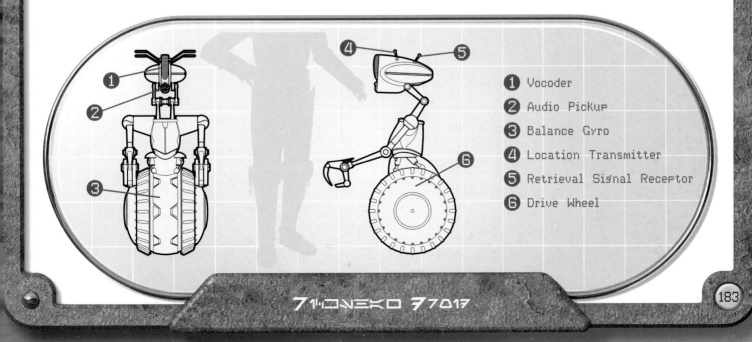

1. Vocoder
2. Audio Pickup
3. Balance Gyro
4. Location Transmitter
5. Retrieval Signal Receptor
6. Drive Wheel

SRT Droid

TECHNICAL READOUT

HEIGHT: 2.75 meters

MANUFACTURER:
Baktoid Combat Automata

PRIMARY FUNCTION:
Cargo hauling

ERA OF INFLUENCE:
Rise of the Empire, Rebellion,
New Republic, New Jedi Order

Baktoid Combat Automata SRT Autonomous Short-Range Transport

The SRT is a heavy industrial droid designed for brutal work. In factory environments, it operates around the clock, and most burn out their original components in less than a standard year.

SRT is an acronym for "short-range transport," an accurate descriptor for a droid designed to carry raw materials, tools, and finished products from one factory hub to another. Inside vast foundries, such as the droidworks of Geonosis, SRT units act as de facto overseers for the entire operation. SRTs cruise through multi-leveled hives on repulsorlifts, ensuring that no conveyer belts are jammed, and that all fuel stores and parts bins are topped off.

An operation like the one on Geonosis consumed incalculable resources and spit out endless numbers of soldiers. SRT droids are responsible for keeping both the input and output ends of the process running smoothly. A power spoke located in the heart of the factory allows SRTs to recharge, though this respite lasts only a few minutes.

The Geonosian SRTs are products of Baktoid Combat Automata, and work inside the same factories where they first came into existence. Each droid has an enormous ellipse of a head featuring heat-shielded photoreceptors and a radar-mapping sensor node. Two multi-jointed arms enable the SRT to heft loads; each hand ends with two fingers that are slender enough to operate factory controls.

"It's a nightmare!"

—C-3PO, carried off by an SRT droid inside the Geonosis factory

A thick front pallet provides the SRT's load-carrying surface, and the droid's commercial-grade repulsorlift engine can support up to ten times its own weight. Baktoid's SRTs are not particularly intelligent, focusing on the job at hand. Although they can communicate only in droid languages, SRTs are in constant contact with the factory central computers, receiving commands input at any remote terminal.

Slight variations on the SRT design are common throughout the galaxy, and are sold by dozens of competing droid companies. Publictechnic's model includes a four-sided bin instead of a flat pallet, and the manufacturer sells the SRT to construction companies. Other groups, including Go-Corp/Utilitech, sell SRTs with fully enclosed, boxcar-like carrying areas. They have met with great success selling the unit to municipal governments as a garbage collector.

On worlds with a great number of construction projects, it's common to see SRTs crisscrossing the sky as they deliver tools or dump loads of rubble. Knowing this, lawbreakers sometimes load contraband—including spice, slaves, and crystalline vertices—into SRT beds in the hope that authorities won't bother to search the big droids. In this fashion, a squad of Republic ARC troopers hijacked a work crew of SRTs in order to sneak behind Separatist lines prior to the Battle of Byblos.

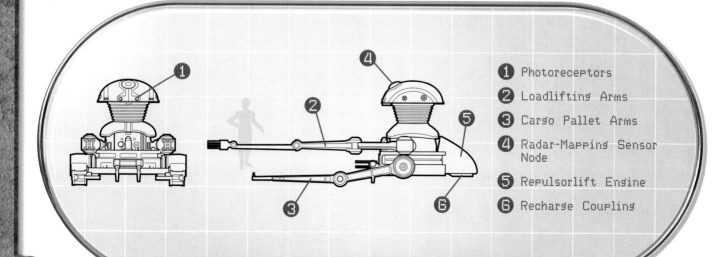

1. Photoreceptors
2. Loadlifting Arms
3. Cargo Pallet Arms
4. Radar-Mapping Sensor Node
5. Repulsorlift Engine
6. Recharge Coupling

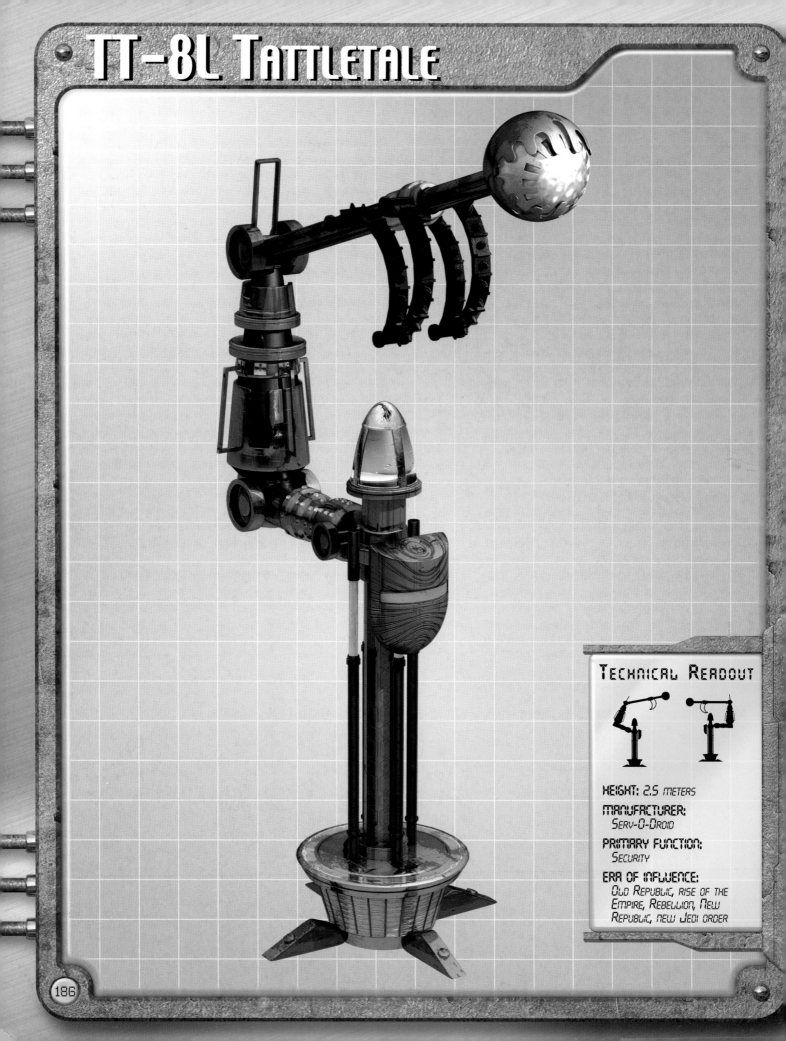

TT-8L Tattletale

Technical Readout

HEIGHT: 2.5 METERS

MANUFACTURER: SERV-O-DROID

PRIMARY FUNCTION: SECURITY

ERA OF INFLUENCE: OLD REPUBLIC, RISE OF THE EMPIRE, REBELLION, NEW REPUBLIC, NEW JEDI ORDER

Serv-O-Droid TT-8L Gatekeeper Droid

When readers of *Popular Automaton* voted, they overwhelmingly named the TT-8L "most annoying" in the holomag's annual rankings of the droid industry. The Tattletale elicits such ire because it acts as a gatekeeper, and not everyone is important enough to make it inside.

Originally built by Serv-O-Droid as a tool for the gentrified rich, the TT-8L Tattletale has been working as a vestibule snoop for more than four thousand standard years. Many models have been produced over the centuries, from the slightly menacing Y7 to the gilded, bauble-trimmed XSS.

The TT-8L is little more than an eye on a stalk. It remains in a fixed position for its operational life, usually installed near a doorway or inside a lobby. An approaching visitor's footfalls trigger the unit's audio sensors, whereupon it scans the newcomer, compares physical parameters against its internal database, and announces the guest's arrival to its master, who can either admit the visitor or request further observation.

The obvious objection—that this job could be easily performed by a nonintelligent security holocam for much less money—explained why Serv-O-Droid initially marketed the TT-8L to wealthy nobles accustomed to servants and hirelings. This elite sales strategy eventually reached its gaudy pinnacle in the fabulously ornate XSS.

Equipped with a snake-like body stalk cast from antique brass, the TT-8L/XSS is bolted to the floor but allowed a limited range of movement through its multiple joints. Its blue-tinted-glass optical lens functions much like a pair of macrobinoculars and is protected by a bronze shutter when inactive. The droid's entire two-and-a-half-meter length is a showcase for intricate scrollwork designs, sparkling silver adornments, and inlaid synthetic gemstones.

The Y7 model was developed when Serv-O-Droid realized that its observation machine had many potential uses beyond simple nosiness. Criminals, recluses, and paranoids had great need for a device that could interrogate suspicious callers and scan them for weapons. Instead of being meekly secretive, this new model was aggressively confrontational.

A TT-8L/Y7 is designed for direct installation in a door, a door frame, or an entranceway alcove. Its rigid body stem lacks the serpentine fluidity of the XSS frame, possessing only a single socket joint at the base of the trunk. All unnecessary ornamentation has been omitted in favor of a basic black shell of resilient durasteel. The Y7's central eye, shielded by a retractable blind, is capable of low-light surveys, spotlight illumination, and scanning sweeps in the ultraviolet and infrared ranges. Because the droid's unremarkable intelligence matrix wasn't always enough to please the truly distrustful, Serv-O-Droid installed a remote-activation subroutine allowing the Y7 to be controlled directly by a security guard at any time.

> **"The overcoat is a nice touch, but white pants with toumon boots? Come back when your eyespots can perceive style."**
>
> *—Glambot, the obnoxious TT-8L gatekeeper at Coruscant's Club Caraveg*

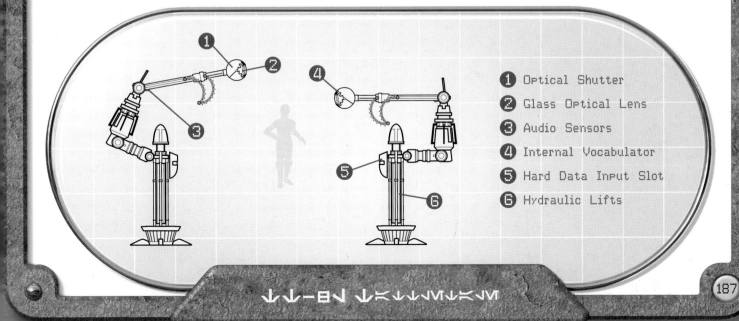

1 Optical Shutter
2 Glass Optical Lens
3 Audio Sensors
4 Internal Vocabulator
5 Hard Data Input Slot
6 Hydraulic Lifts

WED Treadwell

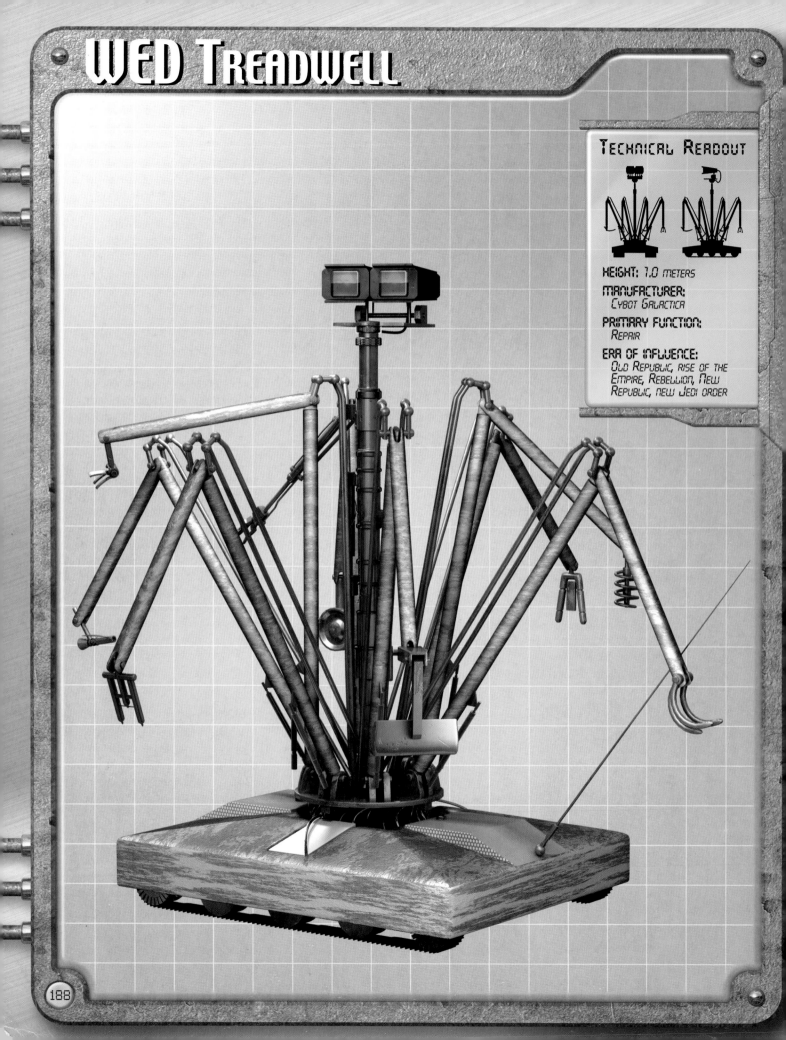

TECHNICAL READOUT

HEIGHT: 1.0 meters

MANUFACTURER: Cybot Galactica

PRIMARY FUNCTION: Repair

ERA OF INFLUENCE: Old Republic, rise of the Empire, Rebellion, New Republic, new Jedi order

Cybot Galactica WED Treadwell Repair Droid

Some pilots swear by their astromechs, but for the vast majority of the galaxy, there's no better repair droid than the WED Treadwell.

Cybot Galactica introduced the current Treadwell line more than seven standard centuries ago, and modifications since then have been mostly cosmetic. The droid *works*. Its simple design is unlikely to be topped anytime soon—at least not at such a low price.

The Treadwell derives its name from the two wide treads that drive it, but its main selling point is its arms. The thin, jointed limbs extend from the droid's base and fold up against the central shaft when not in use, evoking the insectile silhouette of the Storini glass prowler. Four arms come standard, though the Treadwell has sockets for many more. Easily detachable and transposable, each arm contains integrated tools specific to whatever task might be requested by the droid's owner. It's not unusual to encounter Treadwells operating as house painters or tree pruners well outside the confines of repair bays.

Extending from the body is a telescoping neck, which supports a head made up of a pair of binocular photoreceptors capable of magnifying objects up to one thousand times. The Treadwell has a primitive vocabulator that enables it to warble and hoot in a machine language understood by most other droids.

> **"Check this out—arc welder, hydrospanner, fusioncutter, spot sprayer, foam sealant, torque wrench, and power calibrator. My Tread's a mobile multitool."**
>
> *—X-wing mechanic Cubber Daine*

With their long arms, Treadwells can reach areas inaccessible to stubby-bodied astromechs. And the price is hard to beat. Treadwells typically sell for less than similar models, and a thriving pre-owned market exists for used Treadwells and their specialty arms.

The low cost has its drawbacks. Treadwells aren't terribly bright; they sometimes make simple repair mistakes that can cause damage to the job or to themselves. Their arms are easily broken, and the ten wheels that drive the treads can become jammed by grit or sand. On the other hand, a well-maintained Treadwell can remain in service for generations and still be barely distinguishable from a new model on the factory showroom floor. Furthermore, when a Treadwell reaches a point beyond repair, it's no great hardship to simply buy a new one.

The Treadwell's fans—and they are many—point out that the droid's flaws can be overcome by an owner skilled enough to reprogram a diagnostic circuitry matrix. An enthusiast subculture has grown up around the cult of the "tricked-out Treadwell." Many knockoff models exist, including Kalibac Industries' NR-5 maintenance droid, and the Treadwell's radial-arm design has been copied in Medtech's line of FX medical assistants.

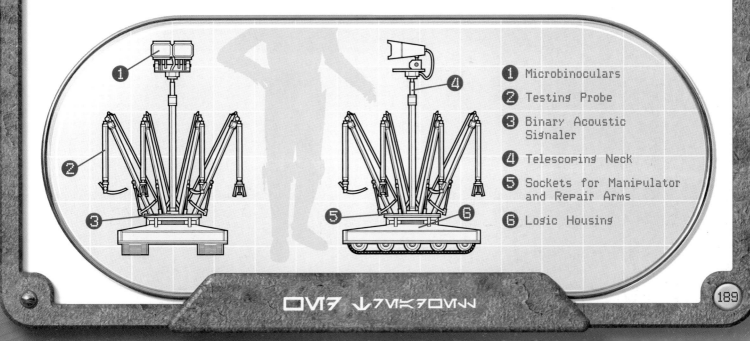

1. Microbinoculars
2. Testing Probe
3. Binary Acoustic Signaler
4. Telescoping Neck
5. Sockets for Manipulator and Repair Arms
6. Logic Housing

CYBORGS

Cyborgs are humans or other organic beings with mechanical parts. As such they are not true droids, but their fates are intertwined with those of automata in the areas of technology and culture.

Cyborgs fall into one of five categories, depending on their type of implant:

- **Prosthetic cyborgs** have artificial limbs. Some prosthetics are constructed from metal or plastic components; others are indistinguishable from organic parts thanks to synthskin coverings. During the Clone Wars, Anakin Skywalker bore a skeletal arm of the first type, while Luke Skywalker received a human-looking artificial hand following his battle at Cloud City.

- **Implant cyborgs** have artificial components not visible to outside eyes. These internal enhancements are used to replace dead or dying parts, or to augment bodies beyond their natural abilities. The replacement of organs is common on worlds such as Bakura, where citizens regularly live to ages of 160 standard years and beyond. All sports-governing bodies have banned the use of muscle-stim implants, corneal-sharpening lenses, adrenaline pumps, and skeletal stiffeners. Mercenaries and private militias, particularly those operating out of Hutt or Bothan space, are known to use augmenting bio-implants.

- **Bio-linked cyborgs** plug their brains into computer bands worn around the head. Such devices provide a wealth of data far beyond what any organic could normally experience, but the interface often leaves the user uninterested in social contact. The Biotech Aj^6 and other computer bands can be wirelessly linked to mainframes for even greater power. Bio-linked cyborgs often act as liaisons between a city's administrative staff and its central computer.

- **Rebuilt cyborgs** have bodies that are almost entirely machines, with the exclusion of their brains, at a minimum. Darth Vader falls at the low end of this category, while the Empire's shadow droids mark the uppermost extreme. Often, rebuilt cyborgs achieve their state as a result of catastrophic injury. Notable examples of rebuilt cyborgs include Kligson, the operator of Droid World, and the bounty hunter Valance, who tried to conceal his condition with a mask of synthskin. The half-mechanical army built by the Arkanian Renegades in 50 B.B.Y., whose members included Gorm the Dissolver, are considered rebuilt cyborgs.

- **Symbiont cyborgs** are not always categorized as true cyborgs, and some are considered a distinct classification unto themselves. Symbionts are droids paired with living beings. A successful symbiont will retain aspects from both intelligences. JK bio-droids and Iron Knights are examples of this rare fusing of the natural and the artificial.

Parts used by a cyborg are similar, or even identical, to those used on droids. While not everyone will wear an arm salvaged from a juggernaut war droid, cyborgs have a vested interest in the advancement of droid technology.

Cultural pressures on cyborgs are great. They bear the weight of anti-droid prejudice, without the mechanical disassociation that allows many droids to live in ignorance.

The Jedi were unconsciously complicit in this bias during the days of the Old Republic. Believing that mechanical devices had no place in the living Force, they viewed cyborging with distaste. Though some exceptions existed among their own ranks, including the Sith War champion Cay Qel-Droma, the study and mastery of machines became the domain of the Sith.

After the rise of the Empire, a number of prominent Imperial officials sported visible cyborg prosthetics, leading many to associate their atrocities with the metal enhancements they wore.

B'omarr Brain Walker

TECHNICAL READOUT

HEIGHT: 1.7 meters

MANUFACTURER:
Arakyd Industries (frame only)

PRIMARY FUNCTION:
Brain locomotion

ERA OF INFLUENCE:
Old Republic, rise of the Empire,
Rebellion, New Republic

Rebuilt Arakyd BT-16 Perimeter Droid

The B'omarr brain walker meets the minimum accepted standard for a cyborg, defined as a brain hooked up to a responsive mechanical frame. In this case, the frame is a modified BT-16 perimeter droid, a fact that has led to some confusion in classification.

To outsiders, the B'omarr cyborging process is off-puttingly disturbing. To the B'omarr monks, however, removing someone's brain is a great privilege. The B'omarr believe that the only way to achieve enlightenment is to rid oneself of the flesh and become a disembodied intellect.

Generations ago, an enclave of B'omarr ascetics set up shop on Tatooine. Among the dunes, the monks constructed a brooding monastery of iron and durasteel, which shut them off from the local population.

After years of meditation, the most advanced believers had no further use for the distractions of the body. In a holy ceremony, the lesser B'omarr acolytes sharpened their scalpels and surgically removed the brains from their masters' skulls. Each lumpy gray mass was dropped into a clear jar of nutrient fluid and arranged on a shelf in the subterranean Great Room of the Enlightened.

But even a brain needs to get out once in a while. For this purpose, the B'omarr attendants assembled a series of armatures built with parts from Arakyd's BT-16. The monks threw out the BT-16's repeating blaster and ventral sensor globe to make room for a brain jar to be affixed to the underbelly of the framework.

The brain walkers have since been modified from their BT-16 origins and no longer follow a single design pattern. Some have gripper claws, some do not; some have only four legs, some have as many as nine. Almost all, however, have speakers and audio sensors and a row of colored lights at the base of the shatterproof jar. These lights glow blue and green under normal conditions. Bright red indicates that the brain is "screaming" and unable to adjust to its strange new state.

Jabba the Hutt turned the B'omarr monastery into his personal pleasure palace and forced the religious order into the lowest subcorridors. This change made the monks even more eager to initiate others into their way of life—so eager, in fact, that they forcibly removed a few reluctant brains following the Hutt's death at the Great Pit of Carkoon.

It's unclear whether Arakyd knew about the bizarre functions their droids had been used to fulfill on Tatooine, but the company introduced a completely redesigned BT-16 just prior to the Battle of Yavin. This new model borrowed heavily from the design of MerenData's TS-Arach pest-control droid. The Empire purchased many for use aboard the first Death Star, but the battle station exploded before the BT-16s could begin their tours of duty.

> **"You have progressed rapidly on your spiritual path, Brother Fortuna. Prepare yourself for enlightenment."**
>
> *—B'omarr monk to Bib Fortuna, prior to forcibly removing the latter's brain*

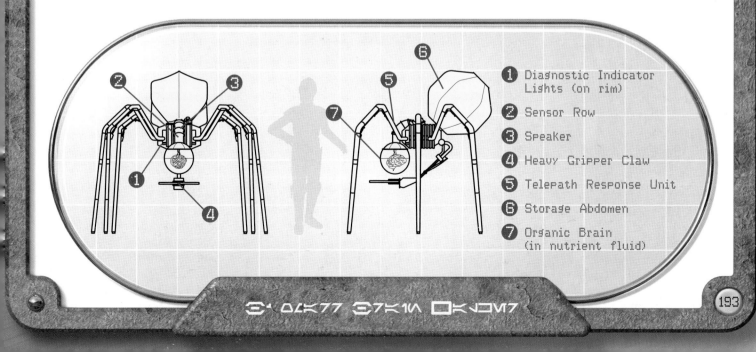

1. Diagnostic Indicator Lights (on rim)
2. Sensor Row
3. Speaker
4. Heavy Gripper Claw
5. Telepath Response Unit
6. Storage Abdomen
7. Organic Brain (in nutrient fluid)

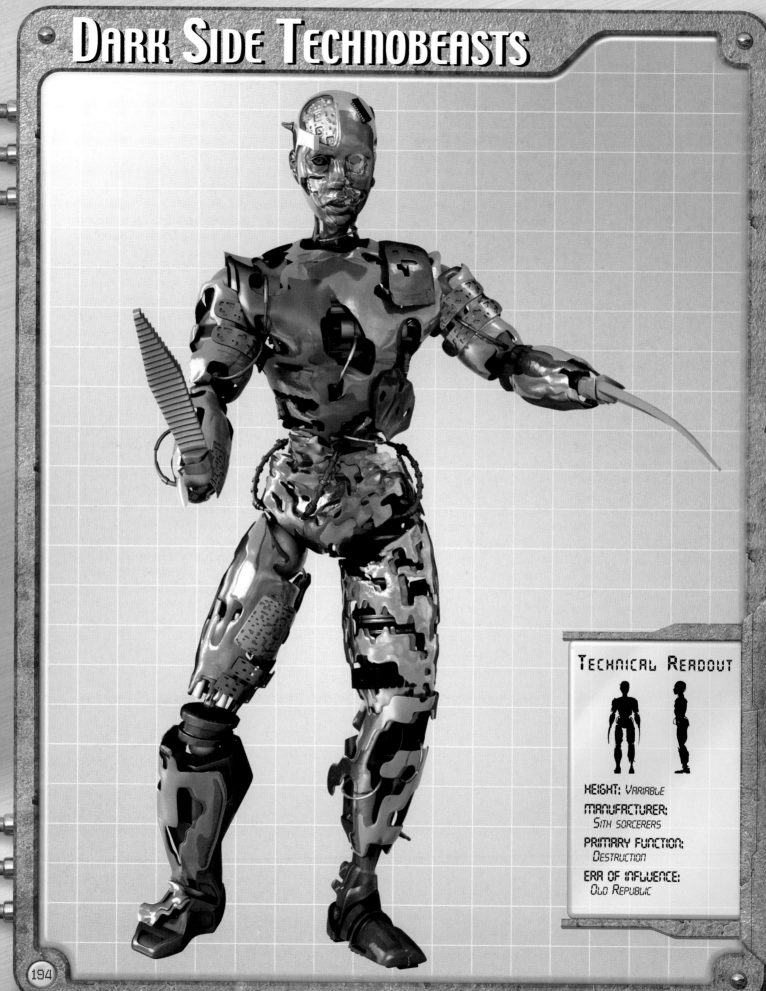

DARK SIDE TECHNOBEASTS

TECHNICAL READOUT

HEIGHT: Variable

MANUFACTURER: Sith sorcerers

PRIMARY FUNCTION: Destruction

ERA OF INFLUENCE: Old Republic

Sith Alchemic Technobeasts

Technobeasts are true Sith abominations. Their very existence is proof of the evils perpetuated during the New Sith Wars, when dark side magicians strove to pervert the balance of the Force.

Because droids are not organic beings, they were a subject few Jedi bothered to understand. Jedi powers that had a technical influence were usually crude, such as the Force ability *mechu macture,* or, as more commonly known, "destroy droid." The Sith went farther than the Jedi ever did, developing the ability *mechu-deru* to allow for Force control over mechanical systems. In true Sith fashion, the power stressed absolute control, turning droids into puppets.

In 1250 B.B.Y., Sith Lord Belia Darzu delved even deeper, using the principles of *mechu-deru* to create alchemic technology that *hungered.* Darzu's technovirus seed could replicate itself by converting organic material into circuitry nodes. A victim infected with the technovirus would rapidly turn into a hideous droid-human hybrid. Lord Darzu called these pitiable creatures technobeasts, and the technique became known as *mechu-deru vitae.*

A technovirus seed could be as small as a mold spore. Once it touched a victim's skin, it replicated by feeding on living tissue, growing to a metallic, fist-size tumor within minutes. The virus's primitive self-preservation instincts caused it to follow neurons up to the brain, where it lobotomized the frontal lobes to make its host incapable of higher thought. At this point, the conversion to technobeast was irreversible.

Technobeasts were never alike, save for their lumpy asymmetry where chunks of metal had replaced living components. The virus sometimes built over its own work multiple times, leaving behind zigzags of metallic scar tissue. The collective consciousness of the technovirus seeds seemed to have a curiosity regarding humanoid biology that expressed itself through experimentation. Technobeasts might have multiple heads, or scuttle about on crab-like pincers. Many had arms that ended in skewers or saw blades. A single technobeast could release a cloud of nanospores that could infect hundreds of other victims.

Technobeasts became the signature horror of the Sictis Wars, a subset of the New Sith Wars that lasted from 1250 to 1230 B.B.Y. One Jedi combatant became infected with the technovirus but kept his identity through the Force, serving the galaxy for decades as the "technobeast Jedi."

The death of Belia Darzu on Tython brought an end to the creation of new hybrids. Nevertheless, subsequent Sith Lords would bring them back in smaller numbers until the end of the New Sith Wars at the Battle of Ruusan.

> **"Maggot of metal, rust, and rot. Sith life draws breath, old life does not."**
>
> —*Sith* mechu-deru vitae *incantation, in the rhyming style popular during the Effulem era*

1. Lobotomized Brain
2. Nanospore Pores
3. Saw Blade
4. Cutting Blade
5. Metallic Tumor
6. Metallic Growths

GENERAL GRIEVOUS

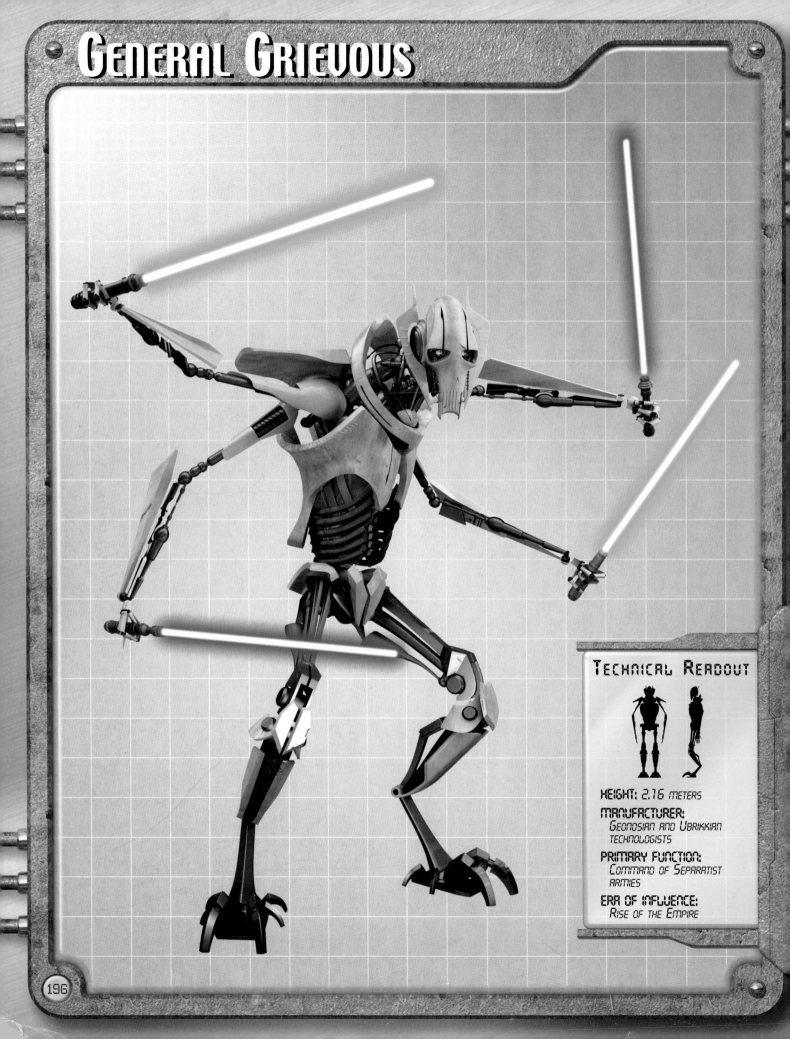

TECHNICAL READOUT

HEIGHT: 2.16 METERS

MANUFACTURER: GEONOSIAN AND UBRIKKIAN TECHNOLOGISTS

PRIMARY FUNCTION: COMMAND OF SEPARATIST ARMIES

ERA OF INFLUENCE: RISE OF THE EMPIRE

Custom Geonosian Cybernetic Frame

Grievous had a body of metal and armorplast, and always appeared in battle flanked by IG 100 MagnaGuards. Most assumed he was a droid himself, but Grievous considered that to be an unforgivable insult. He was a cyborg, though his yellow reptilian eyes remained as the only external evidence of his former life.

On the colony worlds of the Kaleesh, Grievous led his people in battle against the rival Huk. Grievous's appeals for help from the Jedi went unanswered. Darth Sidious, however, noted the warlord's skill, and ensured that Grievous would suffer near-death injuries in a prearranged shuttle crash. Brought back to consciousness inside a bacta tank, Grievous agreed under duress to become a general for the Confederacy of Independent Systems in exchange for aid to the people of Kalee. The only way he would see continued life was as a cyborg.

> ## "I am Grievous, warlord of the Kaleesh and Supreme Commander of the armies of the Confederacy. *And I am not a droid.*"
>
> —*General Grievous*

Geonosian engineers, with funding from the InterGalactic Banking Clan, had achieved a cyborging breakthrough. Their new techniques, tested on a number of tragic victims prior to their use on Grievous, involved brain augmentation to make the subject better able to exploit the increased strength, speed, and reaction time of a computerized droid frame.

The Ubrikkian droids that performed the surgery on Grievous preserved his brain, eyes, spinal cord, and internal organs. But even these parts received cybernetic modifications. Cerebellum implants upgraded Grievous's body coordination, fed him heuristic combat programming, and tampered with his emotions, making him more quick to anger. His eyes received internal implants to increase the sharpness of his vision and to protect them in vacuum. Most reports state that Grievous had no Force abilities, but rumors persist that he received a midi-chlorian-rich blood transfusion from the body of the late Jedi Master Sifo-Dyas.

The general's armorplast body featured magnetized talons to clamp onto the deck of a starship or a hapless victim. His two arms could split at the shoulders and become four, each hand with its own opposable thumb and two fingers. His face became a traditional Kaleesh mask, based on those carved from the skulls of mumuus and marked with dark lines of karabba blood above each eye. The "teeth" of Grievous's mask incorporated the speaker grille of an ultrasonic vocabulator.

Duranium chest plating protected the pressurized gutsac containing Grievous's internal organs. The general wore a cape similar to the one he had worn on Kalee, with inner pockets to hold the lightsabers he collected from vanquished Jedi.

The Geonosian cyborging process used to re-create Grievous wasn't perfect. Injuries sustained in a fight with Mace Windu left Grievous's organs damaged, and the automated armature could not compensate. General Grievous remained plagued by a wheezing cough until his death on Utapau following numerous blaster shots care of Obi-Wan Kenobi. An improved version of the same technology would be used to complete Anakin Skywalker's transformation into Darth Vader.

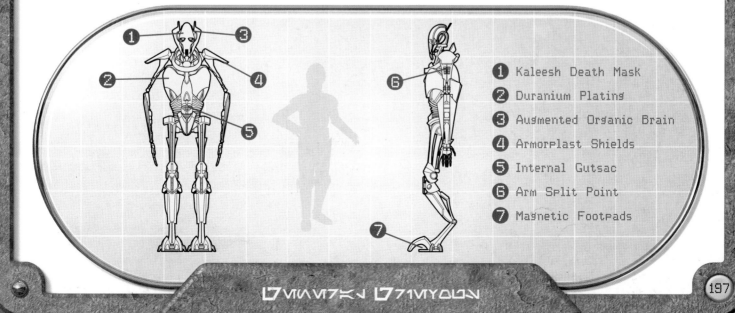

1. Kaleesh Death Mask
2. Duranium Plating
3. Augmented Organic Brain
4. Armorplast Shields
5. Internal Gutsac
6. Arm Split Point
7. Magnetic Footpads

Iron Knight

TECHNICAL READOUT

HEIGHT: Variable (1.6 meters for Justice Droid body)

MANUFACTURER: Various

PRIMARY FUNCTION: Preservation of the Republic

ERA OF INFLUENCE: Rise of the Empire, New Republic, New Jedi Order

198

Unique Crystalline/Electronic Ambulatory Symbiont

The planet Orax is home to an intelligent crystalline species known as the Shard. Like the crystal entities of Nam Chorios, the inhabitants of Orax defy most rules of biology. Immobile and composed of crystalline minerals, they fail most definitions of life, yet are undeniably intelligent.

Some Shards found their way offworld inside the body cavities of droids, where their consciousness and the artificial intelligence of the droids created a unique symbiont relationship. The Shard personality does not overwrite the droid personality; rather, the two meld together into a single persona containing aspects of both.

One Force-sensitive Shard, Ilum, gave birth to crystal splitlings who inhabited their own droids. A nonconformist Sunesi Jedi Master, Aqinos, agreed to train Ilum and her children in the ways of the Jedi on the frozen planet Dweem. After ten years of training, the "Jedi droids" made their public debut during the Arkanian Revolution, where they earned the derogatory nickname, *Iron Knights.*

Aqinos's pupils inhabited the bodies of FLTCH droids, Uulshos justice droids, and ancient juggernaut war droids. They wielded oversize lightsabers of their own construction containing the dead crystal bodies of their ancestors, and comported themselves in a ritualistic parody of courtly manners.

> **"I take no orders from you. So before I lop your head off, I have one question: be ye friend or foe to the Republic?"**
>
> *—High Marshal Dragite, one of the guardians of Dweem*

Though the Jedi Order taught that the Force existed in all things, the notion of droids, or even crystals, using the Force struck many in the Order as perverse. Not only did they lack midi-chlorians, but nonorganic and artificial life-forms were not "living" in the conventional sense. What understanding, therefore, could such beings have of the living Force?

The Jedi Council excommunicated Aqinos for heresy, and did its best to ignore his strange legion of Iron Knights. The Republic gave the Iron Knights the rank of high marshal for their actions during the Arkanian crisis, but the title carried no real weight. A disgraced Aqinos returned to Dweem, where he and the Iron Knights spent decades in exile.

Nine years after the Battle of Endor, Luke Skywalker's Jedi academy reestablished ties with the Iron Knights of Dweem. Luke, who was establishing new Jedi policy as he went along, had no traditionalist objections to the Iron Knights and welcomed their unique perspective on the Force.

During the Yuuzhan Vong invasion, the Iron Knights made it their mission to protect the galaxy's droids from the technology-hating Yuuzhan Vong. One of their number, Luxum, even succumbed to the dark side. Following the victory over the invaders, only a handful of Iron Knights remained active.

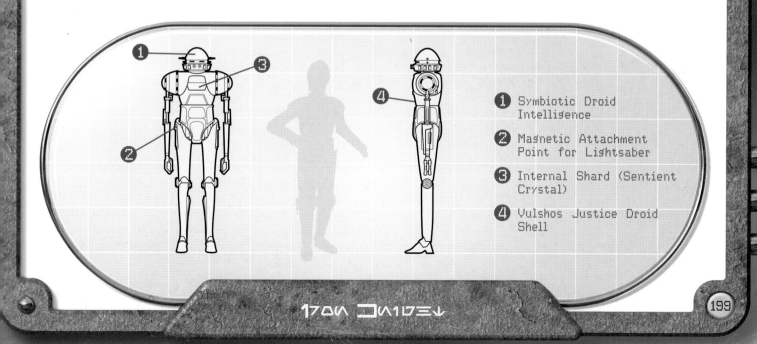

1. Symbiotic Droid Intelligence
2. Magnetic Attachment Point for Lightsaber
3. Internal Shard (Sentient Crystal)
4. Vulshos Justice Droid Shell

About the Author

Daniel Wallace is the author or coauthor of more than a dozen books, such as *The Art of Superman Returns, The Marvel Comics Encyclopedia,* and five previous entries in the Star Wars Essential Guide series, including the *New York Times* bestselling *Star Wars: The New Essential Guide to Characters.* He and his wife live in Detroit with their two sons and daughter.

About the Illustrator

Ian Fullwood lives and works in Herefordshire, England, and has clients both at home and in the USA. He has more than fifteen years' experience in technical illustration and commercial art, and works with a range of clients, including publishing and engineering companies. He produces a variety of work, ranging from science fiction to product visualizing and animation. Ian uses traditional drawing skills combined with computer programs—Illustrator, Photoshop, and Lightwave 3D—to produce technically demanding and visually exciting pieces of art. Visit *www.if3d.com* for more visual indigestion!